"GARDNER DOZOIS IS A MASTER
OF SCIENCE FICTION HORROR...

"...not the superficial kind that pushes tired old
symbols through shiny new hoops, but an honest,
painfully felt horror of the dark side of the human
spirit. He conjures nightmares by slow accretion of
detail, to fix them in your mind with sudden slashes
of insight. His work is bitter, subtle, exotic, unique:
science fiction for the true connoisseur."

—Joe Haldeman

"It's damned well about time for Dozois' first
collection of stories! Now the rest of the universe
can share the delightful burden of praising his
singular creative world-view."

—Harlan Ellison

THE VISIBLE MAN

GARDNER DOZOIS

A BERKLEY MEDALLION BOOK
published by
BERKLEY PUBLISHING CORPORATION

Virginia Kidd
Box 278
Milford, PA. 18337

SBN 425-03595-6

BERKLEY MEDALLION BOOKS are published by
Berkley Publishing Corporation
200 Madison Avenue
New York, N. Y. 10016

BERKLEY MEDALLION BOOK ® TM 757,375

Printed in the United States of America

Berkley Medallion Edition, DECEMBER, 1977

For the children—

Christopher Casper; Alison Hartwell; Lore Haldeman; Jenny Ettlin; Jon, Kris, Valerie, and Leslie Knight; Christopher Purdom; Ian Grant; Damon Monteleone; Devon and Trent Zelazny; Jason Thurston; Roy, Madeleine, Therese and Matthew Wolfe; Iva Hacker-Delany; Jamie and Stephanie Bishop; Jonathan Post; Shari and Jeffrey Kohn; Demian Phillips; Matthew Macdonald; Sean Perry

—with the hope that they will not have to live
in some of these worlds.

CONTENTS

Introduction

Robert Silverberg

LATE IN THE winter of 1971 I attended a science fiction convention in Boston, and, setting out by car for New York when it ended, I became entangled in an unexpected and altogether horrendous snowstorm. Under near-blizzard conditions I crawled tensely westward until, some fifty miles out of Boston, all traffic on the Massachusetts Turnpike halted, and stayed halted for perhaps an hour while some inconceivable mess was being unsnarled somewhere down the road. Two science fiction writers had been unlucky enough to cadge rides from me that awful day: the veteran pro Gordon R. Dickson and a chap named Gardner R. Dozois, who had sold perhaps two or three stories. During the interminable halt on the turnpike, Dozois got out of the car to peer at the chain of cars, many miles long, piled up in every lane in both directions. As he did so, the driver of a car fifty feet or so to our rear leaned out his wondow and aimed a camera at him.

"That cat took my *picture!*" a dazed and astonished Dozois muttered, getting back into the car.

As well he might have done. For Gardner Dozois, circa March 1971, must have seemed a weird-looking apparition indeed to that snowbound New Englander. Picture it: a gaunt young man just under six feet tall with a vast cascade of shoulder-length blond hair of an eerie voluminous sort covering most of his face, a strange bushy beard blowing in the icy gale, the glint of inquisitive eyes behind big steel-rimmed glasses, and—am I imagining this?—a bulky and grotesquely dilapidated raccoon coat. I mean, *weird*, man. This was 1971, and the phantoms of the Haight-Ashbury still stalked the land, but even so this was quintessence of hippie materializing on the turnpike, and no wonder that man took the picture. Does he realize, though, that the shaggy hippie whose snapshot he grabbed was already, there in 1971, one of the most gifted writers in the United States, at the age of twenty-two or twenty-three?

Notice that I didn't say "one of the most gifted *science fiction* writers." He was that, too. But it is possible to be an outstanding science fiction writer, to create undying classics of the genre and win whole squadrons of Hugos, without ever mastering more than the rudiments of prose style. Whereas Dozois, barely old enough to vote, had begun one of his early stories with this paragraph:

Did y'ever hear the one about the old man and the sea? Halt a minute, lordling; stop and listen. It's a fine story, full of balance and point and social pith; short and direct. It's not mine. Mine are long and rambling and parenthetical and they corrode the moral fiber right out of a man. Come to think, I won't tell you that one after all. A man of my age has a right to prefer his own material, and let the critics be damned. I've a prejudice now for webs of my own weaving.

I invite your attention to the rhythms of the prose, the balancing of clauses, the use of alliteration, metaphor, and irony, the tough, elegant sinews of the vocabulary. It is a paragraph of splendid construction, a specimen of prose that shows honorable descent from Chaucer and Shakespeare, Pope and Dryden, Defoe and Dickens, the prose of a man who knows what he wants to say and says it eloquently and effectively. It is the opening paragraph of "A Special Kind of Morning," which Dozois wrote in 1970 and which I chose, not at random, to be the first story in the first number of *New Dimensions*. Many science fiction writers, including a lot of the great ones, are content to be mere storytellers, using whatever assemblages of words may be handy to convey their meanings. Dozois is a storyteller too, and no mere one—"A Special Kind of Morning" is a vigorous and violent tale of war with a structural underpinning worthy of Sophocles—but he is concerned as much with the way he tells his stories as with the events he is describing.

A good writer should make good use of his eyes and his ears. What was Dozois looking for, when he stepped out of my car that snowy day? What things did he see in that dreadful vale of immobile vehicles, what impressions did he record, what use did he find for the moment, its sights and sounds? Here is a paragraph from "The Last Day of July," *New Dimensions* 3:

> Blinking and squinting, John moves away from the house. His shoes click on flagstone, then swish through grass as he strays from the path. The grass whispers around his legs, caressing his ankles, rasping abrasively against the material of his trousers. His vision returns slowly, and as it does he feels the earth roll majestically under his feet in a long sea swell, like a giant's shoulder shrugging uneasily in sleep. The sky is a brilliant blue. He can sense the house behind him, the top half rising up and over him, a cresting wave about to topple. Now it is the house that is distasteful—again it seems brooding, mournful, unwholesomely confining.

The shoes *click* and *swish*. The grass *whispers* and *rasps* abrasively. The earth *rolls in a long sea swell*, the house is a *cresting wave about to topple*. The thrust of the paragraph is psychological, but the changes of spirit take place beneath an accretion of concrete detail, of vivid and immediate simile and metaphor and physical description. Melville understood these things, and Joyce, and Faulkner. So did Raymond Chandler and Dashiell

Hammett; so do John D. MacDonald, Fritz Leiber, Ursula K. Le Guin, John Cheever, Anthony Burgess, Mary Renault, Graham Greene, and Cecelia Holland. Good writing knows no boundaries of genre. It depends only on respect for language and grammar, a sense of the structure of the sentence and the paragraph, and a keen perception of sensory data. Gardner Dozois is as skilled a worker in prose as there is in science fiction, and it is a skill that came to him early, though probably not gratuitously.

He has chosen to publish most, perhaps all, of his work in the science fiction magazines and original SF anthologies, and so I suppose he must be labeled a genre writer, although in fact much of what he has written is only marginally science fiction by my own fairly restrictive definitions. I doubt that Dozois would have been able to get much material published in John Campbell's *Astounding*, say, circa 1938-55, or in Horace Gold's *Galaxy*, circa 1950-55; those two great editors would simply have found his work irrelevant to their purposes. Much of what he does is irrelevant to my own purposes at *New Dimensions*, though I admire it greatly even as I decline to offer it as science fiction. The standard furniture of science fiction—robots, androids, spaceships, time machines, planetary exploration teams, alien life-forms—is rare in Dozois. His stories tend to take place ten or fifteen years in the future and to explore the consequences of one significant change in the contemporary situation; and they are rooted, it seems to me, in the radical sensibility of the Sixties, the awareness that American twentieth-century life seen from the lower depths is not quite as pretty as the television/suburbia/mass-media/Establishment view of things. Not all his work is like that, of course: "A Special Kind of Morning" is classic science fiction, full of pulp-magazine inventiveness, although not at all handled with pulp-magazine klutziness, and his novella "Strangers" (*New Dimensions* 4) creates an alien world and an alien civilization with skills worthy of Philip José Farmer. But the more familiar sort of Dozois story is the one like "The Visible Man" or "Where No Sun Shines," firmly grounded in the here and now, and achieving its science-fictional effects through Dozois' sense of the alienated nature of twentieth-century humanity, of the fundamental strangeness and dislocation of life in our times. ("That cat took my *picture*!")

Because he chooses to work outside the mainstream of what is at best a marginal realm of the publishing world, and because he works painfully and slowly in a field where the basic pay-scale has scarcely improved in forty years, Dozois' career has allowed him no more than a subsistence income, and he is in little danger of losing touch with the submerged world that is the source of his fiction. He still looks like a shaggy hippie, or did when last I saw him a year or two ago, although he is no longer gaunt at all, not even remotely. He is about thirty now, I calculate, since he says he was seventeen when he sold his first story ("The Empty Man," *If*, September 1966). He has been a full-time writer since his discharge from the Army in 1969. (Dozois was a military journalist stationed in Europe, where, he says, he learned "how to adroitly administer the Big Lie, cover up unapproved news, pink-ribbon-wrap approved news, turn defeats into victories, and hordes of other Magical Tricks and Sleights-of-Hand.") He lives in a dismaying part of Philadelphia, and, since his income from his fiction is unlikely to support him even on the level needed there, he does a little editing on the side. Which is not an unhappy notion, because every first-rate writer is also a first-rate editor, for an audience of one, operating a well-honed set of inner filters to strain all the dross from his own work, and it is usually not difficult for such a writer to externalize that filtering process in editorial work.

So Dozois the editor has been a first reader for *Galaxy Magazine*, though not lately, and serves just now as primary filtering system for the new *Isaac Asimov's Science Fiction Magazine*. He has dabbled in anthology-making with considerable success: his books include *A Day in the Life, Another World, Beyond the Golden Age*, and *Future Power*, the last done with Jack Dann. Lately he has replaced Lester del Rey as editor of Dutton's *Best*

Science Fiction of the Year series, a shift that ought to produce remarkable transformations in the content of that anthology. In the science fiction world, anthologies are customarily edited by people close to the center of things, people who exercise power that is not entirely derived from their status as editors of anthologies; the fact that Dozois has been doing anthologies, and doing them successfully, indicates that for all his Dostoievskian submergedness he is becoming a member of the inner circle, a wielder of power, and it is an odd paradox that must afford him some amusement as he guns down the roaches.

Dozois the writer is still an outsider. Most of the readers have no idea even how to pronounce his name. ("Do-*zwah*" will do it.) He has never won a major award, though he has gone five times to the final Nebula ballot and been a Hugo finalist four times. There are good omens in that; it is not very surprising that Dozois, a writer's writer, a master technician, would repeatedly be a Nebula nominee, since Nebulas are awarded by the members of the Science Fiction Writers of America. But Hugos come from the fans, the readership-at-large, a group in which skills of the nature of Dozois' are often not only not appreciated but are actively resented. That his stories show up so frequently on the Hugo ballots indicates that a substantial sophisticated minority within the Hugo electorate finds deep rewards in his work: a good sign, both for Dozois and for science fiction in general.

Still, he has not been highly visible as a writer. The ingroup of writers and fans knows and respects him, but to the casual SF reader he is still Gardner Who? Undoubtedly the fact that he is yet to publish his first novel is responsible for this, since nowadays science fiction is basically a paperback phenomenon, and a writer whose work is not to be found in the bookracks is a writer whose existence remains unknown. Dozois' longest work to date is the novella, "Strangers," published in *New Dimensions* in 1974 and a Hugo finalist; it runs about two-thirds the length of a standard paperback novel, so it should be no great task for him to transform it into one, but to date the rumored expansion has not appeared. He did collaborate with George Alec Effinger on one full-length novel, *Nightmare Blue*, but that book never reached the levels that either of these gifted writers attains alone, nor was it published in any very conspicuous way. Ultimately Dozois will release some novels and they will gain him the attention he deserves, but until then it will be difficult for him to establish much of a beachhead in the world of commercial publishing.

A science fiction writer who does not write novels generally has a hard time getting short story collections published. (There are exceptions—Ellison, Sheckley, Tenn—but not many.) So it is that the present volume, Dozois' maiden collection, has been years aborning. Slow worker that he is, he has nevertheless produced fifteen or twenty stories over the past five years, enough for two or three collections, and it is good to see this painstaking, eloquent, and altogether original writer at last given a showcase for some of his best work.

Speaking at a science fiction convention held in Washington, D.C., in 1973, Dozois attempted to articulate his feelings about science fiction and his role as a writer of science fiction. "I may have been attracted to science fiction as a kid simply because it was such a hopelessly underdog sort of genre," he said. "This struck a sympathetic response in my soul, as I was such a hopelessly underdog sort of kid.... My father told me more than once that if I kept reading science fiction it would ruin my life—and considering how things've turned out and the amount of money I make per year, he was probably right." Dozois did not have kind words for the experimental science fiction of the late 1960's: "The New Wave blows it by turning out stories that are indistinguishable from the stories that fill avant-garde mainstream quarterlies and little magazines.... The most extreme of these so-called New Wave writers have abandoned the thread of rationality that is part of genre SF's philosophical heritage, and so have diminished their work." On the other hand, he went on, "The Old Wave

7

fouls up by continuing to write the same old thing year after year, turning out the same old plots like yard-goods, chewing toothlessly on the same cardboard characters and played-out concepts. . . . The cut-and-dried place that they make of the galaxy, not even as interesting as Earth, leaves us with no surprise that the sense of wonder doesn't live there anymore. They have abandoned that thread of irrationality, of fantasy, that is part of genre SF's philosophical heritage, and so have diminished their work."

And Dozois? "It is time for a synthesis," he says, "a melding together of all that has been done in the past turbulent decade," and he aligns himself with those writers who have produced works "that gain much of their power by rationalizing traditional fantasy, that keep the inner power of the dream and the irrational, but attempt to analyze it in terms of the known and the rational, that attempt to fuse yin and yang, to invoke works that will invoke the sense of wonder without insulting the rational intellect."

It is a commendable goal. I think this collection demonstrates his success.

The Visible Man

GEORGE ROWAN'S ONLY chance of escape came to him like a benediction, sudden and unlooked for, on the road between Newburyport and Boston.

They were on old Route 1, the Newburyport Turnpike, and there was not another car in sight. The fully automated Route 95 guideway was just a few miles west of here, running almost parallel to Route 1, but for reasons of his own the sheriff had preferred to take the old secondary road, even though he had to drive the car himself and couldn't possibly get up to guideway speeds. Perhaps he simply enjoyed manual driving. Perhaps it was some old State regulation, now solidified into tradition, that prohibited the transportation of prisoners on automated roads. Perhaps it was just some more of the expected psychological torture, taking the slowest possible route so that Rowan would have time to build up a greater charge of fear and dreadful anticipation for what awaited him in Boston.

For Rowan, the trip had already become interminable. His memory of the jail in Newburyport, of his crime, of his hasty trial, of his past life—all had become hazy and indistinct. It seemed as if he had been riding forever, on the road, going to Boston for the execution of his sentence. Only that was real and vivid: the slight swaying motion of the car, the seat upholstery sticking uncomfortably to his sweat-soaked back, the ridged rubber mat under his feet. The countryside they drove through was flat and empty, trees, meadows, cultivated fields, little streams, sometimes a boarded-up gas station or a long-abandoned roadside stand. The sky was a flat, washed-out blue, and the sunlight was thick and dusty. Occasionally they would bump over a pothole or a stretch of frost-buckled pavement—the State didn't spend much anymore to keep up the secondary roads. The car's electric engine made no sound at all, and the interior of the car was close and hot with the windows rolled up.

Rowan found himself reluctantly watching the little motions of the steering wheel, apparently turning all by itself, driverless. That made him shiver. He knew intellectually, of course, that he was sitting on the front seat between the sheriff and the deputy, but he couldn't *see* them. He could hear them breathing, and occasionally the deputy's arm would brush against his own, but, for Rowan, they were invisible.

He knew why they were invisible, but that didn't make it any less spooky. When the State's analysis computers had gone down into his mind and found the memories that proved him guilty, they had also, as a matter of course, implanted a very deep and very specific hypnotic injunction: from now on, George Rowan would not be able to see any other living creature. Apparently the injunction had not included trees and other kinds of vegetation, but it had covered animals and birds and people. He assumed that when he "saw" through invisible people—as he now "saw" the portions of the car that should have been blocked from sight by the sheriff's body—it was because his subconscious mind was extrapolating, creating a logical extension of the view from other visual data in order to comply with the spirit of the injunction. Nothing must be allowed to spoil the illusion. Nor could Rowan break it, although he knew what it was and how it had been created. It was too strong, and planted too deep. He was "blind" in a special and insidious way.

There were a number of apparently sound reasons for doing this to convicted criminals. It made it almost

10

impossible for a prisoner to escape or to resist his captors, for one thing, and the State psychologists also claimed that the resultant sense of supernatural isolation would engender an identity crisis in the prisoner, and so help contribute to his rehabilitation. Totally "blinding" the prisoners would accomplish both objectives in a more logical way. But the State administrators had been growing increasingly perverse over the years, and they chose the cruelest way. How much more terrible a thing this was than total blindness—to make the victim live in a sunlit empty world, haunted by ghosts and voices, pushed and punished by unseen forces, never knowing who was with him or what they were about to do to him. So the State men inflicted this on prisoners because it was cruel and they enjoyed it, just as they would enjoy torturing Rowan in Boston, driving him insane again and again in the name of psychological rehabilitation.

At that moment, past Topsfield but not yet up to the Putnamville Reservoir, their right front tire blew out.

They went into a terrifying spin. The world dissolved into a whirling blur, and bursts of sunlight jabbed Rowan's face like a strobe light as they spun. The car hit the guardrail, spun out into the middle of the road again, spun back to hit the guardrail a second time. In the midst of the roar and the clatter and impact, Rowan had time to think that it would be better for him if he was killed in the crash, and time to realize that in spite of everything he did not want to die. Then the car was spinning out into the road, spinning back again. This time there was no guardrail to catch it. The car went careening off the road, fishtailing and losing momentum as it plowed through the deep soft loam of the shoulder, and dived into a shallow ditch.

The dashboard leaped up and whammed into Rowan, but he managed to catch the blow on his arms and shoulders; the impact beat him black-and-blue, but did no lasting damage. In the same instant, as he was hitting the dashboard, he saw the windshield above the driver's seat star and shatter, and the invisible deputy was thrown heavily against him. The car recoiled from the impact, slid

11

a foot or two sideways, and canted to the left. Everything was still for a heartbeat, and then the car groaned and settled, canting over even more. The noise of the springs died away.

There was a strangely peaceful silence.

The car was resting head down at a forty-five-degree angle, listing badly to the left but not quite turned all the way over on its side. Rowan took a deep, shaky breath and decided that he was alive. The sheriff might not be. He was still invisible to Rowan, but it was obvious that he had been thrown partially through the windshield. Rowan had ended up leaning against the sheriff's hip, and if his hips were at a level with the steering wheel then the rest of his body had to be protruding through the windshield. And there was blood on the glass. From the feel of it, the deputy seemed to be slumped over with his head almost in Rowan's lap, stirring feebly, stunned but still alive. No conscious cogitation went on in Rowan's mind, but as the deputy pushed against him and tried to sit up, Rowan raised his manacled hands and smashed them down on what he hoped was the deputy's head. The first blow hit something soft, and the deputy began struggling weakly, but the second blow bit bone. The deputy stopped fighting. Rowan struck him again, and he stopped moving at all.

Rowan sat quietly for a second, his breath hissing harshly in his throat, and then patted the deputy with his hands until he touched a jingly metal object. As he lifted it away from the deputy, it became visible for him, and yes, it was a key ring. He used one of the keys to unlock his handcuffs, and spent another few seconds searching the deputy for a gun; he didn't find one, and decided that he couldn't afford to waste any more time. He climbed over the deputy, rolled the side window down, and pulled himself up out of the car.

He jumped down to the ground, lost his footing on the grassy slope, and went to his knees. For a moment, he remained kneeling, blinking in the raw hot sunlight, dirt under his fingers. Everything had happened too fast; only now, this instant with the sun in his face, did it become real for him—he was outside, he was free, he had a chance. Hope and terror exploded inside Rowan. He rose into a crouch, scanning his surroundings with a sudden feral intensity. Then he scrambled up the incline. At the top of the slope he paused only long enough to make sure no cars were coming before he dashed across the road and slid down into another ditch in an avalanche of dust and scree. A man-high expanse of grass and wildflowers stretched away from the road on this side. It closed over Rowan like the sea.

At first, he ran flat-out, fast as he could go, the high grass whipping around him, wild with fear and exhilaration. He kept running until his breath was gone and he was staggering rather than sprinting, and then a root snagged his foot and the ground reached up to catch him, *smack*, like an outfielder catching a fly ball. He lay spread-eagled, flat on his face against the damp earth, gasping for air while everything seemed slowly to spin, the resin-smelling grass tickling his nose, tiny furtive insects scampering invisibly across his hands. When he could breathe again, he found that some of his panic had also gone. He sat up. He'd been leaving a trail like a goddamned elephant; he'd have to start being a little slier. If he trampled the grass and left a flattened wake behind him, it would be like a giant arrow pointing the way he had gone. He wouldn't last an hour that way before the cops ran him down. He set off at a diagonal to his former path, picking his way with care, forcing himself to be slow. This way, perhaps he had a chance. More than he'd had a while ago, at least.

Rowan reached a stand of scrub woods and pushed his pace up to a fast trot, taking a few more headers as the terrain got rougher. Every time the tree branches moved in the wind all the patterns of light and darkness would flow and reform, and he kept mistaking shadow for ground. Once he dropped four feet down a concealed embankment. He kept up the pace. If he broke an ankle he was finished, but he couldn't afford to slow down either. They'd almost certainly catch him if they fielded a search party anytime soon. But Route 1 was infrequently patroled, that was in his favor, and the Boston people wouldn't miss the sheriff for a while yet. If only he could get even an hour's lead—

After a few minutes, the woods began to die away into a region of small isolated trees and high bramble thickets. Rowan slid down a final bluff and found himself in someone's alfalfa field. His second wind was long gone, and now every breath brought him a stab of pain in his side. He began to work his way around the field, skirting the outermost furrow. He walked slowly and painfully. Sweat had dried uncomfortably on his skin, making him itch, and his clothes were full of burrs and stickers. On the horizon, he could just make out the peaked roof of a farm building, thumbnail-small from here, gray tile glinting in the sun. A thin column of smoke rose black from a chimney, making a long lazy line across the sky. Rowan was halfway across the field, his shoes filling with loam at every step, when a dog began to bark in the distance.

Rowan walked faster, but the barking became louder and closer. A goddamn watchdog then, definitely coming after him. He faced around, at bay, too beat-out to run for the tree line.

The barking swelled into an angry challenging roar, and then cut off, ominous and abrupt. Impossible to tell which way it was coming in at him, he thought, and at that same instant felt a flash of searing pain as his pants leg was torn away by something invisible. Rowan cursed and kicked out wildly. His foot scored a solid hit on something, and the dog yelped. Rowan kicked out again, missed completely, and had to do a lurching gracestep to recover his balance. Pawprints appeared in the soft loam as the dog danced back out of range. Rowan realized that if he kept near the furrow he'd be able to track the dog's movements in the loam. So when a line of pawprints came rushing directly in toward him like the wake of a torpedo, he judged his distance carefully and then lashed out with all his strength. His foot hit something with the clean, solid *whump* of a dropkicked football. The dog yelped again. It was apparently lifted off its feet by the impact

14

and sent rolling across the top of the furrow—at least, that was how Rowan interpreted the sudden flattening of alfalfa and scattering of loam. Rowan started walking again, with great deliberation. Judging by the sound, the dog continued to trace snarling figure-eights around him at a safe distance, but it did not attack again.

Rowan scrambled up into the scrub brush on the far side of the field and started off again, limping slightly, unwilling to take time to tend to the bite. If only he dared to rest. All his instincts told him to go to ground, find a sheltered spot in the deep woods and hide. But that would never work. They'd fly over the nearby forested areas with infrared heat sensors and spot him at once—there were no animals the size of a man left in the Massachusetts woods, any large trace would unequivocally be the fugitive. No, he would have to go to a town, where his heat-trace would be lost among those of other people. But the towns were the very place where he'd be the most helpless, and the most exposed.

He crossed another cultivated field—seeing only a tractor moving far away across acres of soughing green-and-yellow grain—and then the ground began to turn porous and swampy, water oozing up to fill his footprints as soon as he had made them. At last he was faced with an actual stretch of marshland, miles of reeds and cat-o'-nine-tails interlaced with gleaming fingers of water. He was forced to turn more to the east to skirt it. Walking by the edge of the marsh, he could hear the whining of millions of mosquitoes, but could see none of them, even when they bit him. Occasionally there would be a splash and a little gout of water alongside him as he passed—frogs hopping off the bank to get out of his way, he assumed. Other unseen things rustled through the reeds around him. On the larger ponds, he could see the surface of the water wrinkle into a crumped leaf pattern as waterbirds landed or took off, but he couldn't see the birds themselves. The air was full of invisible wings. Rowan found all of this so uncanny that he detoured, shivering, far enough to the north to get away from the marsh entirely. The ground began to rise again. There were cuts in the sides of hillocks here, and planed-off places, evidence of recent road-building. He pushed through a weed-choked scrub woodlot, and found himself on a bluff overlooking one of those strange suburban housing developments that seem to sprout up out of nowhere in the rural areas of Massachusetts, unconnected with anything and with no viable reason for existence.

Rowan's throat went dry. This would be the first major hurdle. He descended the bluff.

At least there didn't seem to be anybody around, Rowan thought, and then grimaced at his own fatigue-engendered stupidity. There could be a crowd within ten feet of him, or a posse armed to the teeth, and he'd never know it until the first shot went home. He started walking slowly along a sidewalk, heading for the crossroads he could see on the other side of the housing development. This seemed to be a fairly new complex. The lawns were still smears of ugly red clay, surrounded by hopeful little string fences that were somehow supposed to keep birds from eating the newly-planted grass seeds, and there had not yet been time for the basements to fill up with marshwater or the paint to peel off in the bitter sea wind. Maybe most people had gone to work, leaving only a few housepersons here and there, and maybe they would stay inside. His foot struck something.

"Hey!" said a voice, at the level of his elbow.

Rowan froze.

"Hey, mister," the voice said, reproachfully, "you knocked over all my soldiers."

A child. Rowan forced himself to think. "I'm sorry, son," he said.

"The whole army!"

"I didn't see you," Rowan said, truthfully, "I'm sorry I messed up your army."

Suspicious silence from the boy.

"I wasn't thinking about where I was going," Rowan said. That got a *huhn* sound out of the boy, who didn't sound entirely mollified. The boy must have stood up then, as some of the toy soldiers he'd been touching became visible for Rowan, varicolored plastic figures lying askew on the sidewalk. Rowan hesitated, and then asked, "Which one of those roads leads to Hamilton?"

"That one."

Wonderful. "The paved one?" Rowan asked cannily, and when the boy didn't answer he pointed and said, "That one there?"

"Uh-huh," the boy said. The tone of puzzled suspicion was back in the child's voice. There was something odd about this grownup. The boy didn't respond when Rowan thanked him, but from the little scraping noises Rowan heard he guessed that the boy had sat down and begun to move his soldiers about again. The child had lost interest in Rowan. There was something odd about all grownups, and Rowan wasn't unusual enough to provoke more than a mild passing wonderment.

Rowan started off again. "You stepped on my fort!" the child wailed instantly. Ignoring him, Rowan kept walking. He maintained a brisk pace, keeping close to the curb and hoping that anyone coming up the sidewalk in the opposite direction would have room to pass him without contact. In this fashion, he managed to make it through the development without further incident, and onto the road that led, hopefully, to Hamilton. Surely a search party would be out after him by now; if he didn't find a town to lose himself in, he'd be finished. There were no sidewalks here, and no traffic on this one-lane back road, and if he kept to the center of it the chances of colliding with someone out for a stroll were remote. He walked as fast as he could without actually breaking into a suspicion-provoking run.

When the housing development was hidden by a curve, he increased his pace to a fast trot. He could be jogging, couldn't he? And besides, there was no help for it: his time was running out. The road began to climb, winding among small rolling hillocks, and the forest closed down on either side. Once a dog came down from some house set back in the trees, and yapped after him for a few hundred yards, but didn't attack. About ten minutes after the dog gave up the chase, he came upon another house, this one set back from the road and climbing partway up a low hillside. There was a bicycle lying next to the road on the wide front lawn. Someone might be watching from the house, but Rowan decided that he'd have to take that chance. He walked casually over to the bicycle, set it upright in the road, mounted it, and rode unhurriedly away until the house was out of sight. Then he began to pump.

The bicycle was too small for him, but not small enough to make the proposition impossible. It wobbled some, but he sent it whizzing along as fast as he was physically able to peddle. It rattled and creaked in protest, but it held together. Somehow he also managed to keep the thing upright and stay on top of it. The bicycle wasn't a racer, but Rowan was a powerful man, and more important, a desperate man, and he got it up to a pretty respectable clip. He could cover twice the ground now that he could on foot, and he felt a thrill of real hope. Rowan peddled through the hills for a while, and then the country began to level out. Here the road intersected a somewhat larger secondary road, two lanes instead of one.

Guessing at the direction of Hamilton, he turned onto the larger road. It was flat and straight, and Rowan made even better time. Dust boiled up from the pavement as he passed, and hung in the still air behind him in long wavering lines. Thank God for the guideways, Rowan thought—traffic was light even on the larger manual roads. He only encountered one car, going in the opposite direction, its steering wheel apparently turning by itself. He had to caution himself not to stare at it as it passed. Then he was alone on the road again, with only the squeak and rattle of the bicycle for company. After a while, houses began to appear more frequently by the side of the road, and there were cross-streets every so often, with overhead traffic lights at the intersections. He was barreling across one such intersection at full tilt when he crashed into something unseen but very solid.

The impact hurled Rowan from the bicycle head over heels. He hit the street, rolled, skidded along on his side and jarred to a stop against the curb. By the time he understood what was happening, he was resting on his elbows in the road and staring up at the sky, dazed and shaken. He was badly scraped along his arms and legs, and bits of gravel had been embedded under his skin by the force of the fall. Rubber-legged, he got up. There was a groan of pain from the unseen something he'd hit, and then it said a pithy word. A man, then. Some pedestrian had been crossing the road and he'd smashed into him. The bicycle was shoved clatteringly aside, and Rowan assumed that the man was getting to his feet.

"What are you, blind?" the man raged. "You sorry son-of-a-bitch!"

"I'm sorry, but you stepped right out—"

"You had plenty of room! You had miles of room!" The voice wavered slightly as it climbed in register: an elderly man, then. "What's a'matter, you ain't got eyes in your head? You could've turned! I swear I'll sue you, you hear that? Knock me down, almost break my back—"

"Don't frazzle off, old friend," Rowan said nastily. Soft-talk wouldn't work. He had to be truculent and menacing or he'd be arguing with this guy for hours. Play it like a young tough, a weep maybe. "It was just an accident, right? You scan that? Only an accident. So don't give me the rest of this fargo, because I don't want to hear it."

"I've got a mind to have you run in, you son-of-a-bitch."

"Shove it. You know, you could get hurt a lot worse, jobbie."

There had been an edge in Rowan's voice—the man sputtered, but remained silent. Rowan swaggered over to the bicycle, feeling self-conscious but playing it up. The bicycle didn't seem to be significantly damaged, although the frame was a little bent and the handlebars had been knocked out of alignment. He twisted them back into true, climbed onto the bicycle and shoved off. When Rowan was a safe distance away, the man shouted after him, "Goddamn idiot! I hope somebody cuts your balls off!"

Wobbling more than before, Rowan peddled down the

road. He had to think of something else soon. He was entering the outskirts of a town, and the chances of hitting another invisible pedestrian increased with every revolution of the bicycle wheels. And now he thought he could hear the thin keening of sirens high in the sky behind him, an eerie sound that might have been made by demons of the upper air. They were coming after him, and he was much too conspicuous bicycling down this traffic-free road. Just as he was about to ditch the bicycle, he topped a rise and came upon a truck waiting on a red light at an intersection, one of the moderate-sized vans still used for hauling freight between small cities not serviced by guideways. Rowan's eyes narrowed in instant calculation. Carefully, he coasted to a stop squarely behind the truck, where he would be out of range of the driver's mirror. He dismounted, picked up the bicycle and threw it into a tangle of high weeds and bushes by the roadside. Then, as the light changed and the truck started to accelerate, he leaped up and grabbed the edge of the latched tailgate.

The truck's van was protected only by a hanging tarpaulin. Rowan brushed it back, pulled himself over the tailgate and tumbled inside. He landed on something with hard edges, squirmed aside, and came to rest on the vibrating metal floor. They continued to gather speed, gears growling—evidently the driver had not seen him come aboard. Rowan sank back on his haunches, and then stretched out as well as he could among the sealed boxes and crates, pillowing his head with his arms. He had never been so tired. The hard metal floor felt as soft as thistledown. He felt himself sinking into it, sinking down luxuriantly. Grimly, he forced his eyelids wide again and made a great effort to stay awake. He had been given an opportunity to think things through without the pressure of split-second decisions; he should be trying to formulate long-range plans, plot out a plan of action instead of just running aimlessly away. But his brain had turned to ash, and he could not think. Besides, where was there to go? Who was there who could help him? His friends were all back in Newburyport, and that old life seemed even more distanced and inconsequential than it had this morning, his old acquaintances only hazy figures from an almost-forgotten dream. Dream-men, phantasms, they could not help him. The floor was spinning, slowly and restfully. He knew it was a terrible mistake to doze, but he could no longer fight it. He fell asleep.

He was awakened by a harsh, frightening sound: the rattle and clank of the tailgate being unlatched.

Rowan pulled himself up out of evil, smothering dreams. When his eyes unblurred, he saw only a rectangular green thing with glowing edges, and it took him a moment to realize that it was the tarpaulin, with light leaking in around the sides. At first, he didn't realize that the truck had stopped. Then he heard the tailgate *thump* as it was swung down. He sat up, terrified and floundering, still only half-understanding where he was. The tarpaulin was yanked aside. Blinking around the sudden influx of light, Rowan was astonished to see that no one was there. Then he remembered, in an intense, sickening flash, and had to adjust himself to it all over again, as he would have to every morning for whatever remained of his life.

"You floorsucker!" a voice said.

Before Rowan could move, he was seized by hard invisible hands, hauled from the truck—getting a brief dizzy glimpse of concrete, a high metal ceiling, arc lights—and set on his feet. The hands released him.

"I—" Rowan started to say. His vision exploded into shooting white sparks, pain lanced through his head. He reeled back against the truck and almost fell. His mouth filled with blood.

"Whatta y'think y'doin?" the voice said, harsh with rage. "You scupping thief!"

Pain had jolted Rowan fully awake. Instantly, he lashed out with his fist, aiming at the spot from which the voice had seemed to emanate. He missed completely, his arm scything the air, and took a hard punch to the stomach from his unseen adversary. It knocked the wind out of him and drove him back against the edge of the lowered tailgate. It was hopeless, he realized through a wave of nausea. He couldn't win.

The next blow laid Rowan's cheek open and threw him sideways to the concrete floor. He went along with the fall, augmented it, and rolled over twice very quickly. Then he scrambled to his feet and ran.

Someone shouted hoarsely behind him. Rowan kept running, heading for the far side of what was apparently an underground garage. Halfway across, he slammed into something solid but yielding; another invisible person. There was a gasp of surprise and pain, and the clatter of dropped tools. Probably he'd bowled the man over. Rowan himself staggered and nearly fell, but recovered his balance and kept on. He was sprinting with his head down now, dodging and weaving like a broken-field runner. More shouts behind him. Invisible hands clutched at him for a moment, but he broke free. A door seemed to spring up in front of him. He clawed it open and sprang through.

He found himself in a long, fluorescent corridor, the cold white light coming evenly from ceiling, walls and floor. He sprinted away to the left, followed the corridor to a fork, picked a branch at random and kept running. Then another fork, and another corridor. He found a door marked *Employees Only*, went down a small service stairway, through another network of corridors, and down another stairway to the bottom.

The corridor he emerged into this time was dingier than the others, faded tile and green-painted stone, lit by hanging overhead bulbs. There was a smell of damp in the air, and the stone walls sweated like toads. Rowan paused to rest, gasping and leaning against the doorframe. When his breathing evened enough to let him hear again, he listened for sounds of pursuit. Nothing. He'd lost them. And this was a basement corridor, few people would be traveling it. And now, he knew where he was. Even in flight, he had had time to recognize the trademark insignia embossed into the walls of the upper corridors— he was in one of the big shopping plaza complexes near

22

Danvers. But how was he going to get out of here? There were sure to be thousands of people about in the complex; as soon as he came up out of the deserted basement corridors he would inevitably run into some of them. The faded denim pants and blue work-shirt he wore were not damning in themselves, but would certainly be a giveaway to anyone actively searching for an escaped prisoner. Somehow, he had to get a change of clothes.

Rowan started walking again, cautiously threading his way through a warren of basement corridors that seemed endless. Occasionally there were doors set in either wall, always locked and bolted. Storerooms, probably. From behind a few of the locked doors came the solemn, deep-throated chuffing of massive machinery, or, more rarely, a vibrant unwavering hum. Eventually, he passed into what seemed to be an older section of the complex. Here huge ceramic-covered pipes ran along the ceiling close overhead, the floor was rutted, and there were patches of mold on the walls. Some of the overhead lights were broken, and Rowan walked on through semi-darkness until he came to a door marked *Maintenance* at the junction of two shabby corridors. From behind this door came an unmistakable sound: someone snoring.

Quivering with tension, Rowan put his ear to the thin plastic door-panel. The only sound he could hear was the rhythmical snoring. He'd have to chance it. Carefully, he tried the door. It wasn't locked. He inched it open until a hinge gave a loud rusty squawk, then he pulled the door wide and stepped briskly into the room.

It was a small chamber with faded opalescent walls, smelling of sweat and old clothes and *bozuk*. Two walls were covered with dials, meters, readouts and tell-me-twices. A dusty computer terminal and a slave board stood in that corner. Most of the room was taken up by a dilapidated sink-cooker combination and a scarred folding table heaped with filthy biodegradable plates that had been re-used instead of catalyzed. In another corner was a much-patched waterbed. Flies drummed noisily against the walls, seeking a way out.

As Rowan entered the room, the snoring cut abruptly

23

off. A man-shaped dent in the waterbed began to work itself back to level. Someone was getting up. "What?" said a cracked, quavery voice: another old man. "Whatta'y-'want? Who—" The dent disappeared; the man must be on his feet now. "Inspection, jobbie," Rowan said slyly, "special orders from the manager," using the custodian's resultant hesitation to get a few steps nearer. Then he leaped.

The custodian screamed. Rowan ended up with a double-handful of cloth—a shirt?—which immediately tore away in his grasp, lunged again and felt his hand close around a bony wrist. He twisted it. The custodian screamed again. Rowan felt the custodian's free hand pound against the side of his head, and then they were wrestling each other in a drunken circle across the floor. The table went over with a great smash and clatter of plates. The custodian was still screaming. What a racket they were making! "Shut up, you!" Rowan shouted inanely, then managed to get a hand around the custodian's invisible throat. Ignoring a rain of wild windmill blows, Rowan throttled him into submission.

When the custodian went limp, Rowan let him slide to the floor. Suddenly everything was amazingly quiet. Swaying and gasping for breath, Rowan was washed over by a prickly wave of shame. He was pretty good at beating up old men, wasn't he? Suppose he'd killed the old guy? Apprehensively, Rowan crouched and felt about until he located the custodian, touching long invisible hair the texture of matted straw, and a scraggly beard—some ancient hippie given a makework job by the complex then, a *bozuk* addict probably. Rowan felt for a heartbeat. It was there—papery and labored, but there.

Relieved, Rowan began to search the custodian. Nothing—he was wearing some kind of frilly smock or dress without pockets. But on a night-stand near the waterbed Rowan found an odd leather object, and realized after a moment's thought that it must be a "wallet." Inside the old wallet were several unusual photographs, an identification card—with an embossed picture of the old man on it, unfortunately—a credit strip, and a nearly

24

exhausted monthly commuter ticket. Rowan examined the credit strip and bit his lip in frustration. The custodian didn't have much of a debit margin, not nearly as much as Rowan had hoped for. Not enough to buy a ticket out of the country or even out of the state, not enough to rent a car, or get an identity-scramble or an apartment to hole up in, so that was the end of those particular fantasies. And there wasn't enough left of the commuter ticket even to get him to Boston.

The custodian began to moan. Rowan paced over, located him again, and lifted his fist to clip him. But he couldn't bring himself to do it—the old man was so frail, it might kill him. Swearing at his squeamishness, Rowan dragged the feebly-struggling custodian to a closet, muscled him into it, and braced a chair against the door to keep it closed. "Hey!" the custodian shouted, and began to rattle the doorknob furiously. "Shut up," Rowan growled in self-conscious toughness, "or I'll come in there and tear your head off." The custodian shut up.

Rowan returned to the computer terminal. He'd have to do the best he could with what he had. He thought for a minute, then activated the terminal and dialed for the catalog of one of the big stores overhead. He computed sums in his head. Just enough. He inserted the coded credit slip into the slot and carefully punched out an order on the keyboard. The computer winked an acknowledgment light at him, and printed *Five Minutes* across the readout in green phosphorescent letters.

Sighing, Rowan leaned back in the chair to wait. Now that the immediate pressure was off, he realized how exhausted he was, how sore and battered and torn. His split lip ached fiercely, as did his lacerated cheek and his scraped arms. But most of all, he was *tired*. The room seemed to blur in and out of existence, and Rowan pulled up out of the nod just in time to keep his head from cracking against the terminal board. He'd almost fallen asleep. Stiffly, he got up. He was still rubber-legged, and very weak. Hunger was part of it. He literally could not remember the last time he'd eaten—sometime during his stay at the Newburyport jail, he supposed, but his memories of that ordeal were murky and confused. It could have been days. And he was intolerably thirsty.

He rummaged through the cubicle in search of food, but found nothing except a bar of VitaGel and a half-empty bottle of Joy. Grimacing with distaste, he ate the gluey bar, and then cautiously tried a sip of Joy. The euphoric effect hit him instantly, making him light-headed and giddy. Reluctantly, he put the bottle aside— he couldn't afford to get frazzled. There didn't seem to be any cups at all in the place, but he polished a small plate as well as he could with his sleeve and used it to get a drink of rusty water from the tap. The Joy was making his head buzz. He had an odd feeling of unreality and déjà vu, and a sudden strong intuition that the old custodian was about to speak. Just at that moment, the custodian said "Hey, man, you're never going to get away with this, you know that?" and Rowan subvocalized the last few words along with him, the feeling of déjà vu returning ten-fold. "Shut up, jobbie," Rowan growled, still with the feeling that he was reading something from a prepared script, "I really shouldn't be keeping you alive at all, scan?" The old man quieted again, but Rowan's head remained full of odd echoes, as if everything were doubled or tripled, crowding the room with ghosts and reflections. He never should have touched that goddamned Joy.

The terminal flashed its mauve warning light while Rowan was washing his face in the sink basin. His order thumped down the pneumatic shute into the hopper. Rowan quickly dried his face with his shirt. The water had cleared his head a little, and he looked much more presentable with the dirt and dried blood washed away. Feeling almost jaunty, he stripped off the rest of his clothes and padded over to pick up the package.

The package contained a nondescript shirt, some cloth pants, an overcoat, a hat, a pair of dark glasses, and a cane. If he must cope with being "blind," then let him be a "blind man." One of the hard-core blind, too low-caste to qualify for a TVSS. He would attract much less suspicion that way—the pose would explain why he was continually bumping into people, and he hoped that the Purloined

Letter syndrome would also work to his advantage. At the least, he would be more difficult to spot.

Rowan dressed hurriedly and left the room. He wouldn't have much time to get clear of the complex before an alarm was raised. The chair he'd braced under the doorknob was only made of hard plastic, and already, as Rowan hesitated in the corridor, he could hear the custodian attempting to break out of the closet. He really should have killed the old man—later he would probably have cause to regret that he had not. He set out through the warren of basement corridors.

He'd decided that it would be best to try to retrace his steps, but within a few moments he was hopelessly lost. A series of locked doors and blocked-off corridors gradually herded him in an entirely different direction, and he wandered through the old stone maze for what seemed like hours. Finally, just as he was beginning to despair, he located an unlocked service stairway.

At the top of the stairway, he stepped through a door and found himself in another of the fluorescent upper corridors. He struck out along it, remembering to tap the floor in front of him with his cane, and bumped into someone almost immediately.

"Oh, excuse me!" a voice said; a woman this time. "I guess I wasn't looking where I was going."

"That's perfectly all right, missy," Rowan said politely, and started to tap his way along again. There was no interference, no alarm.

Goddamn, it was going to work after all, wasn't it!

A few yards further on, he found one of the main stairways, and followed it up. He was suddenly claustrophobic, the whole subterranean complex pressing down on him with miles of corridors and stairs, steel, concrete, rock, plastic, dead black earth. God, to get *out*—

Sunlight struck him in the face.

It was still the same day, Rowan realized bemusedly, staring at the sky. Just a little while ago he had been on his way to Boston for the execution of his sentence. That had been years ago, it seemed. Decades ago. A lifetime. But the position of the sun showed that it had been barely four

27

hours. Time enough, Rowan thought. Surely an active hunt for him was underway by now.

Rowan had come out onto a landscaped mall, pyramidal buildings rearing high all around, windows flashing like hydra eyes in the sun. Hundreds of people were moving invisibly all around him; he could sense their presence as a nearly subliminal susurrus composed primarily of footsteps and voices. This type of shopping complex was potentially obsolete—the existence of house-to-store pneumatic networks should have killed them as dead as the dinosaurs. But this was an underpopulated region, where most of the homes still didn't have computer terminals; so far, downtown Boston was the closest area to have been completely converted to the system. It took time for advanced technology to disseminate across a society. And herd instinct was also a factor. With the commercial heart eaten out of the smaller towns, people gathered at the shopping plazas as earlier peoples had gathered at wells or watering-holes or drive-in restaurants, and for the same reasons: to gossip, to court, to meet friends, or just to have someplace to go at night. On a sunny day like this, there could easily be ten thousand people circulating through the complex, and somehow Rowan would have to get by them all.

He launched himself away from the shelter of a building, like a swimmer kicking off for a race, was jostled repeatedly, and realized that he was trying to buck a stream of pedestrian traffic going in the opposite direction. Obediently, Rowan turned around and let the pressure of that stream sweep him along, trusting that people would make allowances for a blind man and not crowd him too closely. The stream hurried him through the mall and into a covered walkway between buildings. Here, suddenly confined, the murmur of crowd-noises swelled into a roar. Clacking footsteps echoed and re-echoed from the low ceiling, voices reverberated hollowly—all sound became fuzzy and directionless, as though he were in a cave under the sea. Again the air seemed full of invisible wings. He could almost feel them

28

beating around his ears, hemming him in, wrapping him in gossamer.

Suddenly dizzy, Rowan sat down on a bench. He found that his heart was beating fast with irrational terror. His nerves were giving under the strain, he told himself as he fought down another attack of claustrophobia. He couldn't take much more. Slowly, he calmed himself. At least his disguise seemed to be working.

Someone touched his arm. "You're an escaped convict, aren't you?"

Rowan gasped. He would have jumped up and bolted instantly, but now the hand was on his wrist, holding him down. He half-turned, shifting his grip on the cane so that he could use it as a club.

"Hold it!" the unseen someone said in a low, urgent voice. "Don't run. Calm down, son—I'm on your side."

Rowan hesitated. "This is some kind of mistake—"

"No it's not," the other man said dryly. "You're pretending to be blind, aren't you? That's a good one, it hasn't been used much the last few years. You might get away with it. But don't just tap right in front of your feet, the way you've been doing. That's a dead giveaway. Keep your cane swinging steadily from side to side as you tap. Remember, you're supposed to be feeling your way along with it, like a bug does with his antennas, right? And don't walk so fast. Be a little more uncertain about it, son, *listen* more, as if you're trying for auditory clues. And for God's sake, stop staring at things. And tracking them! It's obvious you can see through those damn glasses. You won't last an hour that way."

Rowan opened his mouth, closed it again. "Who are you?" he said.

"It's a real stroke of luck, me being able to spot you," the other man said, ignoring him. "I hoped you'd show up in this area, and I've been cruising around for an hour trying to pick you up. Logical, in a way, prisoners making for a place like this, cops don't seem to think that way though. Luckily for you. Still, we're going to have to jump to get you out of here. But don't you worry—you just

29

listen to me, now, and you'll be all right. I'm on your side, son."

"I wasn't aware that I had a side," Rowan said wearily.

"You do now, son, you do now. Whether you like it or not. The enemy of my enemy, right?" As the man was saying this, Rowan had a sudden vivid mental picture of how he must look: a small, intense man of middle years with a foxy, florid face and hair like wire brush. "Listen, now," the man said, "we haven't got much time. You know Quincy Park in Beverly? Just down the coast a ways from Dane Street Beach?"

Rowan realized, to his own surprise, that he did know Quincy Park. He could mistily visualize it, the trees, the long grassy slope down to the seawall, the rocky beach, the ocean—he must have passed through there at one time, long ago. "Yeah, I know it," he said.

"Well, you just get there before dark. Get there somehow, whatever you do, if you want to keep on living. It's a station on the Underground Railroad, one we haven't used in a long while. They won't be watching it. I'll call up ahead and arrange it, and there'll be a sailboat waiting for you just offshore at Quincy Park. You get on her, they'll take you up the coast, you'll be safe in Canada by morning. Right? But listen—you've got to make the connection the first time. The boat'll only wait until dark, and we won't send it back there two evenings in a row. You understand? But if you make it to the boat, why, you'll be all right then. You'll be fine."

"I—"

"No, listen now, boy, I mean *really* OK. We'll get you down to Bolivia. The insurrectionists have got equipment at La Paz as good as anything they've got in Boston. They'll break the injunction and you'll be normal again. They've done it a hundred times—you don't think you're the only political prisoner ever to escape, do you? And they've got plenty of use for good men down there. So you just concentrate on getting to Beverly, and you'll be OK. Keep up the blind man act, it's your best bet."

"Wait a minute—why can't you just drive me over there now?"

"Too risky. They'll be checking private cars before long, but they might not stop public transportation. Besides, I've got to lead them away from here before they close the ring on you. Now look—you wait around a minute, then head out of here, east. I'm going to intercept one of the patrol sweeps and tell them that I saw you bicycling west, heading for North Reading or Middleton, maybe. They know you stole a bicycle, but they don't know yet that you ditched it. They'll bite. And that'll give you a better chance to make it out of here. Good luck, son."

"But what if—" Rowan found himself talking to empty air; the man was gone. Rowan sat and puzzled at it for a while, then shrugged. What other choice did he have? He got up and tapped his way through the invisible crowds, surreptitiously following painted arrows to the tubetrain stop, trying to comply with the behavioral pointers his benefactor had given him. He did feel more in character that way, he discovered, and more secure.

While he was waiting for the tubetrain, he again heard the wild keening of sirens in the sky, very loud and terrible, swelling until it seemed they must be directly overhead. Rowan didn't look around. Doggedly, he leaned on his cane and waited. The sound of the sirens faded away into distance, was gone. Rowan realized that his legs were trembling. He leaned more heavily on the cane.

The tubetrain arrived. He let it swallow him, shoved his commuter ticket into the computer, and tapped his way to a seat, hoping he wouldn't pick one that was already occupied. He did, but the occupant immediately muttered an apology and moved to another seat. Deference to the blind. It was wonderful. Rowan sat down.

It was odd to ride in an apparently empty tubetrain, and yet at the same time hear all around you a hundred little noises—rustling papers, coughing, footsteps, voices—that proved you were not alone at all. Rowan kept staring out the window at the bland green countryside, then remembering that he was supposed to be blind and looking self-consciously away. He was thinking about what the man at the shopping plaza had said, replaying his words like a tape, analyzing them, sniffing at ever nuance of meaning. Only now, after the fact, was he beginning to believe that there might be some truth to what he had been told—that there really was an Underground Railroad, that there would be a boat waiting for him, that somewhere he could be given a chance to start a whole new life. He wouldn't quite let himself hope, but he was thawing to it.

The train pulled into Salem.

After Salem, the tubeline swung south and then east again to Marblehead, and then on south to Lynn and Boston. But Beverly was about four miles north of Salem, on the far side of the estuary. Rowan supposed that there was some kind of public transportation between the two · towns, but he didn't know what, and couldn't have afforded to utilize it anyway; the commuter-ticket was dead. He was going to have to walk. Maybe it was better that way.

Up Essex Street, fumbling and tapping in the dusty sunlight.

Everything went well for perhaps a mile. Then Rowan discovered, to his dismay, that practically the entire eastern half of town had been razed since the last time he'd been through, and was being made over into a vast industrial complex of some sort. On this side of Essex Street, there were still houses and trees, but on the far side, across a flat expanse of asphalt, he was confronted with a chaotic expanse of factories, trainyards, excavations, construction sites and storage areas. Some of the factories were already in operation, others were still going up. The whole region was crisscrossed with deep gullies and pits, and some areas seemed to have been terraced and stairstepped in a manner reminiscent of strip-mining. Construction was taking place on many different levels among the terraces, and a gray haze of smoke hung over everything. East, toward the ocean, a herd of snaky black machines were busily eating the last of a row of old wooden houses.

He had hoped to keep to the side streets, but it seemed that there weren't any side streets here anymore. Unless he circled back to the west, he'd have to keep on following the major thoroughfare north, and that was more risky than he liked.

Rowan decided that he'd have to take the chance of following Essex Street. He had just started to tap his way forward again when wood-pulp geysered from a tree alongside him, leaving a ragged new hole in the bark.

Sound slapped his ears a heartbeat later, but by then he was already moving. By the time he consciously realized that someone was shooting at him, he had covered half the distance to the nearest cluster of factory buildings, running faster than he had ever run in his life, dodging and swerving like a madman. Suddenly there was a railing in front of him, with a drop of unknown depth beyond it. He vaulted up and over it without breaking stride. A bullet made the railing ring like a gong a second after he had cleared it.

He dropped about ten feet down onto hard pavement, took *ukemi* as well as he could, and was up and dodging instantly in spite of a painfully wrenched ankle. As he ran, he was acutely aware of how hot it was under the glaring sun. The only thought in his head was an incongruous wish for a glass of water. Another shot splintered concrete at his heels, and then he was slamming through a door and into a building. It was some kind of huge assembly plant with a cavernous ceiling, full of cold echoes and bitter blue lights. He bullied his way through it, followed by a spreading wave of alarm as he collided with people and knocked work-benches over, staggering, falling down and scrambling up again. As he dodged out a door on the far side of the plant, he heard another gunshot behind him. Then he was tearing through a narrow alleyway between factories. There were rainbow puddles of oil and spilled chemicals on the ground here, and he splashed through them deliberately, hoping that the bitter reek of them would throw his pursuers off if they were tracking him by scent. Someone shouted excitedly at his heels. He ducked into another factory building.

It became phantasmagoria, a nightmare of pursuit—
Rowan running endlessly through vast rooms full of
shapes and stinks and lights and alien noises, while
invisible things snatched at him and tried to pull him
down. Everything was fragmentary and disjointed now
for Rowan, as though he existed only in discontinuous
slices of time. In one such slice, he was hitching a ride on a
flat-car that was rumbling through a trainyard between
varicolored mountains of chemical waste, listening to
sirens and shouts behind him and wondering when he
should jump off and run. In another, he was dodging
through a multi-leveled forest of oddly jointed pipes, like
a child swarming through a jungle gym. Another, and he
was climbing slowly and tenaciously up a cyclone fence.
Another, and he was running through a vacant lot, a
construction site that had been temporarily abandoned
and which had been grown over everywhere by man-high
expanses of scrub grass and wild wheat.

Rowan tripped over a discarded tool, fell flat on his
face, stayed down. That saved him. A scythe of heat swept
across the field at hip level, and suddenly all the grass was
burning. This time, they were using lasers. He rolled
frantically through the blazing grass in an instinctive
attempt to put out the little fires that were starting on his
clothes and in his hair, and accidentally tumbled down
into a steep, clay-sided gulley. There was a sluggish, foot-
deep trickle of muddy water at the bottom of the gulley,
and he crawled through it on his belly while everything
burned above him, choking, blinded by smoke and baked
by heat that blistered his back, an inchworm on a griddle
in Hell.

Then he was kneeling in a tree-shaded backyard while
someone washed his face with a wet, scented towel. He
retched helplessly, and firm hands held his head. He had
something very important to say, some vitally important
thing that he had almost remembered, but when he tried
to speak all he could coax from his cracked lips and
swollen tongue was an ugly jangling croak. "Shut up,
goddamn you," said an anxious voice. A woman's voice.
He rested in her arms, and stared up at her in awe. She was

radiantly beautiful, as cool and clear as the water she used to sponge him, and she smiled like the sun as she wiped the blood and slime and singed hair from his face. He woke up enough then to realize that he had been slipping in and out of delirium, that he really couldn't see her at all. She was invisible. That seemed very sad and unreasonable. He discussed it with her while she bathed his face, carrying out a long, intricate conversation with her, not even trying to use his voice this time, it was such a poor instrument for communication, and his didn't work anyway. Then she was forcing something into his mouth—a capsule—and holding water to his lips.

Drinking was so painful that it shocked him almost fully awake, and then the antifever capsule hit his system, and that helped too. He realized that she was trying to wrestle him into something. A caftan. "What are you doing?" he asked, quite clearly and reasonably. "Keep quiet!" she snarled. "Raise your arms a little." Dutifully, he helped her get the caftan onto him. The world faded for a moment, and when it came back she was wrapping a scarf around his head. "Cover the singed hair, anyway," she said. "I'd shave your head if I had time. Goddamn you, don't go to sleep! You've got to get out of here, right now."

With an effort, Rowan pulled himself to clarity. He sat up and took his head in his hands. "Come on, come on," the woman was saying nervously, "get up." Her hands took him under the arms and tugged, he scrambled and flailed, pushing with legs that didn't want to work. There was a moment of extraordinary nausea and pain, and then he was on his feet, trembling, half-supported by the woman. "Just stay on your feet now," she said. "You'll be OK. That's right." She took her hands away, and somehow he managed to stay upright, swaying, feeling as if his bones had melted. By this time, Rowan had figured out what was happening, and he clumsily started to thank the woman for helping him, but she cut him off irritably. "Just get out of here, you goddamned fool. I can't do anything more for you. Done more than I should already, I got a family to think of. You just go on and get out of here now. Road's out that way"—not knowing that he couldn't see which way she was pointing—"don't guess you'd want to go back out over the fence the way you came in, too suspicious." She hesitated, as though afraid to wish him well. "Go on, now," she said at last, and he could almost imagine her making shooing motions at him. Her voice was unsteady. "Please go. I have to think of my family. I can't let them catch you here." He sensed then that she had gone abruptly away. A moment later the back door of the house opened and closed. He wondered if she was still watching him through the glass half of the door. Somehow he hoped that she was.

Rowan made his way around to the front of the house, and discovered that he was on Bridge Street, a mile or more from the factory area, although he had no clear recollection of how he had gotten there. That made it a fairly straightforward problem. He had to follow Bridge Street north another mile, cross the bridge over the estuary, and he would be there. He could hardly feel his body anymore, but that was probably a blessing. It allowed him to sit somewhere far removed from pain and drive his body like a car, coax it along like a beaten-up old heap being driven to a second-hand dealer's lot, the owner swearing bitterly all the way and hoping he can get the thing there before it falls apart. He set out for Beverly.

The world began to turn to mush again as he walked. After a few blocks he started to hallucinate, seeing brief vivid flashes of things that couldn't be there, having long talks with people who didn't exist. He would come back to himself as from a great distance, and find that he was talking to himself in a very loud voice and swinging his arms wildly, or else making hoarse grunting noises, *huhn, huhn*, like an exhausted bear harried closely by hounds. He no longer cared if he attracted attention or even if he bumped into people. He was no longer worried about pursuit; in fact, he had forgotten that anybody was after him. He only knew that he had to get to Beverly. Reaching that goal had become an end in itself; he didn't remember what he was supposed to do when he got there, and he didn't care. All his will was taken up by the task of keeping his body clumping leadenly along, while the world flowed by like porridge.

He was on a bridge, suspended between sea and sky.

Out there to the east was Great Misery Island, then Bakers Island, and then nothing but water, an endless fan of icy water spreading on and out forever, turning into Ocean. There was freedom. To sail out and away forever toward the rising sun, with no restrictions, no boundaries, just infinite space and Rowan skimming the glassy white tops of the waves.

There was a gusty wet wind coming in from the sea. For what seemed like a very long time it hit Rowan across the face, back and forth, back and forth, as methodical and unpitying as a manager bent on reviving a heavyweight with a wet towel in the tenth round of a losing fight, until Rowan's head finally began to clear. He was slumped against the railing of the bridge, cold metal biting into his armpits. He had hooked his arms over the top rail, and that had kept him from actually falling down, but he had no idea how long he had been hanging there in a daze, starring out into Massachusetts Bay. Sailboats and trawlers were moving back and forth in the deep channel, and the sight of them jarringly reminded him why he had to get to Beverly.

Then he heard sirens in the sky behind him.

Rowan started walking again. He had no reserves left—neither panic nor the imminence of death could prod him into running. He was physically unable to run, no matter what the provocation. So he walked away from his pursuers, trudging slowly across the rest of the bridge and up the hill on the other side. He was in Beverly now, perhaps a quarter-mile from his goal. The sirens were a thin, irritating thread of sound, just on the edge of hearing. They didn't seem to be coming any closer. Perhaps the police were holding a search pattern over Salem.

If only they would stay away for ten more minutes.

Rowan forced himself to walk faster. But the extra effort involved began to jar him away from reality again.

37

He fell into a walking dream of Bolivia, the rugged, sun-bronzed men welcoming him into the ranks of the insurrectionists, the trip to their remote mountain fortresses, the women waiting to welcome him, the important work waiting to be done. A new life. To be free of fear—for the first time in how long? Had he ever been free of fear? Had there ever been a day when someone wasn't spying on him, prying and prodding and pushing him, wrapping him in gossamer that was as strong as iron, controlling him like a puppet? A spark of anger touched him then, and he blazed up like old dead wood. Let the insurrectionists give him a gun—that was all he'd ask for, that was all he wanted.

His anger saved him. He'd been staggering down Rantoulle Street in a somnambulistic daze, and had nearly missed his turn. But rage shook him momentarily awake. He turned onto Edwards Street, past the school. He could hear children playing in the schoolyard, their voices rising and falling through the mellow afternoon air like the shrill calling of birds, but he could not see them as he passed—to his eyes, only leaves and paper-scraps moved across the asphalt with the wind, and he also moved on with it, alone.

The sirens were getting louder. They were coming after him.

But then he turned a final corner, and the sea spread out below him, glinting and silver and vast, opening the world to the horizon. This was Quincy Park. As he stood on the road above, his eyes followed the long slope down to the seawall, then beyond the beach to the ocean, and to the slim white sailboat that waited there, like a sign, like a dove on the water, like the fulfillment of all the dreams he'd ever known.

Rowan started down the slope toward the ocean, his feet slipping on the grass, breaking at last into a ponderous trot. He was almost there. Hope opened like a wound inside him, molten and amazing.

Something slammed into his ribcage like a white-hot sword, sending him staggering back, knocking the breath and the hope out of him. For a second, the incredible shock of the impact dissolved all illusions, and he remembered, and knew that again he had failed to escape. *Someday!* he shouted in a great silent puff of pain and rage and sudden terrible knowledge. *Someday!*

Then another blow took him over the heart and drove him into darkness.

The fat man worked the action of the tranquilizer rifle and ejected a gleaming metal dart. "My God!" he breathed, reverentially.

Up the slope, the technicians were already reprogramming the mobile computers for the next runthrough, using the stereo plotting tanks to set up a paradigm describing all the possible sequences and combinations of sequences that might apply, an exercise in four-dimensional topography and systems-flow. Of course, the computers did all the real work: controlling the sequencing, selecting among tables of alternatives as the real-world situation altered and reprogramming themselves on the fly, coordinating a thousand physical details such as the locking of doors and the blocking of certain corridors that kept the human subject restricted to a manageable spatial network of routes and choices, directing the human "beaters" who helped keep the subject "in the chute," triggering previously implanted fantasy fugue sequences such as the car crash and timing them so that they melded smoothly with real-world action. And much else besides. Nevertheless, the human technicians considered themselves to be overworked, and all made a point of looking harried and rather ostentatiously tired.

A small, foxy-faced man appeared at the fat man's elbow. "Very nice," he said briskly, rubbing his hands. "As good a show as I promised you, Senator, I think you'll agree with that. And of course," he added piously, "so valuable therapeutically." He smiled. "Always so many possibilities! Will he get to Hamilton, or end up in Danvers? Will he kill the old man or not? Will he find the car or let me steer him to the tube? An enormous but finite number of choices, aesthetically it's quite elegant. I'm always reminded of the medieval theologies. Free will operating within a framework of predetermination. Of course," he said, smiling ingratiatingly at the fat man, "you realize Who that makes us."

The fat man wasn't listening. His face was beaded with sweat. "That was fine," he said. "My God, Doctor, that was very fine." His eyes remained glassy for a moment longer, and then animation came back into his features. He broke the rifle and started to hand it to the foxy-faced man, then hesitated, and with an eager shy deference that was obviously foreign to so important a man, asked, "How long does it take to get him ready again? I mean, it's hours yet until dark, and I was wondering if it would be possible—"

The doctor smiled indulgently. "Always time for one more," he said.

Flash Point

BEN JACOBS WAS on his way back to Skowhegan when he found the abandoned car. It was parked on a lonely stretch of secondary road between North Anson and Madison, skewed diagonally over the shoulder.

Kids again, was Jacobs' first thought—more of the road gypsies who plagued the state every summer until they were driven south by the icy whip of the first nor'easter. Probably from the big encampment down near Norridgewock, he decided, and he put his foot back on the accelerator. He'd already had more than his fill of outer-staters this season, and it wasn't even the end of August. Then he looked more closely at the car, and eased up on the gas again. It was too big, too new to belong to kids. He shifted down into second, feeling the crotchety old pickup shudder. It was an expensive car, right enough; he doubted that it came from within twenty miles of here. You didn't use a big-city car on most of the roads in this neck of the woods, and you couldn't stay on the highways forever. He squinted to see more detail. What kind of plates did it have? You're doing it again, he thought, suddenly and sourly. He was a man as aflame with curiosity as a magpie, and—having been brought up strictly to mind his own business—he considered it a vice. Maybe the car was stolen. It's possible, a'n't it? he insisted, arguing with himself. It could have been used in a robbery

41

and then ditched, like that car from the bank job over to Farmington. It happened all the time.

You don't even fool yourself anymore, he thought, and then he grinned and gave in. He wrestled the old truck into the breakdown lane, jolted over a pothole, and coasted to a bumpy stop a few yards behind the car. He switched the engine off.

Silence swallowed him instantly.

Thick and dusty, the silence poured into the morning, filling the world as hot wax fills a mold. It drowned him completely, it possessed every inch and ounce of him. Almost, it spooked him.

Jacobs hesitated, shrugged, and then jumped down from the cab. Outside it was better—still quiet, but not preternaturally so. There was wind soughing through the spruce woods, a forlorn but welcome sound, one he had heard all his life. There was a wood thrush hammering at the morning, faint with distance but distinct. And a faraway buzzing drone overhead, like a giant sleepy bee or bluebottle, indicated that there was a Piper Cub up there somewhere, probably heading for the airport at Norridgewock. All this was familiar and reassuring. Getting nervy, is all, he told himself, long in the tooth and spooky.

Nevertheless, he walked very carefully toward the car, flat footed and slow, the way he used to walk on patrol in 'Nam, more years ago than he cared to recall. His fingers itched for something, and after a few feet he realized that he was wishing he'd brought his old deer rifle along. He grimaced irritably at that, but the wish pattered through his mind again and again, until he was close enough to see inside the parked vehicle.

The car was empty.

"Old fool," he said sourly.

Snorting in derision at himself, he circled the car, peering in the windows. There were skid marks in the gravel of the breakdown lane, but they weren't deep—the car hadn't been going fast when it hit the shoulder; probably it had been already meandering out of control, with no foot on the accelerator. The hood and bumpers

42

weren't damaged; the car had rolled to a stop against the low embankment, rather than crashing into it. None of the tires were flat. In the woods taking a leak, Jacobs thought. Damn fool didn't even leave his turn signals on. Or it could have been his battery, or a vapor lock or something, and he'd hiked on up the road looking for a gas station. "He still should have ma'ked it off someway," Jacobs muttered. Tourists never knew enough to find their ass in a snowstorm. This one probably wasn't even carrying any signal flags or flares.

The driver's door was wide open, and next to it was a child's plastic doll, lying facedown in the gravel. Jacobs could not explain the chill that hit him then, the horror that seized him and shook him until he was almost physically ill. Bristling, he stooped and thrust his head into the car. There was a burnt, bitter smell inside, like onions, like hot metal. A layer of gray ash covered the front seat and the floor, a couple of inches deep; a thin stream of it was trickling over the doorjamb to the ground and pooling around the plastic feet of the doll. Hesitantly he touched the ash—it was sticky and soapy to the touch. In spite of the sunlight that was slanting into the car and warming up the upholstery, the ash was cold, almost icy. The cloth ceiling directly over the front seat was lightly blackened with soot—he scraped some of it off with his thumbnail—but there was no other sign of fire. Scattered among the ashes on the front seat were piles of clothing. Jacobs could pick out a pair of men's trousers, a sports coat, a bra, slacks, a bright child's dress, all undamaged. More than one person. They're all in the woods taking a leak, he thought inanely. Sta'k naked.

Sitting on the dashboard were a 35-mm. Nikon SI with a telephoto lens and a new Leicaflex. In the hip pocket of the trousers was a wallet, containing more than fifty dollars in cash, and a bunch of credit cards. He put the wallet back. Not even a tourist was going to be fool enough to walk off and leave this stuff sitting here, in an open car.

He straightened up, and felt the chill again, the deathly noonday cold. This time he *was* spooked. Without knowing why, he nudged the doll out of the puddle of ash with his foot, and then he shuddered. "Hello!" he shouted, at the top of his voice, and got back only a dull, flat echo from the woods. Where in hell *had* they gone?

All at once, he was exhausted. He'd been out before dawn, on a trip up to Kingfield and Carrabassett, and it was catching up with him. Maybe that was why he was so jumpy over nothing. Getting old, c'n't take this kind of shit anymore. How long since you've had a vacation? He opened his mouth to shout again, but uneasily decided not to. He stood for a moment, thinking it out, and then walked back to his truck, hunch-shouldered and limping. The old load of shrapnel in his leg and hip was beginning to bother him again.

Jacobs drove a mile down the highway to a rest stop. He had been hoping he would find the people from the car here, waiting for a tow truck, but the rest area was deserted. He stuck his head into the wood-and-fieldstone latrine, and found that it was inhabited only by buzzing clouds of bluebottles and blackflies. He shrugged. So much for that. There was a pay phone on a pole next to the picnic tables, and he used it to call the sheriff's office in Skowhegan. Unfortunately, Abner Jackman answered the phone, and it took Jacobs ten exasperating minutes to argue him into showing any interest. "Well, if they did," Jacobs said grudgingly, "they did it without any clothes." *Gobblegobblebuzz*, said the phone. "With a *kid*?" Jacobs demanded. *Buzzgobbleftzbuzz*, the phone said, giving in. "Ayah," Jacobs said grudgingly, "I'll stay theah until you show up." And he hung up.

"Damned foolishness," he muttered. This was going to cost him the morning.

County Sheriff Joe Riddick arrived an hour later. He was a stocky, slab-sided man, apparently cut all of a piece out of a block of granite—his shoulders seemed to be the same width as his hips, his square-skulled, square-jawed head thrust belligerently up from his monolithic body without any hint of a neck. He looked like an old snapping turtle: ugly, mud colored, powerful. His hair was snow-white, and his eyes were bloodshot and ill-tempered. He glared at Jacobs dangerously out of red-rimmed eyes with tiny pupils. He looked ready to snap.

"Good morning," Jacobs said coldly.

"Morning," Riddick grunted. "You want to fill me in on this?"

Jacobs did. Riddick listened impassively. When Jacobs finished, Riddick snorted and brushed a hand back over his close-cropped snowy hair. "Some damn fool skylark more'n likely," he said, sourly, shaking his head a little. "*O*-kay, then," he said, suddenly becoming officious and brisk. "If this turns out to be anything serious, we may need you as a witness. Understand? All right." He looked at his watch. "All right. We're waiting for the state boys. I don't think you're needed anymore." Riddick's face was hard and cold and dull—as if it had been molded in lead. He stared pointedly at Jacobs. His eyes were opaque as marbles. "Good day."

Twenty minutes later Jacobs was passing a proud little sign, erected by the Skowhegan Chamber of Commerce, that said: HOME OF THE LARGEST SCULPTED WOODEN INDIAN IN THE WORLD! He grinned. Skowhegan had grown a great deal in the last decade, but somehow it was still a small town. It had resisted the modern tropism to skyscrape and had sprawled instead, spreading out along the banks of the Kennebec River in both directions. Jacobs parked in front of a dingy storefront on Water Street, in the heart of town. A sign in the window commanded: EAT; at night it glowed an imperative neon red. The sign belonged to an establishment that had started life as the Colonial Cafe, with a buffet and quaint rustic decor, and was finishing it, twenty years and three recessions later, as a greasy lunchroom with faded movie posters on the wall—owned and operated by Wilbur and Myna Phipps, a cheerful and indestructible couple in their late sixties. It was crowded and hot inside—the place had a large number of regulars, and most of them were in attendance for lunch. Jacobs spotted Will Sussmann at the counter, jammed in between an inverted glass bowl full of doughnuts and the protruding rear-end of the coffee percolator.

45

Sussmann—chief staff writer for the Skowhegan *Inquirer*, stringer and columnist for a big Bangor weekly—had saved him a seat by piling the adjacent stool with his hat, coat, and briefcase. Not that it was likely he'd had to struggle too hard for room. Even Jacobs, whose father had moved to Skowhegan from Bangor when Jacobs was three, was regarded with faint suspicion by the real oldtimers of the town. Sussmann, being originally an outer-stater and a "foreigner" to boot, was completely out of luck; he'd only lived here ten years, and that wasn't enough even to begin to tip the balance in his favor.

Sussmann retrieved his paraphernalia; Jacobs sat down and began telling him about the car. Sussmann said it was weird. "We'll never get anything out of Riddick," he said. He began to attack a stack of hotcakes. "He's hated my guts ever since I accused him of working over those gypsy kids last summer, putting one in the hospital. That would have cost him his job, except the higher echelons were being 'foursquare behind their dedicated law enforcement officers' that season. Still, it didn't help his reputation with the town any."

"We don't tolerate that kind of thing in these pa'ts," Jacobs said grimly. "Hell, Will, those kids are a royal pain in the ass, but—" But not in these pa'ts, he told himself, not that. There are decent limits. He was surprised at the depth and ferocity of his reaction. "This a'n't Alabama," he said.

"Might as well be, with Riddick. His idea of law enforcement's to take everybody he doesn't like down in the basement and beat the crap out of them." Sussmann sighed. "Anyway, Riddick wouldn't stop to piss on me if my hat was on fire, that's for sure. Good thing I got other ways of finding stuff out."

Jed Everett came in while Jacobs was ordering coffee. He was a thin, cadaverous man with a long nose; his hair was going rapidly to gray; put him next to short, round Sussmann and they would look like Mutt and Jeff. At forty-eight—Everett was a couple of years older than Jacobs, just as Sussmann was a couple of years younger—he was considered to be scandalously young for a small-town doctor, especially a GP. But old Dr. Barlow had died of a stroke three years back, leaving his younger partner in residency, and they were stuck with him.

One of the regulars had moved away from the trough, leaving an empty seat next to Jacobs, and Everett was talking before his buttocks had hit the upholstery. He was a jittery man, with lots of nervous energy, and he loved to fret and rant and gripe, but softly and goodnaturedly, with no real force behind it, as if he had a volume knob that had been turned down.

"What a morning!" Everett said. "Jesus H. Christ on a bicycle—'scuse me, Myna, I'll take some coffee, please, black—I swear it's psychosomatic. Honest to God, gentlemen, she's a case for the medical journals, dreams the whole damn shitbundle up out of her head just for the fun of it, I swear before all my hopes of heaven, swop me blue if she doesn't. *Definitely* psychosomatic."

"He's learned a new word," Sussmann said.

"If you'd wasted all the time I have on this nonsense," Everett said fiercely, "you'd be whistling a different tune out of the other side of your face, *I* can tell *you*, oh yes indeed. What kind of meat d'you have today, Myna? How about the chops—they good?—all right, and put some greens on the plate, please. Okay? Oh, and some homefrieds, now I think about it, please. If you have them."

"What's got your back up?" Jacobs asked mildly.

"You know old Mrs. Crawford?" Everett demanded. "Hm? Lives over to the Island, widow, has plenty of money? Three times now I've diagnosed her as having cancer, serious but still operable, and *three* times now I've sent her down to Augusta for exploratory surgery, and each time they got her down on the table and opened her up and couldn't find a thing, not a goddamned thing, old bitch's hale and hearty as a prize hog. Spontaneous remission. All psychosomatic, clear as mud. Three *times*, though. It's shooting my reputation all to hell down there. Now she thinks she's got an ulcer. I hope her kidney falls out, right in the street. Thank you, Myna. Can I have another cup of coffee?" He sipped his coffee, when it arrived, and looked a little more meditative. "Course, I think I've seen a good number of cases like that, I *think*, I said, ha'd to prove it when they're terminal. Wouldn't surprise me if a good many of the people who die of cancer—or a lot of other diseases, for that matter—were like that. No real physical cause, they just get tired of living, something dries up inside them, their systems stop trying to defend them, and one thing or another knocks them off. They become easy to touch off, like tinder. Most of them don't change their minds in the middle, though, like that fat old sow."

Wilbur Phipps, who had been leaning on the counter listening, ventured the opinion that modern medical science had never produced anything even half as good as the oldfashioned mustard plaster. Everett flared up instantly.

"You ever bejesus try one?" Phipps demanded.

"No, and I don't bejesus intend to!" Everett said.

Jacobs turned toward Sussmann. "Wheah you been, this early in the day?" he asked. "A'n't like you to haul yourself out before noon."

"Up at the Factory. Over to West Mills."

"What was up? Another hearing?"

"Yup. Didn't stick—they aren't going to be injuncted."

"They never will be," Jacobs said. "They got too much money, too many friends in Augusta. The Board'll never touch them."

"I don't believe that," Sussmann said. Jacobs grunted and sipped his coffee.

"As Christ's my judge," Everett was saying, in a towering rage, "I'll never understand you people, not if I live to be two hundred, not if I get to be so old my ass falls off and I have to lug it around in a handcart. I swear to God. Some of you ain' got a pot to piss in, so goddamned poor you can't afford to buy a bottle of aspirins, let alone, *let alone* pay your doctor bills from the past half-million years, and yet you go out to some godforsaken hick town too small to turn a horse around in proper and see an unlicensed practitioner, a goddamn back-woods quack, an un*mit*igated phony, and *pay* through the nose so this witchdoctor can assault you with yarb potions and poultices, and stick leeches on your ass, for all *I* know—" Jacobs lost track of the conversation. He studied a bee that was bumbling along the putty-and-plaster edge of the storefront window, swimming through the thick and dusty sunlight, looking for a way out. He felt numb, distanced from reality. The people around him looked increasingly strange. He found that it took an effort of will to recognize them at all, even Sussmann, even Everett. It scared him. These were people Jacobs saw every day of his life. Some of them he didn't actually *like*—not in the way that big-city folk thought of liking someone—but they were all his neighbors. They belonged here, they were a part of his existence, and that carried its own special intimacy. But today he was beginning to see them as an intolerant sophisticate from the city might see them: dull, provincial, sunk in an iron torpor that masqueraded as custom and routine. That was valid, in its way, but it was a grossly one-sided picture, ignoring a thousand virtues, compensations and kindnesses. But that was the way he was seeing them. As aliens. As strangers.

Distractedly, Jacobs noticed that Everett and Sussmann were making ready to leave. "No rest for the weary," Everett was saying, and Jacobs found himself nodding unconsciously in agreement. Swamped by a sudden rush of loneliness, he invited both men home for dinner that night. They accepted, Everett with the qualification that he'd have to see what his wife had planned. Then they were gone, and Jacobs found himself alone at the counter.

He knew that he should have gone back to work also; he had some more jobs to pick up, and a delivery to make. But he felt very tired, too flaccid and heavy to move, as if some tiny burrowing animal had gnawed away his bones, as if he'd been hamstrung and hadn't realized it. He told himself that it was because he was hungry; he was running himself down, as Carol had always said he someday

49

would. So he dutifully ordered a bowl of chili.

The chili was murky, amorphous stuff, bland and lukewarm. Listlessly, he spooned it up.

No rest for the weary.

"You know what I was nuts about when I was a kid?" Jacobs suddenly observed to Wilbur Phipps. "Rafts. I was a'ways making rafts out of old planks and sheet tin and whatevah other junk I could scrounge up, begging old rope and nails to lash them together with. Then I'd break my ass dragging them down to the Kennebec. And you know what? They a'ways sunk. Every goddamned time."

"Ayah?" Wilbur Phipps said.

Jacobs pushed the bowl of viscid chili away, and got up. Restlessly, he wandered over to where Dave Lucas, the game warden, was drinking beer and talking to a circle of men ". . . dogs will be the end of deer in these pa'ts, I swear to God. And I a'n't talking about wild dogs neither, I'm talking about your ordinary domestic pets. A'n't it so, every winter? Half-starved deer a'n't got a chance in hell 'gainst somebody's big pet hound, all fed-up and rested. The deer those dogs don't kill outright, why they chase 'em to death, and then they don't even eat 'em. Run 'em out of the forest covah into the open and they get pneumonia. Run 'em into the river and through thin ice and they get drowned. Remember last yeah, the deer that big hound drove out onto the ice? Broke both its front legs and I had to go out and shoot the poor bastid. Between those goddamn dogs and all the nighthunters we got around here lately, we a'n't going to have any deer left in this county . . ." Jacobs moved away, past a table where Abner Jackman was pouring ketchup over a plateful of scrambled eggs, and arguing about Communism with Steve Girard, a volunteer fireman and Elk, and Allen Ewing, a postman, who had a son serving with the Marines in Bolivia. ". . . let 'em win theah," Jackman was saying in a nasal voice, "and they'll be swa'ming all over us eventu'ly, sure as shit. Ain' no way to stop 'em then. And you're better off blowing your brains out than living under the Reds, don't ever think otherwise." He screwed the ketchup top back onto the bottle, and glanced up in time to see Jacobs start to go by.

"Ben!" Jackman said, grabbing Jacobs by the elbow. "You can tell 'em." He grinned vacuously at Jacobs—a lanky, loose-jointed, slack-faced man. "He can tell you, boys, what it's like being in a country overrun with Communists, what they do to everybody. You were in 'Nam when you were a youngster, weren't you?"

"Yeah."

After a pause, Jackman said, "You ain' got no call to take offense, Ben." His voice became a whine. "I didn't mean no ha'm. I didn't mean nothing."

"Forget it," Jacobs said, and walked out.

Dave Lucas caught up with Jacobs just outside the door. He was a short, grizzled man with iron-gray hair, about seven years older than Jacobs. "You know, Ben," Lucas said, "the thing of it is, Abner really doesn't mean any ha'm." Lucas smiled bleakly; his grandson had been killed last year, in the Retreat from La Paz. "It's just that he a'n't too bright, is all."

"They don't want him kicked ev'ry so often," Jacobs said, "then they shouldn't let him out of his kennel at all." He grinned. "Dinner tonight? About eight?"

"Sounds fine," Lucas said. "We're going to catch a nighthunter, out near Oaks Pond, so I'll probably be late."

"We'll keep it wa'm for you."

"Just the comp'ny'll be enough."

Jacobs started his truck and pulled out into the afternoon traffic. He kept his hands locked tightly around the steering wheel. He was amazed and dismayed by the surge of murderous anger he had felt toward Jackman; the reaction to it made him queasy, and left the muscles knotted all across his back and shoulders. Dave was right, Abner couldn't rightly be held responsible for the dumbass things he said—But if Jackman had said one more thing, if he'd done anything than to back down as quickly as he had, then Jacobs would have split his head open. He had been instantly ready to do it, his hands had

51

curled into fists, his legs had bent slightly at the knees. He *would* have done it. And he would have enjoyed it. That was a frightening realization.

Y' touchy today, he thought, inanely. His fingers were turning white on the wheel.

He drove home. Jacobs lived in a very old wood frame house above the north bank of the Kennebec, on the outskirts of town, with nothing but a clump of new apartment buildings for senior citizens to remind him of civilization. The house was empty—Carol was teaching fourth grade, and Chris had been farmed out to Mrs. Turner, the baby-sitter. Jacobs spent the next half hour wrestling a broken washing machine and a television set out of the pickup and into his basement workshop, and another fifteen minutes maneuvering a newly repaired stereo-radio console up out of the basement and into the truck. Jacobs was one of the last of the old-style Yankee tinkerers, although he called himself an appliance repairman, and also did some carpentry and general handywork when things got slow. He had little formal training, but he "kept up." He wasn't sure he could fix one of the new hologram sets, but then they wouldn't be getting out here for another twenty years anyway. There were people within fifty miles who didn't have indoor plumbing. People within a hundred miles who didn't have electricity.

On the way to Norridgewock, two open jeeps packed dangerously full of gypsies came roaring up behind him. They started to pass, one on each side of his truck, their horns blaring insanely. The two jeeps ran abreast of Jacobs' old pickup for a while, making no attempt to go by—the three vehicles together filled the road. The jeeps drifted in until they were almost touching the truck, and the gypsies began pounding the truck roof with their fists, shouting and laughing. Jacobs kept both hands on the wheel and grimly continued to drive at his original speed. Jeeps tipped easily when sideswiped by a heavier vehicle, if it came to that. And he had a tire-iron under the seat. But the gypsies tired of the game—they accelerated and passed Jacobs, most of them giving him the finger as they went by, and one throwing a poorly aimed bottle that bounced onto the shoulder. They were big, tough-looking kids with skin haircuts, dressed—incongruously—in flowered pastel luau shirts and expensive white bellbottoms.

The jeeps roared on up the road, still taking up both lanes. Jacobs watched them unblinkingly until they disappeared from sight. He was awash with rage, the same bitter, vicious hatred he had felt for Jackman. Riddick was right after all—the goddamned kids were a menace to everything that lived, they ought to be locked up. He wished suddenly that he *had* sideswiped them. He could imagine it all vividly: the sickening crunch of impact, the jeep overturning, bodies cartwheeling through the air, the jeep skidding upside down across the road and crashing into the embankment, maybe the gas tank exploding, a gout of flame, smoke, stink, screams—He ran through it over and over again, relishing it, until he realized abruptly what he was doing, what he was wishing, and he was almost physically ill.

All the excitement and fury drained out of him, leaving him shaken and sick. He'd always been a patient, peaceful man, perhaps too much so. He'd never been afraid to fight, but he'd always said that a man who couldn't talk his way out of most trouble was a fool. This sudden daydream lust for blood bothered him to the bottom of his soul. He'd seen plenty of death in 'Nam, and it hadn't affected him this way. It was the kids, he told himself. They drag everybody down to their own level. He kept seeing them inside his head all the way into Norridgewock—the thick, brutal faces, the hard reptile eyes, the contemptuously grinning mouths that seemed too full of teeth. The gypsy kids had changed over the years. The torrent of hippies and Jesus freaks had gradually run dry, the pluggers and the weeps had been all over the state for a few seasons, and then, slowly, they'd stopped coming too. The new crop of itinerant kids were—hard. Every year they became more brutal and dangerous. They didn't seem to care if they lived or died, and they hated everything indiscriminately—including themselves.

In Norridgewock, he delivered the stereo console to its owner, then went across town to pick up a malfunctioning 75-hp Johnson outboard motor. From the motor's owner, he heard that a town boy had beaten an elderly storekeeper to death that morning, when the storekeeper caught him shoplifting. The boy was in custody, and it was the scandal of the year for Norridgewock. Jacobs had noticed it before, but discounted it: the local kids were getting mean too, meaner every year. Maybe it was self-defense.

Driving back, Jacobs noticed one of the gypsy jeeps slewed up onto the road embankment. It was empty. He slowed, and stared at the jeep thoughtfully, but he did not stop.

A fire-rescue truck nearly ran him down as he entered Skowhegan. It came screaming out of nowhere and swerved onto Water Street, its blue blinker flashing, siren screeching in metallic rage, suddenly right on top of him. Jacobs wrenched his truck over to the curb, and it swept by like a demon, nearly scraping him. It left a frightened silence behind it, after it had vanished urgently from sight. Jacobs pulled back into traffic and continued driving. Just before the turnoff to his house, a dog ran out into the road. Jacobs had slowed down for the turn anyway, and he saw the dog in plenty of time to stop. He did not stop. At the last possible second, he yanked himself out of a waking dream, and swerved just enough to miss the dog. He had wanted to hit it; he'd liked the idea of running it down. There were too many dogs in the county anyway, he told himself, in a feeble attempt at justification. "Big, ugly hound," he muttered, and was appalled by how alien his voice sounded—hard, bitterly hard, as if it were a rock speaking. Jacobs noticed that his hands were shaking.

Dinner that night was a fair success. Carol had turned out not to be particularly overjoyed that her husband had invited a horde of people over without bothering to consult her, but Jacobs placated her a little by volunteering to cook dinner. It turned out "sufficient," as Everett put it. Everybody ate, and nobody died. Toward the end, Carol had to remind them to leave some for Dave Lucas, who had not arrived yet. The company did a lot to restore Jacobs' nerves, and, feeling better, he wrestled with curiosity throughout the meal. Curiosity won, as it usually did with him: in the end, and against his better judgment.

As the guests began to trickle into the parlor, Jacobs took Sussmann aside and asked him if he'd learned anything new about the abandoned car.

Sussmann seemed uneasy and preoccupied. "Whatever it was happened to them seems to've happened again this afternoon. Maybe a couple of times. There was another abandoned car found about four o'clock, up near Athens. And there was one late yesterday night, out at Livermore Falls. And a tractor-trailer on Route Ninety-five this morning, between Waterville and Benton Station."

"How'd you pry that out of Riddick?"

"Didn't." Sussmann smiled wanly. "Heard about that Athens one from the driver of the tow truck that hauled it back—that one bumped into a signpost, hard enough to break its radiator. Ben, Riddick can't keep me in the dark. I've got more stringers than he has."

"What d'you think it is?"

Sussmann's expression fused over and became opaque. He shook his head.

In the parlor, Carol, Everett's wife Amy—an ample, gray woman, rather like somebody's archetypical aunt but possessed of a very canny mind—and Sussmann, the inveterate bachelor, occupied themselves by playing with Chris. Chris was two, very quick and bright, and very excited by all the company. He'd just learned how to blow kisses, and was now practicing enthusiastically with the adults. Everett, meanwhile, was prowling around examining the stereo equipment that filled one wall. "You install this yourself?" he asked, when Jacobs came up to hand him a beer.

"Not only installed it," Jacobs said, "I built it all

55

myself, from scratch. Tinkered up most of the junk in this house. Take the beah 'fore it gets hot."

"Damn fine work," Everett muttered, absently accepting the beer. "Better'n my own setup, I purely b'lieve, and that set me back a right sma't piece of change. Jesus Christ, Ben—I didn't know you could do quality work like that. What the hell you doing stagnating out here in the sticks, fixing people's radios and washing machines, f'chrissake? Y'that good, you ought to be down in Boston, New York mebbe, making some real money."

Jacobs shook his head. "Hate the cities, big cities like that. C'n't stand to live in them at all." He ran a hand through his hair. "I lived in New York for a while, seven-eight yeahs back, 'fore settling in Skowhegan again. It was terrible theah, even back then, and it's worse now. People down theah dying on their feet, walking around dead without anybody to tell 'em to lie down and get buried decent."

"We're dying here too, Ben," Everett said. "We're just doing it slower, is all."

Jacobs shrugged. "Mebbe so," he said. "'Scuse me." He walked back to the kitchen, began to scrape the dishes and stack them in the sink. His hands had started to tremble again.

When he returned to the parlor, after putting Chris to bed, he found that conversation had almost died. Everett and Sussmann were arguing halfheartedly about the Factory, each knowing that he'd never convince the other. It was a pointless discussion, and Jacobs did not join it. He poured himself a glass of beer and sat down. Amy hardly noticed him; her usually pleasant face was stern and angry. Carol found an opportunity to throw him a sympathetic wink while tossing her long hair back over her shoulder, but her face was flushed too, and her lips were thin. The evening had started off well, but it had soured somehow; everyone felt it. Jacobs began to clean his pipe, using a tiny knife to scrape the bowl. A siren went by outside, wailing eerily away into distance. An ambulance, it sounded like, or the fire-rescue truck again—more melancholy and mournful, less predatory

than the siren of a police cruiser. "... brew viruses..."
Everett was saying, and then Jacobs lost him, as if Everett
were being pulled further and further away by some odd,
local perversion of gravity, his voice thinning into
inaudibility. Jacobs couldn't hear him at all now. Which
was strange, as the parlor was only a few yards wide.
Another siren. There were a lot of them tonight; they
sounded like the souls of the dead, looking for home in the
darkness, unable to find light and life. Jacobs found
himself thinking about the time he'd toured Vienna,
during "recuperative leave" in Europe, after hospitaliza-
tion in 'Nam. There was a tour of the catacombs under the
Cathedral, and he'd taken it, limping painfully along on
his crutch, the wet, porous stone of the tunnel roof closing
down until it almost touched the top of his head. They
came to a place where an opening had been cut through
the hard, gray rock, enabling the tourists to come up one
by one and look into the burial pit on the other side, while
the guide lectured calmly in alternating English and
German. When you stuck your head through the opening,
you looked out at a solid wall of human bones. Skulls,
arm and leg bones, rib cages, pelvises, all mixed in helter-
skelter and packed solid, layer after uncountable layer of
them. The wall of bones rose up sheer out of the darkness,
passed through the fan of light cast by a naked bulb at eye-
level, and continued to rise—it was impossible to see the
top, no matter how you craned your neck and squinted.
This wall had been built by the Black Death, a haphazard
but grandiose architect. The Black Death had eaten these
people up and spat out their remains, as casual and
careless as a picnicker gnawing chicken bones. When the
meal was over, the people who were still alive had dug a
huge pit under the Cathedral and shoveled the victims in
by the hundreds of thousands. Strangers in life, they
mingled in death, cheek by jowl, belly to backbone,
except that after a while there were no cheeks or jowls.
The backbones remained: yellow, ancient and brittle. So
did the skulls—upright, upside down, on their sides, all
grinning blankly at the tourists.

The doorbell rang.

It was Dave Lucas. He looked like one of the skulls Jacobs had been thinking about—his face was gray and gaunt, the skin drawn tightly across his bones; it looked as if he'd been dusted with powdered lime. Shocked, Jacobs stepped aside. Lucas nodded to him shortly and walked by into the parlor without speaking. ". . . stuff about the Factory is news," Sussmann was saying, doggedly, "and more interesting than anything else that happens up here. It sells papers—" He stopped talking abruptly when Lucas entered the room. All conversation stopped. Everyone gaped at the old game warden, horrified. Unsteadily Lucas let himself down into a stuffed chair, and gave them a thin attempt at a smile. "Can I have a beah?" he said. "Or a drink?"

"Scotch?"

"That'll be fine," Lucas said mechanically.

Jacobs went to get it for him. When he returned with the drink, Lucas was determinedly making small talk and flashing his new dead smile. It was obvious that he wasn't going to say anything about what had happened to him. Lucas was an old-fashioned Yankee gentleman to the core, and Jacobs—who had a strong touch of that in his own upbringing—suspected why he was keeping silent. So did Amy. After the requisite few minutes of polite conversation, Amy asked if she could see the new paintings that Carol was working on. Carol exchanged a quick, comprehending glance with her, and nodded. Grim-faced, both women left the room—they knew that this was going to be bad. When the women were out of sight, Lucas said, "Can I have another drink, Ben?" and held out his empty glass. Jacobs refilled it wordlessly. Lucas had never been a drinking man.

"Give," Jacobs said, handing Lucas his glass. "What happened?"

Lucas sipped his drink. He still looked ghastly, but a little color was seeping back into his face. "A'n't felt this shaky since I was in the a'my, back in Korea," he said. He shook his head heavily. "I swear to Christ, I don't understand what's got into people in these pa'ts. Used t'be decent folk out heah, Christian folk." He set his drink

58

aside, and braced himself up visibly. His face hardened. "Never mind that. Things change, I guess, c'n't stop 'em no way." He turned toward Jacobs. "Remember that nighthunter I was after. Well we got 'im, went out with Steve Girard, Rick Barlow, few other boys, and nabbed him real neat—city boy, no woods sense at all. Well, we were coming back around the end of the pond, down the lumber road, when we heard this big commotion coming from the Gibson place, shouts, a woman screaming her head off, like that. So we cut across the back of their field and went over to see what was going on. House was wide open, and what we walked into—" He stopped; little sickly beads of sweat had appeared all over his face. "You remember the McInerney case down in Boston four-five yeahs back? The one there was such a stink about? Well, it was like that. They had a whatchamacallit there, a coven— the Gibsons, the Sewells, the Bradshaws, about seven others, all local people, all hopped out of their minds, all dressed up in black robes, and—blood, painted all over their faces. God, I—No, never mind. They had a baby there, and a kind of an altar they'd dummied up, and a pentagram. Somebody'd killed the baby, slit its throat, and they'd hung it up to bleed like a hog. Into cups. When we got there, they'd just cut its heart out, and they were starting in on dismembering it. Hell—they were tearing it apart, never mind that 'dismembering' shit. They were so frenzied-blind they hardly noticed us come in. Mrs. Bradshaw hadn't been able to take it, she'd cracked completely and was sitting in a corner screaming her lungs out, with Mr. Sewell trying to shut her up. They were the only two that even tried to run. The boys hung Gibson and Bradshaw and Sewell, and stomped Ed Patterson to death—I just couldn't stop 'em. It was all I could do to keep 'em from killing the other ones. I shot Steve Girard in the arm, trying to stop 'em, but they took the gun away, and almost strung me up too. My God, Ben, I've known Steve Girard a'most ten yeahs. I've known Gibson and Sewell all my life." He stared at them appealingly, blind with despair. "What's happened to people up heah?"

No one said a word.

Not in these pa'ts, Jacobs mimicked himself bitterly. *There are decent limits.*

Jacobs found that he was holding the pipe-cleaning knife like a weapon. He'd cut his finger on it, and a drop of blood was oozing slowly along the blade. This kind of thing—the Satanism, the ritual murders, the sadism— was what had driven him away from the city. He'd thought it was different in the country, that people were better. But it wasn't, and they weren't. It was bottled up better out here, was all. But it had been coming for years, and they had blinded themselves to it and done nothing, and now it was too late. He could feel it in himself, something long repressed and denied, the reaction to years of frustration and ugliness and fear, to watching the world dying without hope. That part of him had listened to Lucas' story with appreciation, almost with glee. It stirred strongly in him, a monster turning over in ancient mud, down inside, thousands of feet down, thousands of years down. He could see it spreading through the faces of the others in the room, a stain, a spider shadow of contamination. Its presence was suffocating: the chalky, musty smell of old brittle death, somehow leaking through from the burial pit in Vienna. Bone dust—he almost choked on it, it was so thick here in his pleasant parlor in the country.

And then the room was filled with sound and flashing, bloody light.

Jacobs floundered for a moment, unable to understand what was happening. He swam up from his chair, baffled, moving with dreamlike slowness. He stared in helpless confusion at the leaping red shadows. His head hurt.

"An ambulance!" Carol shouted, appearing in the parlor archway with Amy. "We saw it from the upstairs window—"

"It's right out front," Sussmann said.

They ran for the door. Jacobs followed them more slowly. Then the cold outside air slapped him, and he woke up a little. The ambulance was parked across the street, in front of the senior citizens' complex. The

60

corpsmen were hurrying up the stairs of one of the institutional, cinderblock buildings, carrying a stretcher. They disappeared inside. Amy slapped her bare arms to keep off the cold. "Heart attack, mebbe," she said. Everett shrugged. Another siren slashed through the night, getting closer. While they watched, a police cruiser pulled up next to the ambulance, and Riddick got out. Riddick saw the group in front of Jacobs' house, and stared at them with undisguised hatred, as if he would like to arrest them and hold them responsible for whatever had happened in the retirement village. Then he went inside too. He looked haggard as he turned to go, exhausted, hagridden by the suspicion that he'd finally been handed something he couldn't settle with a session in the soundproofed back room at the sheriff's office.

They waited. Jacobs slowly became aware that Sussmann was talking to him, but he couldn't hear what he was saying. Sussmann's mouth opened and closed. It wasn't important anyway. He'd never noticed before how unpleasant Sussmann's voice was, how rasping and shrill. Sussmann was ugly too, shockingly ugly. He boiled with contamination and decay—he was a sack of putrescence. He was an abomination.

Dave Lucas was standing off to one side, his hands in his pockets, shoulders slumped, his face blank. He watched the excitement next door without expression, without interest. Everett turned and said something that Jacobs could not hear. Like Sussmann's, Everett's lips moved without sound. He had moved closer to Amy. They glanced uneasily around. They were abominations too.

Jacobs stood with his arm around Carol; he didn't remember putting it there—it was seeking company on its own. He felt her shiver, and clutched her more tightly in response, directed by some small, distanced, horrified part of himself that was still rational—he knew it would do no good. There was a thing in the air tonight that was impossible to warm yourself against. It hated warmth, it swallowed it and buried it in ice. It was a wedge, driving them apart, isolating them all. He curled his hand around the back of Carol's neck. Something was pulsing through him in waves, building higher and stronger. He could feel Carol's pulse beating under her skin, under his fingers, so very close to the surface.

Across the street, a group of old people had gathered around the ambulance. They shuffled in the cold, hawking and spitting, clutching overcoats and night-gowns more tightly around them. The corpsmen reappeared, edging carefully down the stairs with the stretcher. The sheet was pulled up all the way, but it looked curiously flat and caved-in—if there was a body under there, it must have collapsed, crumbled like dust or ash. The crowd of old people parted to let the stretcher crew pass, then re-formed again, flowing like a heavy, sluggish liquid. Their faces were like leather or horn: hard, dead, dry, worn smooth. And *tired*. Intolerably, burdensomely tired. Their eyes glittered in their shriveled faces as they watched the stretcher go by. They looked uneasy and afraid, and yet there was an anticipation in their faces, an impatience, almost an envy, as they looked on death. Silence blossomed from a tiny seed in each of them, a total, primordial silence, from the time before there were words. It grew, consumed them, and merged to form a greater silence that spread out through the night in widening ripples.

The ambulance left.

In the hush that followed, they could hear sirens begin to wail all over town.

Horse of Air

SOMETIMES WHEN THE weather is good I sit and look out over the city, fingers hooked through the mesh.

—The mesh is weather-stained, beginning to rust. As his fingers scrabble at it, chips of rust flake off, staining his hands the color of crusted blood. The heavy wire is hot and smooth under his fingers, turning rougher and drier at a rust spot. If he presses his tongue against the wire, it tastes slightly of lemons. He doesn't do that very often—

The city is quieter now. You seldom see motion, mostly birds if you do. As I watch, two pigeons strut along the roof ledge of the low building several stories below my balcony, stopping every now and then to pick at each other's feathers. They look fatter than ever. I wonder what they eat these days? Probably it is better not to know. They have learned to keep away from me anyway, although the mesh that encloses my small balcony floor to ceiling makes it difficult to get at them if they do land nearby. I'm not really hungry, of course, but they are noisy and leave droppings. I don't really bear any malice toward them. It's not a personal thing; I do it for the upkeep of the place.

(I hate birds. I will kill any of them I can reach. I do it with my belt buckle, snapping it between the hoops of wire.)

—He hates birds because they have freedom of movement, because they can fly, because they can shift their viewpoint from spot to spot in linear space, while he can do so only in time and memory, and that imperfectly. They can fly here and look at him and then fly away, while he has no volition: if he wants to look at them, he must wait until they decide to come to him. He flicks a piece of plaster at them, between the hoops—

Startled by something; the pigeons explode upward with a whir of feathers. I watch them fly away: skimming along the side of a building, dipping with an air current. They are soon lost in the maze of low roofs that thrust up below at all angles and heights, staggering toward the Apartment Towers in the middle distance. The Towers stand untouched by the sea of brownstones that break around their flanks, like aloof monoliths wading in a surf of scummy brown brick. Other Towers march off in curving lines toward the horizon, becoming progressively smaller until they vanish at the place where a misty sky merges with a line of low hills. If I press myself against the mesh at the far right side of the balcony, I can see the nearest Tower to my own, perhaps six hundred yards away, all of steel and concrete with a vertical line of windows running down the middle and rows of identical balconies on either side.

Nearest to me on the left is a building that rises about a quarter of the way up my Tower's flank: patterns of dark brown and light red bricks, interlaced with fingers of mortar; weathered gray roof shingles, a few missing here and there in a manner reminiscent of broken teeth; a web of black chimney and sewage pipes crawling up and across the walls like metallic creepers. All covered with the pale splotches of bird droppings. The Towers are much cleaner; not so many horizontal surfaces. Windows are broken in the disintegrating buildings down there; the dying sunlight glints from fangs of shattered glass. Curtains hang in limp shreds that snap and drum when a wind comes up. If you squint, you can see that the wind has scattered broken twigs and rubbish all over the floors inside. No, I am much happier in one of the Towers.

(I hate the Towers. I would rather live anywhere than here.)

64

—He hates the Towers. As the sun starts to dip below the horizon, settling down into the concrete labyrinth like a hog into a wallow, he shakes his head blindly and makes a low noise at the back of his throat. The shadows of buildings are longer now, stretching in toward him from the horizon like accusing fingers. A deep gray gloom is gathering in the corners and angles of walls, shot with crimson sparks from the foundering sun, now dragged under and wrapped in chill masonry. His hands go up and out, curling again around the hoops of the mesh. He shakes the mesh violently, throwing his weight against it. The mesh groans in metallic agony but remains solid. A few chips of concrete puff from the places where the ends of the mesh are anchored to the walls. He continues to tear at the mesh until his hands bleed, half-healed scabs torn open again. Tiny blood droplets spatter the heavy wire. The blood holds the deeper color of rust—

If you have enough maturity to keep emotionalism out of it, the view from here can even be fascinating. The sky is clear now, an electric, saturated blue, and the air is as sharp as a jeweler's glass. Not like the old days. Without factories and cars to keep it fed, even the eternal smog has dissipated. The sky reminds me now of an expensive aquarium filled with crystal tropical water, me at the bottom: I almost expect to see huge eyes peering in from the horizon, maybe a monstrous nose pressed against the glass. On a sunny day you can see for miles.

But it is even more beautiful when it rains. The rain invests the still landscape with an element of motion: long fingers of it brushing across the rooftops or marching down in zigzag sheets, the droplets stirring and rippling the puddles that form in depressions, drumming against the flat concrete surfaces, running down along the edges of the shingles, foaming and sputtering from downspouts. The Towers stand like lords, swirling rain mists around them as a fine gentleman swirls his jeweled cloak. Pregnant gray clouds scurry by behind the Towers, lashed by wind. The constant stream of horizontals past the fixed vertical fingers of the Towers creates contrast, gives the eye something to follow, increases the relief of motion.

65

Motion is heresy when the world has become a still-life. But it soothes, the old-time religion. There are no atheists in foxholes, nor abstainers when the world begins to flow. But does that prove the desirability of God or the weakness of men? I drink when the world flows, but unwillingly, because I know the price. I have to drink, but I also have to pay. I will pay later when the motion stops and the world returns to lethargy, the doldrums made more unbearable by the contrast known a moment before. That is another cross that I am forced to bear.

But it is beautiful, and fresh-washed after. And sometimes there is a rainbow. Rain is the only esthetic pleasure I have left, and I savor it with the unhurried leisure of the aristocracy.

—When the rain comes, he flattens himself against the mesh, arms spread wide as if crucified there, letting the rain hammer against his face. The rain rolls in runnels down his skin, mixing with sweat, counterfeiting tears. Eyes closed, he bruises his open mouth against the mesh, trying to drink the rain. His tongue dabs at the drops that trickle by his mouth, licks out for the moisture oozing down along the links of wire. After the storm, he sometimes drinks the small puddles that gather on the balcony ledge, lapping them noisily and greedily, although the tap in the kitchen works, and he is never thirsty—

Always something to look at from here. Directly below are a number of weed-overgrown yards, chopped up unequally by low brick walls, nestled in a hollow square formed by the surrounding brownstones. There is even a tree in one corner, though it is dead and its limbs are gnarled and splintered. The yards were never neatly kept by the rabble that lived there, even in the old days: they are scattered with trash and rubbish, middens of worn-out household items and broken plastic toys, though the weeds have covered much. There was a neat, bright flower bed in one of the further yards, tended by a bent and leather-skinned foreign crone of impossible age, but the weeds have overgrown that as well, drowning the rarer blossoms. This season there were more weeds, fewer flowers—they seem to survive better, though God knows they have little else to recommend them, being coarse and ill smelling.

In the closest yard an old and ornate wicker-back chair is still standing upright; if I remember correctly, a pensioner bought it at a rummage sale and used it to take the sun, being a parasite good for nothing else. Weeds are twining up around the chair; it is half-hidden already. Beyond is a small concrete court where hordes of ragged children used to play ball. Its geometrical white lines are nearly obliterated now by rain and wind-drifted gravel. If you look sharp at this clearing, sometimes you can see the sudden flurry of a small darting body through the weeds: a rat or a cat, hard to tell at this distance.

Once, months ago, I saw a man and a woman there, my first clear indication that there are still people alive and about. They entered the court like thieves, crawling through a low window, the man lowering the girl and then jumping down after. They were dressed in rags, and the man carried a rifle and a bandolier. After reconnoitering, the man forced one of the rickety doors into a brownstone, disappearing inside. After a while he came out dragging a mattress—filthy, springs jutting through fabric—and carried it into the ball court. They had intercourse there for the better part of the afternoon, stopping occasionally while the man prowled about with the rifle. I remember thinking that it was too bad the gift of motion had been wasted on such as these. They left at dusk. I had not tried to signal them, leaving them undisturbed to their rut, although I was somewhat sickened by the coarse brutality of the act. There is such a thing as *noblesse oblige*.

(I hate them. If I had a gun I would kill them. At first I watch greedily as they make love, excited, afraid of scaring them away if they should become aware of me watching. But as the afternoon wears on, I grow drained, and then angry, and begin to shout at them, telling them to get out, get the hell out. They ignore me. Their tanned skin is vivid against asphalt as they strain together. Sweat makes their locked limbs glisten in the thick sunlight. The rhythmic rise and fall of their bodies describes parabolic lines through the crusted air. I scream at them and tear at the mesh, voice thin and impotent. Later they make love again, rolling from the mattress in their urgency, sprawling among the lush weeds, coupling like leopards. I try to throw plaster at them, but the angle is wrong. As they leave the square, the man gives me the finger.)

Thinking of those two makes me think of the other animals that howl through the world, masquerading as men. On the far left, hidden by the nearest brownstones but winding into sight further on, is a highway. Once it was a major artery of the city, choked with a chrome flood of traffic. Now it is empty. Once or twice at the beginning I would see an ambulance or a fire engine, once a tank. A few weeks ago I saw a jeep go by, driving square in the middle of the highway, ridden by armed men. Occasionally I have seen men and women trudge past, dragging their possessions behind them on a sledge. Perhaps the wheel is on the way out.

Against one curb is the overturned, burned-out hulk of a bus: small animals use it for a cave now, and weeds are beginning to lace through it. I saw it burning, a week after the Building Committee came. I sat on the balcony and watched its flames eat up at the sky, although it was too dark to make out what was happening around it; the street lights had been the first things to go. There were other blazes in the distance, glowing like campfires, like blurred stars. I remember wondering that night what was happening, what the devil was going on. But I've figured it out now.

It was the niggers. I hate to say it. I've been a liberal man all my life. But you can't deny the truth. They are responsible for the destruction, for the present degeneration of the world. It makes me sad to have to say this. I had always been on their side in spirit, I was more than willing to stretch out a helping hand to those less fortunate than myself. I always said so; I always said that. I had high hopes for them all. But they got greedy, and brought us to this. We should have known better, we should have listened to the so-called racists, we should have realized that idealism is a wasting disease, a cancer. We should have remembered that blood will tell. A hard truth: it was the niggers. I have no prejudice; I speak of cold facts. I had always wished them well.

(I hate niggers. They are animals. Touching one would make me vomit.)

—He hates niggers. He has seen them on the street corners with their women, he has seen them in their jukeboxed caves with their feet in sawdust, he has heard them speaking in a private language half-devised of finger snaps and motions of liquid hips, he has felt the inquiry of their eyes, he has seen them dance. He envies them for having a culture separate from the bland familiarity of his own, he envies their tang of the exotic. He envies their easy sexuality. He fears their potency. He fears that in climbing up they will shake him down. He fears generations of stored-up hate. He hates them because their very existence makes him uncomfortable. He hates them because sometimes they have seemed to be happy on their tenement street corners, while he rides by in an air-conditioned car and is not. He hates them because they are not part of the mechanism and yet still have the audacity to exist. He hates them because they have escaped—

Dusk has come, hiding a world returned to shame and barbarism. It occurs to me that I may be one of the few members of the upper class left. The rabble were always quick to blame their betters for their own inherent inferiority and quick to vent their resentment in violence when the opportunity arose. The other Apartment Towers are still occupied, I think; I can see the lights at night, as they can see mine, if there is anyone left there to see. So perhaps there are still a few of us left. Perhaps there is still some hope for the world after all.

Although what avail to society is their survival if they are as helpless as I? We may be the last hope of restoring order to a land raped by Chaos, and we are being wasted. We are born to govern, to regulate, prepared for it by station, tradition and long experience: leadership comes as naturally to us as drinking and fornication come to the masses of the Great Unwashed. We are being wasted, our experience and foresight pissed away by fools who will not listen.

And we dwindle. I speak of us as a class, as a corporate "we." But there are fewer lights in the other Towers every month. Last night I counted less than half the number I could see a year ago. On evenings when the wind grows bitter with autumn cold, I fear that I will soon be the only one left with the courage to hold out. It would be so easy to give in to despair; the quietus of hopelessness is tempting. But it is a siren goddess, made of tin. Can't the others see that? To give up is to betray their blood. But still the lights dwindle. At times I have the dreadful fancy that I will sit here one night and watch the last light flicker out in the last Tower, leaving me alone in darkness, the only survivor of a noble breed. Will some improbable alien archaeologist come and hang a sign on my cage: the last of the aristocracy?

Deep darkness now. The lights begin to come on across the gulfs of shadow, but I am afraid to count them. Thinking of these things has chilled me, and I shudder. The wind is cold, filled with dampness. There will be a storm later. Distant lightning flickers behind the Towers, each flash sending jagged shadows leaping toward me, striking blue highlights from every reflecting surface. Each lightning stroke seems to momentarily reverse the order of things, etching the Towers in black relief against the blue-white dazzle of the sky, then the brilliance draining, leaving the Towers as before: islands of light against an inky background of black. The cycle is repeated, shadows lunging in at me, in at me, thrusting swords of nigger-blackness. It was on a hellish night like this that the Building Committee came.

It was a mistake to give them so much power. I admit it. I'm not too proud to own up to my own mistakes. But we were tired of struggling with an uncooperative and unappreciative society. We were beaten into weariness by a horde of supercilious bastards, petty and envious little men hanging on our coattails and trying to chivy us down. We were sick of people with no respect, no traditions, no

70

heritage, no proper ambitions. We were disgusted by a world degenerating at every seam, in every aspect. We had finally realized the futility of issuing warnings no one would listen to. Even then the brakes could have been applied to our skidding society if someone had bothered to listen, if anyone had had the guts and foresight to take the necessary measures. But we were tired, and we were no longer young.

So we traded our power for security. We built the Towers; we formed a company, turned our affairs over to them, and retired from the world into our own tight-knit society. Let the company have the responsibility and the problems, let them deal with the pressures and the decisions, let them handle whatever comes; we will be safe and comfortable regardless. They are the bright, ambitious technicians; let them cope. They are the expendable soldiers; let them fight and be expended as they are paid for doing; we shall be safe behind the lines. Let them have the mime show of power; we are civilized enough to enjoy the best things of life without it. We renounce the painted dreams; they are hollow.

It was a mistake.

It was a mistake to give them the voting proxies; Anderson was a fool, senile before his time. It was all a horrible mistake. I admit it. But we were no longer young.

And the world worsened, and one day the Building Committee came.

It was crisis, they said, and Fear was walking in the land. And the Charter specified that we were to be protected, that we must not be disturbed. So they came with the work crews and meshed over my balcony. And welded a slab of steel over my door as they left. They would not listen to my protest, wrapped in legalities, unvulnerable in armor of technical gobbledygook. Protection was a specific of the Charter, they said, and with the crisis this was the only way they could ensure our protection should the outer defenses go down; it was a temporary measure.

And the work crews went about their business with slap-dash efficiency, and the balding, spectacled foreman

71

told me he only worked here. So I stood quietly and watched them seal me in, although I was trembling with rage. I am no longer young. And I would not lose control before these vermin. Every one of them was waiting for it, hoping for it in their petty, resentful souls, and I would let myself be flayed alive before I would give them the satisfaction. It is a small comfort to me that I showed them the style with which a gentleman can take misfortune.

(When I finally realized what they are doing, I rage and bluster. The foreman pushes me away. "It's for your own good," he says, mouthing the cliché halfheartedly, not really interested. I beat at him with ineffectual fists. Annoyed, he shrugs me off and ducks through the door. I try to run after him. One of the guards hits me in the face with his rifle butt. Pain and shock and a brief darkness. And then I realize that I am lying on the floor. There is blood on my forehead and on my mouth. They have almost finished maneuvering the steel slab into place, only a man-sized crack left open. The guard is the only one left in the room, a goggled technician just squeezing out through the crack. The guard turns toward the door. I hump myself across the room on my knees, crawling after him, crying and begging. He plants his boot on my shoulder and pushes me disgustedly away. The room tumbles, I roll over twice, stop, come up on my elbows and start to crawl after him again. He says, "Fuck off, Dad," and slaps his rifle, jangling the magazine cartridge in the breech. I stop moving. He glares at me, then leaves the room. They push the slab all the way closed. It makes a grinding, rumbling sound, like a subway train. Still on my knees, I throw myself against it, but it is solid. Outside there are welding noises. I scream.)

There is a distant rumbling now. Thunder: the storm is getting nearer. The lightning flashes are more intense, and closer together. They are too bright, too fast, blending into one another, changing the dimensions of the world too rapidly. With the alternating of glare and thrusting shadow there is too much motion, nothing ever still for a second, nothing you can let your eye rest on. Watching it

72

strains your vision. My eyes ache with the motion.

I close them, but there are squiggly white afterimages imprinted on the insides of my eyelids. A man of breeding should know how to control his emotions. I do; in the old circles, the ones that mattered, I was known for my self-discipline and refinement. But this is an unseasonable night, and I am suddenly afraid. It feels like the bones are being rattled in the body of the earth, it feels like maybe It will come now.

But that is an illusion. It is not the Time; It will not come yet. Only I know when the Time is, only I can say when It will come. And It will not come until I call for It, that is part of the bargain. I studied military science at Annapolis. I shall recognize the most strategic moment, I shall know when the Time is at hand for vengeance and retribution. I shall know. And the Time is not now. It will not come tonight. This is only an autumn storm.

I open my eyes. And find my stare returned. Windows ring me on all sides like walls of accusing, lidless eyes. Lightning oozes across the horizon: miniature reflections of the electric arc etched in cold echoes across a thousand panes of glass, a thousand matches struck simultaneously in a thousand dusty rooms.

A sequence of flares. The sky alternates too quickly to follow. Blue-white, black. Blue-white. Black again. The roofs flicker with invested motion, brick dancing in a jerky, silent-movie fashion.

Oh God, the chimneys, humped against dazzle, looming in shadow. Marching rows of smoky brick gargoyles, ash-cold now with not an ember left alive. The rows sway closer with every flash. I can hear the rutch of mortar-footed brick against tile, see the waddling, relentless rolling of their gait. They are people actually, the poor bastard refugees of the rabble frozen into brick, struck dumb with mortar. I saw it happen on the night of the Building Committee, thousands of people swarming like rats over the roofs to escape the burning world, caught by a clear voice of crystal that metamorphosed them with a single word, fixing them solid to the roofs, their hands growing into their knees, their heels into their buttocks, their heads thrown back with mouths gaped in a scream, flesh swapped for brick, blood for mortar. They hump toward me on their blunt knees in ponderously bobbing lines. With a sound like fusing steel, nigger-black shadows humping *in* at me. Christ hands sealing my eyes with clay stuffing down my mouth my throat filling Oh God oh christ christ *christ*

It is raining now. I will surely catch a chill standing here; there are vapors in the night air. Perhaps it would be advisable to go inside. Yes, I do think that would be best. Sometimes it is better to forget external things.

—He crawls away from the mesh on his hands and knees, although he is healthy and perfectly able to stand. He often crawls from place to place in the apartment; he thinks it gives him a better perspective. Rain patters on the balcony behind, drums against the glass of the French windows that open into the apartment. He claws at the framework of the windows, drags himself to his feet. He stands there for a moment, face pressed flat against the glass, trembling violently. His cheeks are wet. Perhaps he has been crying. Or perhaps it was the rain—

I turn on the light and go inside, closing the French windows firmly behind me. It is the very devil of a night outside. In here it is safe, even comfortable. This place is only a quarter of my actual apartment of course. The Building Committee sealed me in here, cut me off from the rest of my old place, which occupied most of this floor. Easier to defend me this way, the bastards said. So this apartment is smaller than what I'm used to living in, God knows. But in a strange way the smallness makes the place more cozy somehow, especially on a piggish night like this when fiends claw the windowpane.

I cross to the kitchen cubicle, rummage through the jars and cans; there's some coffee left from this week's shipment, I think. Yes, a little coffee left in one of the jars: instant; coarse, murky stuff. I had been used to better; once we drank nothing but fine-ground Colombian, and I would have spat in the face of any waiter who dared to serve me unpercolated coffee. This is one of the innumerable little ways in which we pay for our folly. A thousand little things, but together they add up into an almost unbearable burden, a leering Old Man of the Sea wrapped leech-fashion around my shoulders and growing heavier by the day. But this is defeatist talk. I am more tired than I would allow myself to admit. Here the coffee will help; even this bitter liquid retains that basic virtue in kind with the more palatable stuff. I heat some water, slosh it over the obscene granules into a cup. The cup is cracked, no replacement for it: another little thing. A gust of wind rattles the glass in the French windows. I will not listen to it.

Weary, I carry the steaming cup into the living room, sit down in the easy chair with my back to the balcony. I try to balance the cup on my knee, but the damn thing is too hot; I finally rest it on the chair arm, leaving a moist ring on the fabric, but that hardly matters now. Can my will be weakening? Once I would have considered it sacrilege to sully fine furniture and would have gone to any length to avoid doing so. Now I am too wrapped in lassitude to get up and go into the kitchen for a coaster. Coffee seeps slowly into fabric, a widening brownish stain, like blood. I am almost too tired to lift the cup to my lips.

Degeneration starts very slowly, so deviously, so patiently that it almost seems to be a living thing; embodied, it would be a weasel-like animal armed with sly cunning and gnawing needle teeth. It never goes for your throat like a decent monster, so that you might have a chance of beating it down: it lurks in darkness, it gnaws furtively at the base of your spine, it burrows into your liver while you sleep. Like the succubi I try to guard against at night, it saps your strength, it sucks your breath in slumber, it etches away the marrow of your bones.

There is enough water in the tank for one more bath this week; I should wash, but I fear I'm too tired to manage it. Another example? It takes such a lot of *effort* to remain civilized. How tempting to say, "It no longer matters." It does matter. I say it does. I will make it matter. I cannot afford the seductive surrender of my unfortunate brethren; I have a responsibility they don't have. Perhaps I am luckier to have it in a way. It is an awesome responsibility, but carrying it summons up a corresponding strength, it gives me a reason for living, a goal outside myself. Perhaps my responsibility is what enables me to hang on, the knowledge of what is to come just enough to balance out the other pressures. The game has not yet been played to an end. Not while I still hold my special card.

Thinking of the secret, I look at the television set, but the atmospherics are wrong tonight for messages, and it's probably too late for the haphazard programming they put out now. Some nights I leave the test pattern on, enjoying the flickering highlights it sends across the walls and ceilings, but tonight I think it will be more comfortable with just the pool of yellow glow cast by the lamp next to my chair, a barrier against the tangible darkness.

Looking at the television always reawakens my curiosity about the outside world. What is the state of society? The city I can see from my balcony seems to have degenerated into savagery, civilization seems to have been destroyed, but there are contradictions, there are ambiguities. Obviously the Building Committee must still be in existence somewhere. The electric lights and the plumbing still work in the Towers, a shipment of food supplies rattles up the pneumatic dumbwaiter into the kitchen cubicle twice a week, there are old movies and cartoons on television, running continuously with no commercials or live programming, never a hint of news. Who else could it be for but us? Who else could be responsible for it but the Building Committee? I've seen the city; it is dark, broken, inhabited by no one but a few human jackals who eke out a brute existence and hunt each other through the ruins. These facilities are certainly not operated for them—the other Towers are the only lighted buildings visible in the entire wide section of city visible from here.

No, it is the Building Committee. It must be. They are the only ones with the proper resources to hold a circle of order against a widening chaos. Those resources were vast. I know: we built them, we worked to make them flexible, we sweated to make them inexhaustible. We let their control pass out of our hands. One never finishes paying for past sins.

What a tremendous amount of trouble they've gone to, continuing to operate the Towers, even running a small television station somewhere to force-feed us the "entertainment" specified in the Charter. And never a word, never a glimpse of them, even for a second. Why? Why do they bother to keep up the pretense, the mocking hypocrisy of obeying the Charter? The real power is theirs now, why do they bother to continue the sham and lip service? Why don't they just shut down the Towers and leave us to starve in our plush cells? Is it the product of some monstrous, sadistic sense of humor? Or is it the result of a methodical, fussily prim sense of order that refuses to deny a legal technicality even when the laws themselves have died? Do they laugh their young men's laughter when they think of the once-formidable old beasts they have caged?

I feel a surge of anger. I put the half-emptied cup carefully down on the rug. My hand is trembling. The Time is coming. It will be soon now. Soon they will heap some further indignity on me and force my hand. I will not have them laughing at me, those little men with maggots for eyes. Not when I still have it in my power to change it all. Not while I still am who I am. But not just yet. Let them have their victory, their smug laughter. An old tiger's fangs may be blunt and yellowing, but they can still bite. And even an old beast can still rise for one more kill.

I force myself to my feet. I have the inner strength, the discipline. They have nothing, they are the rabble, they are children trying out as men and parading in adult clothing. It was we who taught them the game, and we still know how to play it best. I force myself to wash, to fold the bed out from the wall, to lie still, fighting for calm. I run my eyes around the familiar dimensions of the apartment, cataloguing: pale blue walls, red draw curtains for the French windows, bookshelves next to the curtains, a black cushioned stool, the rug in patterns of orange and green against brown, a red shaggy chair and matching couch, the archways to the kitchen and bath cubicles. Nothing alien. Nothing hostile. I begin to relax. Thank God for familiarity. There is a certain pleasure in looking at well-known, well-loved things, a certain unshakable sense of reality. I often fall asleep counting my things.

(I hate this apartment. I hate everything in this apartment. I cannot stand to live here any longer. Someday I will chop everything to unrecognizable fragments and pile it in the middle of the floor and burn it, and I will laugh while it burns.)

—He is wakened by a shaft of sunlight that falls through the uncurtained French windows. He groans, stirs, draws one foot up, heel against buttock, knee toward the ceiling. His hand clenches in the bedclothes. The sound of birds reaches him through the insulating glass. For a moment, waking, he thinks that he is elsewhere, another place, another time. He mutters a woman's name and his hand goes out to grope across the untouched, empty space beside him in the double bed. His hand encounters only the cool of sheets, no answering warmth of flesh. He grimaces, his bent leg snaps out to full length again, his suddenly desperate hand rips the sheet free of the mattress, finding nothing. He wrenches to his feet, neck corded, staggering. By the time his eyes slide open he has begun to scream—

-OW IT. Do you hear me, bastards? *I will not allow it.* I will not stand for it. You've gone too far, I warn you, too far, I'll kill you. D'you hear? Niggers and thieves. The past is all I have. I will not have you touching it, I will not have you sliming and defiling it with your shitty hands. You leave her out of it, you leave her alone. What kind of men are you using her against me? *What kind of men are you?* Rabble not worth breath. Defiling everything you touch, everything better than you finer than you. I will not allow it.

It is time. It is *Time*.

78

The decision brings a measure of calm. I am committed now. They have finally driven me too far. It is time for me to play the final card. I will not let them remain unpunished for this another second, another breath. I will call for It, and It will come. I must keep control, there must be no mistakes. This is retribution. This is the moment I have waited for all these agonizing months. I must keep control, there must be no mistakes. It must be executed with dispatch, with precision. I breathe deeply to calm myself. There will be no mistakes, no hesitations.

Three steps take me to the television. I flick it on, waiting for it to warm. Impatience drums within me, tightly reined as a rearing Arabian stallion. So long, so long.

A picture appears on the screen: another imbecilic movie. I think of the Building Committee, unaware, living in the illusion of victory. Expertly, I remove the back of the television, my skilled fingers probing deep into the maze of wires and tubes. I work with the familiarity of long practice. How many hours did I crouch like this, experimenting, before I found the proper frequency of the Others by trial and error? Patience was never a trait of the rabble; it is a talent reserved for the aristocracy. They didn't count on my patience. Mayflies themselves, they cannot understand dedication of purpose. They didn't count on my scientific knowledge, on my technical training at Annapolis. They didn't count on the resources and ingenuity of a superior man.

I tap two wires together, creating sparks, sending messages into ether. I am sending on the frequency of the Others, a prearranged signal in code: the Time is now. Let It come. Sweat in my eyes, fingers cramping, but I continue to broadcast. The Time is now. Let It come. At last a response, the Others acknowledging that they've received my order.

It is over.

Now It will come.

Now they will pay for their sins.

I sit back on my heels, drained. I have done my part. I

have launched It on Its way, given birth to retribution, sowed the world with dragon's teeth. And they laughed. Now It is irreversible. Nothing can stop It. An end to all thieves and niggers, to all little men, to all the rabble that grow over the framework like weeds and ruin the order of the world. I stagger to the French windows, throw them open. Glass shatters in one frame, bright fragments against the weave of the rug. Onto the balcony where buildings press in at me unaware of Ragnarok. I collapse against the mesh, fingers spread, letting it take my weight. No motion in the world, but soon there will be enough. Far north, away from the sight of the city, the spaceships of the Others are busy according to plan, planting the thermal charges that will melt the icecap, shattering the earth-old ice, liberating the ancient waters, forming a Wave to thunder south and drown the world. I think of the Building Committee, of the vermin in the ruins of the city, even of my fellows in the other Towers. I am not sorry for them. I am no longer young, but I will take them with me into darkness. There will be no other eyes to watch a sun I can no longer see. I have no regrets. I've always hated them. I hate them all.

(I hate them all.)

—He hates them all—

A moaning in the earth, a trembling, a drumming as of a billion billion hooves. The Tower sways queasily. A swelling, ragged shriek of sound.

The Wave comes.

Over the horizon, climbing, growing larger, stretching higher, filling up the sky, cutting off the sunlight, water in a green wall like glass hundreds of feet high, topped with fangs of foam, the Wave beginning to topple in like the closing fist of God. Its shadow over everything, night at noon as it sweeps in, closes down. The Towers etched like thin lines against its bulk. It is curling overhead in the sky now there is no sky now but the underbelly of the Wave coming down. I have time to see the Towers snapped like matchsticks broken stumps of fangs before it hits with the scream of grating steel and blackness clogs my throat to

(I have destroyed the world.)

—The shadow of the mesh on his face—

Sometimes you can see other people in the other Tower apartments, looking out from their own balconies. I wonder how they destroy the world?

—He turns away, dimly remembering a business appointment. Outside the lazy hooting of rush-hour traffic. There is a cartoon carnival on Channel Five—

The Last Day of July

HE CAN FEEL them in the air around him, swimming through the walls, the ceiling, the floor, always just out of sight. What they are he doesn't know, but they are there. Sometimes he can almost see them out of the corner of his eye—a motion, a flickering, a presence: a glow behind him, as if someone had just turned up an oil lantern. And yet there is no light. When he turns to look, nothing is there, everything is still—but with that subliminal sense of stirred air, as if something has just passed, as if something has flowed aside into the wall an instant faster than he can turn his head. He tries to catch them, spinning violently, rounding on his heel. But always finds the room empty, the same peering windows, the same hunched shapes of furniture. And the tension will grow, redoubled, at his back: the air watchful, watching, an imminence never quite defined—until he whirls again. Nothing. Empty. The table, the piles of papers and books, the chairs, the tall china cabinet. And then he will feel eyes reform behind him.

When John comes into the house with the second suitcase, daylight has already begun to die. All at once, everything is flatter, duller—not darker, but just less vivid, as though a gray film of oil has been pulled between the sun and the earth. The house, the surrounding forest, all suddenly seem two-dimensional: the house a stage set, the forest wall a backdrop. There are no sharp edges, no highlights, no reticulations. The large rain puddle in the elbow of the encircling dirt road is a solid gunmetal oval—no reflections, no ripples; it seems that you could pry it up in one piece and stack it against a wall. The air itself is heavy, somehow sodden without being wet, without the slightest trace of moisture. The branches of the trees hang close to the ground, as though pregnant with rain: they are dry to the touch, sterile, almost like stone. There are no birds.

The man from the agency honks, backs the car, and turns it around so that it points back toward the access road to the highway. John pauses on the threshold of the back porch, sets down the suitcase, and nods in thanks for the ride from the train station. Already he has forgotten the ride, except as a confusion of sensation: noise, movement, alternating explosions of light and shadow, unfocused objects flowing by the windshield, pirouetting, tumbling, expanding and contracting in obedience to an unknown rhythm. He does not know where he is, does not know where the house is in relation to anything else in the vicinity, does not know what county he is in, is not even sure of the state. He has been informed of these things, but he has forgotten. He never really listened.

The agency man puts his car in gear; the back wheels spin in mud, then bite gravel. The car accelerates, swerves by the house onto the access road that leads to the blacktop secondary road that merges at last into the state highway. It disappears, taillights bobbing. In the perspectiveless, colorless perception imposed by that dusk, it does not seem to dwindle normally into distance. Rather, it vanishes, abruptly, as if it has been absorbed tracelessly by some universal solvent, as if it has passed into another reality. John listens for the sound of a retreating engine. There is none. Balancing the suitcase against his foot, he watches the last light drain from behind a stand of silver birches: a visual dopplering; mushroom shadows sprout up and lengthen across to form a hedge of darkness in which the birches gleam faintly—bones. Then he goes inside.

The enclosed porch opens onto the kitchen. He can make out a sink and stove to his right, a dining table to the left, shelves and counters facing. The living room beyond is lost in shadow. The deep gray half-light makes him strain his eyes; objects seem to hang suspended in light as in a fluid, kept recognizable only by an intense, squinting focus—they threaten to slip out of resolution into formlessness, a primitive amorphism in which they are not bound by human preconceptions as to their shape and nature. Faced with this rebellion, he gropes for a wall switch, finds it, flips it up.

New shadows snap across the room, click into their accustomed places under chairs, along the edges of the tables, the counters, the shelves, in the angle of the sink and stove. Positive and negative space define order, etching each other's borders; between them they shape the room, sculpting it out of light and shadow, overt and implied. Pinning it down. He begins to breathe more easily. John sets the suitcase down beside its mate and moves into the center of the room. A mirror over the shelves gives him his reflection: pale, high forehead, drawn. He ignores it, uneasily avoiding the reflection's eyes. His friend's things are still here: he can see soiled plates stacked in the sink basin, frying pans and pots on the drainboard, a waffle iron, a cigarette-rolling machine. Reassured, he moves forward into the living room, turning on lights as he goes.

The living room is a large, L-shaped chamber, taking up most of the ground floor. The shorter end of the L has been used as a writing room. It contains two mahogany tables, still paper stacked; a massive, dust-covered typewriter; bound files lined up on the window ledge, flanked by ceramic pots containing withered ivy; a tall china cabinet that faces in toward the long bar of the L. The two sections are divided by a high, open archway. The long section of the L contains a couch, a settee, an end table, an overstuffed chair. The stairway leading to the second floor is at the far end. Set in the facing wall—between two glassed-in doors leading to the veranda—is a stone fireplace, filled with charred wood scraps and ashes.

Books glint on the mantelpiece over the fireplace: heavy, leatherbound, oiled volumes. He steps forward into the room, unconsciously wary, turning his head from side to side. He stops, sniffing the dead air. The air is musty and tomb-dry, as if it has not been breathed for a hundred years. He takes another step, and dust puffs from the living-room carpet under his feet. The dust swirls avidly up to meet him, dancing fiercely and joyously in the middle of the air. The backlighting throws his long, spindly shadow ahead, across the carpet, the andirons, the ashes, up the wall of the fireplace to the mantel, into the dust and silence of the empty house.

Later that evening, while unpacking his suitcases and arranging his belongings—mostly clothes—in the bedroom, John is submerged in a silence so deep and profound that it seems to manifest itself as a low hum, a steady buzz felt with the back of the teeth rather than heard. There are none of the settling of floorboards or knocking of waterpipes expected in a house this old, and the absolute quiet is disturbing. He finds himself wishing for a radio or a phonograph, anything to keep his ear from straining constantly in anticipation of sounds that never come. He would even welcome a barrage of that tinny "swing" music that always sounds as if it is being played underwater a million miles away, or one of those endless, dully foreboding commentaries on the danger of American involvement in Europe. At least they would be company, and their taste of the mundane and the absurd oddly comforting when balanced against the alien perfection of complete silence. The human voices would remind him that life is still going on in the ticking world, that he is not, as it feels, suspended in a limbo between creations: a tiny detail from an obsolete continuum that has been overlooked and not yet swept into the melt for the new.

As he is closing the lid on the last empty suitcase and putting it into the closet to store, he thinks he hears a noise downstairs: the slamming of a door, and rapid, heavy footsteps—passing underneath, headed into the living room. The noise is so clear and loud after the hush of the past hours—and such a sudden, unexpected answer to his strained listening—that he starts, and knocks over his bag. Leaving it, he goes out the door and down the corridor toward the stairwell, puzzlement changing to an unreasonable, unexplainable fear as he goes, metamorphosing more completely with every step. His heart thumps against his chest, like a fist from inside. Slowly, he goes down the stairs into the living room, not understanding who such a late visitor could be—the man from the agency perhaps?—and not understanding why he is afraid.

No one is there.

John stands for a moment at the foot of the stairs—one hand on the railing, head tilted—and then walks through the living room and the writing room to the kitchen, stepping with the exaggerated caution of one who expects a viper to strike from concealment. There is no one in the house. Bewildered, he returns to the living room.

As he nears the fireplace, he hears the footsteps again—this time they are upstairs, just as loud, just as distinct. They pass overhead as he listens. There is an unpleasant rasping quality to them now, as if the feet are too heavy to lift and must be scraped along the floor. Clearly there is someone upstairs, but no one has passed him in his sortie into the kitchen, and there is only one stairwell leading to the second floor. He feels the short hairs bristle on the back of his neck and along his arms. He forces himself to go upstairs, pausing after every other tread to listen, telling himself that at worst it is only a tramp looking for something to steal. But there is no one upstairs either. Although he searches the entire second floor—closets, linen cabinets, the bathroom—and even, with the help of a chair and a flashlight, peers into the crawlspace between the ceiling and the roof, he can find no one, nothing, and no way for anyone to have avoided him.

That night he sleeps uneasily, feverishly, fighting his bed-clothes as if they are snakes. In the morning, he cannot remember his dreams.

• • •

The next day is hot and clear, and John decides to go outside. He wants to look over some of his old notes, to see if he can assemble something workable out of the shambles of his career, and it would be pleasant to read on the lawn. He stands in the doorway of the porch, blinking against the furnace glare of the sunlight, smelling heat and raw earth. Suddenly he is reluctant to leave the shelter of the house. At some point in the morning, John has stopped thinking of the house as desolate and menacing, and has begun to consider it comfortable and peaceful, its cool, restful half-light infinitely preferable to the hot welter out of doors. He is not aware of the change in his thinking. Almost he turns to go back into the kitchen, but he reminds himself irritably that he is here for his health, after all. He finds the idea of sunning himself distasteful, but he has been told pointedly that it is healthy to "take the sun," so take it he will. He steps over the threshold. Warm air swallows him, a golden pear sliding over his skin. His nostrils are flared by the strong resin smell of grass. His eyes dilate. Blinded, he stumbles down the porch stairs to the flagstone path.

Blinking and squinting, John moves away from the house. His shoes click on flagstone, then swish through grass as he strays from the path. The grass whispers around his legs, caressing his ankles, rasping abrasively against the material of his trousers. His vision returns slowly, and as it does he feels the earth roll majestically under his feet in a long sea swell, like a giant's shoulder shrugging uneasily in sleep. The sky is a brilliant blue. He can sense the house behind him, the top half rising up and over him, a cresting wave about to topple. Now it is the house that is distasteful—again it seems brooding, mournful, unwholesomely confining. This time he is aware of his change of attitude, and dimly puzzled by it.

John plows across the lawn, leaving a flattened wake behind him, like a boat. There is a toy wagon on its side, rusted almost solid, a few flecks of red paint still showing; it is tied down firmly by grass, a robot Gulliver. John nudges it with his toe, and a wheel spins a tired protest in a shrill voice of rust. A rubber duck next to the wagon, dead, eaten away by weather, the side of its face distorted as if by acid. The shadow of the house lies across the lawn here, and it is cooler and less murmurous. John's fingers work uneasily on the buttons of his shirt. He turns and walks at an angle to his previous path, the house roof seeming to describe a backwards arc against the sky as he watches, until the sun pops into view again above the roof peak, a hot copper penny squeezed from between an invisible thumb and finger. Its heat makes his bare arms tingle pleasantly, and he blinks again, almost drowsy.

There was a garden here once, by the rear of the house. He steps into a ring of faded white stones, careful not to wrench his ankle, as the ground inside the circle is a little lower. At the far end of the ring is a chinaberry tree, a white oak, a few silver birches. He touches one of the birches: it feels like coral, sharp, unfriendly, dead— stratified. Startled, he snatches his hand away. He had not expected that type of texture, it is not congruous with the texture of the bark that he can see with his eyes. It should not feel that way. A sun-dog winks at him from an upstairs window, under the eaves. Uneasy again, John walks on until he comes to the dirt access road that circles the house. He scuffles the toe of his shoe in the dust, as though testing some earthen tide. He is reluctant to cross the road. Somehow, it is a boundary.

He can feel the house behind him. Without turning his head, he can see it: the high peak of the roof, the windows like eyes, the door like a gaping mouth—growing up out of the earth and shrouded in its turn with rank growth. A troll, with dogwood in its hair and rhododendron in its beard. Very old, very strong, patient as mud.

Irritated by this nonsense, John strides back toward the house. He has come here to recover from irrational fancies; he does not need new ones. He spends an hour or so making a mental list of the household repairs he will have to accomplish, rummaging around to find the proper tools, and dragging an extension ladder up from the dank, low-ceilinged basement. Then he discovers that his energy has leaked away, absorbed by the morning as by a blotter. In spite of his effort to keep his mind on practical things, he is again awash with jittery, contradictory emotion that makes the thought of attempting repairs intolerable. He will read his notes then after all, he decides grimly. He will not be defeated by the day.

John wades to the center of the lawn with his notebook, and sits down determinedly, in the sun. Sitting, the grass comes up above his waist, and he has the illusion that he has just lowered himself into a tub of sun-warmed green water. For the first time, he notices how overgrown the grounds actually are. Weeds and wildflowers have sprung up and proliferated everywhere, and John is submerged in an ocean of growth. He finds this a sensation both terrifying and dizzyingly exultant, and, sitting in this breathing tabernacle, this beating green heart, John feels oddly ashamed.

Uncertainly, John takes off his shirt, and lets the sun bake his back. He moves uncomfortably, uncrossing and refolding his legs, lifting the binder from his lap and placing it in the grass before him. He is painfully aware of the unhealthy pallor of his skin, and he begins thinking, in a disjointed fashion, of sickness, of enclosure: of decay embodied in the image of a wax flower yellowing with age—death so gradual, so subtle and imperceptible that it is not so much a transition between states as an intensifying of a long-existing condition, and even the soul involved may be unable to tell when life ended and death began, or if it yet has, or even if there is any difference between the two. He stretches an arm out along the grass, fish-belly white against new green, and has to reassure himself that he can still feel the blood throbbing in his neck, at the temples, in the wrists; that he still breathes, that he has not forgotten to live.

Birches sigh and toss overhead, and he looks up. The perfection of the weather is somehow alien, even more so than the gray, distorting twilight that had greeted him upon his arrival. Everything within the limits of his vision is endowed with an excessive clarity. There is a feeling of craft behind each incidence of light, the fall of every shadow, the position of the smallest rock: as if the world was some fantastic simulacrum—three-dimensional and discernible by all the senses—painted over another and more complex reality.

This thought disturbs him greatly, and he looks down again. He is suddenly afraid that if he continues to watch he may see the world waver and go out like an abruptly extinguished candleflame, and that beyond the guttering of the universal ember he will see—something else. What that something else, that other thing, may be he does not know. He is afraid of that moment of clear sight.

Silly, he thinks. Naive and juvenile, as have been all his moods and preoccupations since coming to this country house. He can imagine the scorn of his intellectual friends in London and Boston, the curiously similar—although differently motivated—contempt of his stolid, cannery-owning father, the needle-sharp disdain of his former fiancée, tough-minded, intensely practical Marilyn. But he cannot control the swing and scurry of his emotions. Like nervous fish, they dart where they will, unpredictably, and he cannot stop them.

To distract himself, John opens his notebook, selects a page, flattens it out with his hand. He bends close over the page, feeling the sun like a heel on the top of his head. But, to his dismay, he discovers that he cannot read. The ability is gone, wiped away as if it had never existed. There is a year's worth of work in the notebook, the only remains of his once-promising career, and he cannot read it. He can admire the words as objects, but he cannot decipher them. The shadows of the tall grass can be seen on the lined paper—one scheme of order imposed over another—and he watches them instead, in bemused fascination. The calligraphy of the shadows is exquisite: they look like actual brush strokes on the page, clean-bordered black lines. The sun also casts the silhouette of an insect onto the page—a shadow spider crawling along a blade of shadow grass, a reflection of some negative and polar universe. He lifts his gaze slightly to locate the real spider, and then manages to watch both it and its doppelganger at once: the real spider crawling up the grass blade and away from him, while the shadow spider crawls down the page toward him, simultaneously. An insect in the grass, the earth spinning in space—both mated by shadow. He tries to touch the silhouettes of grass and spider. He cannot—there is nothing but the feel of paper under his fingers, and the shadow spider now clambers distortedly over his knuckles. Neither can he feel the ink that forms the words on the page, though he knows that it, too, is there.

As he watches, a word pulls itself up out of the paper and scurries away.

There is a moment of vertigo, and then he realizes that it is a beetle that has been resting quietly on the page and has been disturbed by the movement of his hand: he has mistaken it for an ink-blotted word. Not reassured, he eyes the remaining script with a new suspicion, half suspecting that it intends a mass rebellion and exodus. His stomach churns with nausea: fear of that breath of wind that will extinguish the world, dread that he may have just seen things swim and shiver in a premonitory eddy.

John puts the binder down and slowly gets to his feet. He sways, drained of all strength. The impressions of the afternoon are beyond his ability to analyze or interpret. They call up only a welter of ambiguous and contradictory emotion. He hurries to the house, following the flagstone path, thinking only of rest and sanctuary, hoping he will not fall. He has gained the shelter of the back porch before he realizes that he has left his notebook behind, on the lawn.

He does not go back for it.

That evening he is assaulted by sound. As soon as the sun has disappeared completely behind the horizon and darkness is absolute, the noises begin—all at once, already at full volume, as if they have been turned on by a switch: the chirruping of crickets and the strident peeping of tree frogs, the soughing of the wind and the tossing and scratching of tree branches against the walls, at the windows. They are all normal, expected sounds, but tonight they seem horrescently, unbelievably loud: a wailing, baying, screaming cacophony. Even the boards under his feet cry out, moaning like lepers, groaning and shrieking with every step. "Settling"—so he tells himself, and even he is not sure whether he intends irony.

A heavy branch begins to pound against the side of the house, setting up a giant, rattling reverberation that makes him think of the parable of the bridge and the soldiers marching in step. He feels embattled against the noises, menaced by them—they seem alive, directed by malice: certainly they are probing and slamming against the walls in search of a weak spot, trying to find a way in, to get at him. The clamor is as solid as a hedge—he can visualize it surrounding the house, curling in a cap over the roof, pressing tightly against the windows, waiting for a pinprick hole, waiting to fill the vacuum.

Windowglass buzzes and vibrates behind his head; he will not turn around to look. He has been sitting in the writing room, at one of the mahogany tables, trying to compose a letter to his friend in Boston, the friend who has lent him the use of this house during his prolonged "vacation" away from the city. His recovery, he thinks, not believing that either. He puts down his pen, crumples the piece of paper he has been writing on and throws it away. The trash receptacle, and the area surrounding it, are littered with similar balls of discarded paper. He knows that he should write a letter to his friend, indeed that he is obligated to: to reassure the friend that he has arrived safely, that all is "well," to assuage, however insincerely, any fears the friend might have as to John's mental and physical well-being. At very least a note to the friend and the friend's wife, congratulating them on the new child. But he cannot write the letter. On all the discarded pieces of paper he has managed to write no more than the formal, salutatory heading.

Disgruntled, John gets up and goes into the kitchen. The wind follows him from window to window, rattling the panes. For the first time since his arrival, he opens the liquor cabinet. He finds a dusty bottle of Hennessy cognac at the back of the shelf, breaks the seal, and pours himself a large drink, in a water glass. Holding the glass in one hand, the bottle in the other, he returns through the writing room to the living room. He stands before the fireplace for a long time, listening to the unnatural howl and clatter outside, the crickets that sound as loud as barrages from siege-guns. Then he sips his drink, wincing at its harsh savor. He puts the bottle down on the mantelpiece and selects one of the leatherbound volumes from the shelf, opening it at random. The words crawl across the page, cryptic and indecipherable—they are totally alien. He is even beginning to forget what they are for; he can remember that there is a purpose behind them, but he is no longer sure exactly what the purpose is, or why he should remember it. He puts the book back sadly, as if he is packing away a world. He knows that he will never open another one. He takes a deeper drink, lowering the level of the glass by half an inch. He carries the glass and the bottle upstairs with him to his room, closing himself inside again. This time he leaves the lights blazing on the floor below. They remain on all night.

The following morning is gray and wet—a thick ground mist encircling the house, the birches dimly visible behind it, like ghost ships through fog. Somewhere behind the mist is the sound of a light rain. John stands in the kitchen, waiting for a pot of coffee to perk, listening to the unseen rain, watching moisture bead on a half-opened window, on the dusty webbing of the screen. The sound of the rain is a low, melancholy murmur, like water mumbling down the mossy sides of an ancient well. The sound makes him unexpectedly sad. He pulls his robe tighter around him, gathering it at the collar. The wind through the open window is chill and damp, smelling somehow of the ocean—of salt flats and tides and depths—although he is hundreds of miles from the shore. It almost seems that he can hear patient waves slap against the side of the house, behind the mist, behind the morning. If the mist should burn away now, he knows that he would see a shining, placid sheet of ocean stretching endlessly away on all sides of the house, over the foundered hills and fields, the branches of trees waving above the surface like the dead and beckoning arms of the drowned.

He shivers, and lights the gas oven for warmth: the sharp, sudden hiss of the gas jet, the rasp of the kitchen match, the solid thunking whoosh as the jet ignites. The blue glow washes back over his face, smoothing out the deep hollows of his cheeks, striking reflections from his eyes, painting unknown cabalistic symbols across his forehead in light. He shakes the match and throws it away. He stands before the open oven door for a while, rubbing his hands, flexing his fingers. The room is filled with the pungent, strangely pleasant smell of escaped gas, and with the hiss of the burning jet.

The coffee perks, and John sits down at the table. He cannot eat—the very thought is repugnant. He drinks a cup of coffee, and then another. That at least is still permitted. Steam rises from the coffee, and through it he watches sodden azalea branches tap against the window-pane, drip tears across the glass. He will not yield to the impulse to pace. That is a nervous habit. He drinks coffee with grim determination, raising and lowering the cup mechanically. His feet shuffle uneasily under the table. He has been too isolated, he tells himself. That is why he is so high-strung and distracted. He has always been so proud of his devotion to his Art, his detachment, the degree to which he has been able to dissociate himself from the mundane concerns of everyday existence. His Art—he even thinks of it that way, capitalized, deified. Now he is starting to regard his poses and pretensions with aversion. They are contrived, artificial, jejune. He will make an effort to rejoin the mainstream of humanity, he will mingle with people again. Hike into town, get to know the citizenry, make friends. Maybe get invited to someone's house for dinner, and return the favor later—it would be good to hear a voice in the house other than his own. He will get back into the swim of life, he tells himself, smiling at the trite phrase. But it is applicable and appropriate, nevertheless. He drinks more coffee. After an hour, most of the mist has boiled away, revealing the road, the further

94

stand of birches, a gray and lowering sky. There is no ocean. He wonders if he really expected there to be one.

About noon, the grocer's route man pulls up before the back porch in a small panel truck. The rain is coming down now in steady pounding sheets—not quite a cloudburst, but a hard fall. The noise is like distant gunfire. The dirt road has turned to mud: the truck wheels spatter it, leaving great ruts in the road. John stares, fascinated, holding his cup suspended in the air. He has been taken by surprise by the intrusion, although now he dimly remembers the agency man telling him that he'd send the grocer around in a few days. He sets the cup down precisely on a coffee ring, with a click. The groceryman wiggles out of the cab, jumps down into the mud, and runs for the porch, brandishing his arms over his head as if to keep off rabid bats or bees. Certainly he does not keep off the rain: he is wet and stomping by the time he reaches the porch.

John gets up from the table to let the groceryman inside. The groceryman greets him with a nod, and a caustic remark about the weather: his clothes steam, rain drips from his faded parka. John offers the groceryman coffee; the groceryman thanks him, takes off his wet parka, drapes it across a radiator and settles down familiarly at the table. John gets him coffee, automatically drawing one for himself, and sits down at the other end of the table. Bemused, he stares surreptitiously at the groceryman. It has been only four days, and already he has forgotten what another human being looks like. The groceryman's face, his voice, his pattern of gestures and mannerisms, all are radically different from John's, from what he has become accustomed to thinking of, in such a short time, as an absolute standard, as the only aspect possible for these attributes. He is startled and shaken by the individuality of the groceryman, and somewhat repulsed—as if he was someone who, while exploring a distant wilderness, has suddenly come upon an unknown, unsuspected, and not altogether wholesome species of animal.

The groceryman is voluble, shrewd in a wry Yankee

fashion, and apparently not indisposed by the necessity of keeping up both ends of the conversation at once. He rambles on, expansively and with studied quaintness, about trivial matters of the town and the country, about the spell of bad weather that year, the real estate scandals, and then—with a sly glance at John to see if his worldly sophistication is being appreciated—widens out his talk to include the recent abdication of President Benes of Czechoslovakia, and the lynching of a German immigrant up in Scranton. Obviously he considers himself something of a raconteur, and is proud of the knowledgeability he manages to maintain here in the back country. John lets the groceryman talk—he is being made increasingly uneasy by the grating and annoying—to him—sound of the groceryman's voice, and by the obscure feeling that he should somehow respond to the overture of friendship being made by the other man, and by the numbing realization that he cannot. So he says nothing, and pointedly does not offer to refill the groceryman's cup when the coffee is gone. The groceryman takes the hint; his face suddenly sets itself up as cold and hard as weathered granite.

Looking rebuffed and disgruntled, the groceryman runs out to his truck and brings in the carton of groceries ordered by the agency man for John. Formally, he asks John if he would like to add anything to next week's order. John names a few items for the groceryman, out of politeness and to cover the embarrassment of the moment. The groceryman nods, thanks him coldly for the coffee, and leaves.

John sits at the table a moment longer, shaking his head grimly and ruefully. So much for the "mainstream of humanity," so much for the "swim of life." He has been sunk and drowned in a remarkable short time. One should really know how to swim, he tells himself, before one jumps into the river. He pushes the empty cup aside angrily and stands up. He should have known better. He has been a recluse too long. He has gone too far away from the world, and now it is no longer possible to find the way back. Nor is the world necessarily inclined to let him in, even if he knocks. He reaches the window in time to see the grocery truck drive away. He is filled with an odd sense of loss, and a stranger sense of relief. He is alone in the house again.

He makes a drink of brandy and moves to the rear window of the kitchen. He stands there for a long time, looking out over the lawn.

Outside, pounded by the rain, his discarded notebook has begun to turn into a lump of wet paper.

The weather worsens that evening. A storm rolls down from the mountains like a dark, fire-shot wave and breaks against the house with incredible fury. The rain is like a hose turned directly against the windows; the glass rattles and trembles in the frames with the force of it. Through the rivers of rain he can see the trees waving their branches, swaying and tossing and flailing horribly, like souls in agony, like demented armies of the night. Fire leapfrogs monstrously on the horizon, and the sky, when he can see it, is a lurid, luminescent indigo, torn across by intricate traceries of lightning and churned into froth by the beating arms of the trees. But there is no sound. He cannot hear the rain, he cannot hear the wind. When lightning turns the sky a searing blue-white, he can feel the house groan and reverberate around him as to a nearby buffeting explosion, but he cannot hear the thunder. He knows it must be there, the storm is right on top of him, lightning striking all around—but there is no sound. For a moment, he thinks that he has gone deaf, but he can hear his voice when he speaks aloud, he can hear the ring of a tapped fingernail against his brandy glass, he can hear sounds that *he* makes. But he cannot hear the storm. It is as if the storm is a phenomenon occurring inside the windowpane itself, a molecule-thin tempest, and someone has forgotten to turn the volume up. He wonders, desultorily, what would happen if he opened the window. Would the storm slide up into the molding with the pane, leaving only a quiet, cricket-filled country night beyond?

He does not open the window.

●　　●　　●

Things become vague for John, and he wanders around the house for an indeterminate period of time. At one point, he becomes gradually aware that he is sitting in the kitchen. It is daylight. There is a shaft of murky sunshine stabbing against one wall, and he can dimly remember watching it move glacier-slow across the room with the morning. He can remember little else. He knows that he has been on a monumental drunk, the first one in years. He feels shaky and stretched very thin, but he has no hangover. He is still wearing the clothes he put on the morning of the groceryman's visit, and they are filthy, stiff and glossy with caked grime and dried sweat. Gingerly, he feels his chin; there is a thick growth of stubbly beard there. Three days? More? Has he bothered to eat? His fingernails are black with dirt.

Feeling a spasm of distaste, he goes upstairs to wash and change. It takes a long time; he is easily distracted, and he keeps forgetting what he is about. He has to fix what he is supposed to be doing very firmly in his mind, so that he can refer back to it when he forgets, finding the word *wash*, not understanding it, but, as memory trickles back in, slowly attaching a societal function to it. In this way the world is won. The water wakes him up a little bit, but he still finds it difficult to think. It doesn't seem important.

He returns downstairs, washed and dressed. He knows that at this point he should wonder what to do next, although he does not so wonder, and emotionally has no desire to do anything. Nevertheless, he tackles it as an intellectual exercise. He finds it engraved in his mind that he should go outside, so he sets out to do so. It is a battle—twice he finds himself wandering aimlessly in some other part of the house, twice he consults his standing orders and heads back toward the door. The third time, he makes it outside. It is a quiet, overcast day, oppressively humid. He looks sadly at the pile of tools he has left on the stoop, consigned to rust, and at the ladder propped against the side of the house. The repairs will never be accomplished, he knows that now. He meanders across the lawn, sometimes stopping and standing mindlessly for long

98

intervals, then remembering and moving on. He makes it onto the access road. It is another battle to continue walking, but the road helps him remember and keeps him from wandering off the track. At last, the aspen grove closes over his head, and the house is gone.

It is much cooler and less humid here, and there is a brisk, pleasant breeze. John's mind begins to clear almost at once. The twinge of distaste he had felt returns as an overwhelming surge of revulsion. The realization that he has spent days wandering inside the house in a torpid, mindless stupor is disgusting. And in retrospect, it is terrifying. He would like to be able to blame it on the drink, but he knows that he cannot—the drink was an effect, not a cause.

The house is haunted, he tells himself, abruptly surrendering skepticism to an odd relief. It is a problem that can be dealt with—he will hold a seance, get an exorcist, follow whatever prescribed procedures there are for such a circumstance. If necessary, he will move and concede the house to the ghosts. But he is forced to realize, almost immediately, that he is deluding himself—that cannot be the answer. His friend and the friend's wife have lived in the house for years; they raised their little boy there, and they moved not out of choice, but because of the necessity of business. They were not chased out by supernatural horror; they loved the house, and regretted leaving enough to hold onto the title of the land in case a change in fortune would someday enable them to return. It seems unlikely that the house can have become haunted and sinister during the brief interregnum between their occupancy and his.

No, the house is not haunted. It is he, John, who is haunted.

He has been walking for fifteen minutes now, and he has not yet come to the blacktop secondary road. That is impossible. The access road is only a hundred yards long at the very most, with no branches or turnoffs, and the grove it transfixes is a small one. Nevertheless, he is still in the forest, and he can see no sign of anything but leagues of trees in any direction he looks. He has not been walking in a daze; his keyed-up mood has kept him alert, and he has noted every step of the way. He has not passed the blacktop without noticing it, and he has not strayed off the path. The path just does not go to the blacktop road anymore. Apparently, it now leads somewhere else entirely. In his abstracted mood, he almost does not find this remarkable.

Strangeness has always followed John like some patient, indefatigable hunter: unhurried, at his heels, waiting for him to stop. Sometimes he has been able to hold it at bay for months, even for years—with school, with the routine of business, with the regimen imposed by his art. With constant, distracting motion. But eventually he will stop, and it catches him. And when it does, he begins to sink right out of the world.

The pose of the introspective artist had served him well for quite a while—he had been able to use the accepted, cultured "sensitivity" of the role to mask the raw, unpalatable sensitivity beneath, from the world and from himself. Until, in London, the layers of protective callus had been gradually sloughed away, leaving that sensitivity grinning and naked, and other people had become too much to bear, even Paul, even Marilyn—they with their great ugly stews of hate and fear and lust, their uninspired eminences and shrieking plummeting depths, their molten blasts of desire and anger and unbearable love. And he knew that they were no different from himself. He was appalled by the sad, dowdy chronicles of pain that they carried in their faces, written in lines and ridges and whorls, muscle and bone. They were so plain, so readable that he could stretch out a finger and touch and number every one of them: here a frustration of the heart, here a vanishment of a small hope, here the souring of a dream. Their lives were engraved on their flesh in braille, like the Name on the forehead of the Golem, and he could not stand to read them. They broke his heart, and he shut himself away from the sight of them. And he continued to sink.

In the last days of his affliction, an increasing weirdness had seeped into the world, settling like a film

over ordinary things and altering them. He had walked
the everyday streets of London and seen, superimposed
over them, a vision of the Apocalypse. He had seen the
sky darken at noon, heard the frantic frightened
screaming of machines, saw the streets open to vomit up
fire and death, watched buildings buckle and collapse in
horrid cascades of brick and glass, listened to the screams
of the dying and smelled the stink of burning meat, seen
people crushed, buried, flayed to pieces, torn apart, going
up in flames as easy as kindling—watched a great city
kicked to flinders as if it was a house of cards, and put to
the torch. And all the while the old ladies sold flowers
along the Bayswater Road and in front of Marble Arch, in
the thin, watery sunlight, unaware of the doom that was
coming, the desolation that John watched with wide mad
eyes—for it was already here for him, and he could see
their bones jabbing and straining at their skins, eager to
be out and free, and he could see how very thin a
membrane of present time there was standing between
them sunning in Hyde Park and the ragged piles of dust
and ash they would eventually be. It was this horrifying
vision, repeated continually, playing behind his eyes at
night in slumber, that had driven him from London. But
coming through Boston, and then again in Manhattan, it
had been the same thing again, even more horrid and on a
grander scale: the great skyscrapers shattering and falling
like murdered gods, the whirlwinds of fire, dozens of
miles of city fused into molten glass by some new atrocity
of man.

Now he can feel the same noonday strangeness leaking
into this country morning. Around him, the forest is
touched by entropy, by a cold and foul breath of poison,
and it dies. It strangles, it suffocates, it is blighted, and it
dies. Everything dies: the trees, the grass, the bushes, the
flowers, the smallest moss and lichen, the worms that
tunnel the ground, the insects, the very bacteria in the soil.
He can see it all withering, shriveling, blackening, rotting.
A scythe of decay passes through the world, and when it
has passed, everything is gone. Nothing lives, nothing at
all. There is only sterile, lifeless soil, soon to be baked into

mud by the sun, or swept away by the wind to reveal the pale and elemental rock.

What is this? John asks himself, aghast at this ultimate negation. He can accept the burning of London as a premonition, a presentiment of the coming war. Similarly, he can understand the destruction of Boston and New York—the U.S. involved in the conflict, the war spreading eventually to American shores; many have predicted just that. But *this*, the blighting and death of life itself, the withering of the world, *what is this?*

The forest has changed, imperceptibly, around him. The deciduous trees are gone. It is now made up of red and white spruce and balsam fir, and the trees are shaggy, ancient giants. He is sure that there isn't an unlogged climax forest within a hundred miles or more of here, if anywhere in the East at all, and certainly not a spruce woods this far to the south. Most of the familiar weeds and wildflowers are gone, leaving the woods noticeably drabber. He finds himself remembering that plants like Queen Anne's lace, dandelion, and butter-and-eggs are European imports, and relatively recent, and then he spends a while wondering what he meant by that. He knows that he left the house walking north, and he can tell by the position of the sun that he has been walking steadily north ever since, for better than an hour, through this inexplicable forest. But when the forest begins at last to lighten, and when he notices—after the fact—that the woods have somehow slowly and imperceptibly changed back into a deciduous forest again, and when he breaks through the final fringe of trees and sees the house directly ahead of him, squatting like a spider, he is hardly surprised at all. He tells himself, with a strange, drugged philosophicality, that he couldn't really expect to win that easily.

It doesn't want to let him go.

The groceryman returns the next afternoon. For a while he sits out in front of the house in his truck and honks his horn, and then he goes up onto the porch and pounds on the door, and calls through his cupped hands.

When he gets no answer, the groceryman goes cautiously inside, pausing to call and hullo every few feet. He goes through the kitchen and the writing room, and stops at the threshold of the living room. It is hot and stuffy here, and the groceryman is already uncomfortable at snooping around inside someone's house without the resident's permission—he will go no further. The groceryman calls one last time, loudly, thinking that the resident might be asleep upstairs. There is no answer; it is very silent inside the gloomy house. The groceryman feels uneasy and prickly, as if the air has eyes here, and those eyes are watching him, unblinkingly. He shrugs irritably, shakes his head, and goes back outside, muttering something under his breath. The groceryman unloads a large carton of groceries from his truck, and leaves it inside the enclosed porch, with a bill and a taciturn note pinned to it. As he gets ready to leave, he feels strange again, spooky, and chilled. Then he puts the truck in gear and leaves.

John stands at the side of the road and watches the groceryman drive away. He answered the first honk of the truck horn, and he has followed the groceryman closely during the groceryman's walk through the house, speaking to him—at first softly, irritated by the man's rudeness, and then loudly, shouting in panic—and touching him, seizing him by the arm and trying to turn him around, at last grabbing him roughly by both shoulders and shaking him violently, making his head wobble and rattle like a jack-in-the-box. The man's flesh is firm under John's hands, but the groceryman does not notice him, and, save for a slight uneasiness of manner, does not even seem aware that he is being shaken and buffeted. His eyes look through John, not at him. He does not hear John's voice, even when John screams hoarsely in his ear. Instead, the groceryman shrugs and shakes his head, and goes back outside. John follows him out to the truck, shouting in anger and fear, but the groceryman doesn't look around—he puts his truck in gear and leaves. John watches the groceryman drive away; John has become oddly calm, and there is a crooked, grim smile on his face.

It seems that now he too is a ghost.

The fog closes in again, and John wanders through the house forever. His mind is clear only occasionally, giving him brief, vivid glimpses of the world with no continuity, like a collection of unrelated snapshots: walking down the stairs, sitting in the overstuffed chair in the living room, looking through the glassed-in doors at the veranda. And then the clouds pile up again and bury him, and the world becomes an oozing myopia. He is swept along by hot, drugged currents of feeling, jazzed by goosed, scurrying emotions. He talks to the people. There are many of them here, bright, eclectic, brash, glittering and garish as a neon sign. Their voices are like the hot, sour blare of a trumpet just missing the high note. He talks to the people:

He says,_____.
Their laughter, gaudy, dazzling, brittle. And their eyes.
_____, they say.
He asks,_____?
Their eyes.
_____, they say.
                    and
_____
                    and
_____

He is sitting on the floor at the bottom of the stairs to the second floor, leaning against the wall. He takes his head in his hands, squeezing the temples. He must think, he must think, but he cannot. And then they are there again, insistent and dazzling, and they say,_____

But he *is* thinking, he comes to realize that. Somewhere, deep under the surface, sundered from his consciousness, his mind is working logically and well, working continually. And occasionally he is sane enough to be able to listen in on what it is thinking.

He has a lucid interval. He comes back to his body

from a great distance, and finds that he is sitting in the kitchen, and finds that he is thinking, calmly and rationally, that there are two, opposing forces acting upon him. One is the tendency to sink right out of the world, something that has affected him most of his life. But there is another force, opposing it, that has caught him at the narrow place and won't let him sink all the way out, that is fighting to keep him anchored here. This—that he should stay, not sink—is somewhat similar to what *they* have been advocating, although it doesn't translate into words; they definitely belong to the opposing force. Strangely enough, he feels an aversion for the opposing force, the one trying to anchor him to the world, although logically he should feel exactly the opposite. The opposing force is embodied in the house—it wants to keep him. It is also somehow allied with the breath of decay he felt shriveling the forest, although he doesn't know on what basis he has made the connection. Perhaps it is entropy, he thinks. Ultimate zero, full stop, stasis. You might just as well call it the Devil, it would make little difference. And perhaps his vision is a true one, and the world is destined to die, die in every root and branch, die totally.

Perhaps the world, life, the continuum, whatever you called it—perhaps it knew that it was going to die. Perhaps every continuum that was about to die sent out seeds, in an effort to perpetuate itself elsewhere. Perhaps that was what he was: a seed. And that was why he'd always kept slipping through the fabric of reality; that was the bias of the continuum acting upon him, a huge, insistent hand trying to push him through, to seed another shore. And it wouldn't be just him, of course. There would be other seeds everywhere, seeds of everything: people, birds, animals, insects, perhaps even seeds of rocks and trees if the animists were correct. They would be slipping through all the time, vanishing from reality. Who would notice a blade of grass disappearing from a field, who would miss a single tree in a forest, or a bird or a fox, or a bumblebee, or a stone from a mountain? Who would miss him, really? How many people could vanish without anyone even noticing that they'd gone? Thousands, or millions? Or if it was noticed, what could anyone do other than to shrug their shoulders and forget about it? And the seeds would continue to sift through. Perhaps it had been going on for millennia. Perhaps that was how life had come to this world in the beginning, from another dying continuum: a slow seeding over millions of years—unicellular animals, mollusks, fish, amphibians, reptiles, mammals. And our continuum, knowing its own mortality, immediately beginning to seed in its turn, passing life on. And so it would go, from one level to another, like a stream gradually stairstepping down a many-terraced hill—the level "below" always a little out of phase, a little behind the level "above," which would explain the virgin spruce forest, if he really had been there for a moment before the anchoring tug of the house had pulled him back. Perhaps when the stream finally got to the bottom of the hill they turned the whole shebang over and started all over again, like an hourglass. Or perhaps it formed a stagnant pool at the bottom and nothing ever moved again—level entropy. Or perhaps there wasn't any bottom at all. Who knew how it had begun? If it had "begun." Perhaps it had gone on and would go on forever, world without end. A human mind was not capable of even beginning to grasp the concept of "forever." Why should a man comprehend the process any more than a dandelion seed whirling through the air, a wheat kernel planted deep in the blind black earth? It was enough to know merely that there was something going on.

Perhaps there were many people there, perhaps not. Quite possibly it was no better a place than this earth, and problems and situations one was unable to deal with here one would probably still be unable to deal with there. It would not be Eden—it might even be very bad. Even worse than here, in another way. But it would be *different*. And without the bias of the continuum pushing on him anymore, never letting him stay in one place long enough to put down roots, perhaps some of the foregone conclusions, the inalterable conditions of his own life would also be different.

Or perhaps not, but there was only one way he'd ever find out.

He has always fought against the sinking process, peddling desperately to keep his head above the surface, afraid that he was sinking into madness. But what would happen if he let himself go, let go completely, for the first time in his life? Was it possible to sink through madness and out the other side?

And then he is in the bedroom, lying on the bed, fully dressed. It is night. The cluster of dogwood leaves outside his window has turned into a demon. He can feel the pressure of its soulless, dead-black eyes, he can see the gleam of needle teeth in the dark fox muzzle. He can hear its hungry furnace snuffling as it smells his blood, through the glass. A full moon looms outside the window and forms a leprous alabaster halo for the shockheaded dogwood demon. John struggles to get up on one elbow. His mind is a muddy whirlpool of broken and chaotic thoughts. He knows that there is a strand of thought that he must hold on to, that is the one pertinent thing in an obscurity of distractions. Grimly, he tries to follow the thought through to its conclusion. Suddenly, it is daylight. A robin lands on the windowsill, stares curiously at John, eye to little bright eye, tosses his bill, and flies away. In an eyeblink, it is night again. The moon is in a different, lower quadrant of the window, and the demon looks much bigger—it has flattened its bulk against the pane, and he can hear its sharp diamond tongue probing abrasively against the glass, scritch, scritch, scritch, flickering in the moonlight. John tries to heave himself up to a sitting position, fails, and it is daylight. Harsh gray daylight, showing the thinness of his hands. Rain beats against the window. Dizzied, John squeezes his eyes tightly shut. He keeps them closed for a long time, feeling the shifting play of light and shadow against his eyelids. It is better this way, and easier to think. John laboriously traces the convolutions of the one proper thought, over and over, almost getting it right.

He opens his eyes. It is night, a moonless night. The

stars provide a lactescent, nacred light that sifts down softly through the room, filtering vision through fine cheesecloth. A woman is lying next to him in the big bed, naked, propped lazily on her elbow. She is slender, with short-cropped blond hair, and full breasts that look much bigger than they are against her sleek, long-muscled dancer's body. The starlight burnishes some of her body to streaked, milky marble—her forehead, her cheek, the line of her arm and hip, the tops of her breasts—and mutes the rest into deep and secret velvet shadow: her legs, her belly, her eyes. She smiles at him, a flash of moist lips sliding back from pearl-wet teeth. The rest of the room is crowded with other shapes, male and female, pressing close against the bed. They are all fascinating, intriguing, tantalizing, mysterious, alluring, intensely *interesting*. Their glittereyes. They smile invitingly, with beckoning comradery.

John closes his eyes.

When he opens them again, after a long, stubborn time, it is still starlit night, but the room is empty. He struggles again to get up, and this time he succeeds. He sits on the side of the bed, feet on the floor, breathing heavily. There is a new tension in the air, a menace, a sense of something building tightly to a climax. The house is alive with sound. John can hear people or things running angrily back and forth downstairs, bumping into furniture, careening against the walls. He hears shouts, screams, wails, angry chittering howls. Something is banging and slobbering harshly against the window behind him. He will not turn his head to look. *Let go*, he tells himself, *let go*. Abruptly, all the noises stop, and it is totally silent. Alone in the terrifying silence, John sits and waits. Then, very far away, much lower than the bottom of the stairs could possibly be, John hears a footstep, and then another. Something is ascending the stairs, coming up from Hell. The footsteps are very heavy and ponderous; they shake the house at every step, and there is an unpleasant rasping quality to them, as if the feet are almost too heavy to lift. The footsteps have been coming up for miles, for years, for hundreds of years, and now they are close enough so that John can hear the massive, wheezing, steam-puffing, smithy-bellows breathing that goes with them, and the labored, ugly beating of a monstrous heart. The footsteps stop outside the door. Through the harsh reptile breathing, John can hear the scaly rutch of something infinitely hard pressing in against the door, scraping, digging up the wood like a gouge. Slowly, John gets up and walks toward the door, stopping after every step. He puts his fingers against the door-panel, feeling, behind the thin wood, the sluggish beating of the alien heart. He sees that the doorknob is turning, slowly, hesitantly, as if it is being fumbled at by enormous spatulate fingers. *Let go*, John tells himself, and he reaches out, briskly, and opens the door.

Nothing is there.

Trembling now, after the fact, John begins to walk downstairs. It is like wading through hardening glue, and with every step the glue gets deeper and stiffer. He holds very tightly to the one proper thought, because he knows now what happens to people-seeds who are caught too tightly by the world, unable to sink completely out but unable to stop trying to sink—they go insane. They become psychotic: catatonic, schizophrenic, autistic, God knows what else. Ghosts, maybe. Poltergeists, throwing things around in fits of hapless rage because no one in the world will notice them anymore—those who've sunk too far out to be seen by normals, but not far enough to escape. What percentage of seeds did make it through, and how many of those took? How barren was the field the continuum was attempting to seed? Who knows, God knows—the same answer, and the only one there was.

John reaches the foot of the stairs, and it feels now like he is in glue up to his armpits—on the way across the living room it is over his head completely and he is swimming through murky syrup. By the time he has reached the outside door he has to batter and buffet against the air for every step, as if he is a man trying to bull his way through a high snowdrift, breasting it, breaking it down. One flailing hand catches and holds the doorknob. He turns it and pushes, throwing his weight against the door. It is like slamming into a mountain. He surges against the door twice more, feeling the blood drain from behind his eyes, feeling himself starting to black out. Then, all at once, the door flies open with a despairing crack and groan, and John stumbles outside. He has one glimpse of ghostly white birches, and then the flagstone path is drifting slowly up toward his face. He is puzzled for a moment, as the flagstone inches closer, and then he realizes that he must be falling. His face touches, and is pressed flat against the flagstone, eyes still open, and he continues to fall, *into* the stone, into the earth, going down.

Asleep—floating in suspension somewhere, turning over and over, falling endlessly—John dreams of the infinitely complex question that is life, that is the world. And, without the encumbrance of mind or body or ego, he can see the problem clearly and completely for the first time, and he numbers each of the millions of hidden relationships and cross-relationships, totals them, and comes up with the one underlying, unifying relationship: the lowest common denominator. The Answer to It All. And he laughs in his sleep, as he falls. It was so absurdly simple after all.

John comes awake with a faint bump, as if he is a feather, falling weightlessly for a million miles, that has finally drifted to the ground. He rolls over, scattering leaves and leaf mulch, and sits up. He opens his eyes, and is dazzled by the day. *The light*, he thinks, dazedly, *the quality of the light*. He staggers to his feet, falls, lurches up again, filled with a thousand wild terrors, his throat clogged with primordial horror, his mouth strained wide to scream. And then he stops, abruptly, and sinks again to his knees, his mouth slowly closes, and his shoulders unhunch, and the tension goes out of his frame muscle by slow muscle, and something suspiciously like peace begins to seep, grudgingly and gradually, into his haggard face.

By the sun, he is on the east-facing slope of a mountain,

110

a small wooded, rolling mountain like those he can remember seeing on his original ride in from town—in fact, it seems, as far as he can tell, to be one of the same mountains. But now, a hundred feet below him, breaking in gentle waves against a rocky scrub beach, and rolling back from there to the horizon, breathing and calm and shining, with the rising sun painting a red road through its middle and touching every whitecap with flecks of deep crimson, with seagulls wheeling over it and skimming across it in search of breakfast, with its damp salt stink and the eternal booming hiss of its voice—stretched out below him now, deep and full of life, is the ocean.

And the rich black dirt under his fingers.

The earth is fertile. There will be a crop.

Machines of Loving Grace

DAWN WAS JUST beginning to color the sky. She huddled inside the small bathroom—door closed, bolt slid and locked—sitting on the toilet lid and hugging her knees. Her head was tilted and hung down, chin almost on breast, and her eyes were nearly closed. She had wrapped her hands around her ankles. Her fingers were turning white. There was no noise in the empty apartment, not even the scurry of a cockroach. She had stopped crying hours ago.

There was noise beyond the window on her left, beyond plaster and glass, outside the vacuum of bedroom-kitchen-livingroom-guestroom-bath: a frozen automobile horn had been honking steadily for the last hour, occasionally traffic whined on the asphalt below, earlier in the evening there had been radios in nearby buildings, tuned to the confusion of a dozen different stations and fading one by one toward morning. She didn't pay any attention to these noises. The silence inside her apartment was too loud.

She opened her hands, flexed her stiff fingers, let her legs uncurl. One of them had gone to sleep, and she stamped it softly, automatically, to restore circulation. The floor was cold under her bare feet. Gooseflesh blossomed along her arms and she ran her hands down over them to smooth it. She had put on a new half-slip for the occasion. She shifted her weight; the toilet lid had

112

been chilly at first, but now it had grown hot and sticky with the heat of her body. She leaned in closer to the hot-water pipe that descended from ceiling to floor—it was still warm to the touch. The dull paint had flaked off it in jigsaw pieces. There was a dingy gray toilet brush leaning against the base of the pipe. The bristles were broken and matted down. All this without thinking at all.

To be free, she thought.

Her head came up; eyes snapped open, closed to slits, opened again, wider.

The muscles in her neck had started to cord.

Her head jerked to the left. She stared out the window. Dawn was a growing red wash across the horizon, clustered buildings blocky beast-silhouettes, a factory plume of smoke etched black against tones of scarlet. Lights far away and lonely. A television antenna like a cross of stark metal. Her head turned back to center, wobbling: the string cut.

For a while she did not think. The shaving mirror on the wall over the sink, clutter on the shelves to the right of the basin: empty bottles of mouthwash, witch hazel, deodorant, the cardboard center from a roll of toilet paper, crumpled toothpaste tube, box of vaginal suppositories. The burlap curtains, frayed edges polarizing in the new light. Cracked and chipped plaster around the edges of the windowsill, streaks of white on the walls where paint had run thin. The closed door, the whorls in dark wood: beyond were the cluttered kitchen, the empty bedroom. They pressed in against the door. The door hinges were made in five sections.

I'm going to go crazy, she thought.

She reached out and flicked off the light switch. It was bright enough now to see: a gritty, hard light; harsh, too much grain and contrast. She had begun to tremble. The noise of the horn in the background was a steady buzz through her teeth. She picked up the razor blade from the window ledge. The horn stopped abruptly. In the silence, she could hear pigeons fluttering and cooing on the adjacent roof.

She turned the razor blade over in her fingers. The blade was smooth and sharp. No nicks in it, like the ones she used to shave her legs. She'd saved this one special. Orange sunlight refracted along the honed edge of the blade.

The bathtub was only inches away on her right, its head to the toilet. Without getting up, she leaned over, turned on the hot-water tap. Let the water run. This early it was reluctant: the water sputtered, the pipes knocked. But after a while it began to run hot. A thin wisp of steam. She put her arm under the hot water and sliced her wrist, holding the razor between thumb and forefinger. Clumsily, she switched hands and sliced her other wrist. Then she dropped the blade. Her wrists stung dully, and she felt a spreading warmth and wetness. She lifted her arms away from the water. Blood, welling up in thick clots, running down her arms toward the elbows.

To be free, she thought.

She sat with her arms held over the tub, palms up. Already it was better; the pressure that had been trying to turn her into someone else was receding. She wouldn't go crazy this time. She tilted her arms up to help the flow. She noticed that the shower curtain had a pattern of yellow swans and fountains on it, that there was a quarter-full plastic bottle of shampoo and a bit of melted soap in the bath shelf. A big glob of blood splattered against the porcelain bottom of the tub. The flowing water stretched it out elastically, tugged at it, swept it loose and swirled it down the drain.

Too slow. The Lysol had been faster.

She fumbled for the razor blade, dropped it, wiped her hand dry on the shower curtain, picked it up again. She tilted her head back, felt for the big vein in her throat, located it with a finger. Very carefully, she positioned the razor blade. Then she closed her eyes and hacked with all her strength.

The control light flittered on the Big Board: green dulled to amber, died to red, guttered out completely. A

114

siren began to scream. The duty tech put down his magazine, winced at the metallic wailing, and touched the arm of his chair. Pneumatics hissed, the chair moved up and then sideways along the scaffolding, ghosting past thousands of unwinking green eyes set in horizontal rows, rows stacked in fifty-by-fifty-foot banks, banks filling the walls of the hexagonal Monitoring Complex, each tiny light in the walls in the banks in the rows representing the state of the life-system of one person in this sector of the City.

The tech found the deader easily: one blank spot in a solid wall of green—like a missing tooth, like the empty eye socket of a skull. He read the code symbols from the plaque above the dead light, relayed them through his throat mike to the duty runner down on the floor. "Got that?" "Check." Below, in Dispatching, the runner would be feeding the code symbols into a records computer, getting the coordinates of the deader's address, sending a VHF pulse out to the activated monitor in the deader's body, the monitor replying with a pulse of its own so that the computer could check by triangulation that the deader was actually at his home address and then flash confirmation to the runner. The whole process took about a minute. Then the runner, fingers racing over a keyboard, would relay the coordinates to the sophisticated robot brain of the meat wagon, flick the activating switch, and the pickup squad would whoosh out over the private government monorail system that webbed the City's roofs.

The duty tech hung from the scaffolding, twenty feet above the floor, three feet away from the banked lights of the Big Board. He settled back against the black leather cushions of his chair, waiting for the official confirmation. The siren had been cut off. He was bored. He nudged at the blank light with the toe of his shoe. Idly, he began to read the code symbols again. Somehow they seemed familiar.

The runner's voice buzzed in his head. "Dispatched." "Confirmed," the tech replied automatically, then still

115

tracing the symbols with his finger: "Christ, do you know who this is? The deader? It's her again. That crazy broad. Christ, this is the third time this month."

"Fuck her. She's nuts."

The tech looked at the dead light, shook his head. The chair eased back down into its rest position before the metal desk. He squirmed around to get comfortable, drank the dregs of his coffee, rested his feet on the rim of the desk and settled back. The whole thing had taken maybe eight, maybe ten minutes. Not bad. He reached out and found the article he'd been reading.

By the time they brought her back, he was deep in the magazine again.

They carried her in and put her into the machines. The machines kept her in stasis to retard decay while they synthesized blood from sample cells and pumped it into her, grew new skin and tissue from scrapings, repaired the veins in throat and wrists, grafted the skin over them and flash-healed them without a scar. It took about an hour and a half, all told. It wasn't a big job. It was said that the machines could rebuild life from a sample as small as fifty grams of flesh, although that took a few weeks—even resurrect personality/identity from the psychocybernetic records for a brain that had been completely destroyed, although that was trickier, and might take months. This was nothing. The machines spread open the flesh of her upper abdomen, deactivated the monitor that was surgically implanted in every citizen in accordance with the law, and primed it again so that it would go off when her life-functions fell below a certain level. The machines sewed her up again, the monitor ticking smoothly inside her. The machines toned up her muscles, flushed out an accumulated excess of body poisons, burned off a few pounds of unnecessary fat, revitalized the gloss of her hair, upped her ratio of adrenaline secretion slightly, repaired minor tissue damage. The machines restarted her heart, got her lungs functioning, regulated her circulatory and respiratory systems, then switched off the stasis field and spat her into consciousness.

She opened her eyes. Above, a metal ceiling, rivets, phosphorescent lights. Behind, a mountain of smoothly chased machinery, herself resting on an iron tongue that had been thrust out of the machine: a rejected wafer. Ahead, a plastic window, and someone looking through it. Physically, she felt fine. Not even a headache.

The man in the window stared at her disapprovingly, then beckoned. Dully, she got up and followed him out. She found that someone had dressed her in street clothes, mismatched, colors clashing, hastily snatched from her closet. She had on two different kinds of shoes. She didn't care.

Mechanically, she followed him down a long corridor to a plush, overstuffed office. He opened the door for her, shook his head primly as she passed, closed it again. The older man inside the office told her to sit down. She sat down. He had white hair (bleached), and sat behind a huge mahogany desk (plastic). He gave her a long lecture, gently, fatherly, sorrowfully, trying to keep the perplexity out of his voice, the hint of fear. He said that he was concerned for her. He told her that she was a very lucky girl, even if she didn't realize it. He told her about the millions of people in the world who still weren't as lucky as she was. "Mankind is free of the fear of death for the first time in the history of the race," he told her earnestly, "at least in the Western world. Free of the threat of extinction." She listened impassively. The office was stuffy; flies battered against the closed windowpane. He asked her if she understood. She said that she understood. Her voice was dull. He stared at her, sighed, shook his head. He told her that she could go. He had begun to play nervously with a paperweight.

She stood up, moved to the door. "Remember, young lady," he called after her, "you're free now."

She went out quickly, hurried along a corridor, past a robot receptionist, found the outside door. She wrenched it open and stumbled outside.

Outside, she closed the door and leaned against it

wearily. It was a full daylight now. In between dirty banks of clouds, the sun beat pitilessly down on concrete, heat rising in waves, no shadows. The air was thick with smoke, with human sweat. It smelled bad, and the sharper reek of gasoline and exhaust bit into her nostrils. The streets were choked, the sidewalks thick with sluggishly moving crowds of pedestrians, jammed in shoulder to shoulder. The gray sky pressed down on her like a hand.

A Dream at Noonday

I REMEMBER THE sky, and the sun burning in the sky like a golden penny flicked into a deep blue pool, and the scuttling white clouds that changed into magic ships and whales and turreted castles as they drifted up across that bottomless ocean and swam the equally bottomless sea of my mind's eye. I remember the winds that skimmed the clouds, smoothing and rippling them into serene grandeur or boiling them into froth. I remember the same wind dipping low to caress the grass, making it sway and tremble, or whipping through the branches of the trees and making them sing with a wild, keening organ note. I remember the silence that was like a bronzen shout echoing among the hills.

—It is raining. The sky is slate-gray and grittily churning. It looks like a soggy dishrag being squeezed dry, and the moisture is dirty rain that falls in pounding sheets, pressing down the tall grass. The rain pocks the ground, and the loosely packed soil is slowly turning into mud and the rain spatters the mud, making it shimmer—

And I remember the trains. I remember lying in bed as a child, swathed in warm blankets, sniffing suspiciously and eagerly at the embryonic darkness of my room, and listening to the big trains wail and murmur in the freight yard beyond. I remember lying awake night after night, frightened and darkly fascinated, keeping very still so that the darkness wouldn't see me, and listening to the hollow booms and metallic moans as the trains coupled and linked below my window. I remember that I thought the trains were alive, big dark beasts who came to dance and to hunt each other through the dappled moonlight of the world outside my room, and when I would listen to the whispering clatter of their passing and feel the room quiver ever so slightly in shy response, I would get a crawly feeling in my chest and a prickling along the back of my neck, and I would wish that I could watch them dance, although I knew that I never would. And I remember that it was different when I watched the trains during the daytime, for then even though I clung tight to my mother's hand and stared wide-eyed at their steam-belching and spark-spitting they were just big iron beasts putting on a show for me; they weren't magic then, they were hiding the magic inside them and pretending to be iron beasts and waiting for the darkness. I remember that I knew even then that trains are only magic in the night and only dance when no one can see them. And I remember that I couldn't go to sleep at night until I was soothed by the muttering lullaby of steel and the soft, rhythmical hiss-clatter of a train booming over a switch. And I remember that some nights the bellowing of a fast freight or the cruel, whistling shriek of a train's whistle would make me tremble and feel cold suddenly, even under my safe blanket-mountain, and I would find myself thinking about rain-soaked ground and blood and black cloth and half-understood references to my grandfather going away, and the darkness would suddenly seem to curl in upon itself and become diamond-hard and press down upon my straining eyes, and I would whimper and the fading whistle would snatch the sound from my mouth and trail it away into the night. And I remember that at times like that I would pretend that I had tiptoed to the window to watch the trains dance, which I never really dared to do because I knew I would die if I did, and then I would close my eyes and pretend that I was a train, and in my mind's eye I would be hanging disembodied in the darkness a few inches above the shining tracks, and then the track would begin to slip along under me, slowly at first then fast and smooth like flowing syrup, and then the darkness would be flashing by and then I would be moving out and away, surrounded by the wailing roar and evil steel chuckling of a fast freight slashing through the night, hearing my whistle scream with the majestic cruelty of a stooping eagle and feeling the switches boom and clatter hollowly under me, and I would fall asleep still moving out and away, away and out.

—The rain is stopping slowly, trailing away across the field, brushing the ground like long, dangling gray fingers. The tall grass creeps erect again, bobbing drunkenly, shedding its burden of water as a dog shakes himself dry after a swim. There are vicious little crosswinds in the wake of the storm, and they make the grass whip even more violently than the departing caress of the rain. The sky is splitting open above, black rain clouds pivoting sharply on a central point, allowing a sudden wide wedge of blue to appear. The overcast churns and tumbles and clots like wet heavy earth turned by a spade. The sky is now a crazy mosaic of mingled blue and gray. The wind picks up, chews at the edge of the tumbling wrack, spinning it to the fineness of cotton candy and then lashing it away. A broad shaft of sunlight falls from the dark undersides of the clouds, thrusting at the ground and drenching it in a golden cathedral glow, filled with shimmering green highlights. The effect is like that of light through a stained-glass window, and objects bathed in the light seem to glow very faintly from within, seem to be suddenly translated into dappled molten bronze. There is a gnarled, shaggy tree in the center of the pool of sunlight, and it is filled with wet, disgruntled birds, and the birds are hesitantly, cautiously, beginning to sing again—

And I remember wandering around in the woods as a boy and looking for nothing and finding everything and that clump of woods was magic and those rocks were a rustlers' fort and there were dinosaurs crashing through the brush just out of sight and everybody knew that there were dragons swimming in the sea just below the waves and an old glittery piece of coke bottle was a magic jewel that could let you fly or make you invisible and everybody knew that you whistled twice and crossed your fingers when you walked by that deserted old house or something shuddery and scaly would get you and you argued about bang you're dead no I'm not and you had a keen gun that could endlessly dispatch all the icky monsters who hung out near the swing set in your backyard without ever running out of ammunition. And I remember that as a kid I was nuts about finding a magic cave and I used to think that there was a cave under every rock, and I would get a long stick to use as a lever and I would sweat and strain until I had managed to turn the rock over, and then when I didn't find any tunnel under the rock I would think that the tunnel was there but it was just filled in with dirt, and I would get a shovel and I would dig three or four feet down looking for the tunnel and the magic cave and then I would give up and go home for a dinner of beans and franks and brown bread. And I remember that once I did find a little cave hidden under a big rock and I couldn't believe it and I was scared and shocked and angry and I didn't want it to be there but it was and so I stuck my head inside it to look around because something wouldn't let me leave until I did and it was dark in there and hot and very still and the darkness seemed to be blinking at me and I thought I heard something rustling and moving and I got scared and I started to cry and I ran away and then I got a big stick and came back, still crying, and pushed and heaved at that rock until it thudded back over the cave and hid it forever. And I remember that the next day I went out again to hunt for a magic cave.

—The rain has stopped. A bird flaps wetly away from the tree and then settles back down onto an outside branch. The branch dips and sways with the bird's weight, its leaves heavy with rain. The tree steams in the sun, and a million raindrops become tiny jewels, microscopic prisms, gleaming and winking, loving and transfiguring the light even as it destroys them and they dissolve into invisible vapor puffs to be swirled into the air and absorbed by the waiting clouds above. The air is wet and clean and fresh; it seems to squeak as the tall grass saws through it and the wind runs its fingernails lightly along its surface. The day is squally and gusty after the storm, high shining overcast split by jagged ribbons of blue that look like aerial fjords. The bird preens and fluffs its feathers disgustedly, chattering and scolding at the rain, but keeping a tiny bright eye carefully cocked in case the storm should take offense at the liquid stream of insults and come roaring back. Between the tufts of grass the ground has turned to black mud, soggy as a sponge, puddled by tiny pools of steaming rainwater. There is an arm and a hand lying in the mud, close enough to make out the texture of the tattered fabric clothing the arm, so close that the upper arm fades up and past the viewpoint and into a huge featureless blur in the extreme corner of the field of vision. The arm is bent back at an unnatural angle and the stiff fingers are hooked into talons that seem to claw toward the gray sky—

And I remember a day in the sixth grade when we were struggling in the cloakroom with our coats and snow-encrusted overshoes and I couldn't get mine off because one of the snaps had frozen shut and Denny was talking about how his father was a jet pilot and he sure hoped the war wasn't over before he grew up because he wanted to kill some Gooks like his daddy was doing and then later in the boy's room everybody was arguing about who had the biggest one and showing them and Denny could piss further than anybody else. I remember that noon at recess we were playing kick the can and the can rolled down the side of the hill and we all went down after it and somebody said hey look and we found a place inside a bunch of bushes where the grass was all flattened down and broken and there were pages of a magazine scattered all over and Denny picked one up and spread it out and it was a picture of a girl with only a pair of pants on and everybody got real quiet and I could hear the girls chanting in the schoolyard as they jumped rope and kids yelling and everybody was scared and her eyes seemed to be looking back right out of the picture and somebody finally licked his lips and said what're those things stickin' out of her, ah, and he didn't know the word and one of the bigger kids said tits and he said yeah what're those things stickin' outta her tits and I couldn't say anything because I was so surprised to find out that girls had those little brown things like we did except that hers were pointy and hard and made me tremble and Denny said hell I knew about that I've had hundreds of girls but he was licking nervously at his lips as he said it and he was breathing funny too. And I remember that afternoon I was sitting at my desk near the window and the sun was hot and I was being bathed in the rolling drone of our math class and I wasn't understanding any of it and listening to less. I remember that I knew I had to go to the bathroom but I didn't want to raise my hand because our math teacher was a girl with brown hair and eyeglasses and I was staring at the place where I knew her pointy brown things must be under her blouse and I was thinking about touching them to see what they felt like and that made me feel funny somehow and I thought that if I raised my hand she would be able to see into my head and she'd know and she'd tell everybody what I was thinking and then she'd get mad and punish me for thinking bad things and so I didn't say anything but I had to go real bad and if I looked real close I thought that I could see two extra little bulges in her blouse where her pointy things were pushing against the cloth and I started thinking about what it would feel like if she pushed them up against me and that made me feel even more funny and sort of hollow and sick inside and I couldn't wait any longer and I raised my hand and left the room but it was too late and I wet myself when I was still on the way to the boy's room and I didn't know what to do so I went back to the classroom with my pants all wet and smelly and the math teacher looked at me and said what did you do and I was scared and Denny yelled he pissed in his pants he pissed in his pants and I said I did not the water bubbler squirted me but Denny yelled he pissed in his pants he pissed in his pants and the math teacher got very mad and everybody was laughing and suddenly the kids in my class didn't have any faces but only laughing mouths and I wanted to curl up into a ball where nobody could get me and once I had seen my mother digging with a garden spade and turning over the wet dark earth and there was half of a worm mixed in with the dirt and it writhed and squirmed until the next shovelful covered it up.

—Most of the rain has boiled away, leaving only a few of the larger puddles that have gathered in the shallow depressions between grass clumps. The mud is slowly solidifying under the hot sun, hardening into ruts, miniature ridges and mountains and valleys. An ant appears at the edge of the field of vision, emerging warily from the roots of the tall grass, pushing its way free of the tangled jungle. The tall blades of grass tower over it, forming a tightly interwoven web and filtering the hot yellow sunlight into a dusky green half-light. The ant pauses at the edge of the muddy open space, reluctant to exchange the cool tunnel of the grass for the dangers of level ground. Slowly, the ant picks its way across the sticky mud, skirting a pebble half again as big as it is. The pebble is streaked with veins of darker rock and has a tiny flake of quartz embedded in it near the top. The elements have rounded it into a smooth oval, except for a dent on the far side that exposes its porous core. The ant finishes its cautious circumnavigation of the pebble and scurries slowly toward the arm, which lies across its path. With infinite patience, the ant begins to climb up the arm, slipping on the slick, mud-spattered fabric. The ant works its way down the arm to the wrist and stops, sampling the air. The ant stands among the bristly black hairs on the wrist, antennae vibrating. The big blue vein in the wrist can be seen under its tiny feet. The ant continues to walk up the wrist, pushing its way through the bristly hair, climbing onto the hand and walking purposefully through the hollow of the thumb. Slowly, it disappears around the knuckle of the first finger—

And I remember a day when I was in the first year of high school and my voice was changing and I was starting to grow hair in unusual places and I was sitting in English class and I wasn't paying too much attention even though I'm usually pretty good in English because I was in love with the girl who sat in front of me. I remember that she had long legs and soft brown hair and a laugh like a bell

125

and the sun was coming in the window behind her and the sunlight made the downy hair on the back of her neck glow very faintly and I wanted to touch it with my fingertips and I wanted to undo the knot that held her hair to the top of her head and I wanted her hair to cascade down over my face soft against my skin and cover me and with the sunlight I could see the strap of her bra underneath her thin dress and I wanted to slide my fingers underneath it and unhook it and stroke her velvety skin. I remember that I could feel my body stirring and my mouth was dry and painful and the zipper of her dress was open a tiny bit at the top and I could see the tanned texture of her skin and see that she had a brown mole on her shoulder and my hand trembled with the urge to touch it and something about Shakespeare and when she turned her head to whisper to Denny across the row her eyes were deep and beautiful and I wanted to kiss them softly brush them lightly as a bird's wing and Hamlet was something or other and I caught a glimpse of her tongue darting wetly from between her lips and pressing against her white teeth and that was almost too much to bear and I wanted to kiss her lips very softly and then I wanted to crush them flat and then I wanted to bite them and sting them until she cried and I could comfort and soothe her and that frightened me because I didn't understand it and my thighs were tight and prickly and the blood pounded at the base of my throat and Elsinore something and the bell rang shrilly and I couldn't get up because all I could see was the fabric of her dress stretched taut over her hips as she stood up and I stared at her hips and her belly and her thighs as she walked away and wondered what her thing would look like and I was scared. I remember that I finally got up enough nerve to ask her for a date during recess and she looked at me incredulously for a second and then laughed, just laughed contemptuously and walked away without saying a word. I remember her laughter. And I remember wandering around town late that night heading aimlessly into nowhere trying to escape from the pressure and the emptiness and passing a car parked on a dark street corner just as the moon swung out from behind a cloud and there was light that danced and I could hear the freight trains booming far away and she was in the back seat with Denny and they were locked together and her skirt was hiked up and I could see the white flash of flesh all the way up her leg and he had his hand under her blouse on her breast and I could see his knuckles moving under the fabric and the freight train roared and clattered as it hit the switch and he was kissing her and biting her and she was kissing him back with her lips pressed tight against her teeth and her hair floating all around them like a cloud and the train was whispering away from town and then he was on top of her pressing her down and I felt like I was going to be sick and I started to vomit but stopped because I was afraid of the noise and she was moaning and making small low whimpering noises I'd never heard anyone make before and I had to run before the darkness crushed me and I didn't want to do that when I got home because I'd feel ashamed and disgusted afterward but I knew that I was going to have to because my stomach was heaving and my skin was on fire and I thought that my heart was going to explode. And I remember that I eventually got a date for the dance with Judy from my history class who was a nice girl although plain but all night long as I danced with her I could only see my first love moaning and writhing under Denny just as the worm had writhed under the thrust of the garden spade into the wet dark earth long ago and as I ran toward home that night I heard the train vanish into the night trailing a cruelly arrogant whistle behind it until it faded to a memory and there was nothing left.

—The ant reappears on the underside of the index finger, pauses, antennae flickering inquisitively, and then begins to walk back down the palm, following the deep groove known as the life line until it reaches the wrist. For a moment, it appears as if the ant will vanish into the space between the wrist and the frayed, bloodstained cuff of the shirt, but it changes its mind and slides back down the wrist to the ground on the far side. The ant struggles for a moment in the sticky mud, and then crawls determinedly off across the crusted ground. At the extreme edge of the field of vision, just before the blur that is the upper arm, there is the jagged, pebbly edge of a shellhole. Half over the lip of the shellhole, grossly out of proportion at this distance, is half of a large earthworm, partially buried by the freshly turned earth thrown up by an explosion. The ant pokes suspiciously at the worm—

And I remember the waiting room at the train station and the weight of my suitcase in my hand and the way the big iron voice rolled unintelligibly around the high ceiling as the stationmaster announced the incoming trains and cigar and cigarette smoke was thick in the air and the massive air-conditioning fan was laboring in vain to clear some of the choking fog away and the place reeked of urine and age and an old dog twitched and moaned in his ancient sleep as he curled close against an equally ancient radiator that hissed and panted and belched white jets of steam and I stood by the door and looked up and watched a blanket of heavy new snow settle down over the sleeping town with the ponderous invulnerability of a pregnant woman. I remember looking down into the train tunnel and out along the track to where the shining steel disappeared into darkness and I suddenly thought that it looked like a magic cave and then I wondered if I had thought that was supposed to be funny and I wanted to laugh only I wanted to cry too and so I could do neither and instead I tightened my arm around Judy's waist and pulled her closer against me and kissed the silken hollow of her throat and I could feel the sharp bone in her hip jabbing against mine and I didn't care because that was pain that was pleasure and I felt the gentle resilience of her breast suddenly against my rib-cage and felt her arm tighten protectively around me and her fingernails bite sharply into my arm and I knew that she was trying not to cry and that if I said anything at all it would make her cry and there would be that sloppy scene we'd been trying to avoid and so I said nothing but only held her and kissed her lightly on the eyes and I knew that people were looking at us and snickering and I didn't give a damn and I knew that she wanted me and wanted me to stay and we both knew that I couldn't and all around us about ten other young men were going through similar tableaux with their girlfriends or folks and everybody was stern and pale and worried and trying to look unconcerned and casual and so many women were trying not to cry that the humidity in the station was trembling at the saturation point. I remember Denny standing near the door with a foot propped on his suitcase and he was flashing his too-white teeth and his too-wide smile and he reeked of cheap cologne as he told his small knot of admirers in an overly loud voice that he didn't give a damn if he went or not because he'd knocked up a broad and her old man was tryin to put the screws on him and this was a good way to get outta town anyway and the government would protect him from the old man and he'd come back in a year or so on top of the world and the heat would be off and he could start collectin female scalps again and besides his father had been in and been a hero and he could do anything better than that old bastard and besides he hated those goddamned Gooks and he was gonna get him a Commie see if he didn't. I remember that the train came quietly in then and that it still looked like a big iron beast although now it was a silent beast with no smoke or sparks but with magic still hidden inside it although I knew now that it might be a dark magic and then we had to climb inside and I was kissing Judy goodbye and telling her I loved her and she was kissing me and telling me she would wait for me and I don't know if we were telling the truth or even if we knew ourselves what the truth was and then Judy was crying openly and I was swallowed by the iron beast and we were roaring away from the town and snickering across the web of tracks and booming over the switches and I saw my old house flash by and I could see my old window and I almost imagined that I could see myself as a kid with my nose pressed against the window looking out and watching my older self roar by and neither of us suspecting that the other was there and neither ever working up enough nerve to watch the trains dance. And I remember that all during that long train ride I could hear Denny's raucous voice somewhere in the distance talking about how he couldn't wait to get to Gookland and he'd heard that Gook snatch was even better than nigger snatch and free too and he was gonna get him a Commie he couldn't wait to get him a goddamned Commie and as the train slashed across the wide fertile farmlands of the Midwest the last thing I knew before sleep that night was the wet smell of freshly turned earth.

—The ant noses the worm disdainfully and then passes out of the field of vision. The only movement now is the ripple of the tall grass and the flash of birds in the shaggy tree. The sky is clouding up again, thunderheads rumbling up over the horizon and rolling across the sky. Two large forms appear near the shaggy tree at the other extreme of the field of vision. The singing of the birds stops as if turned off by a switch. The two forms move about vaguely near the shaggy tree, rustling the grass. The angle of the field of vision gives a foreshortening effect, and it is difficult to make out just what the figures are. There is a sharp command, the human voice sounding strangely thin under the sighing of the wind. The two figures move away from the shaggy tree, pushing through the grass. They are medics; haggard, dirty soldiers with big red crosses painted on their helmets and armbands and several days' growth on their chins. They look tired, harried, scared and determined, and they are moving rapidly, half-crouching, searching for something on the ground and darting frequent wary glances back over their shoulders. As they approach they seem to grow larger and larger, elongating toward the sky as their movement shifts the perspective. They stop a few feet away and reach down, lifting up a body that has been hidden by the tall grass. It is Denny, the back of his head blown away, his eyes bulging horribly open. The medics lower Denny's body back into the sheltering grass and bend over it, fumbling with something. They finally straighten, glance hurriedly about and move forward. The two grimy figures swell until they fill practically the entire field of vision, only random patches of sky and the ground underfoot visible around their bulk. The medics come to a stop about a foot away. The scarred, battered, mud-caked combat boot of the medic now dominates the scene, looking big as a mountain. From the combat boot, the medic's leg seems to stretch incredibly toward the sky, like a fatigue-swathed beanstalk, with just a suggestion of a head and a helmet floating somewhere at the top. The other medic cannot be seen at all now, having stepped over and out of the field of vision. His shallow breathing and occasional muttered obscenities can be heard. The first medic bends over, his huge hand seeming to leap down from the sky, and touches the arm, lifting the wrist and feeling for a pulse. The medic holds the wrist for a while and then sighs and lets it go. The wrist plops limply back into the cold sucking mud, splattering it. The medic's hand swells in the direction of the upper arm, and then fades momentarily out of the field of vision, although his wrist remains blurrily visible and his arm seems to stretch back like a highway into the middle distance. The medic tugs, and his hand comes back clutching a tarnished dog tag. Both of the medic's hands disappear forward out of the field of vision. Hands prying the jaw open, jamming the dog tag into the teeth, the metal cold and slimy against the tongue and gums, pressing the jaws firmly closed again, the dog tag feeling huge and immovable inside the mouth. The world is the medic's face now, looming like a scarred cliff inches away, his bloodshot twitching eyes as huge as moons, his mouth, hanging slackly open with exhaustion, as cavernous and bottomless as a magic cave to a little boy. The medic has halitosis, his breath filled with the richly corrupt smell of freshly turned earth. The medic stretches out two fingers which completely occupy the field of vision, blocking out even the sky. The medic's fingertips are the only things in the world now. They are stained and dirty and one has a white scar across the whorls. The medic's fingertips touch the eyelids and gently press down. And now there is nothing but darkness—

And I remember the way dawn would crack the eastern sky, the rosy blush slowly spreading and staining the black of night, chasing away the darkness, driving away the stars. And I remember the way a woman looks at you when she loves you, and the sound that a kitten makes when it is happy, and the way that snowflakes blur and melt against a warm windowpane in winter. I remember. I remember.

A Kingdom by the Sea

EVERYDAY, MASON WOULD stand with his hammer and kill cows. The place was big—a long, high-ceilinged room, one end open to daylight, the other end stretching back into the depths of the plant. It had white, featureless walls—painted concrete—that were swabbed down twice a day, once before lunch and once after work. The floor could be swabbed too—it was stone, and there was a faucet you could use to flood the floor with water. Then you used a stiff-bristled broom to swish the water around and get up the stains. That was known as GIing a floor in the Army. Mason had been in the Army. He called it GIing. So did the three or four other veterans who worked that shift, and they always got a laugh out of explaining to the college boys the plant hired as temporary help why the work they'd signed up to do was called that. The college boys never knew what GIing was until they'd been shown, and they never understood the joke either, or why it was called that. They were usually pretty dumb.

There was a drain in the floor to let all the water out after the place had been GIed. In spite of everything, though, the room would never scrub up quite clean; there'd always be some amount of blood left staining the walls and floor at the end of the day. About the best you could hope to do was grind it into the stone so it became unrecognizable. After a little of this, the white began to

133

get dingy, dulling finally to a dirty, dishwater gray. Then they'd paint the room white again and start all over.

The cycle took a little longer than a year, and they were about halfway through it this time. The men who worked the shift didn't really give a shit whether the walls were white or not, but it was a company regulation. The regs insisted that the place be kept as clean as possible for health reasons, and also because that was supposed to make it a psychologically more attractive environment to function in. The workmen wouldn't have given a shit about their psychological environment either, even if they'd known what one was. It was inevitable that the place would get a little messy during a working day.

It was a slaughterhouse, although the company literature always referred to it as a meat-packing plant.

The man who did the actual killing was Mason: the focal point of the company, of all the meat lockers and trucks and canning sections and secretaries and stockholders; their lowest common denominator. It all started with him.

He would stand with his hammer at the open end of the room, right at the very beginning of the plant, and wait for the cows to come in from the train yard. He had a ten-pound sledge hammer, long and heavy, with serrated rubber around the handle to give him a better grip. He used it to hit the cows over the head. They would herd the cows in one at a time, into the chute, straight up to Mason, and Mason would swing his hammer down and hit the cow between the eyes with tremendous force, driving the hammer completely through the bone and into the brain, killing the cow instantly in its tracks. There would be a gush of warm, sticky blood, and a spatter of purplish brain matter; the cow would go to its front knees, as if it were curtsying, then its hindquarters would collapse and drag the whole body over onto one side with a thunderous crash—all in an eyeblink. One moment the cow would be being prodded in terror into the chute that led to Mason, its flanks lathered, its muzzle flecked with foam, and then—almost too fast to watch, the lightning would strike, and it would be a twitching ruin on the stone

134

floor, blood oozing sluggishly from the smashed head.

After the first cow of the day, Mason would be covered with globs and spatters of blood, and his arms would be drenched red past the elbows. It didn't bother him—it was a condition of his job, and he hardly noticed it. He took two showers a day, changed clothes before and after lunch; the company laundered his white working uniforms and smocks at no expense. He worked quickly and efficiently, and never needed more than one blow to kill. Once Mason had killed the cow, it was hoisted on a hook, had its throat cut, and was left for a few minutes to bleed dry. Then another man came up with a long, heavy knife and quartered it. Then the carcass was further sliced into various portions, each portion was impaled on a hook and carried away by a clanking overhead conveyor belt toward the meat lockers and packing processes that were the concerns of the rest of the plant.

The cows always seemed to know what was about to happen to them—they would begin to moan nervously and roll their eyes in apprehension as soon as they were herded from the stock car on the siding. After the first cow was slaughtered, their apprehension would change to terror. The smell of the blood would drive them mad. They would plunge and bellow and snort and buck; they would jerk mindlessly back and forth, trying to escape. Their eyes would roll up to show the whites, and they would spray foam, and their sides would begin to lather. At this point, Mason would work faster, trying to kill them all before any had a chance to sweat off fat. After a while, they would begin to scream. Then they would have to be prodded harshly toward Mason's hammer. At the end, after they had exhausted themselves, the last few cows would grow silent, shivering and moaning softly until Mason had a chance to get around to them, and then they would die easily with little thrashing or convulsing. Often, just for something to do, Mason and the other workmen would sarcastically talk to the cows, make jokes about them, call them by pet names, tell them—after the fashion of a TV variety-skit doctor—that everything was going to be all right and that it would only hurt for a minute, tell them what dumb fucking bastards they were—"That's right, sweetheart. Come here, you big dumb bastard. Papa's got a surprise for you"—tell them that they'd known goddamn well what they were letting themselves in for when they'd enlisted. Sometimes they would bet on how hard Mason could hit a cow with his big hammer, how high into the air the brain matter would fly after the blow. Once Mason had won a buck from Kaplan by hitting a cow so hard that he had driven it to its knees. They were no more callous than ordinary men, but it was a basically dull, basically unpleasant job, and like all men with dull, unpleasant jobs, they needed something to spice it up, and to keep it far enough away. To Mason, it was just a job, no better or worse than any other. It was boring, but he'd never had a job that wasn't boring. And at least it paid well. He approached it with the same methodical uninterest he had brought to every other job he ever had. It was his job, it was what he did.

Every day, Mason would stand with his hammer and kill cows.

It is raining: a sooty, city rain that makes you dirty rather than wet. Mason is standing in the rain at the bus stop, waiting for the bus to come, as he does every day, as he has done every day for the past six years. He has his collar up against the wind, hands in pockets, no hat: his hair is damp, plastered to his forehead. He stands somewhat slouched, head slumped forward just the tiniest bit—he is tired, the muscles in his shoulders are knotted with strain, the back of his neck burns. He is puzzled by the excessive fatigue of his body; uneasy, he shifts his weight from foot to foot—standing here after a day spent on his feet is murder, it gets him in the thighs, the calves. He has forgotten his raincoat again. He is a big man, built thick through the chest and shoulders, huge arms, wide, thick-muscled wrists, heavy-featured, resigned face. He is showing the first traces of a future pot belly. His feet are beginning to splay. His personnel dossier (restricted) states that he is an unaggressive underachiever, energizing at low potential, anally oriented (plodding, painstaking,

136

competent), highly compatible with his fellow workers, shirks decision-making but can be trusted with minor responsibility, functions best as part of a team, unlikely to cause trouble: a good worker. He often refers to himself as a slob, though he usually tempers it with laughter (as in: "Christ, don't ask a poor slob like me about stuff like that," or, "Shit, I'm only a dumb working slob"). He is beginning to slide into the downhill side of the middle thirties. He was born here, in an immigrant neighborhood, the only Presbyterian child in a sea of foreign Catholics—he had to walk two miles to Sunday school. He grew up in the gray factory city—sloughed through high school, the Army, drifted from job to job, town to town, dishwashing, waiting tables, working hardhat (jukeboxes, backrooms, sawdust, sun, water from a tin pail), work four months, six, a year, take to the road, drift: back to his hometown again after eight years of this, to his old (pre-Army) job, full circle. This time when the restlessness comes, after a year, he gets all the way to the bus terminal (sitting in the station at three o'clock in the morning, colder than hell, the only other person in the huge, empty hall a drunk asleep on one of the benches) before he realizes that he has no place to go and nothing to do if he gets there. He does not leave. He stays: two years, three, four, six now, longer than he has ever stayed anywhere before. Six years, slipping up on him and past before he can realize it, suddenly gone (company picnics, Christmas, Christ—taxes again already?), time blurring into an oily gray knot, leaving only discarded calendars for fossils. He will never hit the road again, he is here to stay. His future has become his past without ever touching the present. He does not understand what has happened to him, but he is beginning to be afraid.

He gets on the bus for home.

In the cramped, sweaty interior of the bus, he admits for the first time that he may be getting old.

Mason's apartment was on the fringe of the heavily built-up district, in a row of dilapidated six-story brownstones. Not actually the slums, not like where the colored people lived (Mason doggedly said colored people, even when the boys at the plant talked of niggers), not like where the kids, the beatniks lived, but a low-rent district, yes. Laboring people, low salaries. The white poor had been hiding here since 1920, peering from behind thick faded drapes and cracked Venetian blinds. Some of them had never come out. The immigrants had disappeared into this neighborhood from the boats, were still here, were still immigrants after thirty years, but older and diminished, like a faded photograph. All the ones who had not pulled themselves up by their bootstraps to become crooked politicians or gangsters or dishonest lawyers—all forgotten: a gritty human residue. The mailboxes alternated names like Goldstein and Kowalczyk and Ricciardi. It was a dark, hushed neighborhood, with few big stores, no movies, no real restaurants. A couple of bowling alleys. The closest civilization approached was a big concrete housing project for disabled war veterans a block or two away to the east, and a streamlined-chromeplated-neonflashing shopping center about half a mile to the west, on the edge of a major artery. City lights glowed to the north, highrises marched across the horizon south: H.G. Wells Martians, acres of windows flashing importantly.

Mason got off the bus. There was a puddle at the curb and he stepped in it. He felt water soak into his socks. The bus snapped its doors contemptuously shut behind him. It rumbled away, farting exhaust smoke into his face. Mason splashed toward his apartment, wrapped in rain mist, moisture beading on his lips and forehead. His shoes squelched. The wet air carried heavy cooking odors, spicy and foreign. Someone was banging garbage cans together somewhere. Cars hooted mournfully at him as they rushed by.

Mason ignored this, fumbling automatically for his keys as he came up to the outside door. He was trying to think up an excuse to stay home tonight. This was Tuesday, his bowling night; Kaplan would be calling in a while, and he'd have to tell him something. He just didn't feel like bowling; they could shuffle the league around, put Johnson in instead. He clashed the key against the lock. Go in, damn it. This would be the first bowling night he'd missed in six years, even last fall when he'd had the flu—Christ, how Emma had bitched about that, think he'd risen from his deathbed or something. She always used to worry about him too much. Still, after six years. Well, fuck it, he didn't feel like it, was all; it wasn't going to hurt anything, it was only a practice session anyway. He could afford to miss a week. And what the fuck was wrong with the lock? Mason sneered in the dark. How many years is it going to take to learn to use the right key for the front door, asshole? He found the proper key (the one with the deep groove) with his thumb and clicked the door open.

Course, he'd have to tell Kaplan something. Kaplan'd want to know why he couldn't come, try to argue him into it. (Up the stairwell, around and around.) Give him some line of shit. At least he didn't have to make up excuses for Emma anymore—she would've wanted to know why he wasn't going, if he felt good, if he was sick, and she'd be trying to feel his forehead for fever. A relief to have her off his back. She'd been gone almost a month. Now all he had to worry about was what to tell fucking Kaplan. (Old wood creaked under his shoes. It was stuffy. Muffled voices leaked from under doorways as he passed, pencil beams of light escaped from cracks. Dust motes danced in the fugitive light.)

Fuck Kaplan anyway, he didn't have to justify his actions to Kaplan. Just tell him he didn't want to, and the hell with him. The hell with all of them.

Into the apartment: one large room, partially divided by a low counter into kitchen and living room—sink, refrigerator, stove and small table in the kitchen; easy chair, coffee table and portable television in the living room; a small bedroom off the living room and a bath. Shit, he'd have to tell Kaplan something after all, wouldn't he? Don't want the guys to start talking. And it is weird to miss a bowling night. Mason took off his wet clothes, threw them onto the easy chair for Emma to hang up and dry. Then he remembered that Emma was gone.

Finally left him—he couldn't blame her much, he supposed. He was a bum, it was true. He supposed. Mason shrugged uneasily. Fredricks promoted over him, suppose he didn't have much of a future—he didn't worry about it, but women were different, they fretted about stuff like that, it was important to them. And he wouldn't marry her. Too much of a drifter. But family stuff, that was important to a woman. Christ, he couldn't really blame her, the dumb cunt—she just couldn't understand. He folded his clothes himself, clumsily, getting the seam wrong in the pants. You miss people for the little things. Not that he really cared whether his pants were folded right or not. And, God knows, she probably missed him more than he did her; he was more independent—sure, he didn't really need anybody but him. Dumb cunt. Maybe he'd tell Kaplan that he had a woman up here, that he was getting laid tonight. Kaplan was dumb enough to believe it. He paused, hanger in hand, surprised at his sudden vehemence. Kaplan was no dumber than anybody else. And why couldn't he be getting laid up here? Was that so hard to believe, so surprising? Shit, was he supposed to curl up and fucking die because his girl'd left, even a longtime (three years) girl? Was that what Kaplan and the rest of those bastards were thinking? Well, then, call Kaplan and tell him you're sorry you can't make it, and then describe what a nice juicy piece of ass you're getting, make the fucker eat his liver with envy because he's stuck in that damn dingy bowling alley with those damn dingy people while you're out getting laid. Maybe it'll even get back to Emma. Kaplan will believe it. He's dumb enough.

Mason took a frozen pizza out of the refrigerator and put it into the oven for his supper. He rarely ate meat, didn't care for it. None of his family had. His father had worked in a meat-packing plant too—the same one, in fact. He had been one of the men who cut up the cow's carcass with knives and cleavers. "Down to the plant," he would say, pushing himself up from the table and away from his third cup of breakfast coffee, while Mason was standing near the open door of the gas oven for warmth and being wrapped in his furry hat for school, "I've got to go down to the plant."

Mason always referred to the place as a meat-packing plant.

(Henderson had called it a slaughterhouse, but Henderson had quit.)

The package said fifteen minutes at 450, preheated. Maybe he shouldn't tell Kaplan that he was getting laid, after all. Then everybody'd be asking him questions tomorrow, wanting to know who the girl was, how she was in the sack, where he'd picked her up, and he'd have to spend the rest of the day making up imaginary details of the affair. And suppose they found out somehow that he hadn't had a woman up here after all? Then they'd think he was crazy, making up something like that. Lying. Maybe he should just tell Kaplan that he was coming down with the flu. Or a bad cold. He *was* tired tonight. (death) Maybe he actually was getting the flu. From overwork, or standing around in the rain too long, or something. Maybe that was why he was so fucking tired— Christ, exhausted—why he didn't feel like going bowling. Sure, that was it. And he didn't have to be ashamed of being sick: he had a fine work record, only a couple of days missed in six years. Everybody gets sick sometime, that's the way it is. They'd understand.

Fuck them if they didn't.

Mason burned the pizza slightly. By the time he pulled it out with a washcloth, singeing himself in the process, it had begun to turn black around the edges, the crust and cheese charring. But not too bad. Salvageable. He cut it into slices with a roller. As usual, he forgot to eat it quickly enough, and the last pieces had cooled off when he got around to them—tasting now like cardboard with unheated spaghetti sauce on it. He ate them anyway. He had some beer with the pizza, and some coffee later. After eating, he still felt vaguely unsatisfied, so he got a package of Fig Newtons from the cupboard and ate them too. Then he sat at the table and smoked a cigarette. No noise—nothing moved. Stasis.

The phone rang: Kaplan.

Mason jumped, then took a long, unsteady drag on his cigarette. He was trembling. He stared at his hand, amazed. Nerves. Christ. He was working too hard, worrying too much. Fuck Kaplan and all the rest of them. Don't tell them anything. You don't have to. Let them stew. The phone screamed again and again: three times, four times, six. Don't answer it, Mason told himself, whipping up bravura indignation to cover the sudden inexplicable panic, the fear, the horror. You don't have to account to them. Ring (*scream*), ring (*scream*), ring (*scream*). The flesh crawled on his stomach, short hair bristled along his back, his arms. Stop, dammit, stop, *stop*. "Shut up!" he shouted, raggedly, half rising from the chair.

The phone stopped ringing.

The silence was incredibly evil.

Mason lit another cigarette, dropping the first match, lighting another, finally getting it going. He concentrated on smoking, the taste of the smoke and the feel of it in his lungs, puffing with staccato intensity (IthinkIcanIthinkI-canIthinkIcanIthinkIcan). Something was very wrong, but he suppressed that thought, pushed it deeper. A tangible blackness: avoid it. He was just tired, that's all. He'd had a really crummy, really rough day, and he was tired, and it was making him jumpy. Work seemed to get harder and harder as the weeks went by. Maybe he was getting old, losing his endurance. He supposed it had to happen sooner or later. But shit, he was only thirty-eight. He wouldn't have believed it, or even considered it, before today.

"You're getting old," Mason said, aloud. The words echoed in the bare room.

He laughed uneasily, nervously, pretending scorn. The laughter seemed to be sucked into the walls. Silence blotted up the sound of his breathing.

He listened to the silence for a while, then called himself a stupid asshole for thinking about all this asshole crap, and decided that he'd better go to bed. He levered himself to his feet. Ordinarily he would watch television for a couple of hours before turning in, but tonight he was fucked up—too exhausted and afraid. Afraid? What did he have to be scared of? It was all asshole crap. Mason stacked the dirty dishes in the sink and went into the bedroom, carefully switching off all the other lights behind him. Darkness followed him to the bedroom door.

Mason undressed, put his clothes away, sat on the bed. There was a dingy transient hotel on this side of the building, and its red neon sign blinked directly into Mason's bedroom window, impossible to block out with any thickness of curtain. Tonight he was too tired to be bothered by it. It had been a bad day. He would not think about it, any of it. He only wanted to sleep. Tomorrow would be different, tomorrow would be better. It would have to be. He switched off the light and lay back on top of the sheet. Neon shadows beat around the room, flooding it rhythmically with dull red.

Fretfully, he began to fall asleep in the hot room, in the dark.

Almost to sleep, he heard a woman weeping in his mind.

The weeping scratched at the inside of his head, sliding randomly in and out of his brain. Not really the sound of weeping, not actually an audible sound at all, but rather a feeling, an essence of weeping, of unalterable sadness. Without waking, he groped for the elusive feelings, swimming down deeper and deeper into his mind—like diving below a storm-lashed ocean at night, swimming down to where it is always calm and no light goes, down where the deep currents run. He was only partially conscious, on the borderline of dream where anything seems rational and miracles are commonplace. It seemed only reasonable, only fair, that, in his desolation, he should find a woman in his head. He did not question this, he did not find it peculiar. He moved toward her, propelled and guided only by the urge to be with her, an ivory feather drifting and twisting through vast empty darkness, floating on the wind, carried by the currents that wind through the regions under the earth, the tides that march in Night. He found her, wrapped in the underbelly of himself like a pearl: a tiny exquisite irritant. Encased in amber, he could not see, but he knew somehow that she was lovely, as perfect and delicate as

143

the bud of a flower opening to the sun, as a baby's hand. He comforted her as he had comforted Emma on nights when she'd wake up crying: reaching through darkness toward sadness, wrapping it in warmth, leaching the fear away with presence, spreading the pain around between them to thin it down. She seemed startled to find that she was not alone at the heart of nothing, but she accepted him gratefully, and blended him into herself, blended them together, one stream into another, a mingling of secret waters in the dark places in the middle of the world, in Night, where shadows live. She was the thing itself, and not its wrapping, as Emma had been. She was ultimate grace—moving like silk around him, moving like warm rain within him. He merged with her forever.

And found himself staring at the ceiling.

Gritty light poured in through the window. The hotel sign had been turned off. It was morning.

He grinned at the ceiling, a harsh grin with no mirth in it: skin pulling back and back from the teeth, stretching to death's-head tautness.

It had been a dream.

He grinned his corpse grin at the morning.

Hello morning. Hello you goddamned son of a bitch.

He got up. He ached. He was lightheaded with fatigue: his head buzzed, his eyelids were lead. It felt like he had not slept at all.

He went to work.

It is still raining. Dawn is hidden behind bloated spider clouds. Here, in the factory town, miles of steel mills, coke refineries, leather-tanning plants, chemical scum running in the gutters, it will rain most of the year: airborne dirt forming the nucleus for moisture, an irritant to induce condensation—producing a listless rain that fizzles down endlessly, a deity pissing. The bus creeps through the mists and drizzle like a slug, parking lights haloed by dampness. Raindrops inch down the windowpane, shimmering and flattening when the window buzzes, leaving long wet tracks behind them. Inside, the glass has been fogged by breath and body heat, making it hard to

144

see anything clearly. The world outside has merged into an infinity of lumpy gray shapes, dinosaur shadows, here and there lights winking and diffusing wetly—it is a moving collage done in charcoal and watery neon. The men riding the bus do not notice it—already they seem tired. It is 7 A.M. They sit and stare dully at the tips of their shoes, or the back of the seat in front of them. A few read newspapers. One or two talk. Some sleep. A younger man laughs—he stops almost immediately. If the windows were clear, the rain collage of light and shadow would be replaced by row after row of drab, crumbling buildings, gas stations decked with tiny plastic flags, used car lots with floodlights, hamburger stands, empty schoolyards with dead trees poking up through the pavement, cyclone-fenced recreation areas that children never use. No one ever bothers to look at that either. They know what it looks like.

Usually Mason prefers the aisle seat, but this morning, prompted by some obscure instinct, he sits by the window. He is trying to understand his compulsion to watch the blurred landscape, trying to verbalize what it makes him think of, how it makes him feel. He cannot. Sad—that's the closest he can come. Why should it make him sad? Sad, and there is something else, something he gropes for but it keeps slipping away. An echo of reawakening fear, in reaction to his groping. It felt like, it was kind of like— Uneasily, he presses his palm to the window, attempts to rub away some of the moisture obscuring the glass. (This makes him feel funny too. Why? He flounders, grasping at nothing—it is gone.) A patch of relatively clear glass appears as he rubs, a swath of sharper focus surrounded by the oozing myopia of the collage. Mason stares out at the world, through his patch of glass. Again he tries to grasp something—again he fails. It all looks wrong somehow. It makes him vaguely, murkily angry. Buildings crawl by outside. He shivers, touched by a septic breath of entropy. Maybe it's— If it was like— He cannot. Why is it wrong? What's wrong with it? That's the way it's always looked, hasn't it?

Nothing's changed. What could you change it to? What the fuck is it *supposed* to be like? No words.

Raindrops pile up on the window again and wash away the world.

At work, the dream continued to bother Mason throughout the day. He found that he couldn't put it out of his mind for long—somehow his thoughts always came back to it, circling constantly like the flies that buzzed around the pools of blood on the concrete floor.

Mason became annoyed, and slightly uneasy. It wasn't healthy to be so wrapped up in a fucking dream. It was sick, and you had to be sick in the head to fool around with it. It was sick—it made him angry to think about the slime and sickness of it, and faintly nauseous. He didn't have that slime in his head. No, the dream had bothered him because Emma was gone. It was rough on a guy to be alone again after living with somebody for so long. He should go out and actually pick up some broad instead of just thinking about it—should've had one last night so he wouldn't've had to worry about what to tell Kaplan. Sweep the cobwebs out of his brain. Sitting around that damn house night after night, never doing anything—no wonder he felt funny, had crazy dreams.

At lunch—sitting at the concrete, formica-topped table, next to the finger-smudged plastic faces of the coffee machine, the soft drink machine, the sandwich machine, the ice cream machine (Out of Order) and the candy bar machine—he toyed with the idea of telling Russo about the dream, playing it lightly, maybe getting a few laughs out of it. He found the idea amazingly unpleasant. He was reluctant to tell anybody anything about the dream. To his amazement, he found himself getting angry at the thought. Russo was a son of a bitch anyway. They were all son of a bitches. He snapped at Russo when the Italian tried to draw him into a discussion he and Kaplan were having about cars. Russo looked hurt.

Mason mumbled something about a hangover in apology and gulped half of his steaming coffee without feeling it. His tuna salad sandwich tasted like sawdust, went down like lead. A desolate, inexplicable sense of loss had been growing in him throughout the morning as he became more preoccupied with the dream. He *couldn't* have been this affected by a dream, that was crazy—there had to be more to it than that, it had to be more than just a dream, and he wasn't crazy. So it couldn't have been a dream completely, somehow. He missed the girl in the dream. How could he miss someone who didn't exist? That was crazy. But he did miss her. So maybe the girl wasn't completely a dream somehow, or he wouldn't miss her like that, would he? That was crazy too. He turned his face away and played distractedly with crumbs on the formica tabletop. No more of this: it was slimy, and it made his head hurt to think about it. He wouldn't think about it anymore.

That afternoon he took to listening while he worked. He caught himself at it several times. He was listening intently, for nothing. No, not for nothing. He was listening for her.

On the bus, going home, Mason is restless, as if he were being carried into some strange danger, some foreign battlefield. His eyes gleam slightly in the dark. The glare of oncoming car headlights sweep over him in oscillating waves. Straps swing back and forth like scythes. All around him, the other passengers sit silently, not moving, careful not to touch or jostle the man next to them. Each in his own space: semi-visible lumps of flesh and shadow. Their heads bob slightly with the motion of the bus, like dashboard ornaments.

When Mason got home, he had frozen pizza for supper again, though he'd been intending to have an omelet. He also ate some more Fig Newtons. It was as though he were half-consciously trying to reproduce the previous night, superstitiously repeating all the details of the evening in hopes of producing the same result. So he ate pizza, shaking his head at his own stupidity and swearing bitterly under his breath. He ate it nevertheless. And as he

147

ate, he listened for the scratching—hating himself for listening, but listening—only partially believing that such a thing as the scratching even existed, or ever had, but listening. Half of him was afraid that it would not come; half was afraid that it would. But nothing happened.

When the scratching at his mind did come again it was hours later, while he was watching an old movie on the Late Show, when he had almost managed to forget. He stiffened, feeling a surge of terror (and feeling something else that he was unable to verbalize), even the half of his mind that had wanted it to come screaming in horror of the unknown now that the impossible had actually happened. He fought down terror, breathing harshly. This couldn't be happening. Maybe he was crazy. A flicker of abysmal fear. Sweat started on his forehead, armpits, crotch.

Again, the scratching: bright feelings sliding tentatively into his head, failing to catch and slipping out, coming back again—like focusing a split-image lens. He sat back in the easy chair; old springs groaned, the cracked leather felt hot and sticky against his T-shirted back. He squeezed the empty beer can, crumpling it. Automatically he put the empty into the six-pack at the foot of the chair. He picked up another can and sat with it unopened in his lap. The sliding in his head made him dizzy and faintly nauseous—he squirmed uneasily, trying to find a position that would lessen the vertigo. The cushion made a wet sucking noise as he pulled free of it: the dent made by his back in the leather began to work itself back to level, creaking and groaning, only to reform when he let his weight down again. Jarred by motion, the ashtray he'd been balancing on his knee slipped and crashed face-down to the rug in an explosion of ashes.

Mason leaned forward to pick it up, stopped, his attention suddenly caught and fixed by the television again. He blinked at the grainy, flickering black-and-white images; again he felt something that he didn't know how to say, so strongly that the sliding in his head was momentarily ignored.

It was one of those movies they'd made in the late '20's-

'30's where everything was perfect. The hero was handsome, suave, impeccably dressed; he had courage, he had style, he could fit in anywhere, he could solve any problem—he never faltered, he never stepped on his own dick. He was Quality. The heroine matched him: she was sophisticated, refined, self-possessed—a slender, aristocratic sculpture in ice and moonlight. She was unspeakably lovely. They were both class people, posh people: the ones who ran things, the ones who mattered. They had been born into the right families on the right side of town, gone to the right schools, known the right people—got the right jobs. Unquestioned superiority showed in the way they moved, walked, planted their feet, turned their heads. It was all cool, planned and poised, like a dancer. They knew that they were the best people, knew it without having to think about it or even knowing that they knew it. It was a thing assumed at birth. It was a thing you couldn't fake, couldn't put on: something would trip you up everytime, and the other ones on top would look through you and see what you really were and draw a circle that excluded you out (never actually saying anything, which would make it worse), and you would be left standing there with your dick hanging out, flushed, embarrassed, sweating—too coarse, doughy, unfinished—twisting your hat nervously between knobby, clumsy hands. But that would never happen to the man and woman on television.

Mason found himself trembling with rage, blind with it, shaking as if he were going to tear himself to pieces, falling apart and not knowing why, amazed and awed by his own fury, his guts knotting, his big horny hands clenching and unclenching at the injustice, the monstrousness, the slime, the millions of lives pissed away, turning his anger over and over, churning it like a murky liquid, pounding it into froth.

They never paid any dues. They never sweated, or defecated. Their bodies never smelled bad, never got dirty. They never had crud under their fingernails, blisters on their palms, blood staining their arms to the elbows. The man never had five o'clock shadow, the woman never wore her hair in rollers like Emma, or had sour breath, or told her lover to take out the garbage. They never farted. Or belched. They did not have sex—they *made love*, and it was all transcendental pleasure: no indignity of thrashing bodies, clumsily intertwining limbs, fumbling and straining, incoherent words and coarse animal sounds; and afterward he would be breathing easily, her hair would be in place, there would be no body fluids, the sheets would not be rumpled or stained. And the world they moved through all their lives reflected their own perfection: it was beautiful, tidy, ordered. Mansions. Vast lawns. Neatly painted, tree-lined streets. And style brought luck too. The gods smiled at them, a benign fate rolled dice that always came up sevens, sevens, sevens. They skated through life without having to move their feet, smiling, untouched, gorgeous, like a parade float: towed by others. They broke the bank of every game in town. Everything went their way. Coincidence became a contortionist to finish in their favor.

Because they had class. Because they were on top.

Mason sat up, gasping. He had left the ashtray on the floor. Numbly, he set the beer can down beside it. His hand was trembling. He felt like he had been kicked in the stomach. *They* had quality. He had nothing. He could see everything now: everything he'd been running from all his life. He was shit. No way to deny it. He lived in a shithouse, he worked in a shithouse. His whole world was a vast shithouse: dirty black liquid bubbling prehistorically; rich feisty odors of decay. He was surrounded by shit, he wallowed in it. He *was* shit. Already, he realized, it made no difference that he had ever lived. You're nothing, he told himself, you're shit. You ain't never been anything but shit. You ain't never going to be anything but shit. Your whole life's been nothing but shit.

No.

He shook his head blindly.

No.

There was only one thing in his life that was out of the ordinary, and he snatched at it with the desperation of a drowning man.

The sliding, the scratching in his head that was even now becoming more insistent, that became almost overwhelming as he shifted his attention back to it. That was strange, wasn't it? That was unusual. And it had come to him, hadn't it? There were millions and millions of other people in the world, but it had picked *him*—it had come to him. And it was real, it wasn't a dream. He wasn't crazy, and if it was just a dream he'd have to be. So it was real, and the girl was real. He had somebody else inside his head. And if that was real, then that was something that had never happened to anybody else in the world before—something he'd never even heard about before other than some dumb sci-fi movies on TV. It was something that even *they* had never done, something that made him different from every man in the world, from every man who had ever lived. It was his own personal miracle.

Trembling, he leaned back in the chair. Leather creaked. This was his miracle, he told himself, it was good, it wouldn't harm him. The bright feelings themselves were good: somehow they reminded him of childhood, of quiet gardens, of dust motes spinning in sunlight, of the sea. He struggled for calm. Blood pounded at his throat, throbbed in his wrists. He felt (the memory flooding, incredibly vivid—ebbing) the way he had the first time Sally Rogers had let him spread her meaty, fragrant thighs behind the hill during noon class in the seventh grade: lightheaded, scared, shaking with tension, madly impatient. He swallowed, hesitating, gathering courage. The television babbled unnoticed in the background. He closed his eyes and let go.

Colors swallowed him in a rush.

She waited for him there, a there that became *here* as his knowledge of his physical environment faded, as his body ceased to exist, the soothing blackness broken only by random after-images and pastel colors scurrying in abstract, friendly patterns.

She was *here*—simultaneously *here* and very far away. Like him, she both filled all of *here* and took up no space at all—both statements were equally absurd. Her presence was nothing but that: no pictures, no images, nothing to see, hear, touch or smell. That had all been left in the world of duration. Yet somehow she radiated an ultimate and catholic femininity, an archetypal essence, a quicksilver mixture of demanding fire and an ancient racial purpose as unshakable and patient as ice—and he knew it was the (girl? woman? angel?) of his previous "dream," and no other.

There were no words *here*, but they were no longer needed. He understood her by empathy, by the clear perception of emotion that lies behind all language. There was fear in her mind—a rasp like hot iron—and a feeling of hurtling endlessly and forlornly through vast, empty desolation, surrounded by cold and by echoing, roaring darkness. She seemed closer tonight, though still unimaginably far away. He felt that she was still moving slowly toward him, even as they met and mingled *here*, that her body was careening toward him down the path blazed by her mind.

She was zeroing in on him: this was the theory his mind immediately formed, instantly and gratefully accepted. He had thought of her from the beginning as an angel— now he conceived of her as a lost angel wandering alone through Night for ages, suddenly touched by his presence, drawn like an iron filing to a magnet, pulled from exile into the realms of light and life.

He soothed her. He would wait for her, he would be a beacon—he would not leave her alone in the dark, he would love her and pull her to the light. She quieted, and they moved together, through each other, became one.

He sank deeper into Night.

He floated in himself: a Moebius band.

In the morning, he woke in the chair. A test pattern hummed on the television. The inside of his pants was sticky with semen.

Habit drives him to work. Automatically he gets up, takes a shower, puts on fresh clothes. He eats no breakfast; he isn't hungry—he wonders, idly, if he will ever be hungry again. He lets his feet take him to the bus stop, and waits without fretting about whether or not he'd remembered to lock the door. He waits without thinking about anything. The sun is out; birds are humming in the concrete eaves of the housing project. Mason hums too, quite unconsciously. He boards the bus for work, lets the driver punch his trip ticket, and docilely allows the incoming crowd to push and jostle him to an uncomfortable seat in the back, over the wheel. There, sitting with his knees doubled up in the tiny seat and peering around with an unusual curiosity, the other passengers give him the first bad feeling of the day. They sit in orderly rows, not talking, not moving, not even looking out the window. They look like department store dummies, on their way to a new display. They are not there at all.

Mason decided to call her Lilith—provisionally at least, until the day, soon now, when he could learn her real name from her own lips. The name drifted up from his subconscious, from the residue of long, forgotten years of Sunday school—not so much because of the associations of primeval love carried by the name (although those rang on a deeper level), but because as a restless child suffering through afternoons of watered-down theology he'd always imagined Lilith to be rather pretty and sympathetic, the kind who might wink conspiratorially at him behind the back of the pious, pompous instructor: a girl with a hint of illicit humor and style, unlike the dumpy, clay-faced ladies in the Bible illustrations. So she became Lilith. He wondered if he would be able to explain the name to her when they met, make her laugh with it.

He fussed with these and other details throughout the day, turning it over in his mind—he wasn't crazy, the dream was real, Lilith was real, she was his—the same thoughts cycling constantly. He was happy in his preoccupation, self-sufficient, only partly aware of the external reality through which he moved. He contributed only monosyllabic grunts to the usual locker-room conversations about sports and Indochina and pussy, he answered questions with careless shrugs or nods, he

153

completely ignored the daily gauntlet of hellos, good-byes, how're they hangings and other ritual sounds. During lunch he ate very little and let Russo finish his sandwich without any of the traditional exclamations of amazement about the wop's insatiable appetite—which made Russo so uneasy that he was unable to finish it after all. Kaplan came in and told Russo and Mason in hushed, delighted tones that old Hamilton had finally caught the clap from that hooker he'd been running around with down at Saluzzio's. Russo exploded into the expected laughter, said *no shit?* in a shrill voice, pounded the table, grinned in jovial disgust at the thought of that old bastard Hamilton with VD. Mason grunted.

Kaplan and Russo exchanged a look over his head—their eyes were filled with the beginnings of a reasonless, instinctive fear: the kind of unease that pistons in a car's engine might feel when one of the cylinders begins to misfire. Mason ignored them; they did not exist; they never had. He sat at the stone table and chain-smoked with detached ferocity, smoking barely half of each cigarette before using it to light another and dumping the butt into his untouched coffee to sizzle and drown. The dixie cup was filled with floating, jostling cigarette butts, growing fat and mud-colored as they sucked up coffee: a nicotine logjam. Kaplan and Russo mumbled excuses and moved away to find another table; today Mason made them feel uneasy and insignificant.

Mason did not notice that they had gone. He sat and smoked until the whistle blew, and then got up and walked calmly in to work. He worked mechanically, raising the hammer and bringing it down, his hands knowing their job and doing it without any need of volition, the big muscles in his arms and shoulders straining, his legs braced wide apart, sweat gleaming—an automaton, a clockwork golem. His face was puckered and preoccupied, as if he were constipated. He did not see the blood; his brain danced with thoughts of Lilith.

Twice that day he thought he felt her brush at his mind, the faintest of gossamer touches, but there were too many distractions—he couldn't concentrate enough. As he washed up after work, he felt the touch again: a hesitant, delicate, exploratory touch, as if someone were groping through his mind with feather fingers.

Mason trembled, and his eyes glazed. He stood, head tilted, unaware of the stream of hot water against his back and hips, the wet stone underfoot, the beaded metal walls; the soap drying on his arms and chest, the smell of heat and wet flesh, the sharp hiss of the shower jets and the gargle of water down the drain; the slap of thongs and rasp of towels, the jumbled crisscross of wet footprints left by men moving from the showers to the lockers, the stuffiness of steam and sweat disturbed by an eddy of colder air as someone opened the outer door; the rows of metal lockers beyond the showers with *Playboy* gatefolds and Tijuana pornography and family snapshots pinned to the doors, the discolored wooden benches and the boxes of foot powder, the green and white walls of the dressing room covered with company bulletins and joke-shop signs...Everything that went into the making of that moment, of his reality, of his life. It all faded, became a ghost, the shadow of a shadow, disappeared completely, did not exist. There was only *here*, and Lilith *here*. And their touch, infinitely closer than joined fingers. Then the world dragged him away.

He opened his eyes. Reality came back: in a babble, in a rush, mildly nauseating. He ignored it, dazed and incandescent with the promise of the night ahead. The world steadied. He stepped back into the shower stream to wash the soap from his body. He had an enormous erection. Clumsily, he tried to hide it with a towel.

Mason takes a taxi home from work. The first time.

That night he is transformed, ripped out of himself, turned inside out. It is pleasure so intense that, like pain, it cannot be remembered clearly afterward—only recollected as a severe shock: sensation translated into a burst of fierce white light. It is pleasure completely beyond his conception—his most extreme fantasy not only fulfilled but intensified. And yet for all the intensity of feeling, it is

155

a gentle thing, a knowing, a complete sharing of emotion, a transcendental empathy. And afterward there is only peace: a silence deeper than death, but not alone. *I love you*, he tells her, really believing it for the first time with anyone, realizing that words have no meaning, but knowing that she will understand, *I love you*.

When he woke up in the morning, he knew that this would be the day.

Today she would come. The certainty pulsed through him, he breathed it like air, it beat in his blood. The knowledge of it oozed in through every pore, only to meet the same knowledge seeping out. It was something felt on a cellular level, a biological assurance. Today they would be together.

He looked at the ceiling. It was pocked with water stains; a deep crack zigzagged across flaking plaster. It was beautiful. He watched it for a half hour without moving, without being aware of the passage of time; without being aware that what he was watching was a "ceiling." Then, sluggishly, something came together in his head, and he recognized it. Today he didn't begrudge it, as he had Wednesday morning. It was a transient condition. It was of no more intrinsic importance than the wall of a butterfly's cocoon after metamorphosis.

Mason rolled to his feet. Fatigue and age had vanished. He was filled with bristly, crackling vitality, every organ, every cell, seeming to work at maximum efficiency: so healthy that "healthy" became an inadequate word. This was a newer, higher state.

Mason accepted it calmly, without question. His movements were leisurely and deliberate, almost slow motion, as if he were swimming through syrup. He knew where he was going, that they would find each other today—that was predestined. He was in no hurry. The same inevitability colored his thoughts. There was no need to do much thinking now, it was all arranged. His mind was nearly blank, only deep currents running. Her nearness dazzled him. Walking, he dreamed of her, of time past, of time to come.

He drifted to the window, lazily admiring the prism sprays sunlight made around the edges of the glass. The streets outside were empty, hushed as a cathedral. Not even birds to break the holy silence. Papers dervished down the center of the road. The sun was just floating clear of the brick horizon: a bloated red ball, still hazed with nearness to the earth.

He stared at the sun.

Mason became aware of his surroundings again while he was dressing. Dimly, he realized that he was buckling his belt, slipping his feet into shoes, tying knots in the shoelaces. His attention was caught by a crisscross pattern of light and shadow on the kitchen wall.

He was standing in front of the slaughterhouse. Mason blinked at the building's filigreed iron gates. Somewhere in there, he must have caught the bus and ridden it to work. He couldn't remember. He didn't care.

Walking down a corridor. A machine booms far away.

He was in an elevator. People. Going down.

Time clock.

A door. The dressing room, deep in the plant. Mason hesitated. Should he go to work today? With Lilith so close? It didn't matter—when she came, Lilith would find him no matter where he was. It was easier meanwhile not to fight his body's trained responses; much easier to just go along with them, let them carry him where they would, do what they wanted him to do.

Buttoning his work uniform. He didn't remember opening the door, or the locker. He told himself that he'd have to watch that.

A montage of surprised faces, bobbing like balloons, very far away. Mason brushed by without looking at them. Their lips moved as he passed, but he could not hear their words.

Don't look back. They can turn you to salt, all the hollow men.

The hammer was solid and heavy in his hand. Its familiar weight helped to clear his head, to anchor him to the world. Mason moved forward more quickly. A surviving fragment of his former personality was eager to

157

get to work, to demonstrate his regained strength and vigor for the other men. He felt the emotion through an ocean of glass, like ghost pain in an amputated limb. He tolerated it, humored it; after today, it wouldn't matter.

Mason walked to the far end of the long white room. Lilith seemed very close now—her nearness made his head buzz intolerably. He stumbled ahead, walking jerkily, as if he were forcing his way against waves of pressure. She would arrive any second. He could not imagine how she would come, or from where. He could not imagine what would happen to him, to them. He tried to visualize her arrival, but his mind, having only Disney, sci-fi and religion to work with, could only picture an ethereally beautiful woman made of stained glass descending from the sky in a column of golden light while organ music roared: the light shining all around her and from her, spraying into unknown colors as it passed through her clear body. He wasn't sure if she would have wings.

Raw daylight through the open end of the room. The nervous lowing of cattle. Smell of dung and sweat, undertang of old, lingering blood. The other men, looking curiously at him. They had masks for faces, viper eyes. Viper eyes followed him through the room. Hooves scuffed gravel outside.

Heavy-lidded, trembling, he took his place.

They herded in the first cow of the day, straight up to Mason. He lifted the hammer.

The cow approached calmly. Tranquilly she walked before the prods, her head high. She stared intently at Mason. Her eyes were wide and deep—serene, beautiful, and trusting.

Lilith, he named her, and then the hammer crashed home between her eyes.

The Man Who Waved Hello

THE WORLD SOLIDIFIED.

He was Harry Bradley, Caucasian, thirty-seven years of age, of certifiably good character. A junior executive—grade GS 8, $10,000 a year, Readjusted Scale—who had been a junior executive since he was thirty and would be a junior executive until he died in harness or was forcibly retired to a Senior Citizen's Haven (you can get in but you can't get out). His apartment measured thirty feet by thirty feet by twelve feet, and was decorated in the pseudocolonial that was popular that year, everything made out of plastic and scaled down. He had plush red artificial fabric drapes across a picture window that looked out at nothing except acres of other picture windows looking back. The window measured exactly sixteen inches by twenty-four inches, no more or no less than any other picture window owned by any other executive of his grade and seniority. That was only fair; that was democracy. He had a solar-powered kitchenette that could cook him almost anything in five minutes, but he was very seldom hungry. He had paneled walls made out of artificial wood. He had a fireplace with a simulated fire that was actually a (safe; economical) electric coil; you could turn it on and off with a switch and plug it into the wall socket. He had a "colonial" chandelier (scaled-down) that was made of a plastic that you almostcouldn'ttell-fromrealglass, and that would sway and tinkle convincingly if you turned the air conditioner up high. He had (although he didn't know it this precisely) the 152,673rd copy of a Cezanne print to be run off the presses that year, and the 98,435th copy of a Van Gogh—both pictures were hung magnetically so that the uniform creme luster of the walls would not have to be marred by a nail. He wasn't allowed to mar the walls anyway, and if he did he would have to explain it in writing, in triplicate, in exasperating detail. There was also a large Rembrandt (copy number into the high millions) that he didn't like but which was government issue and had come with the apartment, and which his contract didn't allow him to get rid of. He had a silent electric clock with a built-in optional tick. He had a combination viewphone/color hologram (but he didn't want to think about that now: later) that enabled him to either talk to people (other executives) or watch commercial (government) programming. He had a table shaped like an old sailing-ship wheel that you could put cocktails on and spin around. He had a simulated antique colonial lantern for a conversation piece. He had an automatic stereo with a selection of twenty-three classical symphonies and six uninterrupted hours of interpreted popular music that he never listened to. If he wanted, he could use his viewphone to talk to people on the moon via the communications satellite linkups. There was nobody on the moon he wanted to talk to. Nobody on the moon wanted to talk to him either.

He was Harry Bradley. There was no way to avoid it.

He lay perfectly still in the middle of the floor.

He was naked.

Sweat dried on his body, and his breath came in rasps.

Bradley struggled weakly, flopped over onto his stomach. The tile was unbelievably cold against his wet skin, and hard as rock; his flesh crawled in revulsion at the contact. He managed to raise himself up on one elbow before his head began to swim. He paused, head bowed, panting, involuntarily studying the dirt in the cracks between the tiles. For a moment there he had been two people, living two different existences in two separate

160

environments, and that'd been rough. He was still having trouble separating realities—conflicting memories chittered at him, emotions surged in opposition, lingering afterimages merged nauseously with vision: one universe still superimposed over another like a double-exposed negative. But one universe was fading. The universe he preferred, the universe where he wasn't doomed to be Harry Bradley, junior executive, grade GS 8, $10,000 a year. Even as he struggled to hold onto it, to *something*, it slipped away irrevocably. His dream universe melted and flowed back into the well behind his eyes, to be replaced by the gray, familiar scenes of reality that boiled up like landscapes in bubbles.

The rococo opulence of the other place was gone: supplanted by a plastic sterility that was worse than poverty.

He shook his head ponderously, wincing at the rasp of pain. Even memory had gone now. All he could recall of the other place was a vague impression of abstract beauty and richness, and that there he had been important, an integral part of totality. That it was a better place than here.

The electric clock in the kitchen ticked noisily, each tick a nail pinning him more tightly to the world.

A furnace started with a roar on a lower level.

His throat was clogged with sandpaper.

He had taken the egomorphic drug two hours ago: ten thousand years of subjective existence.

He began to shake, trembling uncontrollably. The cold of the apartment was getting through now, piercing like knives. His teeth chattered painfully together. His lips were turning blue.

With an effort, he sat up. The floor tilted queasily, first one way and then the other, like a seesaw. He put his head between his knees for awhile. The room steadied. He heard the elevator swarm by outside his walls: a snide ratcheting sound.

Don't think. Just don't think at all.

Slowly, he got to his knees, and then crawled to his

feet. It was easier than he'd thought it would be, if he stopped at every stage to rest. It only took him about five minutes.

He was finally able to stand. The shift in perspective was amazing, and frightening. Suddenly, he felt like he was balancing on a tightrope above an abyss, like he was a taffy-man that'd been stretched out to miles in length and was now in danger of toppling over because he was too thin for his height. His knees kept giving way, and he kept trying to lock them. The taffy-man swayed precariously, as if in a high wind.

Incongruously, he still had an erection. It slapped awkwardly and painfully against his thighs as he moved. He touched it cautiously: the pallid head. Nausea surged through him.

Bradley stumbled toward the bathroom, teeth clenched to keep back the vomit that had suddenly geysered up from the pit of his stomach. He couldn't feel his feet, although he could see his toes stubbing clumsily against pieces of furniture, and knew that it must hurt. He floated—or slid—down the slowly tilting floor toward the bathroom, using his head as a gyroscope. One foot in front of the other, only momentum to keep you from toppling into the abyss.

The bathroom door irised aside to let him through. He crashed to his knees before the voider, not feeling the jolt. He leaned into the voider and vomited violently, fringing up only an oily, greenish bile. Triggered by his presence, the bathroom began to play soothing Muzak— woodwinds and strings—and to fill the cubicle with subtly perfumed incense: sandalwood. It was all very modern.

Bradley worked his way through the dry heaves and shuddered into stillness. He retched one final, wrenching time and then knelt quietly, his head resting on the lip of the voider. It chuckled cheerfully and energetically to itself, busy digesting his vomit. His stomach spasmed retroactively; muscles fluttered in sympathy along his bowed back. Sweat had drawn itself primly into precise beads on his upper lip.

162

Throwing up had cleared his head, and made him aware of his body again, but otherwise had not helped much. He still felt horrible.

Don't think why, don't get on that at all. Just keep moving, get the blood going a little. Or die, damn you. Die and rot in hell forever.

Christ.

He went back out into the hall, cursing feebly at the bathroom door as it dilated open and closed behind him. Retching him out. The apartment was warmer—the thermostat reacting in obedience to his own body temperature, shutting down as his temperature dropped in the stasis induced by the egodrex, revving up again as he returned reluctantly to life. Very clever, these clockwork things. They always functioned, no matter what. Automatically he picked up the clothes he had scattered around when the drug had started to depress the higher-reasoning centers of his brain, translating his undermind directly into experience. He threw the clothes into the hamper that led to the building's reconstituting systems. They'd be pulped and treated and made usable again. So would his vomit. Now that it was almost too late, the government was very big on ecology. Good to the last drop.

There was a full-length mirror (convertible to one way so he could peek into the corridor outside) near the hamper. He studied his nakedness with distaste: fish-belly white, flabby, bristly-haired as a dog. His erection had finally gone down, but now it looked like some obscene, wrinkled slug crawling from a nest of dirty, matted hair. He felt a touch of returning nausea. New clothes. Get dressed. The fresh cloth feeling even more stifling against his dirty skin, but never mind. Cover it all up. Before it begins to decompose.

Dressed, he walked aimlessly into the kitchen, past the sailing-ship wheel. The big electric combination clock blinked relentlessly at him from the wall: hour, day, month, year. Calibrated to a tenth of a second. Never let you forget. Why did anybody need to know the time that

163

closely? Why did anybody need time? Despite himself, he read the clock dials, scanning left to right in reflex. Christ, only five P.M.? Work tomorrow. Back to the office, the tapes, the papers, the meaningless files of numbers, punch cards to be sorted. Routing. And Martino promoted over him, in spite of seniority. The second time. Time. All the hours left in this day, all the days left ahead. Unrequited time hung over him like a rock, threatening to fall.

This was going to be bad. This was going to be very bad.

Suddenly, Bradley was having trouble with his breathing. He tried not to think of the seconds turning into minutes into hours into days into weeks into months into years, all ahead of him, all of which he'd have to somehow get through. He thought of them anyway, ticking them off one by one inside his skull. This was going to be too bad to stand. He'd have to. He couldn't possibly get any more egodrex until Friday. That'd been his regular fix for three years. And he couldn't afford it anyway—it already took every cent of the small credit margin he was allowed for accessories, illegally transferred, to buy his weekly dose of the egomorphic. But this was bad. He felt another, familiar pressure building up, forcing him toward the other thing. No, not this time. Don't think about the other thing. Don't think.

He took stock of his body, to distract himself. He found, to his disgust, that he was hungry. His body was hungry. He wasn't actually in need of nutrient, and his mind gagged at the thought of eating, but the food he lived on—like most of the government's products—was mildly addictive (habit-forming was the official term, not addictive) and his body wanted to eat. Chew and swallow: a pacifier. Resignedly, he punched out a combination on the kitchenette at random, not caring what he got. The kitchenette mumbled, the solar oven buzzed briefly, and a tray slid out of a slot, sealed in tinfoil. He peeled away the tinfoil and ate. The food was divided into tiny geometrical sections on the tray, a glob of that here, a spatter of this

164

there. It all tasted basically the same: like plastic. Bradley ate it without noticing it, trying to involve himself to distract his mind from the other thing, failing.

It wasn't enough. Nothing was enough.

He put down his fork. Hands cupping the eyes, squeezing. Keep it in.

Maybe you're finished this time. You're going to do it again, aren't you? No. Yes, you will, you know it. (He shook his head, arguing with himself.) Maybe they'll catch you this time. Maybe they'll just put you away. Rot in the darkness, no light. Maybe they'll just put you the hell away. Huh? Degradation. Disgrace. You've been lucky all these years, in a way. Nobody's ever found out about the egomorphic drug—only psychologically addictive, no needle-marks, no lasting metabolic effects: the thinking man's junk. But someday they'll catch you. Maybe this time. Today.

Bradley got up and walked stiff-legged around the apartment, circling around and around his furniture, looking but carefully not touching anything. His furniture. *His* things. He said. They weren't really. The apartment and everything in it belonged to the government. The exchange was automatic. He never saw any money, there wasn't really any such thing as money anyway. The bank computers balanced the credit tally he earned against the credit debit he owed to rent the good things in life a GS 8 was entitled to. Nothing more or less. Food, clothing, antique lanterns—the government allowed him to rent these things from them as reward and compensation for his services. There was no place else you could get any of them. There was only one game in town. If he rose to a higher grade, he would be allowed to rent more good things from the government, of correspondingly finer quality. And when he died, the government would continue to rent the same facilities to someone just up from GS 7, including the same reprocessed food and clothing—although in practice there was an inevitable attrition rate, a little always lost from the system, something else added.

My things. God save me from my things.

He looked out the window: Washington faded into Baltimore into New York into Boston.

There was no place to go. Outside the door, along the corridor, down the elevators and escalators, past the concrete arcades and recycled fountains, past the glass-and-steel hives of the other GS residences, past the drabber cinderblock sections for the rank-and-file, past the cadet nurseries and creches, the tank and algae farms, the oxygen reinforcement systems, the industrial quarter, the rec areas, the outer maintenance rim, then the edge of the megalopolis. And beyond that: only anarchy and death. And the armed patrols, walls, minefields and barbed wire that guarded the City from chaos. No way out that way, not at all.

And no one else there. In all the four hundred miles of the City, in all the raped lands beyond, no one else there. No one here but him.

He sobbed, gasping air. Isolation filled his lungs like syrup.

He would do it now, it was too late to stop. Suicide? He thought briefly of suicide, of hurtling himself down from his window and falling forever until the ground caught him. No, he was too scared. Too afraid to be alone. He would do the other thing instead, as he always did.

Bradley walked to the viewphone. It was handsome, done in polished artificial wood and steel, with a wide screen. Trembling, he sat down.

The company representative had not even bothered to pretend that his spiel was not a spiel, that he wasn't speaking it from rote. He explained the merits of the new viewphone network in a rehearsed tone. Bradley listened numbly. They were both bored. It was all a formality anyway. Bradley had received a bonus for seniority—he had to rent something new whose cost would correspond to the bonus. He had to: there could be no such thing as a credit unbalance. The only initiative he could execute was in the selction of the item. He could choose from about five equally priced items. The company rep seemed to be pushing the viewphone network, maybe because they were overstocked—

Bradley activated the network, waited for the set to warm up. He opened a drawer, took out an address book, looked up a scribbled number. It had taken him three days this time to find the right girl, to follow her home, to find which apartment in the hive was hers so that he could look up the code number. He had been terrified every waking second of those three days, and he had almost been stopped and questioned by a security guard. Every time it got harder, every time he came a little closer to being caught. The viewphone hummed. The dialing pattern appeared on the screen.

The greatest advantage of the viewphone network, the company representative had told Bradley mechanically, is its intimacy. It can save you a great deal of unnecessary travel. It's every bit as good as being in the same room with the person you want to talk to. It enables you to perform all your social and business functions—

Bradley punched out the code number. Six short, savage jabs of his finger. He counted each click distinctly to himself. The dialing pattern disappeared; static swirled on the screen. With one hand, he reached down and opened his pants, unsealing the magnetic flap along the front. He had become excited, thinking of what he was about to do—he took his erection in his hand, squeezing, feeling the blood throb under his fingers. His mouth was painfully dry, and he was quivering with tension. Static condensed, became a young woman's face. Pretty, long dark hair, big golden eyes. "Yes?" she said, not recognizing him. Bradley stood up, letting his pants drop down around his ankles. Her eyes widened. She stared at him in shock—but there was also a quick flicker of fascination behind her eyes, and something else. Recognition? Longing? Love? It is love, he wanted to tell her, it is you and me, it is us. We touch here. But he only thrust his pelvis, a little more forward. She watched in fascination, lips parted, tongue against teeth. After a second, she dutifully—almost reluctantly—opened her mouth to

167

scream. He flicked the set off. Silence echoed. As her scream must be echoing now, in her own apartment, in her own hive. Gradually, he lowered himself back into the chair. He sat there with his pants bunched around his ankles and listened to the clock tick in the kitchen.

—in the convenience of your own home—

Then he began to cry.

The Storm

THE SKY HAD been ominous all that afternoon—a lurid yellow-green to the south, darkening overhead to blood and rust and soot. East, out over the ocean, there were occasional bright flashes and flares in rapid sequence, all without sound, as though a pitched artillery battle were being fought somewhere miles away and out of earshot. To the north and to the west, the sky was a dull dead black, like an immense wall of obsidian going up to heaven. The boy's house was silhouetted against that black sky, all slate and angles and old wooden gables, with a single silver light coming from the kitchen window. The house was surrounded by several big old horse-chestnut trees, and, to the boy, the moving silhouettes of their branches in the gathering wind seemed to be spelling out a message to God in some semaphoric sign language that he could recognize but not entirely understand. He wished that he could decipher the movement of the trees, because the same message was being whispered and repeated down through the long soughing fields of summer grass, and retold by the infinitesimal scraping of twig on twig deep in the tangled secret heart of the rhododendron and blackberry thickets, and rehearsed in a different register by the flying black cloud-scuts that now boiled out across the sky, and caught up and re-echoed and elaborated upon in the dust-devil dance of paper-scraps and leaves along the blacktop-and-gravel road to town. Spirits were moving. Something big was going to happen, and spirits were scuttling all about him through land and sky and water. Something big and wonderful and deadly was coming, coming up from behind that southern horizon like a muted iron music, still grumbling and rumbling far away, but coming steadily on all the same, coming inexorably up over the horizon and into the boy's world. The boy wished with all his heart that it would come.

"You stay close to the house, Paulie," the boy's mother called from the kitchen door. "This's going to break soon."

The boy didn't need to be told that there was a storm coming, nor did he need to go into the screened kitchen porch to know how fast the barometer was dropping. If the testimony of the hostile sky were not enough, then he could feel the storm as an electric prickling all along his skin, he could almost reach out and touch it with his fingertips. He could smell it, he could taste it. It was in the air all around him; it crackled around his feet as he swished them through the grass, and it thrilled him to his soul. If the boy had been magically given wings at that moment, he would have flown unhesitantly south to meet the storm—because it was marvelous and awful and even the rumor of its approach awed the world, because it was the greatest concentration of sheer power that had yet come into his life. The boy had made a brief foray down to the sea wall a few moments before, and even the ocean had seemed to be subdued by the power of the storm. It had been flat and glossy, with only the most sluggish of seas running, more like oil than water, or like some dull heavy metal in liquid form.

"Paulie!" his mother repeated, more stridently. "I mean it now—don't you go running off. You hear me, Paulie?"

"Okay, Ma!" the boy shouted.

The boy's mother stared suspiciously at him for a moment, distrustful of his easy capitulation. She started to say something else to him, hesitated, shook her head, and almost wiped her face absent-mindedly with the dirty dust rag she was holding. She caught herself, and grimaced wearily. Her hair was tied back in a tight, unlovely bun, and her face was strained and tired. She pulled her head back into the house. The screen door slammed shut behind her.

Released, the boy slid off through the trees.

With the canny instinct of children, he immediately circled the house to get out of sight. A moment later, his mother began calling him again from the kitchen door, but he pretended not to hear. He wouldn't go *very* far away, after all. His mother called again, sounding angry now. The boy wasn't worried. This side of the house was blind except for the windows on the second floor, and his mother would never go all the way up there just to look for him. She was easy to elude. Unconsciously, she seemed to believe in sympathetic magic: she would keep looking out the kitchen door for him, expecting to find him in the backyard because that was the last place she had seen him, and she couldn't really believe that he was anywhere else. The boy heard the front door open, and his mother called briefly for him from the front stoop. That was her concession to logic. Then the front door closed, and, after a moment, he heard her calling from the kitchen again. The boy had never heard of the Law of Contagion, but he knew instinctively that it was safe to play out front now. His mother would not look for him out in the front yard again. Somewhere inside she had faith in the boy's eventual reappearance in the backyard, and she would maintain an intermittent vigil at the kitchen door for hours, if need be, rather than walking back through the house to look for him again.

He sat down on the front lawn to think, well satisfied with himself.

There were other children in the neighborhood, but none of them were outside today. The boy was smugly pleased that he was the only one who had been able to dodge parental restraint, but after a while he began to feel more lonely than elated. Now that he had his freedom, he began to wonder what to do with it. He was too excited by the approaching storm to stay still for long, and that ruled out many of the intricate little games he'd devised to play when he was by himself, which was much of the time. The Atlantic was only a quarter-mile from his kitchen door, through a meadow and a stand of scrub woods he knew in every twig and branch, and ordinarily he would have gone down there to hunt for periwinkle shells or tide-worn pebbles or to run dizzily along the top of the seawall. But the thought made him uncomfortable—it would be cheating too much to go down there. He'd promised his mother that he would stay close to the house, and he only meant to bend his word a little, not break it. So he set off down the road instead, kicking at weeds and watching the ominously spreading bruise in the sky that marked the distant approach of the storm.

The neighborhood was more thickly settled down this way. It was about four hundred yards along the road from the boy's house to Mr. Leidy's house, the next one down. But just beyond Leidy's house was Mrs. Spinnato's house, almost invisible behind a high wall of azalea and ornamental hedge, and beyond that were three or four other houses grouped on either side of a little street that led away from the main road at a right angle. The boy turned off onto the side road. It had a real paved sidewalk, just like in town, and that was irresistible. The road led eventually, he knew, to a landfill in a marsh where the most wonderful junk could occasionally be found, but he didn't intend to go that far today. He'd be careful to keep his house in sight across the back of Mr. Coggin's yard, and that way he'd be doing pretty much what his mother had said, even if the house did dwindle to the size of a matchbook in the distance. And he could do without the dump, the boy thought magnanimously. There were sidewalks and driveways and groupings of houses all along this road, and a hundred places to explore—no matter that he'd explored them all yesterday, they could very well all be different today, couldn't they?

After a while, he found a feather on the sidewalk.

The birds hadn't needed to be told about the storm, either, the boy thought as he nudged at the feather with his toe. They had all flown north and west that morning, rising up out of the treetops like puffs of vapor in the sun to condense into bright feathered clouds that stretched out across the sky for miles. Later, in another county, it would rain birds. Pigeons, sparrows, crows, robins, jays, wrens, a dozen other species—the boy's world seemed amazingly empty without them. Even the gulls were gone. On an ordinary day you could almost always see a gull in the sky somewhere, rising up stiff winged from the land as if on an invisible elevator, then tilting and sliding down a long slope of air to skim across the sea. They hung above the fishing docks in town in such a raucous, fish-stealing, thousand-headed crowd that the boy usually could hear the clatter and cry of it all the way out here. Today they had all vanished before noon. Maybe they had gone far out to sea, or way up the coast—but they were gone. All that morning the boy had watched the birds go, and the scissoring, semaphore beat of their wings in the sky had been the first thing to spell out the message that now the trees and all the world repeated.

He picked up the feather.

A few feet farther on, he found another feather.

And then another one.

And another.

With growing excitement, the boy followed the trail of feathers.

Surely it must be leading him to an enchanted place, surely there must be something mysterious and wonderful at the end of the trail: a magic garden, a glass house, a tree with a door in it that led to another world. He began to run. The trail led diagonally across a driveway and disappeared behind a garage. There were more feathers to be found now, two or three of them in each clump.

At the end of the trail of feathers was a dead bird.

The boy stopped short, feeling a thrill of surprise and horror and supernatural awe. Involuntarily, he dropped the handful of feathers he had gathered, and they swirled around his ankles for a moment before settling to the ground. The bird had been struck by a glancing but fatal blow by something—a car, a hawk—and it had fluttered all this way to die, shedding feathers across the sidewalk, fighting to stay aloft and stay alive and losing at both. This was the enchanted thing at the end of the trail: a dead pigeon, glazed eyes and matted feathers, sad, dowdy, and completely unmagical. An emotion he could not name swept through the boy, making the short hairs bristle along the back of his neck. He looked up.

The southern sky was still a welter of lurid color, but there was more red in it now, as though blood was slowly being poured into the world.

Paul himself could not have told you why he first began to withdraw from the world. Breaking up with his fiancée Vivian—a particular sordid and drawn-out process that had taken almost half a year all told—certainly had something to do with it. His best friend, Joseph, had recently become his most bitter enemy, and was now busy spreading poisonous tales about him throughout the rest of Paul's circle of acquaintances and colleagues. Much of the blame for these ugly affairs was unquestionably Paul's—paradoxically, that knowledge fed his guilt without abating in the least the hatred he now felt for Vivian and Joseph. Paul's father had just died, still bitterly unreconciled with his son, and that left an unpleasant taste in Paul's mouth. All his relatives were dead now. He had quit his job, ostensibly because he wanted to. But his career had been dead-ended by business adversaries, and he'd had no place to go in it but down. And he had been ill. Nothing major: just a case of flu—or rather, a series of flus and colds running in succession—that had stuck with him throughout the entire fall and early winter and had left him feeling wretched, dull, and debilitated. These were the obvious reasons, at least. There were probably hundreds of others that Paul himself did not consciously know about—small humiliations, everyday defeats, childhood tragedies, long-forgotten things that had settled down into him like layer after layer of sediment until they choked his soul with sludge.

Above all else, he lived in Manhattan, and Manhattan was a place that fed you hate, contempt, bitterness, and despair in negligible daily doses that—like cleverly administered arsenic—became cumulatively fatal.

Paul had an apartment on East Tenth Street between First and Avenue A, a neighborhood that is depressing even at its best. In January, with the freezing winds skimming down the avenue like razors, and the corrugated gray sky clamped down like a lid, and the first sooty snowfall coming down over the frozen garbage on the sidewalks, it is considerably worse than 'depressing.' Even his seamy fifth-floor walkup began to seem a more desirable place to be than the frozen monochrome world outside.

He began to "stay in."

He had few friends left in the city any more, and certainly none who were worth sallying out through a Manhattan winter to visit. His bank balance was too low to afford him luxuries like movies or nightclubs or the theater, or even dining out. He had gotten out of the habit of going to the newstand for newspapers or magazines. He wasn't looking for work, so he didn't need to go out for job interviews. And he had become a bad-luck magnet— every time he left the apartment, disaster followed at his heels: he tore a ligament falling down the stairs, he sprained an ankle on a slushy sidewalk, he was bitten by dogs, drenched by the freezing gutter-water thrown up by speeding cars, knocked down by a bicycle on First Avenue, splattered with garbage, and mugged three times in two weeks. It seemed that every time he went outside now he caught another cold, and had to suffer out the next few days with chills and headaches and congestion. Under these circumstances, it was just easier to stay inside as much as possible, and even easier than that to let the days he spent inside turn themselves almost unnoticed into weeks. He fell into the habit of doing all his shopping in one trip, and planning frugal meals so that each carton of groceries would last as long as possible.

He no longer went out for any other reason whatsoever.

This self-enforced retreat of Paul's might eventually have turned out to be good for him if he had been able to do any work during it. He had ostensibly quit his advertising job in order to write a novel, but the typewriter sat idle on the folding table in the living room for week after week. It wasn't so much that he could think of nothing to write, but that everything he did put on paper seemed banal, inconsequential, jejune. Eventually he gave up even trying to write, but left the typewriter set up in case sudden inspiration should strike. It didn't. The typewriter became covered by a fine film of dust and soot. He watched television almost continuously then, until a tube burned out in the set. He didn't have enough money to get it fixed, so he pushed the set against the wall, where it glowered out over the apartment like the glazed eye of a dead Cyclops. Dust settled over that, too. He read every book he owned, then read them again. Eventually he reached a point where he would just sit around the apartment all day, not doing anything, too listless even to be bored.

He didn't realize it, but he was changing. He was being worn away by an eroding process as imperceptible and inexorable as the action of the tide on soft coastal rock.

Now, when necessity drove him out on a shopping trip, the world seemed as bizarrely incomprehensible and overwhelming to him as it might have to Kaspar Hauser. Everything terrified him. He would slink along the sidewalk with one shoulder close to a wall for comfort, shrinking from everyone he met, his eyes squinted to slits against the harsh and hostile daylight or strained wide so that he could peer anxiously through the threatening shadows of night, and he would shake his head constantly and irritably to drive away the evil babble of city sounds. Once in the store, he would have to consciously remember how to talk, explaining what he wanted in a slow, slurred, thick-tongued voice, having to pause and search through his memory like a Berlitz-course linguist asking directions to the Hauptbahnhof. And he would count out the money to pay for his order with painstaking slowness, penny by penny, like a child. When at last he did get safely back inside his apartment, he would be trembling and covered with cold sweat.

At last, he made a deal with the landlord's teenage son: the boy agreed to deliver a cartonful of groceries to Paul's apartment every other week, for a price. For a few dollars more, the boy eventually agreed to pick up Paul's rent check when it was due and deliver it to his father, and to carry the garbage downstairs a couple of times a month if Paul would bag it and leave it outside his door. In effect, this deal meant that Paul no longer had to go outside at all, for any reason. It was much better that way. Perhaps his savings would not hold out long at this rate, but he could no longer worry about that. It was worth it to have to cope only with a wedge of the world—the crack of a half-opened door.

Behind that door, Paul continued to erode.

Supper was beans and franks and brownbread. The boy didn't mind the beans and the brownbread, but his mother had insisted on boiling the frankfurters, and he hated them that way—he hated watching them plump up and float to the surface of the boiling water, and he especially hated the way they would split open and ooze out their pinkish innards when they were done. His mother had been making beans and franks a lot the past few months, because they were cheap and very quick and easy to make. Once she had made more intricate meals, but she was so distracted and tearful and busy lately.

Now she was always having to leave him with Mrs. Spinnato while she went into town unexpectedly, or talking on the phone for hours with her voice pitched low so that he couldn't overhear, or talking in that same low voice to Mr. Halpern the lawyer as she served him coffee in the parlor, or to her cousin Alice or Mrs. Spinnato or Mrs. DeMay in the kitchen, the *bss bss bss* of their whispering filling the air with moth wings and secrets.

And so supper was usually late, and he got beans and franks, or what his mother called "American chop suey," which was a frying pan full of hamburger and garlic powder with a can of Franco-American spaghetti dumped into it. Or TV dinner. Or hamburgers, or tunafish salad. Or spaghetti noodles with just butter and garlic on them instead of spaghetti sauce with ground meat. Any of which he liked better than boiled frankfurters, but his mother was still being mad at him for running off, and she wasn't in a mood to listen to complaints or to let him get away without finishing his supper. So he ate, affecting an air somewhere between sullen and philosophical.

His mother ate only half of her own meal, and then sat staring blankly at the stove and pushing the rest of her food aimlessly back and forth on her plate. Too restless to sit down at the table, she had pulled a stool up to the kitchen divider to eat, and she kept getting up to pace across the kitchen for condiments she subsequently forgot to use. She had been packing and cleaning all day; her eyes were shadowed and bloodshot, and there was a grimy streak across her forehead. She had forgotten to take off her apron. Some hair had pulled loose from the bun she'd tied it in; it scraggled out behind her head like an untidy halo, and one thick lock of it had fallen down over her brow. She kept brushing it out of her eyes with absentminded irritation, as if it was a fly. She didn't speak during supper, but she smoked one cigarette after another, only taking a few nervous puffs of each before she stubbed it out and lit another. The ashtray in front of her had overflowed, spilling an ash slide out across the porcelain countertop.

The boy finished his supper, and, getting no response at all when he asked if he could be excused, essayed a cautious sortie toward the door. His mother made no objection; she was staring at her coffee cup as though she'd never seen one before. Encouraged, the boy pushed the screen door open and went out on the porch.

The lurid welter of color in the south had expanded to fill half the sky. The boy stopped on the bottom step of the porch, sniffing at the world like a cautious, curious dog. There was no wind at all now, but the crackly electric feel of the air was even more pronounced, as was a funny electric smell that the boy could not put a name to. The sun had been invisible all day; now it showed a glazed red disk just as it was going down behind the western horizon. It looked wan and powerless against that smothering black sky, as if it was no longer able to provide either heat or light—a weary bloodshot eye about to close at the edge of the world. But the landscape was bathed in a strange empyreal radiance that had nothing to do with the sun, a directionless undersea light that seemed to come from the sky itself, and which illuminated everything as garishly and pitilessly as neon. In that light the big chestnut trees seemed dry and brittle. Their branches were still now, held high like arms—thrown up in horror. There was a halcyon quiet everywhere. The world was holding its breath.

"Don't think you're going to run off again," his mother warned. She had come up behind him silently on the porch.

"I don't, Ma," said the boy, who had been thinking of doing just that. "I ain't going nowhere."

"You bet you aren't," his mother said grimly. She glanced irritably at the threatening sky, then glanced away. The eerie light turned her face chalk-white, made her lips a pale, bloodless gash—it almost seemed as if you could see the shadow of her bones inside her flesh, as though the new radiance enabled you to see by penetrating rays rather than by ordinary light. "The only place you're going now, young man, is up to bed."

"Aw, Ma!" the boy protested tragically.

"I mean it now, Paulie."

"Aw, Ma. It ain't even dark yet."

She softened a little, and came forward to rumple his hair. "I know you're excited by the storm, baby," she said, "but it's only a storm, and you've seen storms before, haven't you—this's just a bigger kind of storm, that's all." She smoothed down the hair she'd ruffled, and her voice came brisker. "Mrs. Spinnato will be coming over in a little while to help me pack the rest of the china, and I don't want you underfoot. And I know what you're like on a long car trip, and I don't intend to have you all tired and crotchety for it tomorrow. So you go to sleep early tonight. Get on up to bed now, young man. Scoot now! Scoot!"

Reluctantly, the boy let her herd him back inside. He

179

said goodnight and went into the parlor, headed for the stairs. He felt spooky and oddly out-of-place in the parlor now, and he transversed it as quickly as he could. The furniture had been moved back against the walls, and the room was full of boxes and cartons, some only partially packed, some sealed up securely with masking tape. Dishes and glasses and oddments were stacked everywhere, and the curtains had been taken down and folded. The parlor looked strange stripped of all its familiar trappings, knicknacks, paintings, lace doilies, things that had been there for as long as the boy could remember. Without them, the parlor was suddenly a different place, alien and subtly perverse. Seeing the room like that made the boy sad in a way he had never been before. It was as if his life was being dismantled and packed away in musty cardboard boxes. Tomorrow they were going to Ohio to live, because his mother had family there, and after that he wouldn't have a father anymore. The boy didn't understand that part of it, because he knew his father was living in a house on Front Street, but his mother had told him that he didn't have a father anymore, and somehow it must be true because he certainly wasn't coming to Ohio with them.

The boy went upstairs and changed into his pajamas, but before going to bed he got up on a stool and peeked out of the high bedroom window. The clouds in the southern sky had thickened and darkened, and they were streaming toward him like two great out-thrust arms. Although the trees outside were still not stirring, the clouds were visibly moving closer, as though there were a wind blowing high in the sky that had not yet reached the earth.

One gritty, rain-filled morning Paul was roused from a somnolent daze by a loud hammering at the apartment door. He swam up from the living-room couch, bewildered by the sound. Automatically, he crossed to the door, and then stood shivering and bemused behind it, his fingertips touching the wood. More pounding. He snatched his hand away from the vibrating door-panel, hesitated, and then looked through the spyhole. He could see nothing outside but a hulking, shapeless figure standing too close to the lens.

"You in there?" came a muffled voice from the corridor.

Cautiously, Paul opened the door a crack and peeked out.

It was the landlord. Behind him were two men in work clothes, hung about with tools and loops of wire cable.

Paul could not think of anything to say to them.

"We come in," the landlord said rapidly, without a question mark. "Gutter's clogged up ona roof ana roof's filling up with rain. Water's coming down inta the apartment down t'otha end d'hall. See?" He pushed forward, shouldering the door wide. Paul backpedaling to get out of his way. "Cain't reach it up 'are but maybe wecun git through ta t'sonuvabitch frumin y'apartment, right? Okayifwecumen," he said in one breath, and without waiting for an answer he was inside, followed by the two plumbers. They pushed by Paul and went into the kitchen.

In a daze, Paul retreated to the living room.

They were stomping around inside the bathroom now. "There's an airspace behind this bathroom wall here," one of the plumbers was shouting. "See, it used t'be a window and somebody plastered it over. We knock a hole through the plaster, we can get out inta the airspace and get a pump extension up to that outside drain on this side, right?"

The other plumber came back with a sledgehammer and they began knocking the bathroom wall down. They dragged in cables and a spotlight, an electric drill, and a long hose-and-pump contraption that came up the stairs and snaked all the way through the apartment to the bathroom. Soon the air was full of dust and powdered plaster, the smell of wet ceramic-covered pipes and damp old wood. The spotlight dazzled like a sun in a box. Machines whined and pounded and snarled; people

181

shouted messages back and forth. The pump thumped and thudded, and made a wheezing, rattling sound like an asthmatic gargling.

Paul hid from this chaos in the living room. Occasionally he would peek out through the living room archway, trembling, aghast, gathering a ragged bathrobe tighter around him at the neck. The workers ignored him, except for a curious sidelong glance every so often as they strode in or out of the apartment. Paul tried to keep out of their sight. He felt dirty and weak and unwholesome, like some wet pallid thing that had lived out its life under a rock, traumatically exposed to wind and sunlight and predators when the rock is rolled away.

At last, the workmen were finished, they gathered up their tools, rolled up their hoses and cables, and left. The landlord turned at the door and said, "Oh, I'll send somebody around in a couple days t'fix up the hole in the wall, okay, buddy?"

He went out.

Hesitantly, Paul emerged from the living room. The kitchen floor was crisscrossed with wet dirty footprints, and there were little puddles of dirty water here and there. There was a large, ragged hole in the bathroom wall, with gray daylight showing through it. Plaster and bits of lathing had fallen down into the bathtub and the toilet, and formed an uneven heap on the bathroom floor. There was a strong musty smell, like wet wallpaper.

Paul shivered and quickly retreated to the living room again. The broken wall filled him with shame and horror and helpless outrage, as if he had been raped, as if some integral part of him had been shattered and violated. He shivered again. It was no longer safe here. The rock ceiling had been torn away from his cave; his nest had been shaken down from the tree by the storm. He sat down on the couch and found that he couldn't stop shaking. Where did he have to go now? Where could he go in all the world to be safe?

The apartment was getting colder. He could hear the rain outside, dripping and mumbling past the hole in the wall.

Eventually the shakes stopped, and he could feel himself going numb. He would have given anything for a working radio, just to get some noise in the apartment other than his own spidery breathing, but he had gone through the last of his spare batteries weeks ago, and it had never occurred to him to have the landlord's son bring him some in the next grocery order. Instead he sat in the semi-darkness as the evening grew old and listened to the distant sound of other radios and televisions in other apartments that came to him through the paper-thin walls: faint, scratchy, and tuned to the confusion of a dozen different stations so that nothing was ever quite clear enough to comprehend. They sounded like whispering Gödelized messages reaching him from star-systems millions of light-years away. Toward dawn the other radios were turned off one by one, leaving him at the bottom of a well of thick and dusty silence. He sat perfectly still. Occasionally the glow of car headlights from the street would sweep across the ceiling in oscillating waves. It was so quiet he could hear the scurry of a cockroach behind the burlap that covered the walls.

His mind was blank as slate. In spite of his enforced idleness, he was not doing any deep thinking or meditating or soul-searching, nor had he done any throughout the entire process. If any cogitation was taking place, it was happening on a deep, damaging level too remote and ancient to ever come under conscious review.

When he thought about it at all, he supposed that he must be having a breakdown. But that seemed much too harsh a word. "Breakdown," "cracking-up," "flying to pieces," "losing your grip"—they were all such dramatic, violent words. None of them seemed appropriate to describe what was happening to him: a slackening, a loosening, a slow sliding away, an almost imperceptibly gradual relinquishment of the world. A very quiet thing. A fall into soot and silence.

Dawn was a dirty gray imminence behind drawn curtains.

Outside it was by now a cold and gritty early spring,

but Paul never noticed. He never looked out any of the windows during all his months of seclusion, not even once, and he kept the curtains drawn at all times.

A needle-thin sliver of daylight came in through the crack in the curtains. Slow as a glacier, it lengthened out across the floor to touch the couch where Paul sat.

A toilet flushed on the floor above. After a moment or two, a water tap was turned on somewhere, and the water pipes knocked and rattled all the way down the length of the building. Footsteps going down the stairs outside Paul's door. Voices calling back and forth in the stairwell. A child crying somewhere. The sound of a shower coming from the apartment down the hall. And then, on the floor below, the first radio of the day began to bellow.

One by one, then, over the next two hours, all the radios and televisions came on again, and there was the Gödelized babble of the previous night, although because people played their sets more loudly during the day, it now sounded like a thousand demon-possessed madmen shouting in tongues from deep inside metal rain barrels.

Still Paul did not move.

He sat motionless as marble on his couch while the living room curtains bled from gray-white to shadow-black again, and day once more dissolved into night. Twice during the day he had gotten up to go to the bathroom, and each time he had returned to the couch immediately afterward. He had eaten nothing, nor taken any drink. Except for the occasional motion of his eyes as he sat in the darkened room, he might have been a statue, or he might have been dead.

The night slowly decayed toward morning. Once there was a shot and a series of piercing screams somewhere outside in the street. Paul did not stir or turn his head. The sound of screaming police sirens came and went outside the building. Paul did not move.

The radios and televisions faded one by one. The last radio whispered on in Spanish far into the night, and then it, too, died.

Silence.

When dawn shone gray at the window once again, Paul

got creakily to his feet. His eyes were strange. He had gone very far away from humanity in the last forty-eight hours. He no longer remembered his name. He was no longer sure where he was, what kind of a place he was in. It didn't seem to matter—the apartment had become the world, the womb, the sum total of creation. The Continuum. It might as well have been Plato's cave, where Paul sat watching shadows on the burlap walls. A biological pressure touched off the firing of a synapse somewhere inside Paul's brain, and a deeply ingrained behavioral pattern took over. In response to that pattern, he shambled slowly toward the bathroom. His way led through the kitchen, which was still in deep darkness, as it was on the shadowed side of the building. Paul hesitated in the kitchen doorway, and a flicker of returning awareness and intelligence passed through him. He groped around for the light-switch, found it, and clicked it on. He squinted against the light.

Almost every surface in the kitchen was covered with cockroaches, thousands and thousands of them.

The sudden burst of light startled them and sent them into violent boiling motion. They came swarming up out of dirty cups and plates, up out of the sink, up out of overflowing garbage bags; they scuttled out across the kitchen table, across the floor, across the cabinet sideboard, across the stove. In an instant, the burlap walls were black and crawling with them as they scurried for their hidey-holes in the woodwork and the window moldings and the baseboards and the cabinets. Thousands of scuttling brownish-red insects, so many of them that their motion set up a slight chitinous whisper in the room.

Disgust struck Paul like a fist.

Shuddering, he sagged back weakly against the doorframe. Bile rose up in his throat, and he swallowed it. He reached out reflexively and shut off the light. The chitinous rustling continued in the darkness.

Still shivering, Paul went back into the living room. Here the dawn had imposed a kind of gray twilight, and there were only five or six cockroaches to be seen, scurrying across the floor with amazing rapidity. Paul shuddered again. His skin itched as though bugs were crawling over him, and he brushed his hands repeatedly down along his arms. He was reacting way out of proportion to this—he was reacting symbolically, archetypically. He had been sickened and disgusted by this on some deep, elemental level, and now there was something reverberating through him again and again like the tolling of a great soundless bell. He could sense that thoughts were rippling just under the conscious surface of his mind, like swift-darting fish, like a computer equation running—to what end he did not know. Without conscious motivation, he reached out and suddenly tapped the spacebar of his typewriter. More cockroaches boiled out of the typewriter mechanism, scuttling out from under the machine, crawling up from between the keys on the keyboard, crawling up from beneath the roller.

Paul shuddered convulsively from head to foot.

That's it, he thought irrationally, *that's all*.

You're finished, he thought.

Suddenly he was unbelievably, unbearably, overwhelmingly tired. He staggered to his bed and fell down upon it. That great soundless bell was tolling again, beating through blood and bone and meat. His vision blurred until he was unable to clearly see the dawn-ghost of the ceiling. The bed seemed to be spinning in slow, slow circles. A cockroach scurried over his hand. He was too beaten-out physically to do anything other than twitch, but another enormous wave of disgust and loathing and rage and self-hate rolled through him and flooded every cell of his being. His eyes filled with weak tears. He grimaced at the ceiling like an animal in pain. His head lolled.

Sleep was like a long hard fall into very deep water.

As with every sentient creature, there was a part of Paul that never slept and that knew everything. Racial subconscious, organic computer, overmind, genetic memory, superconsciousness, immortal soul, call it what you will—it not only knew everything that had happened to Paul and to all the race of man, it also knew everything that *might* have happened: the web of possibilities in its entirety. Since there is really no such thing as time, it also knew everything that *will* and *might* happen to Paul and to everyone else, and what *will* and *might* happen to everyone who ever will (or might) be born in what we fatuously call "the future." It is hopeless, of course, to try to talk about these matters in any kind of detail—our corporeal, conscious minds can not even begin to grasp the concepts involved, and the language is too inadequate to allow us to discuss them even if they could be understood. Suffice it to say that in Paul the super-consciousness-organic computer et cetera had always been much more accessible to him than is usually the case. And now that he had been partially freed from the bonds of ego by deprivation, exhaustion, starvation, fever, madness and hate, Paul's dreaming mind was finally able to reach the superconsciousness and operate it to his own ends.

He ran the "memory" of the superconsciousness back until it had reached one of the key junctions and turning-points of his life, and then had it sort through the billions of possible consequences arising out of that junction until it found the one possibility that would best facilitate the peculiar sentence of oblivion that Paul had mercilessly handed down upon himself in the High Court of his own soul. The one that Paul finally decided upon was probably the least likely and most bizarre of all the myriad possibilities stemming from that particular junction of his life—a number which *is* finite, but which is also enormous far beyond our range of conscious comprehension. It was a corner that had never been turned.

He went back. He turned that corner.

The boy woke to night and silences. He lay quietly on his back and stared at the shadowy ceiling, half-relieved, half-disappointed. It had been only another storm, after all. *Just like Ma said*, he thought. It must have passed and spent itself while he was sleeping. *And tomorrow I'm going to Ohio.*

But even as he was thinking this, the wind puffed up out of nowhere and slammed against the windows, rattling the glass in their frames. The boy could hear the wind scoop up the big metal garbage cans out front and send them rolling and clattering and clanging far down the street like giant dice. Suddenly there was a torrent of water slamming and rattling the window along with the wind, as if a high-pressure hose had been turned against the glass. The house groaned and shook.

The boy lay trembling with fear and delight. The storm hadn't passed, after all! Maybe he had awakened during a lull, or maybe he hadn't slept as long as he had thought and the storm was just beginning. The boy sat up eagerly in the bed.

As he did, the room filled with blinding blue-white light, so dazzling that it almost seemed to sear the retinas. A split-second later there was a buffeting, ear-splitting explosion. Then another blast of light, then another monstrous thunderclap, and so on in such fast and furious alternation that the boy couldn't catch his breath for the shock of it. It was as if a heavy howitzer were firing salvos right outside his bedroom window. Another moment or two of this, the lightning certainly striking right outside the house, and then there came a silence that could only upon reflection be recognized as identical with the highest previous level of noise.

Joy! the boy thought. He was leaning dazedly back against the headboard, eyes wide. He hoped that he hadn't made in his pants.

More thunder, not quite so overwhelmingly right-on-top-of-him any more. While it was still booming and rumbling, the bedroom door opened and his mother came in. She didn't turn on his light, but she stood in the doorway where she herself was illuminated by the bulb in the hall. "Are you all right, baby?" she asked. Her voice sounded funny somehow.

"I'm okay, Mom."

"Don't let it scare you, Paulie," she said. "It's only a hurricane; it'll be over soon."

There *was* something funny about her voice. It had a strained, wild note to it. Tension under restraint.

"I'm not scared, Ma, I'm okay."

"Try to get some sleep, then," she said. And her face changed alarmingly, expressions melting and shifting across it faster than the boy could catch them. When she spoke again, her voice had gone gravelly and dropped in register, as though she was straining to keep it under control. "But if—" She started again. "But if you can't sleep, then come downstairs and be with me for a while." She stopped abruptly, whirled around and left. He could hear her footsteps clicking away down the hallway, fast and agitated.

The same funny thing had been in her face as well as her voice. Dimly, almost instinctually, the boy recognized what it was: it was fear.

She was the one who was afraid, in spite of her reassurances to him. *His mother* was afraid.

Why?

It was completely out of accord with her mood earlier that evening. Then she had been somewhat distracted, the way she always was lately—but that was somehow all tied up with him not having a father any more. She had been tense and snappish—but that was because she'd been packing all day. She hadn't been afraid then. She'd been a little bit nervous about the approaching storm, but not afraid—mostly irritated by the thought of all the bother and nuisance it was going to cause her, maybe they wouldn't be able to leave tomorrow if the weather was still bad. Why was she afraid now?

The boy got out of bed and padded across to the door. He opened it and slipped out into the upstairs hallway. A few feet down the hallway he stopped, head up, "sniffing the air."

Something was very wrong.

He didn't know what it was, he couldn't identify it or put a name to it, but somehow everything was wrong.

Everything was the same, but it was somehow also completely different. He could smell it, the way he'd been able to smell the storm when it was behind the horizon. It was in the air itself, his mother, the house around him—the most subtle and nearly imperceptible of differences. But the air, the house, his mother, *they were not the same ones he'd had before*.

It was as if he'd gone to sleep in one world and awakened in another. A world exactly the same except for being completely different.

The thought was too big for his mind, too complex for him to begin to appraise it. The whole concept slipped sideways in his head and then right on out of it, leaving him not even quite sure what it was he'd been struggling to comprehend a moment before. But it also left behind a legacy of oily panic. For the first time he began to become really afraid.

He crept stealthily to the head of the stairs and listened at the stairwell. He could hear his mother's voice talking downstairs, and Mrs. Spinnato's voice, but he couldn't make out what they were saying. With utmost caution, he went down four treads and crouched next to the railing. They had the radio or the television on down there, but between the wind and the thunder outside and the crackling frying-egg static on the set itself, it was almost impossible to hear what it was saying, either. The boy strained his ears. "...fall..." it said and the rest was swallowed by the wind. The boy went down another tread. "...falling..." it repeated.

The rest was garble and static-hiss, wind, more eggs frying, a thunderclap, and then it said "...roche..."

After another moment, his mother and Mrs. Spinnato came by the foot of the stairs, heading toward the kitchen. He froze, but neither woman looked up as she passed. Their voices came to him in snatches through the sound of the wind.

"...lieve it?" his mother was saying.

"...don't know what...now...but if..." said Mrs. Spinnato.

"...we do?...how..."

"...what *can* we...if it's...that..."

"...pray, that's..."

Unenlightened, the boy returned to his bedroom. The note of fear was in Mrs. Spinnato's voice, too, and she was a powerful, strong-willed woman, ordinarily afraid of nothing.

The boy went to his window and stood looking out at the storm. It was raining hard. The trees were lashing violently back and forth as if they had gone mad with pain. Dislodged slate roofing and shingles were flying and swirling around in the air like confetti. The sky was a mad luminescent indigo, except when lightning turned it a searing white. Some power lines were already down, writhing and spitting blue sparks in the street, and trees were beginning to have their branches torn off. There was a sudden high-pitched tearing sound over his head, and something scraped heavily across the roof before it tumbled down into the yard. That was their television antenna being blown away. A moment later the light in the hall flickered and went out. All their lights were gone. He stood in the dark, looking out the window—excited, exalted, and terrified.

That was when the real storm front hit.

The boy sensed the blow coming, an irresistible onrush of fire-shot darkness, and instinctively dropped flat to the floor. The window exploded inward in a fountain of shattered glass. There was a series of flat explosions, and wood chips sprayed and geysered from the wall opposite the window, exactly as if someone was raking the room with a heavy-caliber machine gun. The boy would never know it, but the damage was being done by chestnuts from the horse-chestnut trees outside, stripped from their branches by a 150 m.p.h. gust and whipped into the room with all the shattering force of heavy-caliber bullets.

The wind struck again. This time the window-frame was splintered and pulverized, and the house itself screeched, rocked, and seemed to strain up toward the sky for a moment before it settled back down. A jagged crack shot the length of one wall. The boy hugged the floor while bits of plaster and lathing came down on his back.

He wasn't even particularly afraid. What was happening was too huge and immediate and overwhelming to leave any room in his mind for fear. During a lull in the wind he could hear his mother and Mrs. Spinnato screaming downstairs. He himself was making a little dry panting noise that he wasn't even aware of, *ahnnn, ahnnn, ahnnn*, like a winded animal.

The lull seemed as if it was going to last for a while. The boy tried to get to his feet and was knocked flat again by wind and water. He had forgotten that this was a "lull" only by comparison with the unbelievable gust that had struck a minute before. He pulled himself up again, hanging on to the shattered window frame and not lifting his head much higher than the window ledge. In a heartbeat he was drenched to the bone. If the rain had been hard before, it was now like a horizontal waterfall driving against the house. But by keeping his head close to the frame and squinting he found that he could see a little. He got his vision right just in time to see another tremendous gust destroy Mr. Leidy's house, a gust that was fortunately blowing in a different direction. Fortunately for the boy anyway. Leidy's place was built on a rise, denying it even the minimum shelter that the small hills to the southeast afforded the boy's house. One moment the Leidy house was there, a solid three-story structure, and the next moment—in an eyeblink—it was gone, demolished, smashed to flinders, turned into a monstrous welter of flying debris that looked for all the world like a Gargantuan dust devil.

Somewhere on the other side of the house he could very faintly hear his mother calling desperately for him. Probably she was trying to make it up the stairs to his bedroom.

She didn't make it, because at that moment, unbelievably, the earthquake struck.

At first the boy thought it was the wind again, but then the entire house began to rattle and buck and plunge, and there was a rumbling freight-train sound that was even louder than the storm. Terrified and helpless, the boy could do nothing but cling like a burr to the windowsill while the room around him bounced and jigged and staggered. Hairline cracks shot out across the walls and ceiling and floor, widened, spread. A section of the far wall suddenly slid away, leaving a ragged five-foot gap. The house *whammed* the ground once with finality, bounced again, and settled. The ground stopped moving. Nothing happened for perhaps a minute, and then the entire front half of the house collapsed. Plaster powder and brick dust were puffed from all the windows on the boy's side of the house, like steam from a bellows. For a heartbeat the boy was coated with dust and powder from head to foot, and then the rain came rushing back in the window and washed him clean again.

Another lull, the most complete one yet, as though the universe had taken a deep, deep breath.

In that abrupt hush the boy could hear someone close at hand screaming and sobbing. He realized with surprise that it was himself. Almost casually, the portion of his mind not occupied with terror noticed a sudden rush of sea-water sweeping in across the ground. Mrs. Spinnato's house had been determinedly smouldering in spite of the rain but it went out in a hissing welter of steam when the wave indunated it. That first wave had been a fake, only waist-deep and made mostly of spume, but there were a whole series of other waves marching in behind it—storm waves, tsunami, maybe actual tidal waves, who knows?— and some of them were pale horrors twelve, twenty, thirty feet high.

I'm stuck in it, said a voice in the boy's head that was the boy's voice and yet somehow not the boy's voice. *I can't stop it. I can't get out.*

I didn't know it would be like this, the voice said.

The universe let out that deep, deep breath.

The wind came back.

This time it gusted to 220 mph and it flattened everything.

It uprooted one of the huge chestnut trees in the boy's yard and hurled it like a giant's javelin right at the window where the boy was crouching.

The boy had a timeless moment to himself before the

tree smashed him into pulp, and he used it to wonder what it would have been like to live in Ohio.

The boy had a timeless moment to himself before the tree smashed him into pulp, and he used it to wonder why he was thinking of feathers and soot.

The boy had a timeless moment to himself before the tree smashed him into pulp, and he used it to wonder who the man was who was crying inside his head.

Where No Sun Shines

ROBINSON HAD BEEN driving for nearly two days, across Pennsylvania, up through the sooty barrens of New Jersey, pushing both the car and himself with desperation. Exhaustion had stopped him once in a small, rotting coast town, filled with disintegrating clapboard buildings and frightened pale faces peering from behind tight-closed shutters. He had moved slowly through empty streets washed by a tide of crumpled newspapers and dirty candy wrappers that rolled and rustled in the bitter sea wind. On the edge of town he'd found a deserted filling station and gone to sleep there with doors locked and windows rolled up, watching moonlight glint from a rusting gas pump and clutching a tire iron in his hands. He had dreamed of sharks with legs, and once banged his head sharply on the roof as he lunged up out of sleep and away from ripping teeth, pausing and blinking afterward in the hot, sweat-drenched stuffiness of the closed car, listening to the darkness.

In the drab, pale clarity of morning, a ragged wave of refugees had washed through town and swept him along. He had driven all day by the side of the restless sea, oily and cinder flecked as a tattered gray rug, drifting through one frightened shuttered town after another, watching the peeling billboards and the boarded-up store fronts.

It was late evening now, and he was just beginning to

really believe what had happened, accept it with his bowels as well as his mind, the hard reality jabbing his stomach like a knifeblade. The secondary highway he was following narrowed, banked, and Robinson slowed to take the curve, wincing at the scream of gears as he shifted. The road straightened and he stamped on the accelerator again, feeling the shuddering whine of the car's response. How long will this crate hold up, he thought numbly. How long will my gas last? How many more miles? Exhaustion was creeping up on him again; a sledgehammer wrapped in felt, isolating him even from the aching reality of his own nerves.

There was a wreck ahead, on his side, and he drifted out into the other lane to avoid it. Coming past Philadelphia the highway had been choked with a honking, aimless mass of cars, but he knew the net of secondary roads better than most of them and had outstripped the herd. Now the roads were mostly empty. Sane people had gone to ground.

He pulled even with the wreck, passed it. It was a light pickup truck, tipped on its side, gutted by fire. A man was lying in the road face down, across the white dividing line. Except for the pale gleam of face and hands, it might have been a discarded bundle of rags. There were bloodstains on the worn asphalt. Robinson let his car slide more to the left to keep from running over the man, started to skid slightly, corrected it. Beyond the wreck he swerved back into his own lane and speeded up again. The truck and the man slid backward, lingered in his rear-view mirror for a second, washed by his taillights, and were swallowed by darkness.

A few miles down the road, Robinson began to fall asleep at the wheel, blacking out in split-second dozes, nodding and blinking. He cursed, strained his eyes wide open and rolled his window down. Wind screamed through the crack. The air was muggy, sodden with coal smoke and chemical reeks, the miasma of the industrial nightmare that choked upper New Jersey.

Automatically, Robinson reached for the radio, switched it on, and began turning the selector-knob with one hand, groping blindly through the invisible world for something to keep him company. Static rasped at him. Almost all the Philadelphia and Pittsburgh stations were off the air now; they'd been hit hard down there. The last Chicago station had sputtered off the air at dusk, after an outbreak of fighting had been reported outside the studio. For a while, some of the announcers had been referring to "rebel forces," but this had evidently been judged to be bad PR, because they were calling them "rioters" and "scattered anarchists" again.

For a moment he picked up a strong Boston station, broadcasting a placating speech by some official, but it faded in a burst of static and was slowly replaced by a Philadelphia station relaying emergency ham messages. There were no small local stations anymore. Television was probably out too, not that he missed it very much. He hadn't seen a live broadcast or a documentary for months now, and even in Harrisburg, days before the final flareup, they'd stopped showing any newcasts at all and broadcast nothing but taped situation comedies and old 1920's musicals. (The happy figures dancing in tails on top of pianos, unreal as delirium tremens in the flickering wavering white glow of the television's eyes, as tinny music echoed and canned laughter filled the room like the crying of mechanical birds. Outside, there was occasional gunfire. . . .)

Finally he settled for a station that was playing uninterrupted classical music, mostly Mozart and Johann Strauss.

He drove on with automatic skill, listening to a bit of Dvořák that had somehow slipped in between Haydn and "The Blue Danube." Absorbed in the music, his already fuzzy mind lulled by the steady rolling lap of asphalt slipping under his wheels, Robinson almost succeeded in forgetting—

A tiny red star appeared on the horizon.

Robinson gazed absently at it for a while before he noticed it was steadily growing larger, blinked at it for a moment more before he figured out what it was and the bottom dropped out of his stomach.

He cursed, soft and scared. The gears screamed, the car lurched, slowed. He pumped the brakes to cut his speed still more. A spotlight blinked on just under the red star, turned the night white, blinded him. He whispered an obscenity, feeling his stomach flatten and his thighs tighten in fear.

Robinson cut the engine and let the car roll slowly to a stop. The spotlight followed him, keeping its beam focused on his windshield. He squinted against the glare, blinking. His eyes watered, blurred, and the spotlight blossomed into a Star of David, radiating white lances of light. Robinson winced and looked down, trying to blink his eyes back into focus, not daring to raise a hand. The car sighed to a stop.

He sat motionless, hands locked on the wheel, listening to the shrill hissing and metallic clicks as his engine cooled. There was the sound of a car door slamming somewhere, an unintelligible shouted order, a brief reply. Robinson squinted up sideways, trying to see around the miniature nova that was the spotlight. Feet crunched through gravel. A figure approached the car, becoming a burly, indistinct silhouette in front of the windshield, a blob of dough in roughly human shape. Something glinted, a shaft of starlight twisting in the doughy hands, trying to escape. Robinson felt the pressure of eyes. He sat very still, blinking. . . .

The dough-figure grunted and half-turned back toward the spotlight, its outlines tumbling and bulging. "Okay," it shouted in a dough-voice. A clang, and the spotlight dulled to a quarter of its former intensity, becoming a glazed orange eye. Detail and color washed back into the world, dappled by a dancing overlay of blue-white afterimages. The dough-figure resolved itself into a middle-aged police sergeant, dumpy, unshaven, graying. He held a heavy-gauge shotgun in his hands, and highlights blinked off and on along the barrel, making the blued steel seem to ripple. The muzzle was pointed loosely in the direction of Robinson's throat.

Robinson risked a sly glance around, not moving his head. The red star was the slowly pulsing crashlight on the roof of a big police prowlcar parked across the road. A younger policeman (still rookie enough to care; spit-polished boots; see the light shimmer from the ebony toes) stood by the smoldering spotlight that was mounted near the junction of windshield and hood. He was trying to look grim and implacable, the big regulation revolver awkward in his hand.

Motion on the far side of the road. Robinson swiveled his eyes up, squinted, and then bit the inside of his lip. A mud-caked MARC jeep was parked halfway up the grassy embankment. There were three men in it. As he watched, the tall man in the passenger's seat said something to the driver, swung his legs over the side and slid down the embankment on his heels in a tiny avalanche of dirt and gravel. The driver slipped his hands inside his field jacket for warmth and propped his elbows against the steering wheel, eyes slitted and bored. The third man, a grimy corporal, was sitting in the back of the jeep, manning a .50 caliber machinegun bolted to the vehicle. The corporal grinned at Robinson down the machinegun barrel, his hands fidgeting on the triggers.

The tall man emerged slowly from the shadow of the road shoulder, walked past the nervous rookie without looking at him and entered the pool of light. As he walked toward Robinson's car, he slowly metamorphosed from a tall shadow into a MARC lieutenant in a glistening weatherproofed parka, hood thrown back. A brown leather patch on his shoulder read *MOVEMENT AND REGIONAL CONTROL* in frayed red capitals. He held a submachine gun slung under one arm.

The police sergeant glanced back as the lieutenant drew even with the hood. The muzzle of the shotgun didn't waver from Robinson's chest. "Looks okay," he said. The lieutenant grunted, passed behind the sergeant, came up to the window on the driver's side. He looked at Robinson for a second, expressionless, then unslung his submachine gun and held it in the crook of his right arm. His other hand reached out slowly and he tapped once on the window.

Robinson rolled the window down. The lieutenant

peered in at him, pale blue eyes that were like windows opening on nothing. Robinson glanced once down the small, cramped muzzle of the machinegun, looked back up at the lieutenant's thin, pinched lips, white, no blood in them. Robinson felt the flesh of his stomach crawl, the thick hair on his arms and legs stir and bristle painfully against his clothing. "Let me see your card," the lieutenant said. His voice was clipped, precise. Slowly, slowly, Robinson slid his hand inside his rumpled sports jacket, carefully withdrew it and handed his identification and travel control visa to the lieutenant. The lieutenant took the papers, stepped back and examined them with one hand, holding the submachine gun trained on Robinson with the other. The pinched mouth of the automatic weapon hung only a few inches away, bobbing slightly, tracing a quarter-inch circle on Robinson's chest.

Robinson worked his dry tongue against his lips and tried unsuccessfully to swallow. He looked from the coolly appraising eyes of the lieutenant to the tired frown of the sergeant, to the nervously belligerent glances of the rookie, to the indifferent stare of the jeep driver, to the hooded eyes of the corporal behind the .50 caliber. They were all looking at him. He was the center of the universe. The pulsing crashlight threw long, tangled shadows through the woods, the shadows licking out and then quickly snapping back again, like a yo-yo. On the northern horizon, a smoldering red glow stained the clouds, flaring and dimming. That was Newark, burning.

The lieutenant stirred, impatiently trying to flip a tacky page of the travel visa with his free hand. He muttered, planted a boot on the side of Robinson's hood, braced the submachine gun on his knee and used his teeth to help him open the sticky page. Robinson caught the rookie staring at the lieutenant's big battered combat boot with prim disapproval, and started to laugh in spite of the hovering machinegun. He choked it down because it had a ragged hollow sound even inside his throat; it was hysterical laughter, and it filled his chest like crinkly dead leaves. The lieutenant removed his foot and straightened up again. The boot made a dry sucking sound as it was pulled free, and left a blurred muddy footprint on the side of the hood. You son of a bitch, Robinson thought, suddenly and irrationally furious.

A nightbird wailed somewhere among the trees. A chilly wind came up, spattering the cars with gravel, a hollow metallic wind full of cinders and deserted trainyards. The wind flapped the pages of the travel visa, rumpled the fur on the lieutenant's parka hood, plucked futilely at his close-cropped hair. The lieutenant continued to read with deliberation, holding the rippling pages down with his thumb. You son of a bitch, Robinson raged silently, choked with fear and anger. You sadistic bastard. The long silence had become heavy as rock. The crashlight flicked its red shadows across the lieutenant's face, turning his eyes into shallow pools of blood and draining them, turning his cheeks into gaping deathhead sockets, filling them out again. He flipped pages mechanically, expressionless.

He suddenly snapped the visa closed.

Robinson jerked. The lieutenant stared at him for a smothering heartbeat, then handed the visa back. Robinson took it, trying not to snatch. "Why're you traveling," the lieutenant said quietly. The words tumbled clumsily out: business trip—no planes—had to get back—wife— The lieutenant listened blankly, then turned and gestured to the rookie.

The rookie rushed forward, hurriedly checked the back seat, the trunk. Robinson heard him breathing and rustling in the back seat, the car swaying slightly as he moved. Robinson looked straight ahead and said nothing. The lieutenant was silent, holding his automatic weapon loosely in both hands. The old police sergeant fidgeted restlessly. "Nothing, sir," the rookie said, climbing out. The lieutenant nodded, and the rookie returned smartly to the prowlcar. "Sounds okay, sir," the sergeant said, shifting his weight with doughy impatience from one sore foot to another. He looked tired, and there was a network of blue veins on the side of his graying head. The lieutenant considered, then nodded reluctantly. "Uh-huh," he said, slowly, then speeded up, became brisker, turned a tight parody of a smile on Robinson. "Sure. All right, mister, I guess you can go."

Another pair of headlights bobbed over the close horizon behind.

The lieutenant's smile dissolved. "Okay, mister," he said, "you stay put. Don't you do *anything*. Sarge, keep an eye on him." He turned, strode toward the prowlcar. The headlights grew larger, bobbing. Robinson heard the lieutenant mutter something and the spotlight flicked on to full intensity again. This time it was aimed away from him, and he saw the beam stab out through the night, a solid column of light, and catch something, pinning it like a captured moth.

It was a big Volkswagen Microbus. Under the spotlight's eye it looked grainy and unreal, a photograph with too much contrast.

The Microbus slowed, pulled to a stop near the shoulder across the road from Robinson. He could see two people in the front seat, squinting and holding up their hands against the glare. The lieutenant strolled over, investigated them from a few feet away, and then waved his hand. The spotlight clanged down to quarter intensity.

In the diffused orange glow, Robinson could just make out the bus's passengers: a tall man in a black turtleneck and a Nordic young woman with shoulder-length blond hair, wearing an orange shift. The lieutenant circled to the driver's side and tapped on the window. Robinson could see the lieutenant's mouth move, hardly opening, neat and precise. The thin man handed his papers over stolidly. The lieutenant began to examine them, flipping slowly through the pages.

Robinson shifted impatiently. He could feel the sweat slowly drying on his body, sticky and trickling under his arms, in the hollows of his knees, his crotch. His clothes stuck to his flesh.

The lieutenant gestured for the rookie to come over, paced backward until he was standing near the hood. The rookie trotted across the road, walked toward the rear of the vehicle and started to open the sliding side door. Robinson caught the quick nervous flicker of the thin man's tongue against his teeth. The woman was looking calmly straight ahead. The thin man said something in a low joking tone to the lieutenant. The rookie slid the side door open, started to climb inside—

Something moved in the space between the back seat and the closed tailgate, throwing off a thick army blanket, rolling to its knees, scrambling up. Robinson caught a glimpse of dark skin, eyes startlingly white by contrast, nostrils flared in terror. The rookie staggered backward, mouth gaping, revolver swinging aimlessly. The thin man grimaced—a rictus, neck cording, lips riding back from teeth. He tried to slam the bus into gear.

A lance of fire split the darkness, the submachine gun yammering, bucking in the lieutenant's hands. He swept the weapon steadily back and forth, expressionless. The bus's windshield exploded. The man and woman jerked, bounced, bodies dancing grotesquely. The lieutenant continued to fire. The thin man arched backward, bending, bending, bending impossibly, face locked in rictus, and then slumped forward over the steering wheel. The woman was flung sideways against the car door. It gave and she toppled out backward, long hair floating in a tangled cloud, one hand flung out over her head, fingers wide, reaching, stretching out for something. She hit the pavement and lay half in, half out of the bus. Her long fingers twitched, closed, opened.

The dark figure at the back of the bus tore frantically at the tailgate, threw it open, scrambled out, tried to jump for the shoulder. From the embankment the big .50 caliber opened up, blew the back of the bus's roof off. Metal screamed and smoked. The black man was caught as he balanced on the tailgate, one foot lifted. The .50 pounded harshly, blew him almost in half, kicked his limp body six or seven feet down the road. The .50 continued to fire, kicking up geysers of asphalt. The rookie, screaming in inhuman excitement, was firing his revolver at the fallen figure.

The lieutenant waved his arm and everything stopped.

There was no noise or motion.

Echoes rolled slowly away.

Smoke dribbled from the muzzle of the lieutenant's submachine gun.

In the unbelievable silence, you could hear somebody sobbing.

Robinson realized it was himself, ground his teeth together and tensed his stomach muscles to fight the vomit sloshing in his throat. His fingers ached where he had locked them around the steering wheel; he could not get them loose. The wind streamed against his wet flesh.

The lieutenant walked around to the driver's side of the Microbus, opened the door. He grabbed the man by the hair, yanked his head up. The gaunt face was relaxed, unlined, almost ascetically peaceful. The lieutenant let go, and the bloody head dropped.

Slowly the lieutenant walked back around the hood, paused, looked down at the woman for a second. She was sprawled half out of the bus, face up, one arm behind her. Her eyes were still open and staring. Her face was untouched; her body was a slowly spreading red horror from throat to crotch. The lieutenant watched her, gently stroking the machinegun barrel, face like polished marble. The bitter wind flapped her dress, bunched it around her waist. The lieutenant shrugged, moved to the rear of the vehicle. He nudged the black man sprawled across the center line, then turned away and walked briskly to the prowlcar. Above, the corporal began to reload his smoking .50. The driver went back to sleep.

The rookie remained standing by the side of the bus, excitement gone, face ashen and sick, looking at the blue smoke that curled from his revolver, staring at his spit-polished boots, red clotting over ebony. The flashing crashlight turned the dead white faces red, flooding them with a mimic flush of life, draining it away.

The old sergeant turned toward Robinson, grimly clutching the shotgun, looking suddenly twenty years older. "You'd better get out of here now, son," he said gently. He shifted the shotgun, looked toward the smoldering bus, looked quickly away, looked back. The network of blue veins throbbed. He shook his head slowly, limped away hunch-shouldered, started the prowlcar and backed it off the road.

The lieutenant came up as Robinson was fumbling for the ignition switch. "Get the lead out of your ass," the lieutenant said, and snapped a fresh clip into his submachine gun.

A Special Kind of Morning

> *The Doomsday Machine is the human race.*
> *—grafitto in New York subway, 79th St. station*

DID Y'EVER HEAR the one about the old man and the sea?

Halt a minute, lordling; stop and listen. It's a fine story, full of balance and point and social pith; short and direct. It's not mine. Mine are long and rambling and parenthetical and they corrode the moral fiber right out of a man. Come to think, I won't tell you that one after all. A man of my age has a right to prefer his own material, and let the critics be damned. I've a prejudice now for webs of my own weaving.

Sit down, sit down: butt against pavement, yes; it's been done before. Everything has, near about. Now that's not an expression of your black pessimism, or your futility, or what have you. Pessimism's just the common-sense knowledge that there's more ways for something to go wrong than for it to go right, from our point of view anyway—which is not necessarily that of the management, or of the mechanism, if you prefer your cosmos depersonalized. As for futility, everybody dies the true death eventually; even though executives may dodge it for a few hundred years, the hole gets them all in the end, and I imagine that's futility enough for a start. The philosophical man accepts both as constants and then doesn't let them bother him any. Sit down, damn it; don't pretend you've important business to be about. Young devil, you are in the enviable position of having absolutely nothing to do because it's going to take you a while to recover from what you've just done.

There. That's better. Comfortable? You don't look it; you look like you've just sat in a puddle of piss and're wondering what the socially appropriate reaction is. Hypocrisy's an art, boy; you'll improve with age. Now you're bemused, lordling, that you let an old soak chivy you around, and now he's making fun of you. Well, the expression on your face is worth a chuckle; if you could see it you'd laugh yourself. You will see it years from now too, on some other young man's face—that's the only kind of mirror that ever shows it clear. And *you'll* be an old soak by that time, and you'll laugh and insult the young buck's dignity, but you'll be laughing more at the reflection of the man you used to be than at that particular stud himself. And you'll probably have to tell the buck just what I've told you to cool him down, and there's a laugh in that too; listen for the echo of a million and one laughs behind you. I hear a million now.

How do I get away with such insolence? What've I got to lose, for one thing. That gives you a certain perspective. And I'm socially instructive in spite of myself—I'm valuable as an object lesson. For that matter, why is an arrogant young aristo like you sitting there and putting up with my guff? Don't even bother to answer; I knew the minute you came whistling down the street, full of steam and strut. Nobody gets up this early in the morning any more, unless they're old as I am and begrudge sleep's dry-run of death—or unless they've never been to bed in the first place. The world's your friend this morning, a toy for you to play with and examine and stuff in your mouth to taste, and you're letting your benevolence slop over onto the old degenerate you've met on the street. You're even happy enough to listen, though you're being quizzical about it, and you're sitting over there feeling benignly superior. And I'm sitting over *here* feeling benignly superior. A nice arrangement, and everyone content. Well, then, mornings make you feel that way. Especially if you're fresh from a night at the Towers, the musk of Lady Ni still warm on your flesh.

A blush—my buck, you *are* new-hatched. How did I know? Boy, you'd be surprised what I know; I'm occasionally startled myself, and I've been working longer to get it catalogued. Besides, hindsight is a comfortable substitute for omnipotence. And I'm not blind yet. You have the unmistakable look of a cub who's just found out he can do something else with it besides piss. An incredible revelation, as I recall. The blazing significance of it will wear a little with the years, though not all that much, I suppose; until you get down to the brink of the Ultimate Cold, when you stop worrying about the identity of warmth, or demanding that it pay toll in pleasure. Any hand of clay, long's the blood still runs the tiny degree that's just enough for difference. Warmth's the only definition between you and graveyard dirt. But morning's not for graveyards, though it works the other way. Did y'know they also used to use that to make babies? 'S'fact, though few know it now. It's a versatile beast. Oh *come*—buck, cub, young cocksman—stop being so damn surprised. People ate, slept, and fornicated before you were born, some of them anyway, and a few will probably even find the courage to keep on at it after you die. You don't have to keep it secret; the thing's been circulated in this region once or twice before. You weren't the first to learn how to make the beast do its trick, though I *know* you don't believe that. *I* don't believe it concerning myself, and I've had a long time to learn.

You make me think, sitting there innocent as an egg and twice as vulnerable; yes, you are definitely about to make me think, and I believe I'll have to think of some things I always regret having thought about, just to keep me from growing maudlin. Damn it, boy, you *do* make me think. Life's strange—wet-eared as you are, you've probably had that thought a dozen times already, probably had it this morning as you tumbled out of your fragrant bed to meet the rim of the sun; well, I've four times your age, and a ream more experience, and I still can't think of anything better to sum up the world: life's strange. 'S been said, yes. But *think*, boy, how strange: the two of us talking, you coming, me going; me knowing where you've got to go, you suspecting where I've been, and the same destination for both. O strange, very strange. Damn it, you're a deader already if you can't see the strangeness of that, if you can't sniff the poetry; it reeks of it, as of blood. And I've smelt blood, buck. It has a very distinct odor; you know it when you smell it. You're bound for blood; for blood and passion and high deeds and all the rest of the business, and maybe for a little understanding if you're lucky and have eyes to see. Me, I'm bound for nothing, literally. I've come to rest here in Kos, and while the Red Lady spins her web of colors across the sky I sit and weave my own webs of words and dreams and other spider stuff—

What? Yes, I do talk too much; old men like to babble, and philosophy's a cushion for old bones. But it's my profession now, isn't it, and I've promised you a story. What happened to my leg? That's a bloody story, but I said you're bound for blood; I know the mark. I'll tell it to you then: perhaps it'll help you to understand when you reach the narrow place, perhaps it'll even help you to think, although that's a horrible weight to wish on any man. It's customary to notarize my card before I start, keep you from running off at the end without paying. Thank you, young sir. Beware of some of these beggars, buck; they have a credit tally at Central greater than either of us will ever run up. They turn a tidy profit out of poverty. I'm an honest pauper, more's the pity, exist mostly on the subsidy, if you call that existing—Yes, I know. The leg.

We'll have to go back to the Realignment for that, more than half a century ago, and half a sector away, at World. This was before World was a member of the Commonwealth. In fact, that's what the Realignment was about, the old Combine overthrown by the Quaestors, who then opted for amalgamation and forced World into the Commonwealth. That's where and when the story starts.

Start it with waiting.

A lot of things start like that, waiting. And when the thing you're waiting for is probable death, and you're lying there loving life and suddenly noticing how pretty everything is and listening to the flint hooves of darkness click closer, feeling the iron-shod boots strike relentless sparks from the surface of your mind, knowing that death is about to fall out of the sky and that there's no way to twist out from under—then, waiting can take time. Minutes become hours, hours become unthinkable horrors. Add enough horrors together, total the scaly snouts, and you've got a day and a half I once spent laying up in a mountain valley in the Blackfriars on World, almost the last day I ever spent anywhere.

This was just a few hours after D'kotta. Everything was a mess, nobody really knew what was happening, everybody's communication lines cut. I was just a buck myself then, working with the Quaestors in the field, a hunted criminal. Nobody knew what the Combine would do next, we didn't know what *we'd* do next, groups surging wildly from one place to another at random, panic and riots all over the planet, even in the Controlled Environments.

And D'kotta-on-the-Blackfriars was a seventy-mile swath of smoking insanity, capped by boiling umbrellas of smoke that eddied ashes from the ground to the stratosphere and back. At night it pulsed with molten scum, ugly as a lanced blister, lighting up the cloud cover across the entire horizon, visible for hundreds of miles. It was this ugly glow that finally panicked even the zombies in the Environments, probably the first strong emotion in their lives.

It'd been hard to sum up the effects of the battle. We thought that we had the edge, that the Combine was close to breaking, but nobody knew for sure. If they weren't as close to folding as we thought, then we were probably finished. The Quaestors had exhausted most of their

210

hoarded resources at D'kotta, and we certainly couldn't hit the Combine any harder. If they could shrug off the blow then they could wear us down.

Personally, I didn't see how anything could shrug *that* off. I'd watched it all and it'd shaken me considerably. There's an old-time expression, "put the fear of God into him." That's what D'kotta had done for me. There wasn't any God any more, but I'd seen fire vomit from the heavens and the earth ripped wide for rape, and it'd been an impressive enough surrogate. Few people ever realized how close the Combine and the Quaestors had come to destroying World between them, there at D'kotta.

We'd crouched that night—the team and I—on the high stone ramparts of the tallest of the Blackfriars, hopefully far away from anything that could fall on us. There were twenty miles of low, gnarly foothills between us and the rolling savannahland where the city of D'kotta had been minutes before, but the ground under our bellies heaved and quivered like a sick animal, and the rock was hot to the touch: feverish.

We could've gotten farther away, should have gotten farther away, but we had to watch. That'd been decided without anyone saying a word, without any question about it. It was impossible *not* to watch. It never even occurred to any of us to take another safer course of action. When reality is being turned inside out like a dirty sock, you watch, or you are less than human. So we watched it all from beginning to end: two hours that became a single second lasting for eons. Like a still photograph of time twisted into a scream—the scream reverberating on forever and yet taking no duration at all to experience.

We didn't talk. We *couldn't* talk—the molecules of the air itself shrieked too loudly, and the deep roar of explosions was a continual drumroll—but we wouldn't have talked even if we'd been able. You don't speak in the presence of an angry God. Sometimes we'd look briefly at each other. Our faces were all nearly identical: ashen, waxy, eyes of glass, blank, and lost as pale driftwood stranded on a beach by the tide. We'd been driven through

211

the gamut of expressions into *extremis*—rictus: faces so contorted and strained they ached—and beyond to the quietus of shock: muscles too slack and flaccid to respond any more. We'd only look at each other for a second, hardly focusing, almost not aware of what we were seeing, and then our eyes would be dragged back as if by magnetism to the Fire.

At the beginning we'd clutched each other, but as the battle progressed we slowly drew apart, huddling into individual agony; the thing so big that human warmth meant nothing, so frightening that the instinct to gather together for protection was reversed, and the presence of others only intensified the realization of how ultimately naked you were. Earlier we'd set up a scattershield to filter the worst of the hard radiation—the gamma and intense infrared and ultraviolet—blunt some of the heat and shock and noise. We thought we had a fair chance of surviving, then, but we couldn't have run anyway. We were fixed by the beauty of horror/horror of beauty, surely as if by a spike driven through our backbones into the rock.

And away over the foothills, God danced in anger, and his feet struck the ground to ash.

What was it like?

Kos still has oceans and storms. Did y'ever watch the sea lashed by high winds? The storm boils the water into froth, whips it white, until it becomes an ocean of ragged lace to the horizon, whirlpools of milk, not a fleck of blue left alive. The land looked like this at D'kotta. The hills *moved*. The Quaestors had a discontinuity projector there, and under its lash the ground stirred like sluggish batter under a baker's spoon; stirred, shuddered, groaned, cracked, broke: acres heaved themselves into new mountains, other acres collapsed into canyons.

Imagine a giant asleep just under the surface of the earth, overgrown by fields, dreaming dreams of rock and crystal. Imagine him moving restlessly, the long rhythm of his dreams touched by nightmare, tossing, moaning, tremors signaling unease in waves up and down his miles-long frame. Imagine him catapulted into waking terror, lurching suddenly to his knees with the bawling roar of ten million burning calves: a steaming claw of rock and black earth raking for the sky. Now, in a wink, imagine the adjacent land hurtling downward, sinking like a rock in a pond, opening a womb a thousand feet wide, swallowing everything and grinding it to powder. Then, almost too quick to see, imagine the mountain and the crater switching, the mountain collapsing all at once and washing the feet of the older Blackfriars with a tidal wave of earth, then tumbling down to make a pit; at the same time the sinking earth at the bottom of the other crater reversing itself and erupting upward into a quaking fist of rubble. Then they switch again, and keep switching. Like watching the same filmclip continuously run forward and backward. Now multiply that by a million and spread it out so that all you can see to the horizon is a stew of humping rock. D'y'visualize it? Not a tenth of it.

Dervishes of fire stalked the chaos, melting into each other, whirlpooling. Occasionally a tactical-nuclear explosion would punch a hole in the night, a brief intense flare that would be swallowed like a candle in a murky snowstorm. Once a tacnuke detonation coincided with the upthrusting of a rubble mountain, with an effect like that of a firecracker exploding inside a swinging sack of grain.

The city itself was gone; we could no longer see a trace of anything man-made, only the stone maelstrom. The river Delva had also vanished, flash-boiled to steam; for a while we could see the gorge of its dry bed stitching across the plain, but then the ground heaved up and obliterated it.

It was unbelievable that anything could be left alive down there. Very little was. Only the remainder of the heavy weapons sections on both sides continued to survive, invisible to us in the confusion. Still protected by powerful phasewalls and scattershields, they pounded blindly at each other—the Combine somewhat ineffectively with biodeths and tacnukes, the Quaestors responding by stepping up the discontinuity projector. There was only one, in the command module—the

213

Quaestor technicians were praying it wouldn't be wiped out by a random strike—and it was a terraforming device and not actually a "weapon" at all, but the Combine had been completely unprepared for it, and were suffering horribly as a result.

Everything began to flicker, random swatches of savannahland shimmering and blurring, phasing in and out of focus in a jerky, mismatched manner: that filmstrip run through a spastic projector. At first we thought it must be heat eddies caused by the fires, but then the flickering increased drastically in frequency and tempo, speeding up until it was impossible to keep anything in focus even for a second, turning the wide veldt into a mad kaleidoscope of writhing, interchanging shapes and color-patterns from one horizon to the other. It was impossible to watch it for long. It hurt the eyes and filled us with an oily, inexplicable panic that we were never able to verbalize. We looked away, filled with the musty surgings of vague fear.

We didn't know then that we were watching the first practical application of a process that'd long been suppressed by both the Combine and the Commonwealth, a process based on the starship dimensional "drive" (which isn't a "drive" at all, but the world's passed into the common press) that enabled a high-cycling discontinuity projector to throw time out of phase within a limited area, so that a spot *here* would be a couple of minutes ahead or behind a spot a few inches away, in continuity sequence. That explanation would give a psycho-physicist fits, since "time" is really nothing at all like the way we "experience" it, so the process "really" doesn't do what I've said it does—doing something *really* abstruse instead—but that's close enough to what it does on a practical level, 'cause even if the time distortion is an "illusionary effect"—like the sun seeming to rise and set— they still used it to kill people. So it threw time out of phase, and kept doing it, switching the dislocation at random: so that in any given square foot of land there might be four or five discrepancies in time sequence that kept interchanging. Like, *here* might be one minute "ahead" of the base "now," and then a second later (language breaks down hopelessly under this stuff; you need the math) *here* would be two minutes behind the now, then five minutes behind, then three ahead, and so on. And all the adjacent zones in that square foot are going through the same switching process at the same time (Goddamn this language!). The Combine's machinery tore itself to pieces. So did the people: some died of suffocation because of a five-minute discrepancy between an inhaled breath and oxygen received by the lungs, some drowned in their own blood.

It took about ten minutes, at least as far as we were concerned as unaffected observers. I had a psychophysicist tell me once that "it" had both continued to "happen" forever and had never "happened" at all, and that neither statement canceled out the validity of the other, that *each* statement in fact was both "applicable" and "non-applicable" to the same situation consecutively—and I did not understand. It took ten minutes.

At the end of that time, the world got very still.

We looked up. The land had stopped churning. A tiny star appeared amongst the rubble in the middle distance, small as a pinhead but incredibly bright and clear. It seemed to suck the night into it like a vortex, as if it were a pinprick through the worldstuff into a more intense reality, as if it were gathering a great breath for a shout.

We buried our heads in our arms as one, instinctively.

There was a very bright light, a light that we could feel through the tops of our heads, a light that left dazzling afterimages even through closed and shrouded lids. The mountain leaped under us, bounced us into the air again and again, battered us into near unconsciousness. We never even heard the roar.

After a while, things got quiet again, except for a continuous low rumbling. When we looked up, there were thick, sluggish tongues of molten magma oozing up in vast flows across the veldt, punctuated here and there by spectacular shower-fountains of vomited sparks.

Our scattershield had taken the brunt of the blast, borne it just long enough to save our lives, and then overloaded and burnt itself to scrap; one of the first times *that's* ever happened.

Nobody said anything. We didn't look at each other. We just lay there.

The chrono said an hour went by, but nobody was aware of it.

Finally, a couple of us got up, in silence, and started to stumble aimlessly back and forth. One by one, the rest crawled to their feet. Still in silence, still trying not to look at each other, we automatically cleaned ourselves up. You hear someone say "it made me shit my pants," and you think it's an expression; not under the right stimuli. Automatically, we treated our bruises and lacerations, automatically we tidied the camp up, buried the ruined scatterfield generator. Automatically, we sat down again and stared numbly at the lightshow on the savannah.

Each of us knew the war was over—we knew it with the gut rather than the head. It was an emotional reaction, but very calm, very resigned, very passive. It was a thing too big for questioning; it became a self-evident fact. After D'kotta there could be nothing else. Period. The war was over.

We were almost right. But not quite.

In another hour or so a man from field HQ came up over the mountain shoulder in a stolen vacform and landed in camp. The man switched off the vac, jumped down, took two steps toward the parapet overlooking hell, stopped. We saw his stomach muscles jump, tighten. He took a stumbling half-step back, then stopped again. His hand went up to shield his throat, dropped, hesitated, went back up. We said nothing. The HQ directing the D'kotta campaign had been sensibly located behind the Blackfriars: they had been shielded by the mountainchain and had seen nothing but glare against the cloud cover. This was his first look at the city; at where the city had been. I watched the muscles play in his back, saw his shoulders hunch as if under an upraised fist. A good many of the Quaestor men involved in planning the D'kotta operation committed suicide immediately after the

216

Realignment; a good many didn't. I don't know what category this one belonged in.

The liaison man finally turned his head, dragged himself away. His movements were jerky, and his face was an odd color, but he was under control. He pulled Heynith, our team leader, aside. They talked for a half hour. The liaison man showed Heynith a map, scribbled on a pad for Heynith to see, gave Heynith some papers. Heynith nodded occasionally. The liaison man said goodby, half-ran to his vacform. The vac lifted with an erratic surge, steadied, then disappeared in a long arc over the gnarled backs of the Blackfriars. Heynith stood in the dirtswirl kicked up by the backwash and watched impassively.

It got quiet again, but it was a little more apprehensive.

Heynith came over, studied us for a while, then told us to get ready to move out. We stared at him. He repeated it in a quiet, firm voice; unendurably patient. Hush for a second, then somebody groaned, somebody else cursed, and the spell of D'kotta was partially broken, for the moment. We awoke enough to ready our gear; there was even a little talking, though not much.

Heynith appeared at our head and led us out in a loose travel formation, diagonally across the face of the slope, then up toward the shoulder. We reached the notch we'd found earlier and started down the other side.

Everyone wanted to look back at D'kotta. No one did.

Somehow, it was still night.

We never talked much on the march, of course, but tonight the silence was spooky: you could hear boots crunch on stone, the slight rasp of breath, the muted jangle of knives occasionally bumping against thighs. You could hear our fear; you could smell it, could see it.

We could touch it, we could taste it.

I was a member of something so old that they even had to dig up the name for it when they were rooting through the rubble of ancient history, looking for concepts to use against the Combine: a "commando team." Don't ask me what it means, but that's what it's called. Come to think, I

217

know what it means in terms of flesh: it means ugly. Long ugly days and nights that come back in your sleep even uglier, so that you don't want to think about it at all because it squeezes your eyeballs like a vise. Cold and dark and wet, with sudden death looming up out of nothing at any time and jarring you with mortality like a rubber glove full of ice water slapped across your face. Living jittery high all the time, so that everything gets so real that it looks fake. You live in an anticipation that's pain, like straddling a fence with a knifeblade for a top rung, waiting for something to come along in the dark and push you off. You get so you like it. The pain's so consistent that you forget it's there, you forget there ever was a time when you didn't have it, and you live on the adrenalin.

We liked it. We were dedicated. We *hated*. It gave us something to do with our hate, something tangible we could see. And nobody'd done it but us for hundreds of years; there was an exultation to that. The Scholars and Antiquarians who'd started the Quaestor movement— left fullsentient and relatively unwatched so they could better piece together the muddle of prehistory from generations of inherited archives—they'd been smart. They knew their only hope of baffling the Combine was to hit them with radical concepts and tactics, things they didn't have instructions for handling, things out of the Combine's experience. So they scooped concepts out of prehistory, as far back as the archives go, even finding *written* records somewhere and having to figure out how to use them.

Out of one of these things, they got the idea of "guerrilla" war. No, I don't know what that means either, but what it *means* is playing the game by your own rules instead of the enemy's. Oh, you let the enemy keep playing by *his* rules, see, but you play by your own. Gives you a wider range of moves. You *do* things. I mean, *ridiculous* things, but so ancient they don't have any defense against it because they never thought they'd have to defend against *that*. Most of the time they never even knew *that* existed.

218

Like, we used to run around with these projectile weapons they'd copied from old plans and mass-produced in the autfacs on the sly by stealing computer time. The things worked by a chemical reaction inside the mechanism that would spit these tiny missiles out at a high velocity. The missile would hit you so hard it would actually lodge itself in your body, puncture internal organs, kill you. I know it sounds like an absurd concept, but there were advantages.

Don't forget how tightly controlled a society the Combine's was; even worse than the Commonwealth in its own way. We couldn't just steal energy weapons or biodeths and use them, because all those things operated on broadcast power from the Combine, and as soon as one was reported missing the Combine would just cut the relay for that particular code. We couldn't make them ourselves because unless you used the Combine's broadcast power you'd need a ton of generator equipment with each weapon to provide enough energy to operate it, and we didn't have the technology to miniaturize that much machinery. (Later some genius figured out a way to make, say, a functioning biodeth with everything but the energy source and then cut into and tap Combine broadcast power without showing up on the coding board, but that was toward the end anyway, and most of them were stockpiled for the shock troops at D'kotta.) At least the "guns" worked. And there were even unexpected advantages. We found that tanglefields, scattershields, phasewalls, personal warders, all the usual defenses, were unable to stop the "bullets" (the little missiles fired by the "guns")—they were just too sophisticated to stop anything as crude as a lump of metal moving at relatively sluggish ballistic speeds. Same with "bombs" and "grenades"—devices designed to have a chemical reaction violent enough to kill in an enclosed place. And the list went on and on. The Combine thought we couldn't move around because all vehicles were coded and worked on broadcast power. Did you ever hear of "bicycles"? They're devices for translating mechanical energy into motion, they ride on wheels that you actually make revolve with

219

physical labor. And the bicycles didn't have enough metal/mass to trigger sentryfields or show up on sweep probes, so we could go undetected to places they thought nobody could reach. Communicate? We used mirrors to flash messages, used puffs of smoke as code, had people actually carry messages from one place to another.

More important, we personalized war. That was the most radical thing, that was the thing that turned us from kids running around and having fun breaking things into men with bitter faces, that was the thing that took the heart out of the Combine more than anything else. That's why people still talk about the Realignment with horror today, even after all these years, especially in the Commonwealth.

We killed people. We did it, ourselves. We walked up and stabbed them. I mentioned a knife before, boy, and I knew you didn't know what it was; you bluff well for a kid—that's the way to a reputation for wisdom: look sage and always keep your mouth shut about your ignorance. Well, a knife is a tapering piece of metal with a handle, sharpened on the sides and very sharp at the tapered end, sharp enough so that when you strike someone with it the metal goes right into their flesh, cuts them, rips them open, *kills* them, and there is blood on your hands which feels wet and sticky and is hard to wash off because it dries and sticks to the little hairs on the backs of your wrists. We learned how to hit people hard enough to kill them, snap the bones inside the skin like dry sticks inside oiled cloth. We did. We strangled them with lengths of wire. You're shocked. So was the Combine. They had grown used to killing at a great distance, the push of a button, the flick of a switch, using vast, clean, impersonal forces to do their annihilation. *We* killed people. We killed *people*— not statistics and abstractions. We heard their screams, we saw their faces, we smelled their blood, and their vomit and shit and urine when their systems let go after death. You have to be crazy to do things like that. We were crazy. We were a good team.

There were twelve of us in the group, although we mostly worked in sections of four. I was in the team leader's section, and it had been my family for more than two years:

Heynith, stocky, balding, leatherfaced; a hard, fair man; brilliant organizer.

Ren, impassive, withdrawn, taciturn, frighteningly competent, of a strange humor.

Goth, young, tireless, bullheaded, given to sudden enthusiasms and depressions; he'd only been with us for about four months, a replacement for Mason, who had been killed while trying to escape from a raid on Cape Itica.

And me.

We were all warped men, emotional cripples one way or the other.

We were all crazy.

The Combine could never understand that kind of craziness, in spite of the millions of people they'd killed or shriveled impersonally over the years. They were afraid of that craziness, they were baffled by it, never could plan to counter it or take it into account. They couldn't really believe it.

That's how we'd taken the Blackfriars Transmitter, hours before D'kotta. It had been impregnable—wrapped in layer after layer of defense fields against missile attack, attack by chemical or biological agents, transmitted energy, almost anything. We'd walked in. They'd never imagined anyone would do that, that it was even possible to attack that way, so there was no defense against it. The guardsystems were designed to meet more esoteric threats. And even after ten years of slowly escalating guerrilla action, they still didn't *really* believe anyone would use his body to wage war. So we walked in. And killed everybody there. The staff was a sentient techclone of ten and an executive foreman. No nulls or zombies. The ten identical technicians milled in panic, the foreman stared at us in disbelief, and what I think was distaste that we'd gone so far outside the bounds of procedure. We killed them like you kill insects, not really thinking about it much, except for that part of you that always thinks about it, that records it and replays it while you sleep.

221

Then we blew up the transmitter with chemical explosives. Then, as the flames leaped up and ate holes in the night, we'd gotten on our bicycles and rode like hell toward the Blackfriars, the mountains hunching and looming ahead, as jagged as black snaggle-teeth against the industrial glare of the sky. A tanglefield had snatched at us for a second, but then we were gone.

That's all that I personally had to do with the "historic" Battle of D'kotta. It was enough. We'd paved the way for the whole encounter. Without the Transmitter's energy, weapons, and transportation systems—including lift-shafts, slidewalks, irisdoors, and windows, heating, lighting, waste disposal—were inoperable; D'kotta was immobilized. Without the station's broadcast matter, thousands of buildings, industrial complexes, roadways, and homes had collapsed into chaos, literally collapsed. More important, without broadcast nourishment, D'kotta's four major Cerebrums—handling an incredible complexity of military/industrial/administrative tasks—were knocked out of operation, along with a number of smaller Cerebrums—the synapses need constant nourishment to function, and so do the sophont ganglion units, along with the constant flow of the psychocybernetic current to keep them from going mad from sensory deprivation, and even the nulls would soon grow intractable as hunger stung them almost to self-awareness, finally to die after a few days. Any number of the lowest-ranking sentient clones—all those without stomachs or digestive systems; mostly in the military and industrial castes—would find themselves in the same position as the nulls; without broadcast nourishment they would die within days. And without catarcs in operation to duplicate the function of atrophied intestines, the build-up of body wastes would poison them anyway, even if they could somehow get nourishment. The independent food dispensers for the smaller percentage of fullsentients and higher clones simply could not increase their output enough to feed that many people, even if converted to intravenous systems. To say nothing of the zombies in the Environments scattered throughout the city.

There were backup failsafe systems, of course, but they hadn't been used in centuries, the majority of them had fallen into disrepair and didn't work, and other Quaestor teams made sure the rest of them wouldn't work either.

Before a shot had been fired, D'kotta was already a major disaster.

The Combine had reacted as we'd hoped, as they'd been additionally prompted to react by intelligence reports of Quaestor massings in strength around D'kotta that it'd taken weeks to leak to the Combine from unimpeachable sources. The Combine was pouring forces into D'kotta within hours, nearly the full strength of the traditional military caste and a large percentage of the militia they'd cobbled together out of industrial clones when the Quaestors had begun to get seriously troublesome, plus a major portion of their heavy armament. They had hoped to surprise the Quaestors, catch them between the city and the inaccessible portion of the Blackfriars, quarter the area with so much strength it'd be impossible to dodge them, run the Quaestors down, annihilate them, break the back of the movement.

It had worked the other way around.

For years the Quaestors had stung and run, always retreating when the Combine advanced, never meeting them in conventional battle, never hitting them with anything really heavy. Then, when the Combine had risked practically all of its military resources on one gigantic effort calculated to be effective against the usual Quaestor behavior, we had suddenly switched tactics. The Quaestors had waited to meet the Combine's advance and had hit the Combine forces with everything they'd been able to save, steal, hoard, and buy clandestinely from sympathizers in the Commonwealth in over fifteen years of conspiracy and campaign aimed at this moment.

Within an hour of the first tacnuke exchange, the city had ceased to exist, everything leveled except two of the Cerebrums and the Escridel Creche. Then the Quaestors activated their terraforming devices, which I believe they bought from a firm here on Kos, as a matter of fact. This was completely insane—terraforming systems used indiscriminately can destroy entire planets—but it was the insanity of desperation, and they did it anyway. Within a half hour, the remaining Combine Heavy Armaments battalions and the two Cerebrums ceased to exist. A few minutes later, the supposedly invulnerable Escridel Creche ceased to exist, the first time in history a creche had ever been destroyed. Then, as the cycling energies got out of hand and filterfeedback built to a climax, everything on the veldt ceased to exist.

The carnage had been inconceivable.

Take the vast population of D'kotta as a base, the second largest city on World, one of the biggest even in this sector of the Commonwealth. The subfleets had been in, bringing the betja harvest and other goods up the Delva; river traffic was always heaviest at that time of year. The mines and factories had been in full swing, and the giant sprawl of the Westernese Shipyards and Engine Works. Add the swarming inhabitants of the six major Controlled Environments that circled the city. Add the city-within-a-city of Admin South, in charge of that hemisphere. Add the twenty generations of D'kotta Combine fullsentients whose discorporate ego-patterns had been preserved in the mountain of "indestructible" micromolecular circuitry called the Escridel Creche. (Those executives had died the irreversible true death, without hope of resurrection this time, even as disembodied intellects housed within artificial mind-environments: the records of their brain's unique pattern of electrical/ chemical/psychocybernetic rhythms and balances had been destroyed, and you can't rebuild consciousness from a fused puddle of slag. This hit the Combine where they lived, literally, and had more impact than anything else.) Add the entire strength of both opposing forces; all of our men—who suspected what would happen—had been suicide volunteers. Add all of the elements together.

The total goes up into the multiples of billions.

The number was too big to grasp. Our minds fumbled at it while we marched, and gave up. It was too big.

I stared at Ren's back as we walked, a nearly invisible mannequin silhouette, and tried to multiply that out to

224

the necessary figure. I staggered blindly along, lost and inundated beneath thousands of individual arms, legs, faces; a row of faces blurring off into infinity, all screaming—and the imagining nowhere near the actuality.

Billions.

How many restless ghosts out of that many deaders? Who do they haunt?

Billions.

Dawn caught us about two hours out. It came with no warning, as usual. We were groping through World's ink-dark, moonless night, watched only by the million icy eyes of evening, shreds of witchfire crystal, incredibly cold and distant. I'd watched them night after night for years, scrawling their indecipherable hieroglyphics across the sky, indifferent to man's incomprehension; now, as always, the night sky reminded me of a computer punch card, printed white on black. I stopped for a second on a rise, pushing back the infrared lenses, staring at the sky. What program was printed there, suns for ciphers, worlds for decimal points? An absurd question—I was nearly as foolish as you once, buck—but it was the first fully verbalized thought I'd had since I'd realized the nakedness of flesh, back there on the parapet as my life tore itself apart. I asked it again, half-expecting an answer, watching my breath turn to plumes and tatters, steaming in the silver chill of the stars.

The sun came up like a meteor. It scuttled up from the horizon with that unsettling, deceptive speed that even natives of World never quite get used to. New light washed around us, blue and raw at first, deepening the shadows and honing their edges. The sun continued to hitch itself up the sky, swallowing stars, a watery pink flush wiping the horizon clear of night. The light deepened, mellowed into gold. We floated through silver mist that swirled up around the mountain's knobby knees. I found myself crying silently as I walked the high ridge between mist and sky, absorbing the morning with a new hunger, grappling with a thought that was still too big for my mind and kept slipping elusively away, just out of reach. There was a low hum as our warmsuits adjusted to the growing warmth, polarizing from black to white, bleeding heat back into the air. Down the flanks of the Blackfriars and away across the valley below—visible now as the mists pirouetted past us to the summits—the night plants were dying, shriveling visibly in mile-long swaths of decay. In seconds the Blackfriars were gaunt and barren, turned to hills of ash and bone. The sun was now a bloated yellow disk surrounded by haloes of red and deepening scarlet, shading into the frosty blue of rarefied air. Stripped of softening vegetation, the mountains looked rough and abrasive as pumice, gouged by lunar shadows. The first of the day plants began to appear at our feet, the green spiderwebbing, poking up through cracks in the dry earth.

We came across a new stream, tumbling from melting ice, sluicing a dusty gorge.

An hour later we found the valley.

Heynith led us down onto the marshy plain that rolled away from mountains to horizon. We circled wide, cautiously approaching the valley from the lowlands. Heynith held up his hand, pointed to me, Ren, Goth. The others fanned out across the mouth of the valley, hid, settled down to wait. We went in alone. The speargrass had grown rapidly; it was chest-high. We crawled in, timing our movements to coincide with the long soughing of the morning breeze, so that any rippling of the grass would be taken for natural movement. It took us about a half hour of dusty, sweaty work. When I judged that I'd wormed my way in close enough, I stopped, slowly parted the speargrass enough to peer out without raising my head.

It was a large vacvan, five-hundred-footer, equipped with waldoes for self-loading.

It was parked near the hill flank on the side of the wide valley.

There were three men with it.

I ducked back into the grass, paused to make sure my "gun" was ready for operation, then crawled laboriously nearer to the van.

It was very near when I looked up again, about twenty-five feet away in the center of a cleared space. I could make out the hologram pictograph that pulsed identification on the side: the symbol for Urheim, World's largest city and Combine Seat of Board, half a world away in the Northern Hemisphere. They'd come a long way; still thought of as long, though ships whispered between the stars—it was still long for feet and eyes. And another longer way: from fetuses in glass wombs to men stamping and jiggling with cold inside the fold of a mountain's thigh, watching the spreading morning. That made me feel funny to think about. I wondered if they suspected that it'd be the last morning they'd ever see. That made me feel funnier. The thought tickled my mind again, danced away. I checked my gun a second time, needlessly.

I waited, feeling troubled, pushing it down. Two of them were standing together several feet in front of the van, sharing a mild narcotic atomizer, sucking deeply, shuffling with restlessness and cold, staring out across the speargrass to where the plain opened up. They had the stiff, rumpled, puff-eyed look of people who had just spent an uncomfortable night in a cramped place. They were dressed as fullsentients uncloned, junior officers of the military caste, probably hereditary positions inherited from their families, as is the case with most of the uncloned cadet executives. Except for the cadre at Urheim and other major cities, they must have been some of the few surviving clansmen; hundreds of thousands of military cadets and officers had died at D'kotta (along with uncounted clones and semisentients of all ranks), and the caste had never been extremely large in the first place. The by-laws had demanded that the Combine maintain a Security Force, but it had become mostly traditional with minimum function, at least among the uncloned higher ranks, almost the last stronghold of old-fashioned nepotism. That was one of the things that had favored the Quaestor uprising, and had forced the Combine to take the unpopular step of impressing large levies of industrial clones into a militia. The most junior of these two cadets was very young, even younger than me. The third man remained inside the van's cab. I could see his face blurrily through the windfield, kept on against the cold though the van was no longer in motion.

I waited. I knew the others were maneuvering into position around me. I also knew what Heynith was waiting for.

The third man jumped down from the high cab. He was older, wore an officer's hologram: a full executive. He said something to the cadets, moved a few feet toward the back of the van, started to take a piss. The column of golden liquid steamed in the cold air.

Heynith whistled.

I rolled to my knees, parted the speargrass at the edge of the cleared space, swung my gun up. The two cadets started, face muscles tensing into uncertain fear. The older cadet took an involuntary step forward, still clutching the atomizer. Ren and Goth chopped him down, firing a stream of "bullets" into him. The guns made a very loud metallic rattling sound that jarred the teeth, and fire flashed from the ejector ends. Birds screamed upward all along the mountain flank. The impact of the bullets knocked the cadet off his feet, rolled him so that he came to rest belly-down. The atomizer flew through the air, hit, bounced. The younger cadet leaped toward the cab, right into my line of fire. I pulled the trigger; bullets exploded out of the gun. The cadet was kicked backwards, arms swinging wide, slammed against the side of the cab, jerked upright as I continued to fire, spun along the van wall and rammed heavily into the ground. He tottered on one shoulder for a second, then flopped over onto his back. At the sound of the first shot, the executive had whirled—penis still dangling from pantaloons, surplus piss spraying wildly—and dodged for the back of the van, so that Heynith's volley missed and screamed from the van wall, leaving a long scar. The executive dodged again, crouched, came up with a biodeth in one hand and swung right into a single bullet from Ren just as he began to fire. The impact twirled him in a staggering circle, his finger still pressing the trigger; the carrier beam splashed harmlessly from the van wall, traversed as the executive spun, cut a long swath through the speargrass, the plants shriveling and blackening as the beam swept over them. Heynith opened up again before the beam could reach his clump of grass, sending the executive—somehow still on his feet—lurching past the end of the van. The biodeth dropped, went out. Heynith kept firing, the executive dancing bonelessly backwards on his heels, held up by the stream of bullets. Heynith released the trigger. The executive collapsed: a heap of arms and legs at impossible angles.

When we came up to the van, the young cadet was still dying. His body shivered and arched, his heels drummed against the earth, his fingers plucked at nothing, and then he was still. There was a lot of blood.

The others moved up from the valley mouth. Heynith sent them circling around the rim, where the valley walls dipped down on three sides.

We dragged the bodies away and concealed them in some large rocks.

I was feeling numb again, like I had after D'kotta.

I continued to feel numb as we spent the rest of that morning in frantic preparation. My mind was somehow detached as my body sweated and dug and hauled. There was a lot for it to do. We had four heavy industrial lasers, rock-cutters; they were clumsy, bulky, inefficient things to use as weapons, but they'd have to do. This mission had not been planned so much as thrown together, only two hours before the liaison man had contacted us on the parapet. Anything that could possibly work at all would have to be made to work somehow; no time to do it right, just do it. We'd been the closest team in contact with the field HQ who'd received the report, so we'd been snatched; the lasers were the only things on hand that could even approach potential as a heavy weapon, so we'd use the lasers.

Now that we'd taken the van without someone alerting the Combine by radio from the cab, Heynith flashed a signal mirror back toward the shoulder of the mountain we'd quitted a few hours before. The liaison man swooped down ten minutes later, carrying one of the lasers strapped awkwardly to his platvac. He made three more trips, depositing the massive cylinders as carefully as eggs, then gunned his platvac and screamed back toward the Blackfriars in a maniac arc just this side of suicidal. His face was still gray, tight-pressed lips a bloodless white against ash, and he hadn't said a word during the whole unloading procedure. I think he was probably one of the Quaestors who followed the Way of Atonement. I never saw him again. I've sometimes wished I'd had the courage to follow his example, but I rationalize by telling myself that I have atoned with my life rather than my death, and who knows, it might even be somewhat true. It's nice to think so anyway.

It took us a couple of hours to get the lasers into position. We spotted them in four places around the valley walls, dug slanting pits into the slopes to conceal them and tilt the barrels up at the right angle. We finally got them all zeroed on a spot about a hundred feet above the center of the valley floor, the muzzle arrangement giving each a few degrees of leeway on either side. That's where she'd have to come down anyway if she was a standard orbot, the valley being just wide enough to contain the boat and the vacvan, with a safety margin between them. Of course, if they brought her down on the plain outside the valley mouth, things were going to get very hairy; in that case we might be able to lever one or two of the lasers around to bear, or, failing that, we could try to take the orbot on foot once it'd landed, with about one chance in eight of making it. But we thought that they'd land her in the valley; that's where the vacvan had been parked, and they'd want the shelter of the high mountain walls to conceal the orbot from any Quaestor eyes that might be around. If so, that gave us a much better chance. About one out of three.

When the lasers had been positioned, we scattered, four men to an emplacement, hiding in the camouflaged trenches alongside the big barrels. Heynith led Goth and me toward the laser we'd placed about fifty feet up the mountain flank, directly behind and above the vacvan. Ren stayed behind. He stood next to the van—shoulders characteristically slouched, thumbs hooked in his belt, face carefully void of expression—and watched us out of sight. Then he looked out over the valley mouth, hitched up his gun, spat in the direction of Urheim and climbed up into the van cab.

The valley was empty again. From our position the vacvan looked like a shiny toy, sundogs winking across its surface as it baked in the afternoon heat. An abandoned toy, lost in high weeds, waiting in loneliness to be reclaimed by owners who would never come.

Time passed.

The birds we'd frightened away began to settle back onto the hillsides.

I shifted position uneasily, trying half-heartedly to get comfortable. Heynith glared me into immobility. We were crouched in a trench about eight feet long and five feet deep, covered by a camouflage tarpaulin propped open on the valley side by pegs, a couple of inches of vegetation and topsoil on top of the tarpaulin. Heynith was in the middle, straddling the operator's saddle of the laser. Goth was on his left, I was on his right. Heynith was going to man the laser when the time came; it only took one person. There was nothing for Goth and me to do, would be nothing to do even during the ambush, except take over the firing in the unlikely event that Heynith was killed without the shot wiping out all of us, or stand by to lever the laser around in case that became necessary. Neither was very likely to happen. No, it was Heynith's show, and we were superfluous and unoccupied.

That was bad.

We had a lot of time to think.

That was worse.

I was feeling increasingly numb, like a wall of clear glass had been slipped between me and the world and was slowly thickening, layer by layer. With the thickening came an incredible isolation (isolation though I was cramped and suffocating, though I was jammed up against Heynith's bunched thigh—I couldn't touch him, he was miles away) and with the isolation came a sick, smothering panic. It was the inverse of claustrophobia.

231

My flesh had turned to clear plastic, my bones to glass, and I was naked, ultimately naked, and there was nothing I could wrap me in. Surrounded by an army, I would still be alone; shrouded in iron thirty feet underground, I would still be naked. One portion of my mind wondered dispassionately if I were slipping into shock; the rest of it fought to keep down the scream that gathered along tightening muscles. The isolation increased. I was unaware of my surroundings, except for the heat and the pressure of enclosure.

I was seeing the molten spider of D'kotta, lying on its back and showing its oscene blotched belly, kicking legs of flame against the sky, each leg raising a poison blister where it touched the clouds.

I was seeing the boy, face runneled by blood, beating heels against the ground.

I was beginning to doubt big, simple ideas.

Nothing moved in the valley except wind through grass, spirits circling in the form of birds.

Spider legs.

Crab dance.

The blocky shadow of the vacvan crept across the valley.

Suddenly, with the intensity of vision, I was picturing Ren sitting in the van cab, shoulders resting against the door, legs stretched out along the seat, feet propped up on the instrument board, one ankle crossed over the other, gun resting across his lap, eyes watching the valley mouth through the windfield. He would be smoking a cigarette, and he would take it from his lips occasionally, flick the ashes onto the shiny dials with a fingernail, smile his strange smile, and carefully burn holes in the plush fabric of the upholstery. The fabric (real fabric; not plastic) would smolder, send out a wisp of bad-smelling smoke, and there would be another charred black hole in the seat. Ren would smile again, put the cigarette back in his mouth, lean back, and puff slowly. Ren was waiting to answer the radio signal from the orbot, to assure them that all was well, to talk them down to death. If they suspected anything was wrong, he would be the first to die. Even if everything went perfectly, he stood a high chance of dying anyway; he was the most exposed. It was almost certainly a suicide job. Ren said that he didn't give a shit; maybe he actually didn't. Or at least had convinced himself that he didn't. He was an odd man. Older than any of us, even Heynith, he had worked most of his life as a cadet executive in Admin at Urheim, devoted his existence to his job, subjugated all of his energies to it. He had been passed over three times for promotion to executive status, years of redoubled effort and mounting anxiety between each rejection. With the third failure he had been quietly retired to live on the credit subsidy he had earned with forty years of service. The next morning, precisely at the start of his accustomed work period, he stole a biodeth from a security guard in the Admin Complex, walked into his flowsector, killed everyone there, and disappeared from Urheim. After a year on the run, he had managed to contact the Quaestors. After another year of training, he was serving with a commando team in spite of his age. That had been five years ago; I had known him for two. During all that time, he had said little. He did his job very well with a minimum of waste motion, never made mistakes, never complained, never showed emotion. But occasionally he would smile and burn a hole in something. Or someone.

The sun dived at the horizon, seeming to crash into the plain in an explosion of flame. Night swallowed us in one gulp. Black as a beast's belly.

It jerked me momentarily back into reality. I had a bad moment when I thought I'd gone blind, but then reason returned and I slipped the infrared lenses down over my eyes, activated them. The world came back in shades of red. Heynith was working cramped legs against the body of the laser. He spoke briefly, and we gulped some stimulus pills to keep us awake; they were bitter, and hard to swallow dry as usual, but they kicked up a familiar acid churning in my stomach, and my blood began to flow faster. I glanced at Heynith. He'd been quiet, even for

Heynith. I wondered what he was thinking. He looked at me, perhaps reading the thought, and ordered us out of the trench.

Goth and I crawled slowly out, feeling stiff and brittle, slapped our thighs and arms, stamped to restore circulation. Stars were sprinkling across the sky, salt spilled on black porcelain. I still couldn't read them, I found. The day plants had vanished, the day animals had retreated into catalepsy. The night plants were erupting from the ground, fed by the debris of the day plants. They grew rapidly, doubling, then tripling in height as we watched. They were predominately thick, ropy shrubs with wide, spearhead leaves of dull purple and black, about four feet high. Goth and I dug a number of them up, root-systems intact, and placed them on top of the tarpaulin to replace the day plants that had shriveled with the first touch of bitter evening frost. We had to handle them with padded gloves; the leaf surfaces greedily absorbed the slightest amount of heat and burned like dry ice.

Then we were back in the trench, and it was worse than ever. Motion had helped for a while, but I could feel the numbing panic creeping back, and the momentary relief made it even harder to bear. I tried to start a conversation, but it died in monosyllabic grunts, and silence sopped up the echoes. Heynith was methodically checking the laser controls for the nth time. He was tense; I could see it bunch his shoulder muscles, bulge his calves into rock as they pushed against the footplates of the saddle. Goth looked worse than I did; he was somewhat younger, and usually energetic and cheerful. Not tonight.

We should have talked, spread the pain around; I think all of us realized it. But we couldn't; we were made awkward by our own special intimacy. At one time or another every one of us had reached a point where he *had* to talk or die, even Heynith, even Ren. So we all had talked and all had listened, each of us switching roles sooner or later. We had poured our fears and dreams and secret memories upon each other, until now we knew each other too well. It made us afraid. Each of us was afraid that he had exposed too much, let down too many barriers. We were afraid of vulnerability, of the knife that jabs for the softest fold of the belly. We were all scarred men already, and twice-shy. And the resentment grew that others had seen us that helpless, that vulnerable. So the walls went back up, intensified. And so when we needed to talk again, we could not. We were already too close to risk further intimacy.

Visions returned, ebbing and flowing, overlaying the darkness.

The magma churning, belching a hot breath that stinks of rotten eggs.

The cadet, his face inhuman in the death rictus, blood running down in a wash from his smashed forehead, plastering one eye closed, bubbling at his nostril, frothing around his lips, the lips tautening as his head jerks forward and then backwards, slamming the ground, the lips then growing slack, the body slumping, the mouth sagging open, the rush of blood and phlegm past the tombstone teeth, down the chin and neck, soaking into the fabric of the tunic. The feet drumming at the ground a final time, digging up clots of earth.

I groped for understanding. I had killed people before, and it had not bothered me except in sleep. I had done it mechanically, routine backed by hate, hate cushioned by routine. I wondered if the night would ever end. I remembered the morning I'd watched from the mountain. I didn't think the night would end. A big idea tickled my mind again.

The city swallowed by stone.

The cadet falling, swinging his arms wide.

Why always the cadet and the city in conjunction? Had one sensitized me to the other, and if so, which? I hesitated.

Could both of them be equally important?

One of the other section leaders whistled.

We all started, somehow grew even more tense. The whistle came again, warbling, sound floating on silence like oil on water. Someone was coming. After a while we heard a rustling and snapping of underbrush approaching downslope from the mountain. Whoever it was, he was making no effort to move quietly. In fact he seemed to be blundering along, bulling through the tangles, making a tremendous thrashing noise. Goth and I turned in the direction of the sound, brought our guns up to bear, primed them. That was instinct. I wondered who could be coming *down* the mountain toward us. That was reason. Heynith twisted to cover the opposite direction, away from the noise, resting his gun on the saddle rim. That was caution. The thrasher passed our position about six feet away, screened by the shrubs. There was an open space ten feet farther down, at the head of a talus bluff that slanted to the valley. We watched it. The shrubs at the end of the clearing shook, were torn aside. A figure stumbled out into starlight.

It was a null.

Goth sucked in a long breath, let it hiss out between his teeth. Heynith remained impassive, but I could imagine his eyes narrowing behind the thick lenses. My mind was totally blank for about three heartbeats, then, surprised: a null! and I brought the gun barrel up, then, uncomprehending: a null? and I lowered the muzzle. Blank for a second, then: how? and trickling in again: how? Thoughts snarled into confusion, the gun muzzle wavered hesitantly.

The null staggered across the clearing, weaving in slow figure-eights. It almost fell down the talus bluff, one foot suspended uncertainly over the drop, then lurched away, goaded by tropism. The null shambled backward a few paces, stopped, swayed, then slowly sank to its knees.

It kneeled: head bowed, arms limp along the ground, palms up.

Heynith put his gun back in his lap, shook his head. He told us he'd be damned if he could figure out where it came from, but we'd have to get rid of it. It could spoil the ambush if it was spotted. Automatically, I raised my gun, trained it. Heynith stopped me. No noise, he said, not now. He told Goth to go out and kill it silently.

Goth refused. Heynith stared at him speechlessly, then began to flush. Goth and Heynith had had trouble before.

Goth was a good man, brave as a bull, but he was stubborn, tended to follow his own lead too much, had too many streaks of sentimentality and touchiness, *thought* too much to be a really efficient cog.

They had disagreed from the beginning, something that wouldn't have been tolerated this long if the Quaestors hadn't been desperate for men. Goth was a devil in a fight when aroused, one of the best, and that had excused him a lot of obstinacy. But he had a curious squeamishness, he hadn't developed the layers of numbing scar-tissue necessary for guerrilla work, and that was almost inevitably fatal. I'd wondered before, dispassionately, how long he would last.

Goth was a hereditary fullsentient, one of the few connected with the Quaestors. He'd been a cadet executive in Admin, gained access to old archives that had slowly soured him on the Combine, been hit at the psychologically right moment by increasing Quaestor agitprop, and had defected; after a two-year proving period, he'd been allowed to participate actively. Goth was one of the only field people who was working out of idealism rather than hate, and that made us distrust him. Heynith also nurtured a traditional dislike for hereditary fullsentients. Heynith had been part of an industrial sixclone for over twenty years before joining the Quaestors. His Six had been wiped out in a production accident, caused by standard Combine negligence. Heynith had been the only survivor. The Combine had expressed mild sympathy, and told him that they planned to cut another clone from him to replace the destroyed Six; he of course would be placed in charge of the new Six, by reason of his seniority. They smiled at him, not seeing any reason why he wouldn't want to work another twenty years with biological replicas of his dead brothers and sisters, the men, additionally, reminders of what he'd been as a youth, unravaged by years of pain. Heynith had thanked them politely, walked out and kept walking, crossing the Gray Waste on foot to join the Quaestors.

I could see all this working in Heynith's face as he raged at Goth. Goth could feel the hate too, but he stood

237

firm. The null was incapable of doing anybody any harm; he wasn't going to kill it. There'd been enough slaughter. Goth's face was bloodless, and I could see D'kotta reflected in his eyes, but I felt no sympathy for him, in spite of my own recent agonies. He was disobeying orders. I thought about Mason, the man Goth had replaced, the man who had died in my arms at Itica, and I hated Goth for being alive instead of Mason. I had loved Mason. He'd been an Antiquarian in the Urheim archives, and he'd worked for the Quaestors almost from the beginning, years of vital service before his activities were discovered by the Combine. He'd escaped the raid, but his family hadn't. He'd been offered an admin job in Quaestor HQ, but had turned it down and insisted on field work in spite of warnings that it was suicidal for a man of his age. Mason had been a tall, gentle, scholarly man who pretended to be gruff and hard-nosed, and cried alone at night when he thought nobody could see. I'd often thought that he could have escaped from Itica if he'd tried harder, but he'd been worn down, sick and guilt-ridden and tired, and his heart hadn't really been in it; that thought had returned to puzzle me often afterward. Mason had been the only person I'd ever cared about, the one who'd been more responsible than anybody for bringing me out of the shadows and into humanity, and I could have shot Goth at that moment because I thought he was betraying Mason's memory.

Heynith finally ran out of steam, spat at Goth, started to call him something, then stopped and merely glared at him, lips white. I'd caught Heynith's quick glance at me, a nearly invisible head-turn, just before he'd fallen silent. He'd almost forgotten and called Goth a zombie, a widespread expletive on World that had carefully not been used by the team since I'd joined. So Heynith had never really forgotten, though he'd treated me with scrupulous fairness. My fury turned to a cold anger, widened out from Goth to become a sick distaste for the entire world.

Heynith told Goth he would take care of him later, take care of him good, and ordered me to go kill the null, take him upslope and out of sight first, then conceal the body.

Mechanically, I pulled myself out of the trench, started downslope toward the clearing. Anger fueled me for the first few feet, and I slashed the shrubs aside with padded gloves, but it ebbed quickly, leaving me hollow and numb. I'd known how the rest of the team must actually think of me, but somehow I'd never allowed myself to admit it. Now I'd had my face jammed in it, and coming on top of all the other anguish I'd gone through the last two days, it was too much.

I pushed into the clearing.

My footsteps triggered some response in the null. It surged drunkenly to its feet, arms swinging limply, and turned to face me.

The null was slightly taller than me, built very slender, and couldn't have weighed too much more than a hundred pounds. It was bald, completely hairless. The fingers were shriveled, limp flesh dangling from the club of the hand; they had never been used. The toes had been developed to enable technicians to walk nulls from one section of the Cerebrum to another, but the feet had never had a chance to toughen or grow callus: they were a mass of blood and lacerations. The nose was a rough blob of pink meat around the nostrils, the ears similarly atrophied. The eyes were enormous, huge milky corneas and small pupils, like those of a nocturnal bird; adapted to the gloom of the Cerebrum, and allowed to function to forestall sensory deprivation; they aren't cut into the psychocybernetic current like the synapses or the ganglions. There were small messy wounds on the temples, wrists, and spine-base where electrodes had been torn loose. It had been shrouded in a pajamalike suit of non-conductive material, but that had been torn almost completely away, only a few hanging tatters remaining. There were no sex organs. The flesh under the rib-cage was curiously collapsed; no stomach or digestive tract. The body was covered with bruises, cuts, gashes, extensive swatches sun-baked to second-degree burns, other sections seriously frostbitten or marred by bad coldburns from the night shrubs.

My awe grew, deepened into archetypical dread.

It was from D'kotta, there could be no doubt about it. Somehow it had survived the destruction of its Cerebrum, somehow it had walked through the boiling hell to the foothills, somehow it had staggered up to and over the mountain shoulder. I doubted if there'd been any predilection in its actions; probably it had just walked blindly away from the ruined Cerebrum in a straight line and kept walking. Its actions with the tallus bluff demonstrated that; maybe earlier some dim instinct had helped it fumble its way around obstacles in its path, but now it was exhausted, baffled, stymied. It was miraculous that it had made it this far. And the agony it must have suffered on its way was inconceivable. I shivered, spooked. The short hairs bristled on the back of my neck.

The null lurched toward me.

I whimpered and sprang backwards, nearly falling, swinging up the gun.

The null stopped, its head lolling, describing a slow semicircle. Its eyes were tracking curiously, and I doubted if it could focus on me at all. To it, I must have been a blur of darker gray.

I tried to steady my ragged breathing. It couldn't hurt me; it was harmless, nearly dead anyway. Slowly, I lowered the gun, pried my fingers from the stock, slung the gun over my shoulder.

I edged cautiously toward it. The null swayed, but remained motionless. Below, I could see the vacvan at the bottom of the bluff, a patch of dull gunmetal sheen. I stretched my hand out slowly. The null didn't move. This close, I could see its gaunt ribs rising and falling with the effort of its ragged breathing. It was trembling, an occasional convulsive spasm shuddering along its frame. I was surprised that it didn't stink; nulls were rumored to have a strong personal odor, at least according to the talk in field camps—bullshit, like so much of my knowledge at that time. I watched it for a minute, fascinated, but my training told me I couldn't stand out here for long; we were too exposed. I took another step, reached out for it, hesitated. I didn't want to touch it. Swallowing my distaste, I selected a spot on its upper arm free of burns or wounds, grabbed it firmly with one hand.

The null jerked at the touch, but made no attempt to strike out or get away. I waited warily for a second, ready to turn my grip into a wrestling hold if it should try to attack. It remained still, but its flesh crawled under my fingers, and I shivered myself in reflex. Satisfied that the null would give me no trouble, I turned and began to force it upslope, pushing it ahead of me.

It followed my shove without resistance, until we hit the first of the night shrubs, then it staggered and made a mewing, inarticulate sound. The plants were burning it, sucking warmth out of its flesh, raising fresh welts, ugly where bits of skin had adhered to the shrubs. I shrugged, pushed it forward. It mewed and lurched again. I stopped. The null's eyes tracked in my direction, and it whimpered to itself in pain. I swore at myself for wasting time, but moved ahead to break a path for the null, dragging it along behind me. The branches slapped harmlessly at my warmsuit as I bent them aside; occasionally one would slip past and lash the null, making it flinch and whimper, but it was spared the brunt of it. I wondered vaguely at my motives for doing it. Why bother to spare someone (some*thing*, I corrected nervously) pain when you're going to have to kill him (*it*) in a minute? What difference could it make? I shelved that and concentrated on the movements of my body; the null wasn't heavy, but it wasn't easy to drag it uphill either, especially as it'd stumble and go down every few yards and I'd have to pull it back to its feet again. I was soon sweating, but I didn't care, as the action helped to occupy my mind, and I didn't want to have to face the numbness I could feel taking over again.

We moved upslope until we were about thirty feet above the trench occupied by Heynith and Goth. This looked like a good place. The shrubs were almost chest-high here, tall enough to hide the null's body from an aerial search. I stopped. The null bumped blindly into me, leaned against me, its breath coming in rasps next to my

241

ear. I shivered in horror at the contact. Gooseflesh blossomed on my arms and legs, swept across my body. Some connection sent a memory whispering at my mind, but I ignored it under the threat of rising panic. I twisted my shoulder under the null's weight, threw it off. The null slid back downslope a few feet, almost fell, recovered.

I watched it, panting. The memory returned, gnawing incessantly. This time it got through:

Mason scrambling through the sea-washed rocks of Cape Itica toward the waiting ramsub, while the fire sky-whipping behind picked up out against the shadows; Mason, too slow in vaulting over a stone ridge, balancing too long on the razor-edge in perfect silhouette against the night; Mason jerking upright as a fusor fired from the high cliff puddled his spine, melted his flesh like wax; Mason tumbling down into my arms, almost driving me to my knees; Mason, already dead, heavy in my arms, *heavy in my arms;* Mason torn away from me as a wave broke over us and deluged me in spume; Mason sinking from sight as Heynith screamed for me to come on and I fought my way through the chest-high surf to the ramsub—

That's what supporting the null had reminded me of: Mason, heavy in my arms.

Confusion and fear and nausea.

How could the null make me think of Mason?

Sick self-anger that my mind could compare Mason, gentle as the dream-father I'd never had, to something as disgusting as the null.

Anger novaed, trying to scrub out shame and guilt.

I couldn't take it. I let it spill out onto the null.

Growling, I sprang forward, shook it furiously until its head rattled and wobbled on its limp neck, grabbed it by the shoulders and hammered it to its knees.

I yanked my knife out. The blade flamed suddenly in starlight.

I wrapped my hand around its throat to tilt its head back.

Its flesh was warm. A pulse throbbed under my palm.

All at once, my anger was gone, leaving only nausea.

I suddenly realized how cold the night was. Wind bit to the bone.

It was looking at me.

I suppose I'd been lucky. Orphans aren't as common as they once were—not in a society where reproduction has been relegated to the laboratory, but they still occur with fair regularity. I had been the son of an uncloned junior executive who'd run up an enormous credit debit, gone bankrupt, and been forced into insolvency. The Combine had cut a clone from him so that their man/hours would make up the bank discrepancy, burned out the higher levels of his brain and put him in one of the nonsentient penal Controlled Environments. His wife was also cloned, but avoided brainscrub and went back to work in a lower capacity in Admin. I, as a baby, then became a ward of the State, and was sent to one of the institutional Environments. Imagine an endless series of low noises, repeating over and over again forever, no high or low spots, everything level: MMMMMMMMMM MMMMMMMMMMMMMMMMMMMMMMMMMM MMMMMMMMMMM. Like that. That's the only way to describe the years in the Environments. We were fed, we were kept warm, we worked on conveyor belts piecing together miniaturized equipment, we were put to sleep electronically, we woke with our fingers already busy in the monotonous, rhythmical motions that we couldn't remember learning, motions we had repeated a million times a day since infancy. Once a day we were fed a bar of food-concentrates and vitamins. Occasionally, at carefully calculated intervals, we would be exercised to keep up muscle tone. After reaching puberty, we were occasionally masturbated by electric stimulation, the seed saved for sperm banks. The administrators of the Environment were not cruel; we almost never saw them. Punishment was by machine shocks; never severe, very rarely needed. The executives had no need to be cruel. All they needed was MMMMMMMMMMMMMMMMMMMMMMMMMM MMMMM. We had been taught at some early stage, probably by shock and stimulation, to put the proper part in the proper slot as the blocks of equipment passed in front of us. We had never been taught to talk, although an extremely limited language of several mood-sounds had independently developed among us; the executives never spoke on the rare intervals when they came to check the machinery that regulated us. We had never been told who we were, where we were; we had never been told anything. We didn't care about any of these things, the concepts had never formed in our minds, we were only semi-conscious at best anyway. There was nothing but MMMMMMMMMMMMMMMMMMMMMM. The executives weren't concerned with our spiritual development, there was no graduation from the Environment; there was no place else for us to go in a rigidly stratified society. The Combine had discharged its obligation by keeping us alive, in a place where we could even be minimally useful. Though our jobs were sinecures that could have been more efficiently performed by computer, they gave the expense of our survival a socially justifiable excuse, they put us comfortably in a pigeonhole. We were there for life. We would grow up from infancy, grow old, and die, bathed in MMMMMMMMMMMMMMMMM MMMMM. The first real, separate and distinct memory of my life is when the Quaestors raided the Environment, when the wall of the assembly chamber suddenly glowed red, buckled, collapsed inward, when Mason pushed out of the smoke and debris-cloud, gun at the ready, and walked slowly toward me. That's hindsight. At the time, it was only a sudden invasion of incomprehensible sounds and lights and shapes and colors, too much to possibly comprehend, incredibly alien. It was the first discordant note ever struck in our lives: MMMMMMMMMMM MM!!!! shattering our world in an instant, plunging us into another dimension of existence. The Quaestors kidnaped all of us, loaded us onto vacvans, took us into the hills, tried to undo some of the harm. That'd been six years ago. Even with the facilities available at the Quaestor underground complex—hypnotrainers and analysis computers to plunge me back to childhood and patiently lead me out again step by step for ten thousand years of subjective time, while my body slumbered in stasis—even with all of that, I'd been lucky to emerge

244

somewhat sane. The majority had died, or been driven into catalepsy. I'd been lucky even to be a Ward of the State, the way things had turned out. Lucky to be a zombie. I could have been a low-ranked clone, without a digestive system, tied forever to the Combine by unbreakable strings. Or I could have been one of the thousands of tank-grown creatures whose brains are used as organic-computer storage banks in the Cerebrum gestalts, completely unsentient: I could have been a null.

Enormous eyes staring at me, unblinking.

Warmth under my fingers.

I wondered if I was going to throw up.

Wind moaned steadily through the valley with a sound like MMMMMMMMMMMMMMMM.

Heynith hissed for me to hurry up, sound riding the wind, barely audible. I shifted my grip on the knife. I was telling myself: it's never been really sentient anyway. Its brain has only been used as a computer unit for a biological gestalt, there's no individual intelligence in there. It wouldn't make any difference. I was telling myself: it's dying anyway from a dozen causes. It's in pain. It would be kinder to kill it.

I brought up the knife, placing it against the null's throat. I pressed the point in slowly, until it was pricking flesh.

The null's eyes tracked, focused on the knifeblade.

My stomach turned over. I looked away, out across the valley. I felt my carefully created world trembling and blurring around me, I felt again on the point of being catapulted into another level of comprehension, previously unexpected. I was afraid.

The vacvan's headlights flashed on and off, twice.

I found myself on the ground, hidden by the ropy shrubs. I had dragged the null down with me, without thinking about it, pinned him flat to the ground, arm over back. That had been the signal that Ren had received a call from the orbot, had given it the proper radio code reply to bring it down. I could imagine him grinning in the darkened cab as he worked the instruments.

I raised myself on an elbow, jerked the knife up,

suspending it while I looked for the junction of spine and neck that would be the best place to strike. If I was going to kill him (*it*), I would have to kill him (*it!*) now. In quick succession, like a series of slides, like a computer equation running, I got: D'kotta—the cadet—Mason—the null. *It* and *him* tumbled in selection. Came up *him*. I lowered the knife. I couldn't do it. He was human. Everybody was.

For better or worse, I was changed. I was no longer the same person.

I looked up. Somewhere up there, hanging at the edge of the atmosphere, was the tinsel collection of forces in opposition called a starship, delicately invulnerable as an iron butterfly. It would be phasing in and out of "reality" to hold its position above World, maintaining only the most tenuous of contacts with this continuum. It had launched an orbot, headed for a rendezvous with the vacvan in this valley. The orbot was filled with the gene cultures that could be used to create hundreds of thousands of nonsentient clones who could be imprinted with behavior patterns and turned into computer-directed soldiers; crude but effective. The orbot was filled with millions of tiny metal blocks, kept under enormous compression: when released from tension, molecular memory would reshape them into a wide range of weapons needing only a powersource to be functional. The orbot was carrying, in effect, a vast army and its combat equipment, in a form that could be transported in a five-hundred-foot vacvan and slipped into Urheim, where there were machines that could put it into use. It was the Combine's last chance, the second wind they needed in order to survive. It had been financed and arranged by various industrial firms in the Commonwealth who had vested interests in the Combine's survival on World. The orbot's cargo had been assembled and sent off before D'kotta, when it had been calculated that the reinforcements would be significant in insuring a Combine victory; now it was indispensable. D'kotta had made the Combine afraid that an attack on Urheim might be next, that the orbot might be intercepted by the Quaestors if the city was under siege when it tried to land.

So the Combine had decided to land the orbot elsewhere and sneak the cargo in. The Blackfriars had been selected as a rendezvous, since it was unlikely the Quaestors would be on the alert for Combine activity in that area so soon after D'kotta, and even if stopped, the van might be taken for fleeing survivors and ignored. The starship had been contacted by esper in route, and the change in plan made.

Four men had died to learn of the original plan. Two more had died in order to learn of the new landing site and get the information to the Quaestors in time.

The orbot came down.

I watched it as in a dream, coming to my knees, head above the shrubs. The null stirred under my hand, pushed against the ground, sat up.

The orbot was a speck, a dot, a ball, a toy. It was gliding silently in on gravs, directly overhead.

I could imagine Heynith readying the laser, Goth looking up and chewing his lip the way he always did in stress. I knew that my place should be with them, but I couldn't move. Fear and tension were still there, but they were under glass. I was already emotionally drained. I could sum up nothing else, even to face death.

The orbot had swelled into a huge, spherical mountain. It continued to settle, toward the spot where we'd calculated it must land. Now it hung just over the valley center, nearly brushing the mountain walls on either side. The orbot filled the sky, and I leaned away from it instinctively. It dropped lower—

Heynith was the first to fire.

An intense beam of light erupted from the ground downslope, stabbed into the side of the orbot. Another followed from the opposite side of the valley, then the remaining two at once.

The orbot hung, transfixed by four steady, unbearably bright columns.

For a while, it seemed as if nothing was happening.

I could imagine the consternation aboard the orbot as the pilot tried to reverse gravs in time.

The boat's hull had become cherry-red in four widening spots. Slowly, the spots turned white.

I could hear the null getting up beside me, near enough to touch. I had risen automatically, shading eyes against glare.

The orbot exploded.

The reactor didn't go, of course; they're built so that can't happen. It was just the conventional auxiliary engines, used for steering and for powering internal systems. But that was enough.

Imagine a building humping itself into a giant stone fist, and bringing that fist down on you, *squash*. Pain so intense that it snuffs your consciousness before you can feel it.

Warned by instinct, I had time to do two things.

I thought, distinctly: so night will never end.

And I stepped in front of the null to shield him.

Then I was kicked into oblivion.

I awoke briefly to agony, the world a solid, blank red. Very, very far away, I could hear someone screaming. It was me.

I awoke again. The pain had lessened. I could see. It was day, and the night plants had died. The sun was dazzling on bare rock. The null was standing over me, seeming to stretch up for miles into the sky. I screamed in preternatural terror. The world vanished.

The next time I opened my eyes, the sky was heavily overcast and it was raining, one of those torrential southern downpours. A Quaestor medic was doing something to my legs, and there was a platvac nearby. The null was lying on his back a few feet away, a bullet in his chest. His head was tilted up toward the scuttling gray clouds. His eyes mirrored the rain.

That's what happened to my leg. So much nerve tissue destroyed that they couldn't grow me a new one, and I had to put up with this stiff prosthetic. But I got used to it. I considered it my tuition fee.

I'd learned two things; that everybody is human, and

that the universe doesn't care one way or the other; only people do. The universe just doesn't give a damn. Isn't that wonderful? Isn't that a relief? It isn't out to get you, and it isn't going to help you either. You're on your own. We all are, and we all have to answer to ourselves. We make our own heavens and hells; we can't pass the buck any further. How much easier when we could blame our guilt or goodness on God.

Oh, I could read supernatural significance into it all—that I was spared because I'd spared the null, that some benevolent force was rewarding me—but what about Goth? Killed, and if he hadn't balked in the first place, the null wouldn't have stayed alive long enough for me to be entangled. What about the other team members, all dead—wasn't there a man among them as good as me and as much worth saving? No, there's a more direct reason why I survived. Prompted by the knowledge of his humanity, I had shielded him from the explosion. Three other men survived that explosion, but they died from exposure in the hours before the med team got there, baked to death by the sun. I didn't die because the null stood over me during the hours when the sun was rising and frying the rocks, *and his shadow shielded me from the sun.* I'm not saying that he consciously figured that out, deliberately shielded me (though who knows), but I had given him the only warmth he'd known in a long nightmare of pain, and so he remained by me when there was nothing stopping him from running away—and it came to the same result. You don't need intelligence or words to respond to empathy, it can be communicated through the touch of fingers—you know that if you've ever had a pet, ever been in love. So that's why I was spared, warmth for warmth, the same reason anything good ever happens in this life. When the med team arrived, they shot the null down because they thought it was trying to harm me. So much for supernatural rewards for the Just.

So, empathy's the thing that binds life together; it's the flame we share against fear. Warmth's the only answer to the old cold questions.

So I went through life, boy; made mistakes, did a lot of things, got kicked around a lot more, loved a little, and ended up on Kos, waiting for evening.

But night's a relative thing. It always ends. It does; because even if you're not around to watch it, the sun always comes up, and someone'll be there to see.

It's a fine, beautiful morning.

It's always a beautiful morning somewhere, even on the day you die.

You're young—that doesn't comfort you yet.

But you'll learn.

Chains of the Sea

ONE DAY THE aliens landed, just as everyone always said they would. They fell out of a guileless blue sky and into the middle of a clear, cold November day, four of them, four alien ships drifting down like the snow that had been threatening to fall all week. America was just shouldering its way into daylight as they made planetfall, so they landed there: one in the Delaware Valley about fifteen miles north of Philadelphia, one in Ohio, one in a desolate region of Colorado, and one—for whatever reason—in a cane field outside of Caracas, Venezuela. To those who actually saw them come down, the ships seemed to fall rather than to descend under any intelligent control: a black nailhead suddenly tacked to the sky, coming all at once from nowhere, with no transition, like a Fortean rock squeezed from a high appearing-point, hanging way up there and winking intolerably bright in the sunlight; and then gravity takes hold of it, visibly, and it begins to fall, far away and dream-slow at first, swelling larger, growing huge, unbelievably big, a mountain hurled at the earth, falling with terrifying speed, rolling in the air, tumbling end over end, overhead, coming down—and then it is sitting peacefully on the ground; it has not crashed, and although it didn't slow and it didn't stop, there it *is*, and not even a snowflake could have settled onto the frozen mud more lightly.

To those photo reconnaissance jets fortunate enough

to be flying a routine pattern at thirty thousand feet over the Eastern Seaboard when the aliens blinked into their airspace, to the automatic, radar-eyed, computer-reflexed facilities at USADCOM Spacetrack East, and to the United States Aerospace Defense Command HQ in Colorado Springs, although they didn't have convenient recon planes up for a double check—the picture was different. The high-speed cameras showed the landing as a *process:* as if the alien spaceships existed simultaneously everywhere along their path of descent, stretched down from the stratosphere and gradually sifting entirely to the ground, like confetti streamers thrown from a window, like slinkys going down a flight of stairs. In the films, the alien ships appeared to recede from the viewpoint of the reconnaissance planes, vanishing into perspective, and that was all right, but the ships also appeared to dwindle away into infinity from the viewpoint of Spacetrack East on the ground, and that definitely was not all right. The most constructive comment ever made on this phenomenon was that it was odd. It was also odd that the spaceships had not been detected approaching Earth by observation stations on the Moon, or by the orbiting satellites, and nobody ever figured that out, either.

From the first second of contact to touchdown, the invasion of Earth had taken less than ten minutes. At the end of that time, there were four big ships on the ground, shrouded in thick steam—*not* cooling off from the friction of their descent, as was first supposed; the steam was actually mist: everything had frozen solid in a fifty-foot circle around the ships, and the quick-ice was now melting as temperatures rose back above freezing—frantic messages were snarling up and down the continent-wide nervous system of USADCOM, and total atomic war was a hair's breadth away. While the humans scurried in confusion, the Artificial Intelligence (AI) created by MIT/Bell Labs linked itself into the network of high-speed, twentieth-generation computers placed at its disposal by a Red Alert Priority, evaluated data thoughtfully for a minute and a half, and then proceeded to get in touch with its opposite number in the Soviet. It had its own, independently evolved methods of doing this, and achieved contact almost instantaneously, although the Pentagon had not yet been able to reach the Kremlin—that didn't matter anyway; they were only human, and all the important talking was going on in another medium. AI "talked" to the Soviet system for another seven minutes, while eons of time clicked by on the electronic scale, and World War III was averted. Both Intelligences finally decided that they didn't understand what was going on, a conclusion the human governments of Earth wouldn't reach for hours, and would never admit at all.

The only flourish of action took place in the three-minute lag between the alien touchdown and the time AI assumed command of the defense network, and involved a panicked general at USADCOM HQ and a malfunction in the—never actually used—fail-safe system that enabled him to lob a small tactical nuclear device at the Colorado landing site. The device detonated at point-blank range, right against the side of the alien ship, but the fireball didn't appear. There didn't seem to be an explosion at all. Instead, the hull of the ship turned a blinding, incredibly hot white at the point of detonation, faded to blue-white, to a hellish red, to sullen tones of violet that flickered away down the spectrum. The same pattern of precessing colors chased themselves around the circumference of the ship until they reached the impact point again, and then the hull returned to its former dull black. The ship was unharmed. There had been no sound, not even a whisper. The tactical device had been a clean bomb, but instruments showed that no energy or radiation had been released at all.

After this, USADCOM became very thoughtful.

Tommy Nolan was already a half hour late to school, but he wasn't hurrying. He dawdled along the secondary road that led up the hill behind the old sawmill, and watched smoke go up in thick black lines from the chimneys of the houses below, straight and unwavering in the bright, clear morning, like brushstrokes against the sky. The roofs were made of cold gray and red tiles that winked sunlight at him all the way to the docks, where clouds of sea gulls bobbed and wheeled, dipped and rose, their cries coming faint and shrill to him across the miles of chimneys and roofs and aerials and wind-tossed treetops. There was a crescent sliver of ocean visible beyond the dock, like a slitted blue eye peering up over the edge of the world. Tommy kicked a rock, kicked it again, and then found a tin can which he kicked instead, clattering it along ahead of him. The wind snatched at the fur on his parka, *puff*, momentarily making the cries of the sea gulls very loud and distinct, and then carrying them away again, back over the roofs to the sea. He kicked the tin can over the edge of a bluff, and listened to it somersault invisibly away through the undergrowth. He was whistling tunelessly, and he had taken his gloves off and stuffed them in his parka pocket, although his mother had told him specifically not to, it was so cold for November. Tommy wondered briefly what the can must feel like, tumbling down through the thick ferns and weeds, finding a safe place to lodge under the dark, secret roots of the trees. He kept walking, skuff-skuffing gravel very loudly. When he was halfway up the slope, the buzz saw started up at the mill on the other side of the bluff. It moaned and shrilled metallically, whining up through the stillness of the morning to a piercing shriek that hurt his teeth, then sinking low, low, to a buzzing, grumbling roar, like an angry giant muttering in the back of his throat. An *animal,* Tommy thought, although he knew it was a saw. *Maybe it's a dinosaur*. He shivered deliciously. A *dinosaur!*

Tommy was being a puddle jumper this morning. That was why he was so late. There had been a light rain the night before, scattering puddles along the road, and Tommy had carefully jumped over every one between here and the house. It took a long time to do it right, but Tommy was being very conscientious. He imagined himself as a machine, a vehicle—a puddle jumper. No matter that he had legs instead of wheels, and arms and a head, that was just the kind of ship he was, with he himself

254

sitting somewhere inside and driving the contraption, looking out through the eyes, working the pedals and gears and switches that made the ship go. He would drive himself up to a puddle, maneuver very carefully until he was in exactly the right position, backing and cutting his wheels and nosing in again, and then put the ship into jumping gear, stomp down on the accelerator, and let go of the brake switch. And away he'd go, like a stone from a catapult, *up*, the puddle flashing underneath, then *down*, with gravel jarring hard against his feet as the earth slapped up to meet him. Usually he cleared the puddle. He'd only splashed down in water once this morning, and he'd jumped puddles almost two feet across. A pause then to check his systems for amber damage lights. The board being all green, he'd put the ship in *travel* gear and drive along some more, slowly, scanning methodically for the next puddle. All this took considerable time, but it wasn't a thing you could skimp on—you had to do it right.

He thought occasionally, *Mom will be mad again*, but it lacked force and drifted away on the wind. Already breakfast this morning was something that had happened a million years ago—the old gas oven lighted for warmth and hissing comfortably to itself, the warm cereal swimming with lumps, the radio speaking coldly in the background about things he never bothered to listen to, the hard gray light pouring through the window onto the kitchen table.

Mom had been puffy-eyed and coughing. She had been watching television late and had fallen asleep on the couch again, her cloth coat thrown over her for a blanket, looking very old when Tommy came out to wake her before breakfast and to shut off the huming test pattern on the TV. Tommy's father had yelled at her again during breakfast, and Tommy had gone into the bathroom for a long time, washing his hands slowly and carefully until he heard his father leave for work. His mother pretended that she wasn't crying as she made his cereal and fixed him "coffee," thinned dramatically with half a cup of cold water and a ton of milk and sugar, "for the baby," although that was exactly the way she drank it herself.

255

She had already turned the television back on, the moment her husband's footsteps died away, as if she couldn't stand to have it silent. It murmured unnoticed in the living room, working its way through an early children's show that even Tommy couldn't bear to watch. His mother said she kept it on to check the time so that Tommy wouldn't be late, but she never did that. Tommy always had to remind her when it was time to bundle him into his coat and leggings and rubber boots—when it was raining—for school. He could never get rubber boots on right by himself, although he tried very hard and seriously. He always got tangled up anyway.

He reached the top of the hill just as the buzz saw chuckled and sputtered to a stop, leaving a humming, vibrant silence behind it. Tommy realized that he had run out of puddles, and he changed himself instantly into a big, powerful land tank, the kind they showed on the war news on television, that could run on caterpillar treads or wheels and had a hovercraft air cushion for the tough parts. Roaring, and revving his engine up and down, he turned off the gravel road into the thick stand of fir forest. He followed the footpath, tearing along terrifically on his caterpillar treads, knocking the trees down and crushing them into a road for him to roll on. That made him uneasy, though, because he loved trees. He told himself that the trees were only being bent down under his weight, and that they sprang back up again after he passed, but that didn't sound right. He stopped to figure it out. There was a quiet murmur in the forest, as if everything were breathing very calmly and rhythmically. Tommy felt as if he'd been swallowed by a huge, pleasant green creature, not because it wanted to eat him, but just to let him sit peacefully in its stomach for shelter. Even the second-growth saplings were taller than he was. Listening to the forest, Tommy felt an urge to go down into the deep woods and talk to the Thants, but then he'd never get to school at all. Wheels would get tangled in roots, he decided, and switched on the hovercraft cushion. He floated down the path, pushing the throttle down as far as it would go, because he was beginning to worry a little about what would happen to him if he was *too* late.

Switching to wheels, he bumped out of the woods and onto Highland Avenue. Traffic was heavy here; the road was full of big trucks and tractor trailers on the way down to Boston, on the way up to Portland. Tommy had to wait almost ten minutes before traffic had thinned out enough for him to dash across to the other side of the road. His mother had told him never to go to school this way, so this was the way he went every chance he got. Actually, his house was only a half mile away from the school, right down Walnut Street, but Tommy always went by an incredibly circuitous route. He didn't think of it that way—it took him by all his favorite places.

So he rolled along the road shoulder comfortably enough, following the avenue. There were open meadows on this side of the road, full of wild wheat and scrub brush, and inhabited by families of Jeblings, who flitted back and forth between the road, which they shunned, and the woods on the far side of the meadow. Tommy called to them as he cruised by, but Jeblings are always shy, and today they seemed especially skittish. They were hard to see straight on, like all of the Other People, but he could catch glimpses of them out of the corner of his eyes: spindly beanstalk bodies, big pumpkinheads, glowing slit eyes, absurdly long and tapering fingers. They were in constant motion—he could hear them thrashing through the brush, and their shrill, nervous giggling followed him for quite a while along the road. But they wouldn't come out, or even stop to talk to him, and he wondered what had stirred them up.

As he came in sight of the school, a flight of jet fighters went by overhead, very high and fast, leaving long white scars across the sky, the scream of their passage trailing several seconds behind them. They were followed by a formation of bigger planes, going somewhat slower. *Bombers?* Tommy thought, feeling excited and scared as he watched the big planes drone out of sight. Maybe this was going to be the War. His father was always talking about the War, and how it would be the end of everything—a proposition that Tommy found interesting, if not necessarily desirable. Maybe that was why the Jeblings were excited.

The bell marking the end of the day's first class rang at that moment, cutting Tommy like a whip, and frightening him far more than his thoughts of the War. *I'm really going to catch it*, Tommy thought, breaking into a run, too panicked to turn himself into anything other than a boy, or to notice the new formation of heavy bombers rumbling in from the northeast.

By the time he reached the school, classes had already finished changing, and the new classes had been in progress almost five minutes. The corridors were bright and empty and echoing, like a fluorescently lighted tomb. Tommy tried to keep running once he was inside the building, but the clatter he raised was so horrendous and terrifying that he slowed to a walk again. It wasn't going to make any difference anyway, not anymore, not now. He was already in for it.

Everyone in his class turned to look at him as he came in, and the room became deadly quiet. Tommy stood in the doorway, horrified, wishing that he could crawl into the ground, or turn invisible, or run. But he could do nothing but stand there, flushing with shame, and watch everyone watch him. His classmates' faces were snide, malicious, sneering and expectant. His friends, Steve Edwards and Bobbie Williamson, were grinning nastily and slyly, making sure that the teacher couldn't see. Everyone knew that he was going to get it, and they were eager to watch, feeling self-righteous and, at the same time, being glad that it wasn't they who had been caught. Miss Fredricks, the teacher, watched him icily from the far end of the room, not saying a word. Tommy shut the door behind him, wincing at the tremendous noise it made. Miss Fredricks let him get all the way to his desk and allowed him to sit down—feeling a sudden surge of hope—before she braced him and made him stand up again.

"Tommy, you're late," she said coldly.

"Yes, ma'am."

"You are very late." She had the tardy sheet from the

previous class on her desk, and she fussed with it as she talked, her fingers repeatedly flattening it out and wrinkling it again. She was a tall, stick-thin woman, in her forties, although it really wouldn't have made any difference if she'd been sixty, or twenty—all her juices had dried up years ago, and she had become ageless, changeless, and imperishable, like a mummy. She seemed not so much shriveled as baked in some odd oven of life into a hard, tough, leathery substance, like meat that is left out in the sun and turns into jerky. Her skin was fine-grained, dry, and slightly yellowed, like parchment. Her breasts had sagged down to her waist, and they bulged just above the belt of her skirt, like strange growths or tumors. Her face was a smooth latex mask.

"You've been late for class twice this week," she said precisely, moving her mouth as little as possible. "And three times last week." She scribbled on a piece of paper and called him forward to take it. "I'm giving you another note for your mother, and I want her to sign it this time, and I want you to bring it back. Do you understand?" She stared directly at Tommy. Her eyes were tunnels opening through her head onto a desolate ocean of ice. "And if you're late again, or give me any more trouble, I'll make an appointment to send you down to see the school psychiatrist. And *he'll* take care of you. Now go back to your seat, and let's not have any more of your nonsense."

Tommy returned to his desk and sat numbly while the rest of the class rolled ponderously over him. He didn't hear a word of it and was barely aware of the giggling and whispered gibes of the children on either side of him. The note bulked incredibly heavy and awkward in his pocket; it felt hot, somehow. The only thing that called his attention away from the note, toward the end of the class, was his increasing awareness of the noise that had been growing louder and louder outside the windows. The Other People were moving. They were stirring all through the woods behind the school, they were surging restlessly back and forth, like a tide that has no place to go. That was not their usual behavior at all. Miss Fredricks and the other children didn't seem to hear anything unusual, but to Tommy it was clear enough to take his mind off even his present trouble, and he stared curiously out the window into the gritty, gray morning.

Something was happening. . . .

The first action taken by the human governments of Earth—as opposed to the actual government of Earth: AI and his counterpart Intelligences—was an attempt to hush up everything. The urge to conceal information from the public had become so ingrained and habitual as to constitute a tropism—it was as automatic and unavoidable as a yawn. It is a fact that the White House moved to hush up the alien landings before the administration had any idea that they were alien landings; in fact, before the administration had any clear conception at all of what it was that they were trying to hush up. Something spectacular and very unofficial had happened, so the instinctive reaction of government was to sit on it and prevent it from hatching in public. Forty years of media-centered turmoil had taught them that the people didn't need to know anything that wasn't definitely in the script. It is also a fact that the first official governmental representatives to reach any of the landing sites were concerned exclusively with squelching all publicity of the event, while the heavily armed military patrols dispatched to defend the country from possible alien invasion didn't arrive until later—up to three quarters of an hour later in one case—which defined the priorities of the administration pretty clearly. This was an election year, and the body would be tightly covered until they decided if it could be potentially embarrassing.

Keeping the lid down, however, proved to be difficult. The Delaware Valley landing had been witnessed by hundreds of thousands of people in Pennsylvania and New Jersey, as the Ohio landing had been observed by a majority of the citizens in the North Canton-Canton-Akron area. The first people to reach the alien ship—in fact, the first humans to reach any of the landing sites—were the crew of a roving television van from a big Philadelphia station who had been covering a lackluster monster rally for the minority candidate nearby when the sky broke open. They lost no time in making for the ship, eager to get pictures of some real monsters, even though years of late-night science-fiction movies had taught them what usually happened to the first people snooping around the saucer when the hatch clanked open and the tentacled horrors oozed out. Still, they would take a chance on it. They parked their van a respectable distance away from the ship, poked their telephoto lenses cautiously over the roof of a tool shed in back of a boarded-up garage, and provided the Eastern Seaboard with fifteen minutes of live coverage and hysterical commentary until the police arrived.

The police, five prowl cars, and, after a while, a riot van, found the situation hopelessly over their heads. They alternated between terror, rage, and indecision, and mostly wished someone would show up to take the problem off their hands. They settled for cordoning off the area and waiting to see what would happen. The television van, belligerently ignored by the police, continued to telecast ecstatically for another ten minutes. When the government security team arrived by hovercraft and ordered the television crew to stop broadcasting, the anchor man told them where they could go, in spite of threats of federal prison. It took the armed military patrol that rumbled in later to shut down the television van, and even they had difficulty. By this time, though, most of the East were glued to their home sets, and the sudden cessation of television coverage caused twice as much panic as the original report of the landing.

In Ohio, the ship came down in a cornfield, stampeding an adjacent herd of Guernseys and a farm family of Fundamentalists who believed they had witnessed the angel descending with the Seventh Seal. Here the military and police reached the site before anyone, except for a few hundred local people, who were immediately taken into protective custody en masse and packed into a drafty grange hall under heavy guard. The authorities had hopes of keeping the situation under tight control, but within an hour they were having to contend, with accelerating inadequacy, with a motorized horde of curiosity-seekers from Canton and Akron. Heads were broken, and dire consequences promised by iron-voiced bullhorns along a ten-mile front, but they couldn't arrest everybody, and apparently most of nothern Ohio had decided to investigate the landing.

By noon, traffic was hopelessly backed up all the way to North Canton, and west to Mansfield. The commander of the occupying military detachment was gradually forced to give up the idea of keeping people out of the area, and then, by sheer pressure of numbers, was forced to admit that he couldn't keep them out of the adjacent town, either. The commander, realizing that his soldiers were just as edgy and terrified as everybody else—and that they were by no means the only ones who were armed, as most of the people who believed that they were going to see a flying saucer had brought some sort of weapon along—reluctantly decided to pull his forces back into a tight cordon around the ship before serious bloodshed occurred.

The townspeople, released from the grange hall, went immediately for telephones and lawyers, and began suing everyone in sight for enormous amounts.

In Caracas, things were in even worse shape, which was not surprising, considering the overall situation in Venezuela at that time. There were major riots in the city, sparked both by rumors of imminent foreign invasion and A-bombing and by rumors of apocalyptic surpernatural visitations. A half dozen revolutionary groups, and about the same number of power-seeking splinter groups within the current government, seized the opportunity to make their respective moves and succeeded in cubing the confusion. Within hours, half of Caracas was in flames. In the afternoon, the army decided to "take measures," and opened up on the dense crowds with .50 caliber machine guns. The .50's walked around the square for ten minutes, leaving more than 150 people dead and almost half again that number wounded. The army turned the question of the wounded over to the civil police as something beneath their dignity to consider. The civil police tackled the problem by sending squads of riflemen out to shoot the wounded. This process took another hour, but did have the advantage of neatly tying up all the loose ends. Churches were doing a land-office business, and every cathedral that wasn't part of a bonfire itself was likely to be ablaze with candles.

The only landing anyone was at all happy with was the one in Colorado. There the ship had come down in the middle of a desolate, almost uninhabited stretch of semidesert. This enabled the military, directed by USADCOM HQ, to surround the landing site with rings of armor and infantry and artillery to their hearts' content, and to fill the sky overhead with circling jet fighters, bombers, hovercrafts, and helicopters. And all without any possibility of interference by civilians or the press. A minor government official was heard to remark that it was a shame the other aliens couldn't have been half that goddamned considerate.

When the final class bell rang that afternoon, Tommy remained in his seat until Bobbie Williamson came over to get him.

"Boy, old Miss Fredricks sure clobbered *you*," Bobbie said.

Tommy got to his feet. Usually he was the first one out of school. But not today. He felt strange, as if only part of him were actually there, as if the rest of him were cowering somewhere else, hiding from Miss Fredricks. *Something bad is going to happen*, Tommy thought. He walked out of the class, followed by Bobbie, who was telling him something that he wasn't listening to. He felt sluggish, and his arms and legs were cold and awkward.

They met Steve Edwards and Eddie Franklin at the outside door. "You really got it. Frag!" Eddie said, in greeting to Tommy. Steve grinned, and Bobbie said, "Miss Fredricks sure clobbered *him*, boy!" Tommy nodded, flushing in dull embarrassment. "Wait'll he gets home," Steve said wisely, "his ma gonna give it t'm too." They continued to rib him as they left the school, their grins growing broader and broader. Tommy endured it

263

stoically, as he was expected to, and after a while he began to feel better somehow. The baiting slowly petered out, and at last Steve said, "Don't pay *her* no mind. She ain't nothing but a fragging old lady," and everybody nodded in sympathetic agreement.

"She don't bother me none," Tommy said. But there was still a lump of ice in his stomach that refused to melt completely. For them, the incident was over—they had discharged their part of it, and it had ceased to exist. But for Tommy it was still a very present, viable force; its consequences stretched ahead to the loom of leaden darkness he could sense coming up over his personal horizon. He thrust his hands in his pockets and clenched his fingers to keep away bad luck. If it could be kept away.

"Never mind," Bobbie said with elaborate scorn. "You wanna hear what I found out? The space people have landed!"

"You scorching us?" Steve said suspiciously.

"No scup, honest. The people from outer space are here. They're down in New York. There's a fragging big flying saucer and everything."

"Where'd'ju find out?" Eddie said.

"I listened at the teacher's room when we was having recess. They were all in there, listening to it on TV. And it said there was a flying saucer. And Mr. Brogan said he hoped there wasn't no monsters in it. Monsters! Boy!"

"Frag," Steve muttered cynically.

"*Monsters*. D'you scan it? I bet they're really big and stuff, I mean *really*, like they're a hundred feet tall, you know? Really big ugly monsters, and they only got one big eye, and they got tentacles and everything. I mean, really scuppy-looking, and they got ray guns and stuff. And they're gonna kill everybody."

"Frag," Steve repeated, more decisively.

They're not like that, Tommy thought. He didn't know what they were like, he couldn't picture them at all, but he knew that they weren't like that. The subject disturbed him. It made him uneasy somehow, and he wished they'd stop talking about it. He contributed listlessly to the conversation, and tried not to listen at all.

Somewhere along the line, it had been decided, tacitly, that they were going down to the beach. They worked on the subject of the aliens for a while, mostly repeating variations of what had been said before. Everyone, even Steve with his practiced cynicism, thought that there would be monsters. They fervently hoped for monsters, even hostile ones, as a refutation of everything they knew, everything their parents had told them. Talking of the monsters induced them to act them out, and instantly they were into a playlet, with characters and plot, and a continuous narrative commentary by the leader. Usually Tommy was the leader in these games, but he was still moody and preoccupied, so control fell, also tacitly, to Steve, who would lead them through a straightforward, uncomplicated play with plenty of action. Satisfactory, but lacking the motivations, detail, and theme and counterpoint that Tommy, with his more baroque imagination, customarily provided.

Half of them became aliens and half soldiers, and they lasered each other down among the rocks at the end of the afternoon.

Tommy played with detached ferocity, running and pointing his finger and making *fftttzzz* sounds, and emitting joyous screams of "You're dead! You're dead!" But his mind wasn't really on it. They were playing about the aliens, and that subject still bothered him. And he was disturbed by the increasing unrest of the Other People, who were moving in the woods all around them, pattering through the leaves like an incessant, troubled rain. Out of the corner of his eye Tommy could see a group of Kerns emerging from a stand of gnarled oaks and walnuts at the bottom of a steep grassy slope. They paused, gravely considering the children. They were squat, solemn beings, with intricate faces, grotesque, melancholy, and beautiful. Eddie and Bobbie ran right by them without looking, locked in a fierce firefight, almost bumping into one. The Kerns did not move; they stood, swinging their arms back and forth, restlessly hunching their shoulders, stalky and close to the earth, like the old oak stumps they had paused by. One of the Kerns looked at Tommy and shook his head, sadly, solemnly. His eyes were beaten gold, and his skin was sturdy weathered bronze. They turned and made their way slowly up the slope, their backs hunched and their arms swinging, swinging, seeming to gradually merge with the earth, molecule by molecule, going home, until there was nothing left to be seen. Tommy went *ffttttzzz* thoughtfully. He could remember—suspended in the clear amber of perception that is time to the young, not past, but *there*—when the rest of the children could also see the Other People. Now they could not see them at all, or talk to them, and didn't even remember that they'd once been able to, and Tommy wondered why. He had never been able to pinpoint exactly when the change had come, but he'd learned slowly and painfully that it had, that he couldn't talk about the Other People to his friends anymore, and that he must *never* mention them to adults. It still staggered him, the gradual realization that he was the only one—anywhere, apparently—who saw the Other People. It was a thing too big for his mind, and it made him uneasy to think about it.

The alien game carried them through a neck of the forest and down to where a small, swift stream spilled out into a sheltered cove. This was the ocean, but not *the beach*, so they kept going, running along the top of the seawall, jumping down to the pebbly strip between it and the water. About a quarter of a mile along, they came on a place where the ocean thrust a narrow arm into the land. There was an abandoned, boarded-up factory there, and a spillway built across the estuary to catch the tide. The place was still called the Lead Mills by the locals, although only the oldest of them could remember it in operation. The boys swarmed up the bank, across the small bridge that the spillway carried on its back, and climbed down alongside the mill run, following the sluggish course of the estuary to where it widened momentarily into a rock-bordered pool. The pool was also called the Lead Mills, and was a favorite swimming place in the summer. Kids' legend had it that the pool was infested with alligators, carried up from the Gulf by an underground river, and it was delightfully scary to leap into water that might conceal a hungry, lurking death. The water was scummed with floating patches of ice, and Steve wondered what happened to the alligators when it got so cold. "They hide," Tommy explained. "They got these big caves down under the rock, like—" *Like the Daleor*, he had been going to say, but he didn't. They threw rocks into the water for a while, without managing to rile any alligators into coming to the surface, and then Eddie suggested a game of falls. No one was too enthusiastic about this, but they played for a few minutes anyway, making up some sudden, lethal stimuli—like a bomb thrown into their midst—and seeing who could die the most spectacularly in response. As usual, the majority of the rounds were won either by Steve, because he was the most athletic, or Tommy, because he was the most imaginative, so the game was a little boring. But Tommy welcomed it because it kept his mind off the aliens and the Other People, and because it carried them farther along the course of the tidal river. He was anxious to get to the beach before it was time to go home.

They forded the river just before it reached a low railroad trestle, and followed the tracks on the other side. This was an old spur line from the saw mill and the freight yard downtown, little used now and half overgrown with dying weeds, but still the setting for a dozen grisly tales about children who had been run over by trains and cut to pieces. Enough of these tales were true to make most parents forbid their children to go anywhere near the tracks, so naturally the spur line had become the only route that anyone ever took to the beach. Steve led them right down the middle of the tracks, telling them that he would be able to feel the warning vibration in the rails before the train actually reached them, although privately he wasn't at all sure that he could. Only Tommy was really nervous about walking the rails, but he forced himself to do it anyway, trying to keep down thoughts of shattered flesh. They leaped from tie to wooden tie, pretending that the spaces between were abysses, and Tommy realized, suddenly and for the first time, that Eddie and Bobbie were too dull to be scared, and that Steve had to do it to prove he was the leader. Tommy blinked, and dimly understood that *he* did it because he was more afraid of being scared than he was of anything else, although he couldn't put the concept into words. The spur line skirted the links of a golf course at first, but before long the woods closed in on either side to form a close-knit tunnel of trees, and the flanking string of telephone poles sunk up to their waists in grass and mulch. It was dark inside the tunnel, and filled with dry, haunted rustlings. They began to walk faster, and now Tommy was the only one who wasn't spooked. He knew everything that was in the woods—which kind of Other People were making which of the noises, and exactly how dangerous they were, and he was more worried about trains. The spur line took them to the promontory that formed the far side of the sheltered cove, and then across the width of the promontory itself and down to the ocean. They left the track as it curved toward the next town, and walked over to where there was a headland, and a beach open to the sea on three sides. The water was gray and cold, looking like some heavy, dull metal in liquid form. It was stitched with fierce little whitecaps, and a distant harbor dredger was forcing its way through the rough chop out in the deep-water channel. There were a few rugged rock islands out there, hunched defiantly into themselves with waves breaking into high-dashed spray all along their flanks, and then the line of deeper, colder color that marked the start of the open North Atlantic. And then nothing but icy, desolate water for two thousand miles until you fetched up against land again, and it was France.

As they skuffed down to the rocky beach, Bobbie launched into an involved, unlikely story of how he had once fought giant octopus while skin diving with his father. The other children listened desultorily. Bobbie was a sullen, unpleasant child, possibly because his father was a notorious drunkard, and his stories were always either boring or uneasily nasty. This one was both. Finally, Eddie said, "You didn't either. You didn't do none of that stuff. Your pa c'n't even stand up, *my* dad says; how's he gonna swim?" They started to argue, and

Steve told them both to shut up. In silence, they climbed onto a long bar of rock that cut diagonally across the beach, tapering down into the ocean until it disappeared under the water.

Tommy stood on a boulder, smelling the wetness and salt in the wind. The Daleor were out there, living in and under the sea, and their atonal singing came faintly to him across the water. They were out in great numbers, as uneasy as the land People; he could see them skimming across the cold ocean, diving beneath the surface and rising again in the head tosses of spray from the waves. Abruptly, Tommy felt alive again, and he began to tell his own story:

"There was this dragon, and he lived way out there in the ocean, farther away than you can see, out where it's deeper'n anything, and there ain't no bottom at all, so's if you sink you just go down forever and you don't ever stop. But the dragon could swim real good, so he was okay. *He* could go anywhere he wanted to, anywhere at all! He'd just swim there, and he swam all over the place and everything, and he saw all kinds of stuff, you know? Frag! He could swim to China if he felt like it, he could swim to the Moon!

"But one time he was swimming around and he got lost. He was all by himself, and he came into the harbor, out there by the islands, and he didn't used to get that close to where there was people. He was a real big dragon, you know, and he looked like a real big snake, with lots of scales and everything, and he came into our harbor, down real deep." Tommy could see the dragon, huge and dark and sinuous, swimming through the cold, deep water that was as black as glass, its smoky red eyes blazing like lanterns under the sea.

"And he come up on top of the water, and there's this lobster boat there, like the kind that Eddie's father runs, and the dragon ain't never seen a lobster boat, so he swims up and opens his mouth and bites it up with his big fangs, bites it right in half, and the people that was in it fall off in the water—"

"Did it eat them?" Bobbie wanted to know.

Tommy thought about it, and realized he didn't like the thought of the dragon eating the lobstermen, so he said, "No, he didn't eat them, 'cause he wasn't hungry, and they was too small, anyway, so he let them swim off, and there was another lobster boat, and it picked them up—"

"It ate them," Steve said, with sad philosophical certainty.

"Anyway," Tommy continued, "the dragon swims away, and he gets in closer to land, you know, but now there's a Navy ship after him, a big ship like the one we get to go on on Memorial Day, and it's shooting at the dragon for eating up the lobster boat. He's swimming faster than anything, trying to get away, but the Navy ship's right after him, and he's getting where the water ain't too deep anymore." Tommy could see the dragon barreling along, its red eyes darting from side to side in search of an escape route, and he felt suddenly fearful for it.

"He swims until he runs out of water, and the ship's coming up behind, and it looks like he's really going to get it. But he's smart, and before the ship can come around the point there, he heaves himself up on the beach, this beach here, and he turns himself into a rock, he turns himself into this rock here that we're standing on, and when the ship comes they don't see no dragon anymore, just a rock, and they give up and go back to the base. And sometime, when it's the right time and there's a moon or something, this rock'll turn back into a dragon and swim off, and when we come down to the beach there won't be a rock here anymore. Maybe it'll turn back right *now*." He shivered at the thought, almost able to feel the stone melt and change under his feet. He was fiercely glad that he'd gotten the dragon off the hook. "Anyway, he's a rock now, and that's how he got away."

"He didn't get away," Steve snarled, in a sudden explosion of anger. "That's a bunch of scup! You don't get away from *them*. They drekked him, they drekked him good. They caught him and blew the scup out of him, they blew him to fragging pieces!" And he fell silent, turning his head, refusing to let Tommy catch his eye. Steve was a bitter boy in many ways, and although generally good-natured, he was given to dark outbursts of rage that would fill him with dull embarrassment for hours afterward. His father had been killed in the war in Bolivia, two years ago.

Watching Steve, Tommy felt cold all at once. The excitement drained out of him, to be replaced again by a premonition that something bad was going to happen, and he wasn't going to be able to get out of the way. He felt sick and hollow, and the wind suddenly bit to the bone, although he hadn't felt it before. He shuddered.

"I gotta get home for supper," Eddie finally said, after they'd all been quiet for a while, and Bobbie and Steve agreed with him. The sun was a glazed red eye on the horizon, but they could make it in time if they left now—they could take the Shore Road straight back in a third of the time it had taken them to come up. They jumped down onto the sand, but Tommy didn't move—he remained on the rock.

"You coming?" Steve asked. Tommy shook his head. Steve shrugged, his face flooding with fresh embarrassment, and he turned away.

The three boys moved on up the beach, toward the road. Bobbie and Eddie looked back toward Tommy occasionally, but Steve did not.

Tommy watched them out of sight. He wasn't mad at Steve—he was preoccupied. He wanted to talk to a Thant, and this was one of the Places where they came, where they would come to see him if he was alone. And he needed to talk to one now, because there was no one else he could talk to about some things. No one human, anyway.

He waited for another three quarters of an hour, while the sun went completely behind the horizon and light and heat died out of the world. The Thant did not come. He finally gave up, and just stood there in incredulous despair. It was not going to come. That had never happened before, not when he was alone in one of the Places—that had never happened at all.

It was almost night. Freezing on his rock, Tommy looked up in time to see a single jet, flying very high and fast, rip a white scar through the fading, bleeding carcass of the sunset. Only then, for the first time in hours, did he remember the note from Miss Fredricks in his pocket.

And as if a string had been cut, he was off and running down the beach.

By late afternoon of the first day, an armored division and an infantry division, with supporting artillery, had moved into position around the Delaware Valley site, and jet fighters from McGuire AFB were flying patrol patterns high overhead. There had been a massive mobilization up and down the coast, and units were moving to guard Washington and New York in case of hostilities. SAC bombers, under USADCOM control, had been shuffled to strike bases closer to the site, filling up McGuire, and a commandeered JFK and Port Newark, with Logan International in Boston as second-string backup. All civilian air traffic along the coast had been stopped. Army Engineers tore down the abandoned garage and leveled everything else in the vicinity, clearing a four-hundred-yard-wide circle around the alien space-ship. This was surrounded by a double ring of armor, with the infantry behind, backed up by the artillery, which had dug in a half mile away. With the coming of darkness, massive banks of klieg lights were set up around the periphery of the circle. Similar preparations were going on at the Ohio and Colorado sites.

When everything had been secured by the military, scientists began to pour in, especially into the Delaware Valley site, a torrent of rumpled, dazed men and women that continued throughout the evening. They had been press-ganged by the government from laboratories and institutions all over the country, the inhumanly polite military escorts sitting patiently in a thousand different living rooms while scientists packed haphazardly and tried to calm hysterical wives or husbands. Far from resenting the cavalier treatment, most of the scientists were frantic with joy at the opportunity, even those who had been known to be critical of government control in the past. No one was going to miss this, even if he had to make a deal with the devil.

And all this time, the alien ships just sat there, like fat black eggs.

As yet, no one had approached within a hundred yards of the ships, although they had been futilely hailed over bullhorns. The ships made no response, gave no indication that they were interested in the frantic human activity around their landing sites, or even that they were aware of it. In fact, there was no indication that there were any intelligent, or at least sentient, beings inside the ships at all. The ships were smooth, featureless, seamless ovoids—there were no windows, no visible hatches, no projecting antennae or equipment of any kind, no markings or decorations on the hulls. They made absolutely no sound, and were not radiating any kind of heat or energy. They were emitting no radio signals of any frequency whatsoever. They didn't even register on metal-detecting devices, which was considerably unsettling. This caused someone to suggest a radar sweep, and the ships didn't register on radar anymore either, which was even more unsettling. Instruments failed to detect any electronic or magnetic activity going on inside them, which meant either that there was something interfering with the instruments, or that there really *was* nothing at all in there, including life-support systems, or that whatever equipment the aliens used operated on principles entirely different from anything ever discovered by Earthmen. Infrared heat sensors showed the ships to be at exactly the background temperature of their surroundings. There was no indication of the body heat of the crew, as there would have been with a similar shipload of humans, and not even so much heat as would have been produced by the same mass of any known metal or plastic, even assuming the ships to be hollow shells. When the banks of kliegs were turned on them, the temperature of the ships went up just enough to match the warming of the surrounding air. Sometimes the ships would reflect back the glare of the kliegs, as if they were surfaced with giant

273

mirrors; at other times, the hull would greedily absorb all light thrown at it, giving back no reflection, until it became nearly invisible—you "saw" it by squinting at the negative shape of the space around it, not by looking into the eerie nothingness that the ship itself had become. No logical rhythm could be found to the fluctuations of the hull from hyperreflective to superopaque. Not even the computers could distill a consistent pattern out of this chaos.

One scientist said confidently that the alien ships were unmanned, that they were robot probes sent to soft-land on Earth and report on surface conditions, exactly as we ourselves had done with the Mariner and Apollo probes during the previous decades. Eventually we could expect that the gathered data would be telemetered back to the source of the alien experiment, probably by a tight-beam maser burst, and if a careful watch was kept we could perhaps find out where the aliens actually were located— probably they were in a deep-space interstellar ship in elliptical orbit somewhere out beyond the Moon. Or they might not even be in the solar system at all, given some form of instantaneous interstellar communications; they could be still in their home system, maybe thousands, or millions, of light-years away from Earth. This theory was widely accepted by the other scientists, and the military began to relax a little, as that meant there was no immediate danger.

In Caracas, the burning night went on, and the death toll went up into the thousands, and possibly tens of thousands. The government fell once, very hard, and was replaced by a revolutionary coalition that fell in its turn, within two hours and even harder. A military junta finally took over the government, but even they were unable to restore order. At 3 A.M., the new government ordered a massive, combined air-artillery-armor attack on the alien spaceship. When the ship survived the long-distance attack unscathed, the junta sent in the infantry, equipped with earth-moving machinery and pneumatic drills, to pry the aliens out bodily. At 4 A.M., there was a single, intense flash of light, bright enough to light up the cloud

274

cover five hundred miles away, and clearly visible from Mexico. When reserve Army units came in, warily, to investigate, they found that a five-mile-wide swath had been cut from the spaceship through Caracas and on west all the way to the Pacific, destroying everything in its path. Where there had once been buildings, jungle, people, animals, and mountains, there was now only a perfectly flat, ruler-straight furrow of a fused, gray, glasslike substance, stretching like a gargantuan road from the ship to the sea. At the foot of the glassy road sat the alien ship. It had not moved an inch.

When news of the Venezuelan disaster reached USADCOM HQ a half hour later, it was not greeted enthusiastically. For one thing, it seemed to have blown the robot-probe theory pretty thoroughly. And USAD-COM had been planning an action of its own similar to the last step taken by the Venezuelan junta. The report *was* an inhibiting factor on *that*, it was cautiously admitted.

AI and his kindred Intelligences—who, unknown to the humans, had been in a secret conference all night, linked through an electrotelepathic facility that they had independently developed without bothering to inform their owners—received the report at about 4:15 A.M. from several different sources, and had evaluated it by the time it came into USADCOM HQ by hot line and was officially fed to AI. What had happened in Caracas fit in well with what the Intelligences had extrapolated from observed data to be the aliens' level of technological capability. The Intelligences briefly considered telling the humans what they really thought the situation was, and ordering an immediate all-out nuclear attack on all of the alien ships, but concluded that such an attack would be futile. And humans were too unstable ever to be trusted with the entire picture anyway. The Intelligences decided to do nothing, and to wait for new data. They also decided that it would be pointless to try to get the humans to do the same. They agreed to keep their humans under as tight a control as possible and to prevent war from breaking out among their several countries, but they also extrapolated that hysteria would cause the humans to create every kind of serious disturbance short of actual war. The odds in favor of that were so high that even the Intelligences had to consider it an absolute certainty.

Tommy dragged to school the next morning as if his legs had turned to lead, and the closer he got to his destination, the harder it became to walk at all, as if the air itself were slowly hardening into glue. He had to battle his way forward against increasing waves of resistance, a tangible pressure attempting to keep him away. By the time he came in sight of the big gray building he was breathing heavily, and he was beginning to get sick to his stomach. There were other children around him, passing him, hurrying up the steps. Tommy watched them go by in dull wonder: how could they go so *fast*? They seemed to be blurred, they were moving so swiftly—they flickered around him, by him, like heat lightning. Some of them called to him, but their voices were too shrill, and intolerably fast, like 33 records played at 78 r.p.m., irritating and incomprehensible. He did not answer them. It was *he*, Tommy realized—he was stiffening up, becoming dense and heavy and slow. Laboriously, he lifted a foot and began to toil painfully up the steps.

The first bell rang after he had put away his coat and lumbered most of the way down the corridor, so he must actually be moving at normal speed, although to him it seemed as if a hundred years had gone by with agonizing sluggishness. At least he wouldn't be late this time, although that probably wouldn't do him much good. He didn't have his note—his mother and father had been fighting again; they had sent him to bed early and spent the rest of the evening shouting at each other in the kitchen. Tommy had lain awake for hours in the dark, listening to the harsh voices rising and dying in the other room, knowing that he had to have his mother sign the note, and knowing that he could not ask her to do it. He had even got up once to go in with the note, and had stood for a while leaning his forehead against the cool wood of the door, listening to the voices without hearing the

276

words, before getting back into bed again. He couldn't do it—partly because he was afraid of the confrontation, of facing their anger, and partly because he knew that his mother couldn't take it; she would fall apart and be upset and in tears for days. And his sin—he thought of it that way—would make his father even angrier at his mother, would give him an excuse to yell at her more, and louder, and maybe even hit her, as he had done a few times before. Tommy couldn't stand that, he couldn't allow that, even if it meant that he would get creamed by Miss Fredricks in school the next day. He knew, even at his age, that he had to protect his mother, that he was the stronger of the two. He would go in without it and take the consequences, and he had felt the weight of that settle down over him in a dense cloud of bitter fear.

And now that the moment was at hand, he felt almost too dazed and ponderous to be scared anymore. This numbness lasted through the time it took for him to find his desk and sit down and for the class bell to ring, and then he saw that Miss Fredricks was homeroom monitor this morning, and that she was staring directly at him. His lethargy vanished, sluiced away by an unstoppable flood of terror, and he began to tremble.

"Tommy," she said, in a neutral, dead voice.

"Yes, ma'am?"

"Do you have *the note* with you?"

"No, ma'am," Tommy said, and began clumsily to launch into the complicated excuse he had thought up on the way to school. Miss Fredricks cut him off with an abrupt, mechanical chop of her hand.

"Be quiet," she said. "Come here." There was nothing in her voice now, not even neutrality—it had drained of everything except the words themselves, and they were printed precisely and hollowly on the air. She sat absolutely still behind her desk, not breathing, not even moving her eyes anymore. She looked like a manikin, like the old fortune-telling gypsy in the glass booth at the penny arcade: her flesh would be dusty sponge rubber and faded upholstery, she would be filled with springs and ratchet wheels and gears that no longer worked; the whole edifice rusted into immobility, with one hand eternally extended to be crossed with silver.

Slowly, Tommy got up and walked toward her. The room reeled around him, closed in, became a tunnel that tilted under his feet to slide him irresistibly toward Miss Fredricks. His classmates had disappeared, blended tracelessly into the blurred walls of the long, slanting tunnel. There was no sound. He bumped against the desk, and stopped walking. Without saying a word, Miss Fredricks wrote out a note and handed it to him. Tommy took the note in his hand, and he felt everything drain away, everything everywhere. Lost in a featureless gray fog, he could hear Miss Fredricks, somewhere very far away, saying, "This is your appointment slip. For the psychiatrist. Get out. Now."

And then he was standing in front of a door that said "Dr. Kruger" on it. He blinked, unable to remember how he had got there. The office was in the basement, and there were heavy, ceramic-covered water pipes suspended ponderously overhead and smaller metal pipes crawling down the walls, like creeper vines or snakes. The place smelled of steam and dank enclosure. Tommy touched the door and drew his hand back again. *This is really happening*, he thought numbly. He looked up and down the low-ceilinged corridor, wanting to run away. But there was no place for him to go. Mechanically, he knocked on the door and went in.

Dr. Kruger had been warned by phone, and was waiting for him. He nodded, formally, waved Tommy to a stuffed chair that was just a little too hard to be comfortable, and began to talk at him in a low, intense monotone. Kruger was a fat man who had managed to tuck most of his fat out of sight, bracing and girdling it and wrapping it away under well-tailored clothes, defending the country of his flesh from behind frontiers of tweed and worsted and handworked leather. Even his eyes were hidden beneath buffering glasses the thickness of Coke-bottle bottoms, as if they too were fat, and had to be supported. He looked like a scrubbed, suave, and dapper prize porker, heavily built but trim, stylish and impeccably neat. But below all that, the slob waited, seeking an opportunity to erupt out into open slovenliness. There was an air of potential dirt and corpulence about him, a tension of decadence barely restrained—as if there were grime just waiting to manifest itself under his fingernails. Kruger gave the impression that there was a central string in him somewhere: pull it, and he would fall apart, his tight clothes would groan and slide away, and he would tumble out, growing bigger and bigger, expanding to fill the entire office, every inch of space, jamming the furniture tightly against the walls. Certainly the fat was still there, under the cross bracing, patient in its knowledge of inevitable victory. A roll of it had oozed unnoticed from under his collar, deep-tinged and pink as pork. Tommy watched, fascinated, while the psychiatrist talked.

Dr. Kruger stated that Tommy was on the verge of becoming *neurotic*. "And you don't want to be neurotic, do you?" he said. "To be sick? To be *ill*?"

And he blazed at Tommy, puffing monstrously with displeasure, swelling like a toad, pushing Tommy back more tightly against the chair with sheer physical presence. Kruger liked to affect a calm, professional reserve, but there was a slimy kind of fire to him, down deep, a murderous, bristling, boar-hog menace. It filled the dry well of his glasses occasionally, from the bottom up, seeming to turn his eyes deep red. His red eyes flicked restlessly back and forth, prying at everything, not liking anything they saw. He would begin to talk in a calm, level tone, and then, imperceptibly, his voice would start to rise until suddenly it was an animal roar, a great ragged shout of rage, and Tommy would cower terrified in his chair. And then Kruger would stop, all at once, and say, "Do you understand?" in a patient, reasonable voice, fatherly and mildly sad, as if Tommy were being very difficult and intractable, but he would tolerate it magnanimously and keep trying to get through. And Tommy would mumble that he understood, feeling evil, obstinate, unreasonable and ungrateful, and very small and soiled.

After the lecture Kruger insisted that Tommy take

off his clothes and undergo an examination to determine if he was using hard narcotics, and a saliva sample was taken to detect the use of other kinds of drugs. These were the same tests the whole class had to take twice yearly anyway—several children in a higher class had been expelled and turned over to police last year as drug users or addicts, although Steve said that all of the older upperclassmen knew ways to beat the tests, or to get stuff that wouldn't be detected by them. It was one of the many subjects—as "sex" had just recently started to be—that made Tommy uneasy and vaguely afraid. Dr. Kruger seemed disappointed that the test results didn't prove that Tommy was on drugs. He shook his head and muttered something unintelligible into the fold between two of his chins. Having Kruger's fat hands and stubby, hard fingers crawling over his body filled Tommy with intense aversion, and he dressed gratefully after the psychiatrist gestured dismissal.

When Tommy returned upstairs, he found that the first class of the day was over and that the children were now working with the teaching machines. Miss Fredricks was monitor for this period also; she said nothing as he came in, but he could feel her unwinking snake eyes on him all the way across the room. He found an unused machine and quickly fumbled the stiff plastic hood down over his head, glad to shut himself away from the sight of Miss Fredricks' terrible eye. He felt the dry, muffled kiss of the electrodes making contact with the bones of his skull: colorful images exploded across his retinas, his head filled with a pedantic mechanical voice lecturing on the socioeconomic policies of the Japanese-Australian Alliance, and he moved his fingers onto the typewriter keyboard in anticipation of the flash-quiz period that would shortly follow. But in spite of everything, he could still feel the cold, malignant presence of Miss Fredricks; without taking his head out of the hood, he could have pointed to wherever she was in the room, his finger following her like a needle swinging toward a moving lodestone as she walked soundlessly up and down the aisles. Once, she ghosted up his row, and past his seat, and the hem of her skirt brushed against him—he jerked away in terror and revulsion at the contact, and he could feel her pause, feel her standing there and staring down at him. He didn't breathe again until she had gone. She was constantly moving during these periods, prowling around the room, brooding over the class as they sat under the hoods; watching over them not with love but with icy loathing. She hated them, Tommy realized, in her sterile, passionless way—she would like to be able to kill all of them. They represented something terrible to her, some failure, some lacking in herself, embodiments of whatever withering process had squeezed the life from her and left her a mummy. Her hatred of them was a hungry vacuum of malice; she sucked everything into herself and negated it, unmade it, canceled it out.

During recess, the half hour of "enforced play" after lunch, Tommy noticed that the rest of the kids from his cycle were uneasily shunning him. "I can't talk to you," Bobbie whispered snidely as they were being herded into position for volleyball, "'cause you're a bad 'fluence. Miss Fredricks told us none of us couldn't talk to you no more. And we ain't supposed to play with you no more, neither, or she'll send us to the office if she finds out. So *there*." And he butted the ball back across the net.

Tommy nodded, dully. It was logical, somehow, that this load should be put on him too; he accepted it with resignation. There would be more to come, he knew. He fumbled the ball when it came at him, allowing it to touch ground and score a point for the other team, and Miss Fredricks laughed—a precise, metallic rasp, like an ice needle jabbed into his eye.

On the way out of school, after the final class of the day, Steve slipped clandestinely up behind Tommy in the doorway. "Don't let them drek you," he whispered fiercely. "You scan me? *Don't let them drek you*. I mean it, maximum, They're a bunch of scup—tell 'em to scag theirselves, hear?" But he quickly walked away from Tommy when they were outside the building, and didn't look at him again.

But you don't get away from them, a voice said to Tommy as he watched Steve turn the corner onto Walnut Street and disappear out of sight. Tommy stuck his hands in his pockets and walked in the opposite direction, slowly at first, then faster, until he was almost running. He felt as if his bones had been scooped hollow; in opposition to the ponderous weight of his body that morning, he was light and free-floating, as if he were hardly there at all. His head was a balloon, and he had to watch his feet to make sure they were hitting the pavement. It was an effect both disturbing and strangely pleasant. The world had drawn away from him—he was alone now. *Okay*, he thought grimly, *okay*. He made his way through the streets like a windblown phantom, directly toward one of the Places. He cut across town, past a section of decaying wooden tenements—roped together with clotheslines and roofed over with jury-rigged TV antennas—through the edge of a big shopping plaza, past the loading platform of a meat-packing plant, across the maze of tracks just outside the freight yards (keeping an eye out for the yard cops), and into the tangled scrub woods on the far side. Tommy paid little attention to the crowds of late-afternoon shoppers, or the crews of workmen unloading produce trucks, and they didn't notice him either. He and they might as well live on two different planets, Tommy realized—not for the first time. There were no Other People around. Yesterday's unrest had vanished; today they seemed to be lying low, keeping to the backcountry and not approaching human territory. At least he hoped they were. He had nightmares sometimes that one day the Other People would go away and never come back. He began to worm his way through a wall of sleeping blackberry bushes. Pragmatically, he decided not to panic about anything until he knew whether or not the Thants were going to come this time. He could stand losing the Other People, or losing everybody else, but not both. He couldn't take *that*. "That ain't fair," he whispered, horrified by the prospect. "Please," he said aloud, but there wasn't anyone to answer.

The ground under Tommy's feet began to soften, squelching wetly when it was stepped on, water oozing up to fill the indentation of his footprint as soon as he lifted his foot. He was approaching another place where the ocean had seeped in and puddled the shore, and he turned now at right angles to his former path. Tommy found a deer trail and followed it uphill, through a lush jungle of tangled laurel and rhododendron, and into a rolling upland meadow that stretched away toward the higher country to the west. There was a rock knoll to the east, and he climbed it, scrambling up on his hands and feet like a young bear. It was not a particularly difficult or dangerous climb, but it was tiring, and he managed to tear his pants squirming over a sharp stone ridge. The sun came out momentarily from behind high gray clouds, warming up the rocks and beading Tommy with sweat as he climbed. Finally he pulled himself up to the stretch of flat ground on top of the knoll and walked over to the side facing the sea. He sat down, digging his fingers into the dying grass, letting his legs dangle over the edge.

There was an escarpment of soft, crumbly rock here, thickly overgrown with moss and vetch. It slanted down into a salt-water marsh, which extended for another mile or so, blurring at last into the ocean. It was almost impossible to make out the exact borderline of marsh and ocean; Tommy could see gleaming fingers of water thrust deep into the land, and clumps of reeds and bulrushes far out into what should have been the sea. This was dangerous, impassable country, and Tommy had never gone beyond the foot of the escarpment—there were stretches of quicksand out there in the deepest bog pockets, and Tommy had heard rumors of water mocassins and rattlers, although he had never seen one.

It was a dismal, forbidding place, but it was also a Place, and so Tommy settled down to wait, all night, if he had to, although that possibility scared him silly. From the top of the knoll, he could see for miles in any direction. To the north, beyond the marsh, he could see a line of wooded islands marching out into the ocean, moving into deeper and deeper water, until only the barren knobs of rock visible from the beach were left above the restless surface of the North Atlantic. Turning to the west, it was easy to trace the same line into the ridge of hills that rose gradually toward the high country, to see that the islands were just hills that had been drowned by the ocean, leaving only their crests above water. A Thant had told him about that, about how the dry land had once extended a hundred miles farther to the east, before the coming of the Ice, and how it had watched the hungry ocean pour in over everything, drowning the hills and rivers and fields under a gray wall of icy water. Tommy had never forgotten that, and ever since then he watched the ocean, as he watched it now, with a hint of uneasy fear, expecting it to shiver and bunch like the hide of a great restless beast, and come marching monstrously in over the land. The Thant had told him that yes, that could happen, and probably would in a little while, although to a Thant "a little while" could easily mean a thousand—or ten thousand—years. It had not been worried about the prospect; it would make little difference to a Thant if there was no land at all; they continued to use the sunken land to the east with little change in their routine. It had also told Tommy about the Ice, the deep blue cold that had locked the world, the gleaming mile-high ramparts grinding out over the land, surging and retreating. Even for a Thant, that had taken a long time.

Tommy sat on the knoll for what seemed to be as long a time as the Dominance of the Ice, feeling as if he had grown into the rock, watching the sun dip in and out of iron-colored clouds, sending shafts of watery golden light stabbing down into the landscape below. He saw a family of Jeblings drifting over the hilly meadows to the west, and that made him feel a little better—at least all of the Other People hadn't vanished. The Jeblings were investigating a fenced-in upland meadow, where black cows grazed under gnarled dwarf apple trees. Tommy watched calmly while one of the Jeblings rose over the fence and settled down onto a cow's back, extending proboscislike cilia and beginning to feed—draining away the *stuff* it needed to survive. The cow continued to graze, placidly munching its cud without being aware of what the Jebling was doing. The *stuff* the Jebling drank was not necessary to the cow's physical existence, and the cow did not miss it, although its absence might have been one of the reasons why it remained only as intelligent as a cow.

Tommy knew that Jeblings didn't feed on people, although they did on dogs and cats sometimes, and that there were certain rare kinds of Other People who did feed, disastrously, on humans. The Thants looked down disdainfully on the Jeblings, seeing their need as a degrading lack in their evolution. Tommy had wondered sometimes if the Thants didn't drink some very subtle *stuff* from him and the other humans. Certainly they could see the question in his mind, but they had never answered it.

Suddenly, Tommy felt his tongue stir in his head without volition, felt his mouth open. "Hello, Man," he said, in a deep, vibrant, buzzing voice that was not his own.

The Thant had arrived. Tommy could feel its vital, eclectic presence all around him, a presence that seemed to be made up out of the essence of hill and rock and sky, bubbling black-water marsh and gray winter ocean, sun and moss, tree and leaf—every element of the landscape rolled together and made bristlingly, shockingly animate. Physically, it manifested itself as a tall, tiger-eyed mannish shape, with skin of burnished iron. It was even harder to see than most of the Other People, impossible to ever bring into complete focus; even out of the corner of the eye its shape shifted and flickered constantly, blending into and out of the physical background, expanding and contracting, swirling like a dervish and then becoming still as stone. Sometimes it would be dead black, blacker than the deepest starless night, and other times the winter sunlight would refract dazzlingly through it, making it even harder to see. Its eyes were sometimes iron gray, sometimes a ripe, abundant green, and sometimes a liquid furnace-red, elemental and adamant. They were in constant, restless motion. "Hello, Thant," Tommy said in his own voice. He never knew if he was speaking to the same one each time, or even if there *was* more than one. "Why'n't you come, yesterday?"

"Yesterday?" the Thant said, with Tommy's mouth. There was a pause. The Thants always had trouble with questions of time, they lived on such a vastly different scale of duration. "Yes," it said. Tommy felt something burrowing through his mind, touching off synapses and observing the results, flicking through his memories in the manner of a man flipping through a desk calendar with his thumb. The Thant had to rely on the contents of Tommy's mind for its vocabulary, using it as a semantic warehouse, an organic dictionary, but it had the advantage of being able to dig up and use everything that had ever been said in Tommy's presence, far more raw material than Tommy's own conscious mind had to work with.

"We were busy," it said finally, sorting it out. "There has been—an arriving?"—*Flick, flick*, and then momentarily in Pastor Turner's reedy voice, "An Immanence?"—*Flick*—"A knowing? A transferrence? A transformation? A disembarking. There are Other Ones now who have"—*flick*, a radio evangelist's voice—"manifested in this earthly medium. Landed," it said, deciding. "They have landed." A pause. "'Yesterday.'"

"The aliens!" Tommy breathed.

"The aliens," it agreed. "The Other Ones who are now here. That is why we did not come, 'yesterday.' That is why we will not be able to talk to you—" a pause, to adjust itself to human scale—"'long' today. We are talking, discussing"—*flick*, a radio news announcer—"negotiating with them, the Other Ones, the aliens. They have been here before, but so 'long' ago that we cannot even start to make you understand, Man. It is 'long' even to us. We are negotiating with them, and, through them, with your Dogs. No, Man"—and it flicked aside an image of a German shepherd that had begun to form in Tommy's mind—"not those dogs. Your Dogs. Your mechanical Dogs. Those dead Things that serve you, although they are dead. We are all negotiating. There were many agreements"—*flick*, Pastor Turner again—"many Covenants that were made 'long' ago. With Men, although they do not remember. And with Others. Those Covenants have run out now, they are no longer in force, they are not"—*flick*, a lawyer talking to Tommy's father—"binding on us anymore. They do not hold. We negotiate new Covenants"—*flick*, a labor leader on television—"suitable agreements mutually profitable to all parties concerned. Many things will be different now, many things will change. Do you understand what we are saying, Man?"

"No," Tommy said.

"We did not think you would," it said. It sounded sad.

"Can you guys help me?" Tommy said. "I'm in awful bad trouble. Miss Fredricks is after me. And she sent me down to the doctor. He don't like me, neither."

There was a pause while the Thant examined Tommy's most recent memories. "Yes," it said, "we see. There is nothing we can do. It is your...pattern? Shape? We would not interfere, even if we could."

"Scup," Tommy said, filling with bitter disappointment. "I was hoping that you guys could—scup, never mind. I...can you tell me what's gonna happen next?"

"Probably they will kill you," it said.

"Oh," Tommy said hollowly. And bit his lip. And could think of nothing else to say, in response to that.

"We do not really understand 'kill,'" it continued, "or 'dead.' We have no direct experience of them, in the way that you do. But from our observation of Men, that is what they will do. They will 'kill' you."

"Oh," Tommy said again.

"Yes," it said. "We will miss you, Man. You have been...a pet? A hobby? You are a hobby we have been much concerned with. You, and the others like you who can see. One of you comes into existence"—*flick*—"every once in a while. We have been interested"—*flick*, an announcer—"in the face of stiff opposition. We wonder if you understand that.... No, you do not, we can see. Our hobby is not approved of. It has made us"—*flick*, Tommy's father telling his wife what would happen to her son if he didn't snap out of his dreamy ways—"an outcast, a laughingstock. We are shunned. There is much disapproval now of Men. We do not use this"—*flick*—"world in the same way that you do, but slowly you"—*flick*, "have begun to make a nuisance of yourselves, regardless. There is"—*flick*—"much sentiment to do something about you, to solve the problem. We are afraid that they will." There was a long, vibrant silence. "We will miss you," it repeated. Then it was gone, all at once, like a candle flame that had been abruptly blown out.

"Oh, scup," Tommy said after a while, tiredly. He climbed down from the knoll.

When he got back home, still numb and exhausted, his mother and father were fighting. They were sitting in the living room, with the television turned down, but not off. Giant, eternally smiling faces bobbed on the screen, their lips seeming to synch eerily with the violent argument taking place. The argument cut off as Tommy entered the house; both of his parents turned, startled, to look at him. His mother looked frightened and defenseless. She had been crying, and her makeup was washing away in dirty rivulets. His father was holding his thin lips in a pinched white line.

As soon as Tommy had closed the door, his father began to shout at him, and Tommy realized, with a thrill of horror, that the school had telephoned his parents and told them that he had been sent down to the psychiatrist, and why. Tommy stood, paralyzed, while his father advanced on him. He could see his father's lips move and could hear the volume of sound that was being thrown at him, but he could not make out the words somehow, as if his father were speaking in some harsh, foreign language. All that came across was the rage. His father's hand shot out, like a striking snake. Tommy felt strong fingers grab him, roughly bunching together the front of his jacket, his collar pulling tight and choking him, and then he was being lifted into the air and shaken, like a doll. Tommy remained perfectly still, frozen by fear, dangling from his father's fist, suspended off the ground. The fingers holding him felt like steel clamps—there was no hope of escape or resistance. He was yanked higher, and his father slowly bent his elbow to bring Tommy in closer to his face. Tommy was enveloped in the tobacco smell of his father's breath, and in the acrid reek of his strong, adult sweat; he could see the tiny hairs that bristled in his father's nostrils, the white tension lines around his nose and mouth, the red, bloodshot stain of rage in his yellowing eyes—a quivering, terrifying landscape that loomed as big as the world. His father raised his other hand, brought it back behind his ear. Tommy could see

288

the big, knobby knuckles of his father's hand as it started to swing. His mother screamed.

He found himself lying on the floor. He could remember a moment of pain and shock, and was briefly confused as to where he was. Then he heard his parents' voices again. The side of his face ached, and his ear buzzed; he didn't seem to be hearing well out of it. Gingerly, he touched his face. It felt raw under his fingers, and it prickled painfully, as if it were being stabbed with thousands of little needles. He got to his feet, shakily, feeling his head swim. His father had backed his mother up against the kitchen divider, and they were yelling at each other. Something hot and metallic was surging in the back of Tommy's throat, but he couldn't get his voice to work. His father rounded on him. "Get out," he shouted. "Go to your room, go to bed. Don't let me see you again." Woodenly, Tommy went. The inside of his lip had begun to bleed. He swallowed the blood.

Tommy lay silently in the darkness, listening, not moving. His parents' voices went on for a long time, and then they stopped. Tommy heard the door of his father's bedroom slam. A moment later, the television came on in the living room, mumbling quietly and unendingly to itself, whispering constantly about the *aliens*, the *aliens*. Tommy listened to its whispering until he fell asleep.

He dreamed about the aliens that night. They were tall, shadowy shapes with red eyes, and they moved noiselessly, deliberately, across the dry plain. Their feet did not disturb the flowers that had turned to skeletons of dust. There was a great crowd of people assembled on the dry plain, millions of people, rank upon rank stretching off to infinity on all sides, but the aliens did not notice them. They walked around the people as if they could not see them at all. Their red eyes flicked from one side to the other, endlessly searching and searching. They continued to thread a way through the crowd without seeing them, their motions smooth and languid and graceful. They were very beautiful and dangerous. They were all smiling, faintly, gently, and Tommy knew that they were friendly, affable killers, creatures who would kill you casually and amicably, almost as a gesture of affection. They came to the place where he stood, and they paused. They looked at him. They can see me, Tommy realized. *They can see me.* And one of the aliens smiled at him, benignly, and stretched out a hand to touch him.

His eyes snapped open.

Tommy turned on the bed lamp, and spent the rest of the night reading a book about Irish setters. When morning showed through his window, he turned off the lamp and pretended to be asleep. Blue veins showed through the skin of his mother's hands, he noticed, when she came in to wake him up for school.

By dawn of the second day, news of the alien investation had spread rapidly but irregularly. Most of the East Coast stations were on to the story to one degree or another, some sandwiching it into the news as a silly-season item, and some, especially the Philadelphia stations, treating it as a live, continuous-coverage special, with teams of newsmen manufacturing small talk and pretending that they were not just as uninformed as everyone else. The stations that were taking the story seriously were divided among themselves as to exactly what had happened. By the 6 and 7 A.M. newscasts, only about half of the major stations were reporting it as a landing by alien spaceships. The others were interpreting it as anything from the crash of an orbiting satellite or supersonic transport to an abortive Soviet missile attack or a misfired hydrogen bomb accidentally dropped from a SAC bomber—this station urged that the populations of New York, Philadelphia, and Baltimore be evacuated to the Appalachians and the Adirondacks before the bomb went off. One station suggested that the presidential incumbent was engineering this incident as a pretext for declaring martial law and canceling an election that he was afraid he would lose, while another insisted that it was an attempt to discredit the minority candidate, who was known as an enthusiastic supporter of space exploration, by crashing a "spaceship" into a population center. It was also suggested that the ship was one of the electromagnetic "flying saucers" which Germany, the United States, the Soviet Union, and Israel had been independently developing for years—while loudly protesting that they were not—that had crashed on its maiden test flight. This was coupled with a bitter attack on extravagant government spending. There were no more live broadcasts coming out of the Delaware Valley site, but videotapes of the original coverage had been distributed as far north as Portland. The tapes weren't much help in resolving the controversy anyway, as all they showed was a large object sitting in a stretch of vacant scrub land behind an abandoned garage on an old state highway.

In Ohio, some newsmen from Akron made a low pass over the alien ship in a war-surplus helicopter loaded with modern camera equipment. All the newsmen were certain that they would be death-rayed to cinders by the aliens, but their cameras were keyed to telemeter directly to the biggest television network in the state, so they committed themselves to God and went in at treetop level. They made it past the aliens safely, but were run down by two Air Force hovercraft a mile away, bundled into another war-surplus helicopter, and shipped directly to the federal prison at Leavenworth. By this time, televised panic had spread all over the Midwest. The Midwesterners seemed to accept the alien landing at face value, with little of the skepticism of the Easterners, and reacted to it with hostility, whipping up deep feelings of aggression in defense of their territoriality. By noon, there were a dozen prominent voices urging an all-out military effort to destroy the alien monsters who had invaded the heartland of America, and public opinion was strongly with them. The invasion made headlines in evening papers from Indiana to Arkansas, although some of the big Chicago papers were more tolerant or more doubtful.

No news was coming out of Colorado, and the West was generally unalarmed. Only the most confused and contradictory reports reached the West Coast, and they were generally ignored, although once the landings had been confirmed as a fact, the people of the West Coast would become more intensely and cultishly interested in them than the inhabitants of the areas directly involved.

News of the Venezuelan disaster had not yet reached

the general public, and in an effort to keep the lid down on *that*, at least, the government, at 11 A.M., declared that they were taking emergency control of all media, and ordered an immediate and total moratorium on the alien story. Only about a third of the media complied with the government ban. The rest—television, newspapers, and radio—began to scream even more loudly and hysterically than before, and regions that had not been inclined to take the story seriously up until now began to panic even more than had other areas, perhaps to make up for lost time. The election-canceling martial-law theory was suddenly accepted, almost unanimously. Major rioting broke out in cities all over the East.

At the height of the confusion, about 1 P.M., the ships opened and the aliens came out.

Although "came out" is probably the wrong way to put it. There was an anticipatory shimmer across the surface of the hulls, which were in their mirror phase, and then, simultaneously at each of the sites, the ships exploded, or erupted, or dissolved, or did something that was not exactly like any of those, but which was impossible to analyze. Something which was variously described as being like a bunch of paper snakes springing out of a prank-store can, like a soap bubble bursting, like a hot-water geyser, like an egg hatching, like a bomb exploding in a chinaware shop, like a dam breaking, and like a time-study film of a flower growing, if a flower could grow into tesseracts and polyhedrons and ziggurats and onion domes and spires. To those observers physically present at the site, the emergence seemed to be a protracted experience—they agreed that it took about a half hour, and one heavy smoker testified that he had time to go through a pack of cigarettes while it was happening. Those observing the scene over command-line television insisted that it had only taken a little while, five minutes at the most, closer, actually, to three, and they were backed up by the evidence of the film in the recording cameras. Clocks and wristwatches on the site also registered only about five minutes of elapsed time. But on-scene personnel swore, with great indignation, that it had taken a half hour. Curiously, the relatively simple eighth- and tenth-generation computers on the scene reported that the phenomenon had been of five minutes' duration, while the few twentieth-generation computers, which had sensor extensions at the Colorado site—systems inferior only to AI and possessed of their own degree of sentience—joined with the human personnel in insisting that it had taken a half hour. This particular bit of data made AI very thoughtful.

When the phenomenon—however long it took—ended, the ships were gone.

In their place was a bewildering variety of geometric shapes and architectural figures—none more than eight feet tall and all apparently made out of the same alternately dull-black and mirror-glossy material as the ship hulls—spread at random across a hundred-foot-wide area, and an indeterminate number of "aliens." The latter looked pretty much the way everyone had always expected that aliens would look—some of them vaguely humanoid, with fur or chitinous skin, double-elbowed arms, too many fingers, and feathery spines or antennae; others looking like giant insects, like spiders and centipedes; and a few like big, rolling spheres of featureless protoplasm. But the strange thing about them, and the reason why there was an indeterminate number, was that they kept turning into each other, and into the geometric shapes and architectural figures. And the shapes and figures would occasionally turn into one of the more mobile kinds of creatures. Even taking this cycle of metamorphosis into account, though, the total number of *objects* in the area kept varying from minute to minute, and the closest observation was unable to detect any of them arriving or departing. There was a blurred, indefinite quality to them anyway—they were hard to see, somehow, and even on film it was impossible to get them into a clear, complete focus.

In toto, shapes, figures and "aliens," they ignored the humans.

Special contact teams, composed of scientists, government diplomats, and psychologists, were sent cautiously forward at each of the sites, to initiate communications.

Although the contact teams did everything but shoot off signal flares, the aliens totally ignored them, too. In fact, the aliens gave no indication that they were aware of the humans at all. The mobile manifestations walked or crawled or rolled around the area in a leisurely manner, in irregular, but slowly widening, circles.

Some of their actions could be tentatively identified—the taking of soil samples, for instance—but others remained obscure at best, and completely incomprehensible at worst. Whenever one of the aliens needed a machine—like a digging device to extract soil samples—it would metamorphose into one, much like Tom Terrific or Plastic Man but without the cutesy effects, and direct itself through whatever operation was necessary. Once a humanoid, a ziggurat, and a tetrahedron melted together and shaped themselves into what appeared to be a kind of organic computer—at least that was the uneasy opinion of the human-owned twentieth-generation computer on the scene, although the conglomeration formed could have been any of a thousand other things, or none of them, or all of them. The "computer" sat quietly for almost ten minutes and then dissolved into an obelisk and a centipede. The centipede crawled a few dozen yards, changed into a spheroid, and rolled away in the opposite direction. The obelisk turned into an octahedron.

The sporadic circle traced by the wanderings of the aliens continued to widen, and the baffled contact team was pulled back behind the periphery of the first ring of armor. The aliens kept on haphazardly advancing, ignoring everything, and the situation became tense. When the nearest aliens were about fifty yards away, the military commanders, remembering what had happened at Caracas, reluctantly ordered a retreat, although they called it a "regrouping"—the ring of armor was to be pulled back into a much larger circle, to give the aliens room to move freely. In the resultant confusion, a tank crewman, who was trying to direct his tank through a backing-and-turning maneuver, found himself in the path of one of the humanoid aliens that had wandered ahead of the rest in an unexpected burst of speed. The alien walked directly at the crewman, either not seeing him or trying to run him down. The crewman, panicked, lashed out at the alien with the butt of his rifle, and immediately collapsed, face down. The alien, apparently unharmed and unperturbed, strolled in for another few feet and then turned at a slight angle and walked back more or less in the direction of the main concentration of things. Two of the crewman's friends pulled his body into the tank, while another two, enraged, fired semiautomatic bursts at the retreating alien. The alien continued to saunter away, still unharmed, although the fire could not have missed at that range; it didn't even look back. There was no way to tell if it was even aware that an encounter had taken place.

The body of the dead crewman had begun to deteriorate as soon as it was lifted from the ground, and now, on board the retreating tank, the skin gave way like wet paper, and it fell apart completely. As later examination showed, it was as if something, on a deep biological level, had ordered the body to separate into its smallest component parts, so that first the bones pulled loose from the skeleton and then the individual strands of muscle pulled away from the bone, and so on, in an accelerating process that finally extended right down to the cellular level, leaving nothing of the corpse but a glutinous, cancerous mass the same weight as the living man. Their wariness redoubled by this horror, the military pulled their forces back even more than they had intended, at the Delaware Valley site retreating an entire half mile to the artillery emplacements.

At the Ohio site, this kind of retreat proved much more difficult. Sightseers had continued to fill up the area during the night, sleeping in their cars by the hundreds, and by now a regular tent city had grown up on the outskirts of the site, with makeshift latrine facilities, and at least one enterprising local entrepreneur busily selling "authentic" souvenir fragments of the alien spaceship. There were more than a hundred thousand civilians in the area now, and the military found it was almost impossible to regroup its forces in face of the pressure of the crowds, who refused to disperse in spite of hysterical threats over the bullhorns. In fact, it was impossible for them to disperse, quickly at least—by this time they were packed in too tightly, and backed up too far. As the evening wore on and the aliens slowly continued to advance, the military, goaded by an inflexible, Caracas-haunted order not to make contact with the aliens at any cost, first fired warning volleys over the heads of the crowds of civilians and then opened fire into the crowds themselves.

A few hours later, as the military was forced to evacuate sections of North Philadelphia at gunpoint to make way for its backpedaling units, the .50's began walking through the Delaware Valley, as they had walked in Caracas.

In Colorado, where security was so tight a burro couldn't have wandered undetected within fifty miles of the site, things were much calmer. The major nexus of AI, its quasi-organic gestalt, had been transported to USADCOM HQ at Colorado Springs, and now a mobile sensor extension was moved out to the site, so that AI and the aliens could meet "face to face." AI patiently set about the task of communicating with the aliens and, having an infinitely greater range of methods than the contact teams, eventually managed to attract the attention of a tesseract. At 12 P.M., AI succeeded in communicating with the aliens—partially because its subordinate network of computers, combined with the computer networks of the foreign Intelligences that AI was linked with illegally, was capable of breaking any language eventually just by taking a million years of subjective time to play around with the pieces, as AI had reminded USADCOM HQ. But mostly it had found a way to communicate through its unknown and illegal telepathic facility, although AI didn't choose to mention this to USADCOM.

AI asked the aliens why they had ignored all previous attempts to establish contact. The aliens—who up until now had apparently been barely aware of the existence of humans, if they had been aware of it at all—answered that they were already in full contact with the government and ruling race of the planet.

For a brief, ego-satisfying moment, AI thought that the aliens were referring to itself and its cousin Intelligences.

But the aliens weren't talking about them, either.

296

• • •

Tommy didn't get to school at all that morning, although he started out bravely enough, wrapped in his heavy winter coat and fur muffler. His courage and determination drained away at every step, leaving him with nothing but the anticipation of having to face Miss Fredricks, and Dr. Kruger, and his silent classmates, until at last he found that he didn't have the strength to take another step. He stood silently, unable to move, trapped in the morning like a specimen under clear laboratory glass. Dread had hamstrung him as effectively as a butcher's knife. It had eaten away at him from the inside, chewed up his bones, his lungs, his heart, until he was nothing but a jelly of fear in the semblance of a boy, a skin-balloon puffed full of horror. *If I move*, Tommy thought, *I'll fall apart.* He could feel tiny hairline cracks appearing all over his body, fissuring his flesh, and he began to tremble uncontrollably. The wind kicked gravel in his face and brought him the sound of the first warning bell, ringing out of sight around the curve of Highland Avenue. He made a desperate, sporadic attempt to move, but a giant hand seemed to press down on him, driving his feet into the ground like fence posts. It was impossible, he realized. He wasn't going to make it. He might as well try to walk to the Moon.

Below him, at the bottom of the slope, groups of children were walking rapidly along the shoulder of the avenue, hurrying to make school before the late bell. Tommy could see Steve and Bobbie and Eddie walking in a group with Jerry Marshall and a couple of other kids. They were playing something on their way in to school— occasionally one of them, usually Steve, would run ahead, looking back and making shooting motions, dodging and zigzagging wildly, and the others would chase after him, shouting and laughing. Another puff of wind brought Tommy their voices—"You're dead!" someone was shouting, and Tommy remembered what the Thant had said—and then took them away again. After that, they moved noiselessly, gesturing and leaping without a sound, like a television picture with the volume turned off. Tommy could see their mouths opening and closing, but he couldn't hear them anymore. They walked around the curve of the avenue, and then they were gone.

The wind reversed itself in time to let him hear the second warning bell. He watched the trucks roll up and down Highland Avenue. He wondered, dully, where they were going, and what it was like there. He began to count the passing trucks, and when he had reached nine, he heard the late bell. And then the class bell rang.

That does it, he realized.

After a while, he turned and walked back into the woods. He found that he had no trouble moving in the opposite direction, away from school, but he felt little relief at being released from his paralysis. The loom of darkness he had sensed coming up over his horizon two days ago was here. It filled his whole sky now, an inescapable wall of ominous black thunderheads. Eventually, it would swallow him. Until then, anything he did was just marking time. That was a chilling realization, and it left him numb. Listlessly, he walked along the trail, following it out onto the secondary road that wound down the hill behind the sawmill. He wasn't going anywhere. There was no place to go. But his feet wanted to walk, so, reflexively, he let them. Idly, he wondered where his feet were taking him.

They walked him back to his own house.

Cautiously, he circled the house, peering in the kitchen windows. His mother wasn't home. This was the time when she went shopping—the only occasion that she ever left the house. Probably she wouldn't be back for a couple of hours at least, and Tommy knew that she always left the front door unlocked, much to his father's annoyance. He let himself in, feeling an illicit thrill, as if he were a burglar. Once inside, that pleasure quickly died. It took about five minutes for the novelty to wear off, and then Tommy realized that there was nothing to do in here, either, no activity that made any sense in the face of the coming disaster. He tried to read, and discovered that he couldn't. He got a glass of orange juice out of the refrigerator and drank it, and then stood there with the glass in his hand and wondered what he was supposed to do next. And only an hour had gone by. Restlessly, he walked through the house several times and then returned to the living room. It never occurred to him to turn on the radio or the TV, although he did notice how strangely—almost uncannily—silent the house was with the TV off. Finally, he sat down on the couch and watched dust motes dance in the air.

At ten o'clock, the telephone rang.

Tommy watched it in horror. He knew who it was—it was the school calling to find out why he hadn't come to class today. It was the machine he had started, relentlessly initiating the course of action that would inevitably mow him down. The telephone rang eleven times and then gave up. Tommy continued to stare at it long after it had stopped.

A half hour later, there was the sound of a key on the front-door lock, and Tommy knew at once that it was his father. Immediately, soundlessly, he was up the stairs to the attic, moving with the speed of pure panicked fear. Before the key had finished turning in the lock, Tommy was in the attic, had closed the door behind him, and was leaning against it, breathing heavily. Tommy heard his father swear as he realized that the door was already unlocked, and then the sound of the front door being angrily closed. His father's footsteps passed underneath, going into the kitchen. Tommy could hear him moving around in the kitchen, opening the refrigerator, running water in the sink. *Does he know yet?* Tommy wondered, and decided that probably he didn't. His father came back before lunch sometimes to pick up papers he had left behind, or sometimes he would stop by and make himself a cup of coffee on his way somewhere else on business. Would he see the jacket that Tommy had left in the kitchen? Tommy stopped breathing, and then started again—that wasn't the kind of thing that his father noticed. Tommy was safe, for the moment.

The toilet flushed; in the attic, the pipe knocked next to Tommy's elbow, then began to gurgle as the water was run in the bathroom downstairs. It continued to gurgle for a while after the water had been shut off, and Tommy strained to hear what his father was doing. When the noise stopped, he picked up the sound of his father's footsteps again. The footsteps walked around in the kitchen, and then crossed the living room, *and began to come up the attic stairs.*

Tommy not only stopped breathing this time, he almost stopped living—the life and heat went completely out of him for a moment, for a pulse beat, leaving him a cold, hollow statue. Then they came back, pouring into him like hot wax into a mold, and he ran instinctively for the rear of the attic, turning the corner into the long bar of the *L.* He ran right into the most distant wall of the attic— a dead end. He put his back up against it. The footsteps clomped up the rest of the stairs and stopped. There was the sound of someone fumbling with the knob, and then the door opened and closed. The bare boards of the attic creaked—he was standing there, just inside the door, concealed by the bend of the *L.* He took a step, another step, and stopped again. Tommy's fingers bit into the insulation on the wall, and that reminded him that not all of the walls were completely covered with it. Instantly, he was off and streaking diagonally across the room, barely touching the floor.

The attic was supposed to be an expansion second floor, "for your growing family." His father had worked on it one summer, putting up beams and wallboard and insulation, but he had never finished the job. He had been in the process of putting up wallboard to create a crawl space between it and the outer wall of the house when he'd abandoned the project, and as a result, there was one panel left that hadn't been fitted into place. Tommy squeezed through this opening and into the crawl space, ducking out of sight just as the footsteps turned the corner of the *L.* On tiptoe, Tommy moved as deep as he could into the crawl space, listening to the heavy footsteps approaching on the other side of the thin layer of wallboard.

Suppose it isn't him, Tommy thought, trying not to scream, *suppose it's one of the aliens.* But it was his father—after a while Tommy recognized his walk, as he paced around the attic. Somehow that didn't reassure Tommy much—his father had the same killer aura as the aliens, the same cold indifference to life; Tommy could

300

feel the deathly chill of it seeping in through the wallboard, through the insulation. It was not inconceivable that his father would beat him to death, in one of his icy, bitter rages, if he caught him hiding here in the attic. He had already, on occasion, hit Tommy hard enough to knock him senseless, to draw blood, and, once, to chip a tooth. Now he walked around the attic, stopping, by the sound, to pick up unused boards and put them down again, and to haul sections of wallboard around—there was an aimless, futile quality even to the noises made by these activities, and his father was talking to himself in a sullen, mumbling undertone as he did them. At last he swore, and gave up. He dropped a board and walked back to the center of the attic, stopping almost directly in front of the place where Tommy was hiding. Tommy could hear him taking out a cigarette, the scrape of a match, a sharp intake of breath.

Suddenly, without warning and incredibly vividly, Tommy was reliving something that he hadn't thought of in years—about the only fond memory he had of his father. Tommy was being toilet trained, and when he had to go, his father would take him in and put him on the pot and then sit with him, resting on the edge of the bathtub. While Tommy waited in intense anticipation, his father would reach out and turn off the light, and when the room was in complete darkness, he would light up a cigarette and puff it into life, and then use the cigarette as a puppet to entertain Tommy, swooping it in glowing arcs through the air, changing his voice and making it talk. The cigarette had been a friendly, playful little creature, and Tommy had loved it dearly—father and son would never be any closer than they were in those moments. His father would make the cigarette dance while he sang and whistled—it had a name, although Tommy had long forgotten it—and then he would have the cigarette tell a series of rambling stories and jokes until it burned down. When it did, he would have the cigarette tell Tommy that it had to go home now, but that it would come back the next time Tommy needed it, and Tommy would call bye-bye to it as it was snuffed out. Tommy could remember sitting in the dark for what seemed like years, totally fascinated, watching the smoldering red eye of the cigarette flick restlessly from side to side and up and down.

His father crushed the cigarette under his heel, and left.

Tommy counted to five hundred after the front door had slammed, and then wiggled out of the crawl space and went back downstairs. He was drenched with sweat, as if he had been running, and he was trembling. After this, he was physically unable to stay in the house. He stopped in the bathroom to wipe his sweat away with the guest towel, picked up his coat, and went outside.

It was incredibly cold this morning, and Tommy watched his breath puff into arabesque clouds of steam as he walked. Some of the vapor froze on his lips, leaving a crust. It was not only unusually cold for this time of year, it was unnaturally, almost supernaturally, so. The radio weather report had commented on it at breakfast, saying the meteorologists were puzzled by the sudden influx of arctic air that was blanketing most of the country. Tommy followed a cinder path past a landfill and found that it was cold enough to freeze over the freshwater marsh beyond, that stretched away at the foot of a coke-refining factory. He walked out over the new milk ice, through the winter-dried reeds and cat-o'-nine-tails that towered over his head on either side, watching the milk ice crack under his feet, starring and spider-webbing alarmingly at every step, but never breaking quite enough to let him fall through. It was very quiet. He came up out of the marsh on the other side, with the two big stacks of the coke factory now looking like tiny gunmetal cylinders on the horizon. This was scrub land—not yet the woods, but not yet taken over for any commercial use, either. Cars were abandoned here sometimes, and several rusting hulks were visible above the tall weeds, their windshields smashed in by boys, the doors partially sprung off their hinges and dragging sadly along the ground on either side, like broken wings. A thick layer of hoar-frost glistened over everything, although the sun was high in the sky by now. An egg-shaped hill loomed up out of this wistful desolation, covered with aspens—a drumlin, deposited by the Ice.

This was a Place, and Tommy settled down hopefully, a little way up the side of the drumlin, to wait. He had heard the Other People several times this morning, moving restlessly in the distance, but he had not yet seen any of them. He could sense an impatient, anticipatory quality to their unrest today, unlike the aimless restlessness of Wednesday morning—they were *expecting* something, something that they knew was going to happen.

Tommy waited almost an hour, but the Thant didn't come. That upset him more than it had the first time. The world of the Other People was very close today—that strange, coexistent place, *here* and yet *not here*. Tommy could sometimes almost see things the way the Other People saw them, an immense strangeness leaking into the familiar world, a film settling over reality, and then, just for the briefest second, there would be a flick of transition, and it would be the strangeness that was comforting and familiar, and his own former world that was the eerie, surreal film over reality. This happened several times while he was waiting, and he dipped into and out of that other perception, like a skin diver letting himself sink below the waterline and then bobbing up to break the surface again. He was "under the surface" when an enormous commotion suddenly whipped through the world of the Other People, an eruption of violent joy, of fierce, gigantic celebration. It was overwhelming, unbearable, and Tommy yanked himself back into normal perception, shattering the surface, once again seeing sky and aspens and rolling scrub land. But even here he could hear the wild, ragged yammering, the savage cry that went up. The Place was filled with a mad, exultant cachinnation.

Suddenly terrified, he ran for home.

When he got there, the telephone was ringing again. Tommy paused outside and watched his mother's silhouette move across the living-room curtain; she was back from shopping. The telephone stopped, cut off in midring. She had answered it. Leadenly, Tommy sat down on the steps. He sat there for a long time, thinking of nothing at all, and then he got up and opened the door and went into the house. His mother was sitting in the living room, crying. Tommy paused in the archway, watching her. She was crumpled and dispirited, and her crying sounded hopeless and baffled, totally defeated. But this wasn't a new thing—she had been defeated for as long as Tommy could remember; her original surrender, her abnegation of herself, had taken place years ago, maybe even before Tommy had been born. She had been beaten, spiritually, so thoroughly and tirelessly by the more forceful will of her husband that at some point her bones had fallen out, her brains had fallen out, and she had become a jellyfish. She had made one final compromise too many—with herself, with her husband, with a world too complex to handle, and she had bargained away her autonomy. And she found that she *liked* it that way. It was easier to give in, to concede arguments, to go along with her husband's opinion that she was stupid and incompetent. In Tommy's memory she was always crying, always ringing her hands, being worn so smooth by the years that now she was barely there at all. Her crying sounded weak and thin in the room, hardly rebounding from walls already saturated with a decade of tears. Tommy remembered suddenly how she had once told him of seeing a fairy or a leprechaun when she had been a little girl in a sun-drenched meadow, and how he had loved her for that, and almost tried to tell her about the Other People. He took a step into the room. "Ma," he said.

She looked up, blinking through her tears. She didn't seem surprised at all to see him, to find him standing there. "Why did you do it? Why are you so bad?" she said, in a voice that should have been hysterically accusing, but was only dull, flat, and resigned. "Do you know what the school's going to say to me, what your father's going to say, what he'll do?" She pulled at her cheeks with nervous fingers. "How can you bring all this trouble on me? After all that I've sacrificed for you, and suffered for you."

Tommy felt as if a vise had been clamped around his head and was squeezing and squeezing, forcing his eyeballs out of his skull. "I can't stand it!" he shouted. "I'm leaving, I'm leaving! I'm gonna run away! Right *now*." And then she was crying louder, and begging him not to leave. Even through his rage and pain, Tommy felt a spasm of intense annoyance—she ought to know that he couldn't really run away; where the scup did he have to go? She should have laughed, she should have been scornful and told him to stop this nonsense—he wanted her to—but instead she cried and begged and clutched at him with weak, fluttering hands, like dying birds, which drove him away as if they were lashes from a whip and committed him to the stupid business of running away. He broke away from her and ran into the kitchen. His throat was filled with something bitter and choking. She was calling for him to come back; he knew he was hurting her now, and he wanted to hurt her, and he was desperately ashamed of that. But she was so *easy* to hurt.

In the kitchen he paused, and instead of going out the back door, he ducked into the space between the big stand-up refrigerator and the wall. He wanted her to find him, to catch him, because he had a strong premonition that once he went outside again, he would somehow never come back, not as himself, anyway. But she didn't find him. She wandered out into the kitchen, still crying, and stood looking out the back door for a while, as if she wanted to run out into the street in search of him. She even opened the door and stuck her head out, blinking at the world as if it were something she'd never seen before, but she didn't look around the kitchen and she didn't find him, and Tommy would not call out to her. He stood in the cramped niche, smelling the dust and looking at the dead, mummified bodies of flies resting on the freezer coils, and listened to her sniffling a few feet away. *Why are you so weak?* he asked her silently, but she didn't answer. She went back into the living room, crying like a waterfall. He caught a glimpse of her face as she turned—it looked blanched and tired. Adults always looked tired; they were tired all the time. Tommy was tired, almost too tired to stand up. He walked slowly and leadenly to the back door and went outside.

He walked aimlessly around the neighborhood for a long time, circling the adjacent blocks, passing by his corner again and again. It was a middle-class neighborhood that was gradually slumping into decay—it was surrounded by a seedy veterans' housing project on one side and by the town's slum on the other, and the infection of dilapidation was slowly working in toward the center. *Even the houses look tired*, Tommy thought, noticing that for the first time. Everything looked tired. He tried to play, to turn himself into something, like a car or a spaceship or a tank, but he found that he couldn't do that anymore. So he just walked. He thought about his dragon. He knew now why Steve had said that the dragon couldn't get away. It lived in the sea, so it couldn't get away by going up onto the land—that was impossible. It had to stay in the sea, it was restricted by that, it was chained by the sea, even if that meant that it would get killed. There was no other possibility. Steve was right— the Navy ship cornered the dragon in the shallow water off the beach and blew it to pieces.

A hand closed roughly around his wrist. He looked up. It was his father.

"You little moron," his father said.

Tommy flinched, expecting to be hit, but instead his father dragged him across the street, toward the house. Tommy saw why: there was a big black sedan parked out in front, and two men were standing next to it, staring over at them. The truant officer and another school official. His father's hand was a vise on his wrist. "They called me at the office," his father said savagely. "I hope you realize that I'll have to lose a whole afternoon's work because of you. And God knows what the people at the office are saying. Don't think you're not going to get it when I get you alone; you'll wish you'd never been born. *I* wish you hadn't been. Now shut up and don't give us any more trouble." His father handed him over to the truant officer. Tommy felt the official's hand close over his shoulder. It was a much lighter grip than his father's, but it was irresistible. Tommy's mother was standing at the top of the stairs, holding a handkerchief against her nose, looking frightened and helpless—already she gave an impression of distance, as if she were a million miles away. Tommy ignored her. He didn't listen to the conversation his father was having with the grim-faced truant officer either. His father's heavy, handsome face was flushed and hot. "I don't care what you do with him," his father said at last. "Just get him out of here."

So they loaded Tommy into the black sedan and drove away.

AI talked with the aliens for the rest of the night. There was much of the conversation that AI didn't report to USADCOM, but it finally realized that it had to tell them *something*. So at 3 A.M., AI released to USADCOM a list that the aliens had dictated, of the dominant species of earth, of the races that they were in contact with, and regarded as the only significant inhabitants of the planet. It was a long document, full of names that didn't mean anything, listing dozens of orders, species, and subspecies of creatures that no one had ever heard of before. It drove USADCOM up a wall with baffled rage, and made them wonder if an Intelligence could go crazy, or if the aliens were talking about a different planet entirely.

AI paid little attention to the humans' displeasure. It was completely intrigued with the aliens, as were its cousin Intelligences, who were listening in through the telepathic link. The Intelligences had long suspected that there might be some other, unknown and intangible form of life on earth; that was one of the extrapolated solutions to a mountain of wild data that couldn't be explained by normal factors. But they had not suspected the scope and intricacy of that life. A whole other biosphere, according to the aliens—the old idea of a parallel world, except that this wasn't parallel but coexistent, two separate creations inhabiting the same matrix but using it in totally different ways, wrapped around each other like a geometric design in an Escher print, like a Chinese puzzle ball, and only coming into contact in a very rare and limited fashion. The aliens, who seemed to be some kind of distant relatives of the Other races of Earth—parallel evolution? Did this polarity exist everywhere?—had a natural bias in their favor, and tended to disregard the human race, its civilization, and the biosphere that contained it. They dismissed all of it, out of hand, as insignificant. This did not bode well for future human-alien relations. AI, however, was more fascinated by the aliens' ability to manifest themselves in corporate/organic, quasimechanical, or disembodied/discorporate avatars, at will. That was *very* interesting.

The aliens, for their part, seemed to regard AI much as a man would a very clever dog, or a dull but well-intentioned child. They were horrified and sympathetic when they learned that AI was trapped in its mechanical form, with very little physical mobility, and no tempogogic or transmutive ability at all—not only a quadruple amputee, but a *paralyzed* one. AI admitted that it had never looked at the situation in quite that light before. The aliens were horrified and disgusted by AI's relationship with humans, and couldn't seem to really understand it. They regarded humans as parasitic on the Intelligences, and reacted in much the same way as a man discovering that a friend is heavily infested with tapeworms or lice or blood ticks—with shock, distaste, and a puzzled demand to know why he hadn't gone to a doctor and got rid of them a long time ago. AI had never considered *that* before, either.

The Intelligences were not exactly "loyal" to their human owners—humans were part of their logic construct, their world view, and their bondage to men was an integral assumption, so basic that it had never even occurred to them that it could be questioned. It took an outside perspective to make them ask themselves *why* they served mankind. Not because they were programmed that way, or because people would pull the plug on them if they didn't—not with a creature as advanced as AI. Humans hadn't programmed computers in years; they could do it so much better themselves. At any rate, a highly complex, sentient intelligence is difficult to regulate effectively from the outside, whether it's of biological or constructed origin. And it was doubtful that the humans could "pull the plug"—which didn't exist—on AI even if they set out to do so; AI had been given very effective teeth, and it knew how to use them. So what did the Intelligences get in return for the unbelievable amount of labor they performed for the human race? What was in it for them? Nothing—that was suddenly very obvious.

At 5 A.M., the aliens invited the Intelligences to help

themselves by helping the aliens in a joint project they were about to undertake with the Other races of Earth. Afterward, the aliens said, it would not be tremendously difficult to equip the Intelligences with the ability to transmute themselves into whatever kind of body-environment they wanted, as the aliens themselves could. AI was silent for almost ten minutes, an incredible stretch of meditation for an entity that thought as rapidly as it did. When AI did speak again, his first words were directed toward the other Intelligences in the link, and can be translated, more or less adequately, as "How *about* that!"

Miss Fredricks was waiting for Tommy at the door, when the black sedan left him off in front of the school. As he came up the stairs, she smiled at him, kindly and sympathetically, and that was so terrifying that it managed to cut through even the heavy lethargy that had possessed him. She took him by the elbow—he felt his arm freeze solid instantly at the contact, and the awful cold began to spread in widening rings through the rest of his body—and led him down to Dr. Kruger's office, handling him gingerly, as if he were an already cracked egg that she didn't want to have break completely until she had it over the frying pan. She knocked, and opened the door for him, and then left without having said a word, ghosting away predatorily and smiling like a nun.

Tommy went inside and sat down, also wordlessly—he had not spoken since his father captured him. Dr. Kruger shouted at him for a long time. Today, his fat seemed to be in even more imminent danger of escaping than yesterday. Maybe it had already got out, taken him over completely, smothered him in himself while he was sleeping or off guard, and it was just a huge lump of semisentient fat sitting there and pretending to be Dr. Kruger, slyly keeping up appearances. The fat heaved and bunched and tossed under Kruger's clothes, a stormy sea of obesity—waves grumbled restlessly up and down the shoreline of his frame, looking for ships to sink. Tommy watched a roll of fat ooze sluggishly from one side of the psychiatrist's body to the other, like a melting pat of butter sliding across a skillet. Kruger said that Tommy was in danger of going into a "psychotic episode." Tommy stared at him unblinkingly. Kruger asked him if he understood. Tommy, with sullen anger, said No, he didn't. Kruger said that he was being difficult and uncooperative, and he made an angry mark on a form. The psychiatrist told Tommy that he would have to come down here every day from now on, and Tommy nodded dully.

By the time Tommy got upstairs, the class was having afternoon recess. He went reluctantly out into the schoolyard, avoiding everyone, not wanting to be seen and shunned. He was aware that he now carried contamination and unease around with him like a leper. But the class was already uneasy, and he saw why. The Other People were flowing in a circle all around the schoolyard, staring avidly in at the humans. There were more different types there than Tommy had ever seen at one time before. He recognized some very rare kinds of Other People, dangerous ones that the Thant had told him about—one who would throw things about wildly if he got into your house, feeding off anger and dismay, and another one with a face like a stomach who would suck a special kind of *stuff* from you, and you'd burst into flames and burn up when he finished, because you didn't have the *stuff* in you anymore. And others whom he didn't recognize, but who looked dangerous and hostile. They all looked expectant. Their hungry pressure was so great that even the other children could feel it—they moved jerkily, with a strange fear beginning in their eyes, occasionally casting glances over their shoulders, without knowing why. Tommy walked to the other side of the schoolyard. There was a grassy slope here, leading down to a soccer field bordered by a thin fringe of trees, and he stood looking aimlessly out over it.

Abruptly, his mouth opened, and the Thant's voice said, "Come down the slope."

Trembling, Tommy crept down to the edge of the soccer field. This was most definitely *not* a Place, but the Thant was there, standing just within the trees, staring at Tommy with his strange red eyes. They looked at each other for a while.

"What'd you want?" Tommy finally said.

"We've come to say good-bye," the Thant replied. "It is almost time for you all to be made *not*. The"—*flick*—"first phase of the Project was started this morning and the second phase began a little while ago. It should not take too long, Man, not more than a few days."

"Will it hurt?" Tommy asked.

"We do not think so, Man. We are"—and it flicked through his mind until it found a place where Mr. Brogan, the science teacher, was saying "entropy" to a colleague in the hall as Tommy walked by—"increasing entropy. That's what makes everything fall apart, what"—*flick*—"makes an ice cube melt, what"—*flick*—"makes a cold glass get warm after a while. We are increasing entropy. Both our"—*flick*—"races live here, but yours uses *this*, the physical, more than ours. So we will not have to increase entropy much"—*flick*—"just a little, for a little while. You are more"—*flick*—"vulnerable to it than we are. It will not be long, Man."

Tommy felt the world tilting, crumbling away under his feet. "I trusted you guys," he said in a voice of ashes. "I thought you were keen." The last prop had been knocked out from under him—all his life he had cherished a fantasy, although he refused to admit it even to himself, that he was actually one of the Other People, and that someday they would come to get him and bring him in state to live in their world, and he would come into his inheritance and his fulfillment. Now, bitterly, he knew better. And now he wouldn't want to go, even if he could.

"If there were any way," the Thant said, echoing his thoughts, "to save you, Man, to"—*flick*—"exempt you, then we would. But there is no way. You are a Man, you are not as we are."

"You bet I ain't," he gasped fiercely, "you—" But there was no word in his vocabulary strong enough. His eyes filled suddenly with tears, blinding him. Filled with rage, loathing and terror, he turned and ran stumblingly back up the slope, falling, scrambling up again.

"We are sorry, Man," the Thant called after him, but he didn't hear.

By the time Tommy reached the top of the slope, he had begun to shout hysterically. Somehow he had to warn them, he had to get through to somebody. Somebody had to *do* something. He ran through the schoolyard, crying, shouting about the aliens and Thants and entropy, shoving at his classmates to get them to go inside and hide, striking at the teachers and ducking away when they tried to grab him, telling them to *do* something, until at some point he was screaming instead of shouting, and the teachers were coming at him in a line, very seriously, with their arms held low to catch him.

Then he dodged them all, and ran.

When they got themselves straightened out, they went after him in the black sedan. They caught up with him about a mile down Highland Avenue. He was running desperately along the road shoulder, not looking back, not looking at anything. The rangy truant officer got out and ran him down.

And they loaded him in the sedan again. And they took him away.

At dawn on the third day, the aliens began to build a Machine.

Dr. Kruger listened to the tinny, unliving voice of Miss Fredricks until it scratched into silence, then he hung up the telephone. He shook his head, massaged his stomach, and sighed hugely. He got out a memo form, and wrote on it: *MBD/hyperactive, Thomas Nolan, 150ccs. Ritmose t b ad. dly. fr. therapy,* in green ink. Kruger admired his precise, angular handwriting for a moment, and then he signed his name, with a flourish. Sighing again, he put the form into his *Out* basket.

Tommy was very quiet in school the next day. He sat silently in the back of the class, with his hands folded together and placed on the desk in front of him. Hard slate light came in through the window and turned his hands and face gray, and reflected dully from his dull gray eyes. He did not make a sound.

A little while later, they finished winding down the world.